BEYOND EIGHT SECONDS

CARLY KADE

PRAISE FOR IN THE REINS

If you love horse stories and are looking for a book to draw you into its pages and not let go until that last page is read, check out *In the Reins* – you won't be disappointed.

— FEATHERED QUILL BOOK REVIEWS

I loved getting lost in Devon's transformation as she faced her need for change head-on. What's more, I loved the complexity of each of the characters: JD, the reckless yet tenderhearted bull rider, McKennon, the strong and intuitive cowboy, and Sophia, the matriarch and Devon's confidant and guardian angel throughout the novel. I would recommend this to any equestrian who loves getting lost in a great story.

— HORSE ROOKIE EQUESTRIAN LIFESTYLE SITE

PRAISE FOR COWBOY AWAY

Carly Kade hits another home run with her sequel to *In the Reins*. As much as I enjoyed the first book, I like this one even more. She strikes the perfect balance between making her characters human and revealing their flaws, while still allowing us to love them and root for their success. I loved the backstory she developed for McKennon – he's even sexier in this book than he was in the original.

— AMY ELIZABETH, AUTHOR OF THE ASPEN EYES SERIES

If you love horses, then I give *Cowboy Away* five blue ribbons, and if you love the romance genre, then I'd give it five golden hearts. And if you love both those things ... that makes it a solid 10!!!

— SARAH EVERS CONRAD, EQUINE JOURNALIST

PRAISE FOR SHOW PEN PROMISE

Carly Kade has built a beautiful life at Green Briar in her *In the Reins* series with characters the horse world has come to love. The other day, I was out with my horses, mucking and doing barn chores, and caught myself thinking about Green Briar and how I wished I lived there!

— LAURIE BERGLIE, AUTHOR OF THE EQUESTRIAN ROMANCE SERIES

As an equestrian exhibitor, it's so nice to read details about a setting and with terminology I live each day. But even if that's not your cup of tea, the romance itself will draw you in to the point where you don't want to put the book down. I'm not a romance reader – ever – other than Kade's books, and she never disappoints! Highly recommend.

— DELORES KUHLWEIN, EQUINE JOURNALIST

Beyond Eight Seconds
A Novel by Carly Kade
Copyright © 2021 by Carly Kade

Developmental Editor: Ann Luu
Copy Editor: Laurie Berglie
ISBN: 9781733476317
Library of Congress Control Number: 2021908688
Carly Kade Creative, Phoenix, AZ
http://www.carlykadecreative.com

JD's fans — This one's for you!

Thank you to the readers who reached out asking for a book that gets up close and personal with JD McCall, my handsome bull riding heartthrob.

You recognize JD's driven, never-give-up attitude and understand his attempts to lighten the mood by providing a good giggle now and then. You know he's a good guy underneath it all.

1

JD

I still remember the day McKennon pulled away from Green Briar. I hovered at the rail, watching Devon ride Faith. I was hopeful then that maybe Devon would want me in the end, but I was wrong. She is marrying McKennon today.

McKennon's a lucky bastard. He's hit the jackpot twice. Me? Not so much.

I am standing under a trellis covered with white flowers as some lame classical music plays from somewhere off to the side. I am McKennon's best man. *Again.*

Now that a video of McKennon proposing to Devon at Congress has been viewed a million times over, everyone in the industry wants a piece of M&D Quarter Horses and Services. Students are lining up to work with McKennon again. The training business is blowing up – so much so, that I'm helping McKennon build an additional barn at Green Briar to house the horses that keep coming in. Star's foals are selling before they even hit the ground. And today Sophia is hosting the horse industry's wedding of the year — potential clients, horse buyers, sponsors, friends, and family fill the seats on the sprawling lawn of the hillside.

Because of that dang video, McKennon's been offered all sorts of magazine spreads on the business, and brands have been banging on the doors to offer sponsorships. McKennon's so darn private, though. He turns everything away. 'Been there, done that,' he says to me.

Dang stupid if you ask me! I'd be all over that kind of publicity if I had the chance.

As I stand next to McKennon – did I mention *again* –, I can't help but notice that Devon's maid of honor is staring at me rather intensely. I look her up and down.

Redhead. Long legs. Not too shabby. Haven't had me too many redheads.

She is obviously older than me, but I liked the look of her right away. She seems different from my usual conquest. Classy, polished, regal even. I can see the big city on her. It's easy to assume she's loaded. I don't see a ring on her finger. She probably divorced some rich guy, took half of his money or more with her, and hasn't had sex in ages.

I'd be happy to remedy that in a jiffy.

I make a mental note to sniff her out later. I plan to poke around after the ceremony because I can't quite put a finger on the way she is looking at me.

Is it lust or is it somethin' else? Did I bed her already? Was I too drunk to remember her? Nah.

My attention is diverted from the cougar by McKennon's fidgeting. I roll my eyes and put a palm to McKennon's shoulder. His nervousness is obvious as he readjusts his black Stetson over and over again.

"Give it a rest, man," I say. "You've got this, brother. Devon is the best thing that's happened to you since Madison." He nods and gives me a thankful smile. Just then, the music stops, and the guests turn in awe as a horse and carriage trot up the drive.

Sophia sure has pulled out all the stops for McKennon and Devon today. Don't suppose it should be any other way.

As the carriage comes to a stop at the end of the aisle, I roll my eyes at the wedding theatrics but am mesmerized as Devon takes the driver's hand and steps down from the buggy. I can hear the wedding guests murmur their approvals, too. The late afternoon sun hovers over Green Briar as Devon pauses at the end of the aisle.

She is absolutely stunning in her white gown. The top hugs her figure in the best sort of way. The skirt is full and fluffy. Everything about her glimmers in the sunlight, particularly her smile. I can't take my eyes off of her, although I probably should. She clutches her bouquet of red roses. The awful classical music begins again, and Devon walks slowly toward us, smiling at people she knows as she makes her way down the aisle. She walks alone, the bottom of her gown moving around her lower half in waves. Dad had offered to accompany her, but she declined.

"You are so beautiful," McKennon whispers when Devon reaches his side.

Groan. Lucky bastard.

Devon simply smiles as her cheeks grow a deeper shade of pink, and she presses her lips together. McKennon sure has a hold on the woman. I can sense that if she speaks right now, there will be waterworks. I force myself not to roll my eyes again.

Girls!

I stand by McKennon's side as they recite their vows. I hand over the ring at the right moment. I swallow hard as they seal the deal.

McKennon strokes Devon's cheek after they say 'I do.' My gut turns when he presses his lips to her mouth. I'm not sure if it is because I wish I were kissing Devon, that my sister was once in Devon's place, or if it's the aching resemblance she has to someone I once knew. I shake my head, lift my hat, and run a hand through my hair.

I turn my attention to the regal, redheaded cougar in Devon's bridal party, the one who's been staring at me the whole ceremony.

Perhaps I'll soak myself in a little whiskey at the reception and give her a go ... to take my mind off of things.

2

DEVON

6 Months Earlier

I've never been more certain of anything. I can't wait to start my life with McKennon as husband and wife. However, I can't shake the lingering doom about seeing friends and relatives again, some of whom I haven't seen in years.

I am such a different person now.

"Devon?" Sophia's lilting voice calls me out of my trance.

"Yes, Sophia?" I respond, turning from the window of her master bedroom.

"My husband and I tied the knot here at Green Briar. I'd be honored if you and McKennon would do the same. It would make this old woman so happy."

"Oh, Sophia ... I wouldn't have it any other way. Green Briar is perfect." I kiss Sophia on the cheek and give her frail body a squeeze. "Thank you, Sophia. I can't think of a more wonderful place to say 'I do' to the man of my dreams."

"Ahem, that'll be cowboy of your dreams, miss," Sophia teases.

"You're right there," I say with a smile. "He's all cowboy."

"You leave all the planning to me, dear. I know just what to do. Of course, Devon, I'll run everything by you," Sophia chimes. She is luminescent, and her peach skin glows.

She just might be giddier about our wedding than I am.

"Have at it, Sophia. My cowboy and I have horses to train and a business to run. I really am too busy for wedding planning, plus I just think you might be a little better at it than I am. I'll get a guest list prepared and take care of my dress, but by all means, if you really want to do the planning, I would be honored."

"Are you comfortable with an elegant Western theme?"

"Oh, yes! That would be lovely. McKennon probably wouldn't want it any other way either. I can just picture it now."

"Wouldn't want what any other way?" McKennon asks, sneaking up behind me and planting his perfect lips on my cheek.

"Hi, cowboy," I breathe, turning to face him. "Where did you come from?"

"Just checkin' in on my girls. What are we up to in here?" he asks, blue eyes scanning the bedroom, landing on Sophia. She is mumbling to herself while rummaging through her closet. "Rather, what is she up to?"

"Sophia asked to plan our wedding for us. Is that OK with you?" I ask.

"Is that what you were talking about when I came in?"

"Yes, she'd like for us to have it at Green Briar. Western-themed. What do you think?" I ask, putting my head on his strong shoulder as he wraps his arms around my frame.

"Hmmm," he purrs. "Sounds perfect." I don't have to look up to know he is smiling.

"Oh, McKennon! I didn't hear you come in," Sophia says, padding out of her closet with an aged brown box in her grasp. "Come, come. Let me show you my wedding album, dear. We can start brewing up some ideas."

McKennon chuckles and releases me from his embrace.

I take a seat on the bed next to Sophia and eye the worn leather scrapbook she's just lifted from the timeworn box. She clasps her hands, bites her lower lip, scrunches her petite shoulders, and looks at me with glee. The corners of her thin peach lips lift.

She looks so happy.

"I'll leave you ladies to it then," McKennon drawls. With a tip of his hat, he skedaddles out of the room like a long-tail cat in a room full of rocking chairs.

Sophia and I watch him gallop out of the room and giggle to each other.

"Men and wedding planning," Sophia sighs. "Not sure there is a man on the planet who really wants to sit around and discuss it in detail. My husband, Andrew, was the same way. He told me as long as I was happy, spare no expense. I'm sure McKennon feels the same way. Just leave it to me, dear," Sophia confirms.

"I am so happy you want to plan our special day, Sophia. To be honest, I was a little worried about it before you asked. I might be more like McKennon and Andrew than you think."

"Ah, yes. A woman who would rather be out in the barn and riding the horses than talking about stationery, flowers, lace, twinkle lights, and such. Doesn't surprise me one bit, Devon."

"Twinkle lights?" I shake my head with a grin.

Sophia is always one step ahead of me.

I watch Sophia's weathered, purple veined, baubled hands glide over the front of her wedding album. Sophia sighs that pretty sigh of hers and shifts the big diamond on her left hand.

"It's been a while since I've looked through this," she murmurs, fingering the edges of the yellowed pages.

"We don't have to if it makes you sad, Sophia," I say, cupping her slight shoulder with the palm of my hand.

Sophia shifts on the mattress and gazes upon me. An angelic expression relaxes across her face.

"My memories of Andrew don't make me sad, dear. Though, I often think that perhaps we should have had children, but I was so fearful to have them. I always worried that something would happen to Andrew and me. I didn't want my children to become orphans like I once was. It gets me thinking."

"I understand. I think to have children or not is a very difficult decision for anyone."

"I would really like to have an heir to Green Briar one day," Sophia continues. "I'm not going to live forever, you know. I want this property to stay in the family. I plan to leave everything to McKennon when I go, but what happens after that? Have you and McKennon talked about starting a family?"

Gulp.

"We haven't exactly gotten that far yet, Sophia," I answer nervously. "McKennon and I did discuss it in a fleeting kind of way, but not seriously."

My mind flits back to our conversation just before the first time we made love when McKennon had so thoughtfully provided a box of protection, and I assured him I was on the pill. I feel my cheeks start to flush and put a palm to my face.

Kids? I'm not sure how I feel about kids. Maybe?

"I understand, dear," Sophia adds, not meeting my eyes. She pats my free hand with her cool, aged one. "All in due time. I didn't mean to pry. I hope you understand I will be all right with whatever decisions you make for your family. It's *your* family, but I would really love to be a grandmother." I look at her. She winks at me and opens the cover to her wedding album.

"This was the happiest day of my life," she whispers, lovingly stroking her fingertips over a particular photo.

"May I?" I ask. Sophia turns the album toward me, and I lift it onto my lap. I take a closer look. The photograph is sepia in tone, but I can still tell that Sophia is luminous. Her smile beams up at Andrew. He is much taller and well-built. He is impressive standing over her slight frame, looking down upon her with an expression of love.

"Sophia! You are so beautiful."

"Marrying Andrew Clark was my fairytale come true," Sophia sighs.

"Your dress is amazing!" I exclaim.

"Do you like it, dear?"

"Yes, yes, I do. It's exquisite."

"Would you like to see it?"

"You still have it? Yes, please!"

"Of course, I have it, dear. I'd never be able to part with it," Sophia says over her shoulder as she glides back into her dressing room. I flip through the album, admiring her wedding photos. I long for the same happiness she experienced that day. I say a little prayer that I never experience the despair of losing a spouse. I don't think anyone at Green Briar could handle death for a third time. I shudder as I turn to the last page of the album. I furrow my brows and hold the album closer to my face.

Is that a tombstone?

Sophia returns from the closet with a garment bag and hangs it next to the full-length mirror in her bedroom.

"What is this picture doing in your wedding album?" I ask. Sophia returns to her position on the bed. She is so lightweight that the mattress doesn't even bow when she sits.

"That is Andrew's last photograph, dear."

"In your wedding album? Isn't that kind of morbid?"

"No. That's life, Devon. Our loved ones live, and our loved ones die. That photo is a tribute to Andrew's life well lived and well loved. It may be the end of his life, but it isn't the end of his story. He is still a very large part of Green Briar and me. And you. He lives right now as we discuss this picture and reminisce about our wedding day."

"Where is this picture taken, Sophia?"

"Here at Green Briar. It's my special spot."

I ask nothing more. It is her special place on the farm. I don't need to know where it is. My heart hurts when I see the making of a tear glint in Sophia's eye. She clears her throat.

"Let us look at my wedding dress, shall we?" she whispers.

"I would be honored, Sophia." She turns her back and heads toward the dress. I see her wipe her eyes with a handkerchief in the mirror. She pauses for a moment, closes her eyes, takes a deep breath, then nods to herself as she unzips the garment bag.

Gently, Sophia lifts the dress from the bag and carries it toward me. I can hardly see her behind all the fluffy white layers of tulle and lace.

"Would you like to try it on, dear?"

"Oh, Sophia. I couldn't possibly," I gasp, putting my fingertips to my chest. "It's beautiful." I rise from the bed and touch the satin sweetheart bodice. It's romantic with a universe of tiny gleaming crystals adhered to it.

"Please, dear, try it on," Sophia encourages.

"Are you sure, Sophia?" I ask, hesitantly. "It's so special."

"Yes, I'm sure. It would please me to see a youthful body occupy it again. I was about your size back then."

"Well, if you insist." I hastily strip out of my shirt and jeans. Sophia holds the gown open in front of the mirror, I step carefully into the full skirt, and she lifts the top of it over me. The eight layers of lace and tulle of the ball gown, no longer a pool on the floor, flutter around my legs, and a chill pricks to my skin as I stare at the reflection in the mirror.

"My fingers don't quite work like they used to. Bear with me, dear, as this old woman fumbles with these slippery little buttons."

"Take your time, Sophia," I whisper.

As the dress shapes to my form, I am even more enchanted by the reflection in the mirror. Each button tightens the corset top on my frame. I smooth my hand over the delicate clear jewels glinting in the light from the satin of the bodice. I glide my fingertips over the billowing skirts of white at the bottom of the dress. I feel a lump form in my throat.

It's perfect.

"Ah, last button, Devon. Phew! That was a workout for these old hands," Sophia admits, wringing her hands as she steps out from behind me. She lifts her eyes from her aching fingers and meets mine in the mirror. She draws in a sharp breath and covers her mouth.

"What do you see, Sophia?" I ask.

"Me!" she exclaims. "You look just like me when I was younger."

I had noticed our similarities, too, while browsing her album, but didn't say anything.

"You look stunning," she whispers, touching the handkerchief to the corners of her timeworn eyes.

"Tell me about the dress, Sophia."

"I had it handmade in France by Coco Chanel," she replies, the beginning of a coy smile lifting a corner of her lips.

"What?" I shriek as my eyes go wide. "Sophia! This dress must be worth a fortune."

"Well, Andrew told me price had no bounds when it came to his future wife's happiness on her wedding day, so I took his word for it. Plus, I loved how Coco said, 'A girl should be two things: classy and fabulous.' I think she hit the nail on the head with this creation. Wouldn't you agree?"

I nod my head enthusiastically. There are no words. I am shocked to be standing in front of the mirror adorned in vintage Chanel. It is a full-blown ball gown for sure, but it is not over the top. It is delicate, glittery, beautiful, and ultra-feminine at the same time.

"I am glad to still have it," Sophia continues, touching my arm. "Would you like to wear it on your wedding day, too?"

I gasp and put my hand to my mouth, matching Sophia's reaction to me in the dress. I close my eyes and feel the tears well. The dread I've been harboring about the hunt for a perfect wedding dress is undeniable. I never imagined the first one I tried on would be *the one*, not to mention, Sophia's vintage designer dress that she wore right here at Green Briar for her own wedding no less.

Fate strikes again.

"Are you all right, dear?" Sophia asks.

"I'm perfect, Sophia," I whisper. "This is perfect. It's perfect. I would be honored to wear your dress when I marry McKennon."

"I had a feeling," Sophia says, stroking my cheek. "You are a vision, my dear."

I turn back to the mirror and give Sophia's dress a spin. She giggles as it swirls around my body in a white shimmering tidal wave.

3

DAY BEFORE THE WEDDING

My side of the wedding list certainly wasn't long. When we started sending out wedding invitations, I had scribbled down a few names and handed the list over to Sophia, and she blinked at me.

"Is this it?" she asked in disbelief.

"Yes, that's it," I said, not offering any explanation.

"All right, then," Sophia answered, not asking for one.

When Sophia had wandered down the drive to put the invitations in the mailbox a few weeks later, my throat closed off, and my chest tightened.

When the RSVPs started coming in, I found it hard to catch my breath.

Now that guests will be arriving, I need to clear my head.

How am I going to explain my actual family and lack of maintained friendships?

The only constants in my life over the last years have been my writing, my editor, the horses, and my Green Briar clan. Faith, Cash, and Willa just accept me for who I am. Perhaps this is why I am so devoted to the horses, because they are not turned off by the outward appearances other humans so often judge us by. McKennon is more horse than man, so perhaps this is why I feel so completed by him, too.

I've never been one for a whole herd of friends. In the city, I had a couple girlfriends, a lot of acquaintances, my editor, and, of course, Michael. I could keep busy on my own for hours and often found being invited out for get-togethers spoiled how I had planned to spend my alone time. Being a writer is a solitary occupation and requires space for thought and silence, aloneness. I lost touch with most of those people when I left Michael and the city. They didn't call me, but I didn't call them either. I figure they think I have gone crazy leaving him and New York. I don't mind. I prefer being alone or with my horses, anyway.

When I was young, I'd wrap my arms around the furry tuft of our family dog's neck when my parents went from screaming to throwing things. When I wasn't able to stand listening to their arguments any longer, I would sneak out to the boarding stable to lean against Cricket's soft shoulder. I'd bury my face in her soft fur and let the tears roll. My childhood animals brought me comfort. Animals silently understood me then and offered a different sort of companionship, same as they do now. They were beings I could trust when I couldn't trust the humans in my life to take care of me, protect me, or even see me.

Shaking thoughts of my broken family's nuclear implosion from my mind, I step into the stirrup and lift myself onto my horse's back. I glance to the end of Green Briar's drive. I'm going to ignore the fact that people will arrive shortly. I guide Faith out to where the foals are. I need a good dose of innocence. All this thinking about real world, grown up stuff is exhausting.

My head is clouded with thoughts. A ride through Green Briar's pastures to get away from life for a while will hopefully do the trick. As usual, I quickly realize my mind isn't interested in quieting down. In fact, it just gets louder.

With my mind in its usual overdrive, I ride out on horseback to the pasture where Green Briar's newest foals will be grazing next to their mamas. For a moment, I wish I wasn't such a loner, that I wasn't an only child, that I had kept in touch with some of my college friends, that I had a sane mom to call, or that my dad was still alive to confide in.

My childhood home was too sad, too crazy, too embarrassing for me. I never invited anyone over for fear they would witness my reality, so I coped with my crazy family through my imagination and my animals. When I was old enough to leave, I left. The only hard part of that decision was finding my childhood horse a new child to love her, but that will never happen again. Faith will be with me forever.

The day the trailer pulled away with Cricket inside, I decided that my mission was to remain portable and keep my life full, yet simple. After I left home and went to college, I had plenty of friends, but I have long since lost touch with them. We all ended up moving to distant cities, in search of achieving our dreams, building our careers, and starting families. Occasionally, I will comment on someone's work promotion or the birth of a baby on social media, but scrolling past pictures of their faces just isn't the same as genuine connection.

After I graduated from college, I let work take over my life. Ambition became more important than relationships. I was always caught up in the constant demands of being a journalist, buried under voicemails from my editor, and emails on projects that needed to be written yesterday. There was always another article to be written on the road to success.

My heavy heart swells with a hurricane of emotion, but I know these melancholy feelings are temporary, and eventually will pass. I shake the thoughts of my broken family and lost friendships out of my head. I run a hand beneath Faith's pearly white mane.

Stop it, Devon. Life is good.

I have McKennon. I have Faith. I have Willa. I have Cash. I have Sophia. I have JD. I have my editor, who is also my agent. I have my writing. I have M&D Kelly Quarter Horses. I have Green Briar. That feels like enough.

It is enough.

Green Briar and all that it provides is all I ever wanted. I realize that when I left the city and came to Green Briar, I finally gave myself permission to slow down a little and think about what I really wanted out of life. Finding Green Briar saved me. I don't think I could go back to the life I held in the city, even if I wanted to. I can't be without the close friendships I've developed here.

Thank heaven for Sophia, JD, and especially, McKennon.

I am smart and successful. I am strong. I'd made a mistake along the way shacking up with Michael, but oh well. It was fate. All my choices led me to the life I have now. I'll never be able to go back and make all my choices pretty. All I can do now is move forward and make the whole of my life beautiful.

That begins with marrying McKennon. My heart swells at the thought of walking down the aisle toward him.

Faith and I circle the pasture's edge. Willa spots us, and she releases a grown-up version of her whinny. She's the mama now. We are betting the future on her giving M&D Kelly Quarter Horses our next champion. Willa streaks across the pasture like a blaze of sunshine. Her belly swells with the tiny foal growing inside of her. She slows and lopes up to the gate to greet us with a nicker, then sniffs noses with Faith.

"How you doing, girl?"

I am grateful for Willa. She was my salvation during the dark days when my cowboy was away. She was my mount while Faith healed, and she helped me earn my first buckle. I am happy to be back in Faith's saddle now, but my heart holds an extra special space for Willa. When she nudges the pocket of my jeans over the fence, I retrieve an apple slice, which she hungrily accepts from the palm of my hand. I rub her forehead and gaze lovingly at her belly. I remember when Willa was all legs and lashes, just a few months old.

McKennon and I will have a foal to name soon.

"See you later, girl," I coo. Willa turns on her heels with a swish of her tail and a toss of her golden head. She trots off toward the weepy willow tree she has always favored in the pasture. I sit in the saddle and watch for a while. My heart pings in my chest when she frolics in the shade of the gigantic tree like she always has. I giggle when she takes a hold of one of the elastic branches with her mouth before letting it snap back into place. The other mares in the herd pay her no mind as they meander through the pasture, tearing at Green Briar's lush grasses.

I cluck Faith forward. A visit with Willa always makes me feel better. I ride by our house, hoping to catch a glimpse of my future husband. Butterflies zip through my stomach when I see him sitting out front in one of the rockers, sipping a cup of coffee, his boots up on the porch railing, reading a book.

"Morning, cowgirl," he calls. I smile and pull Faith up. His blue eyes are luminous in the morning sun. "Have I told you lately that I can't wait to be your husband?"

"Yes, you have. In fact, I think I hear it about a hundred times a day," I tease.

"Does that please you?"

"Yes. Very much."

"I aim to please, miss," he says through his heart-stopping smile. "I'm a little sad that you didn't invite me out to ride with you this morning."

"I'm sorry. Needed to clear my head."

He takes a sip from his mug and nods.

"I know the guests are gonna start arriving soon. I figured you needed a little alone time, so I took the opportunity for a little alone time of my own." He winks at me and lifts the book in his lap.

How can one man understand me so well?

"I can't wait to be your wife, Mr. Kelly."

"Music to my ears, cowgirl. Music to my ears. So how are our mamas in foal lookin' this mornin'?"

"They look healthy and happy."

"Good, good," McKennon says, dropping his boots from the railing and leaning forward in his chair. "Tell me more."

"Well, Willa's playing in the willows, as usual. We are going to have to name her baby one of these days."

"I reckon we will. I just know that little one is going to be Green Briar's next champion. That baby will follow in his parent's hoof prints, too."

"Being with you is like a dream come true," I sigh.

"I aim to please," McKennon replies.

"I'm going to head back to the barn and put Faith up. Try to get ready for the arrivals."

"See you later, cowgirl." McKennon replaces his boots on the railing. I blow him a kiss, and he tips his cowboy hat to me before picking his book back up. I smile and cue Faith on.

As I ride back to the barn, I survey the land and reminisce about our early horseback jaunts through Green Briar's acres. Faith's white mane shimmers in the sunlight, and I am beyond happy.

I lift my face to the sun, letting it warm my cheeks as my hips sway to the rhythm of Faith's stride below me. After a moment, I open my eyes in time to see the gleam of a black town car as it pulls into Green Briar's drive. It is coming fast and with purpose, a whirl of dust kicks up behind it. I pick up the pace and lope down the hill.

Who just arrived?

4

The car comes to a stop in front of the barn. I dismount Faith and walk toward it. With my horse in tow, I knock on the tinted window. It instantly rolls down, and I peer in.

"Is this Green Briar farm?" a regal redhead asks, staring straight ahead into a compact. "And are you Devon Brooke?" She presses her ruby red lips together, snaps the mirror shut, and then turns toward me, shifting slightly on the rich leather backseat.

"Ev! I can't believe you came!" I exclaim. "You're actually in the country and on a horse farm!"

My editor shoots me a devilish grin.

"I can't believe it either," she says, shaking her head as her crimson hair waterfalls over her shoulders. "I hardly ever leave the city, but I just couldn't pass up the invitation of the century," she says, waving our wedding stationery through the open window.

"Get out of that car, and give me a hug!" I exclaim, opening the door before her driver can. Ev teeters in high heels on Green Briar's gravel driveway. She slams the door of her town car with gusto. Faith's head shoots up with the bang.

"Oops. Did I scare that horse?" she asks.

"A little. I'll give you some equine etiquette lessons later."

"That's good. It's been a while since I've been in the company of horses, but what I really don't know the first thing about is cowboys or the country. I'm going to need plenty of lessons in that department." She says it seriously, like the city woman she is.

"No problem," I chuckle. "This is Faith, Ev. She's the horse I told you so much about. The one my book is about."

Ev softens and gingerly picks her way in her designer heels over to my mare. She lifts her perfectly manicured red fingertips as if to touch my horse's neck, but then stops, hesitant.

"Can I pet her?"

"Of course."

"Hi, girl," she whispers. "You had one heck of a time last year, huh?"

"Where would you like your bags, miss?" the chauffeur asks, interrupting Ev's tender moment. It's a moment not typical of my tough, big city agent.

"Please put them in the back of the four-wheeler over there, sir," I pipe up. "I'll take you up to the main house after I put Faith away, Ev."

"Actually, please leave them in the car."

"What do you mean? Sophia's invited you to stay in the house for the wedding."

"Oh, I will, but I am going to stay in a nice hotel in Fort Worth until I get used to things. I have to take this country thing slow. I have to get used to things first. I like my space, plus I need my room service, bellhops, mini-bar, spa, and all the amenities for a day. I'll stay at Green Briar on your wedding night because I plan to drink way too much."

"Ev. You are a hoot."

"Before I check in to the hotel, I just had to see for myself that the city girl I once knew actually turned country and is marrying a real live cowboy. With that horse at your side, it looks like it's true, too."

I laugh as Ev pulls her sunglasses down the bridge of her nose and looks at my attire.

"Clearly, I'll be needing a pair of those," she says, pointing to my boots.

"Done. I know a great place in Fort Worth. We'll go there once you get settled. After all, this wedding is a Western affair. I'm glad to hear you're willing to dress the part."

"Yes, I noticed that on the invite," Ev says, staring down the manure pile next to the barn. I laugh when she scrunches up her nose.

"You're here. You're really here. Thank you for coming! I still can't believe it." I loop Faith's reins over my shoulder and hug her.

"Believe it," she whispers near my ear. "I have to feast my city eyes on this McKennon Kelly fellow for myself, you know. As for being your maid of honor, that's just a bonus."

"You'll meet him soon enough, but probably not before the bach-elorette party tonight because I'm taking you shopping for some country clothes," I announce.

"And a pair of boots?" Ev asks with a lift of her brow.

"Of course!"

5

Later that afternoon, Ev and I collapse on the king-size bed in her fancy five-star hotel. Bags upon bags surround us, having just gone on a spending spree for the ages.

"That was fun," I giggle.

"I never knew there were so many kinds of cowboy boots," Ev replies. "I wanted to buy them all, but I don't know that I'll have that much use for them. I think five pairs should suffice for this trip."

"Yes, you've got the bases covered with classic Western to exotic leathers," I add.

Ev sits up and lifts the lid on one of the boxes.

"I think that pair is my favorite. I love the detail," I admit as I run a finger along the boot's leather uppers inset with flowers, hearts, and little blue birds. "The leather cut-outs and stitching details are divine."

"Well, I am glad to hear it because I bought this pair for you. I saw you eyeing them."

"Ev!" I gasp. "How did you manage to do that behind my back?"

"I have my ways. Consider them your something new. You can wear them under your wedding dress, can't you?"

"Yes! I was planning to wear my black boots, but I suppose they have done their duty."

"Black boots? Under your wedding dress?" Ev asks with a frown.

"It's a sentimental thing."

"Ah, I see. Would it be a Madison thing?"

"Yes, I wanted to honor Madison's memory, but I think your gift is perfect for my special day. It's time to let the past be the past."

"I agree. It's the right thing to do to wear something new."

"Thank you for your generosity, Ev. These are beautiful." I lift the boots from the box and hug them to my chest.

"Think nothing of it. Your writing is part of what's made me a rich woman, so technically, you contributed to that purchase," she admits with a wave of her slender hand. "I'm looking forward to the money that book of yours is going to bring in, too."

"I still can't believe I won a buckle, wrote a book, *and* I'm getting married. Speaking of my book ..." I cross the room and lift the flap of my messenger bag. I pull out my manuscript and hand it to Ev.

"Is this it?" Ev asks, fingering the edges of the paper.

"Yes, that's it! I can't believe I did it."

"It's been a heck of a year for you, Devon. I am happy for you. Can I read it?"

"Not now, silly! We have other things to do. I was going to send it to the office, but then I figured I'd just give it to you in person. Should be good material for reading on the plane ride back to Manhattan. I'm not sure it's publishable though. How much interest could there be in a memoir about my experience relearning about horses?'

"I'll be the judge of that, Devon. I'll find it a suitable home, make sure it gets published, and stir up that interest you are so worried about. It's what I do. Now help me pick out one of these outfits to wear to your bachelorette party tonight. I want everyone to think 'look what just rode into Dodge' when I walk in. I want eye-catching pizazz! I'm ready to party."

"I'm afraid it will not be that crazy, Ev. It's just a dinner here in the city. You, me, Sophia, and Sallie Mae."

"You call that a bachelorette party? We'll figure something out," she says with a raise of her thin red eyebrow. "We are going to find a way to put ourselves in the saddle of attention tonight."

Uh oh.

"Come on, let's get dressed. I've decided I'm wearing the buckskin suede skirt with the fringe, the red halter-top, and the red boots. That should heat things up a notch."

"Ev, it's just a dinner."

"Uh-uh. You are not getting off that easy," Ev says, turning back to the pile of bags on the bed. She rummages through them for a moment. "Here, wear this."

"Another gift?" I ask, holding up a very short, very hot little black suede dress with fringe for sleeves at the shoulders.

"Go on, try it on," Ev orders.

I gallop to the bathroom, strip out of my jeans and T-shirt, and I slip on the dress. It fits like a glove. I pull my black boots back on and look in the mirror.

I look hot.

Ev bursts into the bathroom in her own getup and hollers, "You look hot!"

Knew it!

We touch up our makeup, spritz ourselves with perfume, primp our hair, and nod in approval as we stand side by side in the full-length mirror hanging on the wall.

"All right. Let's go!" I grin and shake my head as we slip out of Ev's hotel room. We drive my car back to Green Briar and then call for a cab to the Fort Worth honkytonk for a 6 p.m. reservation. I spot Sophia and Sallie Mae already seated in the booth, chatting easily when we arrive. They stop speaking and look up when we make our way toward them.

"Ah, to be young again," Sallie Mae blurts with a raised eyebrow as she looks us up and down with a whistle.

"I just love suede," Sophia chimes in. She clasps her hands together with a giddy look in her weathered eyes. "You look lovely, ladies."

"Thank you, Sophia. Thank you for coming, Sallie Mae. This is my editor and agent, Ev. She's from New York City. We went on a shopping spree today. She ... um ... picked out my dress."

I slide into the booth. Sophia and Sallie Mae exchange looks as they watch Ev hold the edges of her very short mini-skirt, so not to expose her lower region, as she scoots into the booth after me. We all lift our menus to make our selections.

"Hello, ladies," the waitress greets us with a too-wide smile and tray full of drinks. "I heard it was someone's bachelorette party," she says as she sets a shot glass down in front of each of us.

"Ev!" I demand, popping her lightly in the shoulder. "Shots? This is just supposed to be dinner."

"It wasn't me," she shoots back with a green-eyed glare and a shoulder punch of her own. "Somebody has the right idea, though! Watch my shot for me, will you? I have to go to the little ladies' room."

I rub my shoulder as she slips back out of the booth. I watch the sway of her hips as she heads for the bathroom for a moment and then look to Sophia. She shakes her head.

"Sallie Mae?"

"Wasn't me, Devon." They both shrug their shoulders and eyeball the drinks on the table.

"Who the heck?" I wonder aloud.

"Ladies, ladies, ladies," I hear over our server's shoulder. I know the voice instantly.

JD.

JD saunters out from behind the waitress and releases his gleaming white megawatt smile. It's an attempt to dazzle us.

"The drinks are on me," he announces, holding his own shot glass in the air. "In honor of Devon on the eve of her wedding day."

"Oh, what the heck," Sophia says, raising her glass.

My mouth drops when Sallie Mae raises hers, too. I give JD the evil eye. He just smirks and nods toward my glass, still sitting on the table. I swear I see a star twinkle in his eye as I glower at him.

My bachelorette party is admittedly pretty lame, but that was the point!

"Fine," I huff and hoist my shot glass. "I'm not looking to get drunk tonight though."

"Down the hatch," Sallie Mae grunts. She, JD, and I toss the liquor down our throats. I watch Sophia as she sips from her glass. It's difficult to suppress my smile when her eyes go wide.

"My goodness. What on earth is this concoction? I don't believe I've ever had anything quite like this," she wheezes, clutching her throat.

"It's a mind eraser, Sophia. Want another one?" JD teases.

"No, thank you, JD. One sip of that was quite enough for me."

"OK, Sophia. No more mind erasers for you, but Devon, when you are finished eatin' with the ladies, I've arranged for a little fun. I'm making sure you stay up past your bedtime." He points his finger across the empty dance floor toward the front door.

"JD, what have you done?" I groan, following the direction of his index finger.

In an instant, a gaggle of buckle bunnies burst into the bar. They are all wearing pink feathery boas and have bags of what I can only imagine might be inappropriate items strung up their arms. My mouth drops open as they rowdily order drinks from the lone bartender, then with bottles and glasses in hand, accost the DJ with requests for songs that promise to get the dance floor moving.

In the corner of the bar just beyond the dance floor is a mechanical bull circled by an inflatable mat. The gentleman manning the controls pushes a button and the cowhide-covered bull whirls around riderless in the middle of the bar, inviting someone to give it a go. He lets out a long slow whistle as he moves the joystick controlling the bull. His eyes wander all over the scantily clad ladies JD has apparently invited to *my* bachelorette party.

"JD! This is supposed to be low key. I didn't want to do anything crazy tonight. I don't even know any of those girls. What the heck are *you* doing here, anyway?" I ask, putting an annoyed finger in his chest.

"Hey, I have every right to be here," he says, rubbing the shirt pocket I've just poked. "I've been the closest thing you've had to a girlfriend since you came to Green Briar. Would've liked it to be more, but at least I got a woman for a best friend out of the deal. I wouldn't miss your bachelorette party for anything."

I am touched. JD *is* a good friend.

"Fine, I will come hang out with you for a little while once we've finished our nice meal." I smile apologetically at Sophia and Sallie Mae.

"Terrific," JD responds before waltzing over to his groupies.

"What did I miss?" Ev asks when she returns moments later from the ladies' room.

"Nothing," I reply with a huff as she shoots her drink.

"Mmm, mind eraser. I love these."

"Let's order, shall we?" I say, changing the subject. "This place has amazing food, even though it becomes a honkytonk in the evenings."

We eventually place our orders and have a lovely meal, chatting easily and enjoying each other's company. As we finish our dessert, I grow concerned about what will happen once I bid Sophia and Sallie Mae good night. I watch JD in the distance. He has ditched his ball-capped boyish look for his full-on bull rider persona and several women surround him, all bubbly, busty, and babbling. He has the women hanging on his every word. While his lips move, his eyes survey their plunging necklines. I know he has finished one of his trademark jokes because all of his harlots toss their heads back in laughter.

"Well, dear, this has been a wonderful evening. I have a few last touches I need to make for the big day, so I need to say adieu."

"Thank you for coming, Sophia. I can't believe you did a shot," I reply.

"There's still some spunk in this old body, young lady. Don't be getting in too much trouble now," she orders, slivering her eyes at JD on the dance floor sandwiched between two women.

"I won't, Sophia," I groan.

"He's trying to be nice, dear, but JD can be a troublemaker."

"Don't I know it," I reply.

"Who's JD?" Ev pipes up.

"You'll see," I say as I walk Sophia and Sallie Mae to the door.

"Thanks for driving Sophia home, Sallie Mae."

"My pleasure, dear. McKennon and I have plans for a nightcap this evening, anyway. Looking forward to tomorrow. Take care now," she says, raising an eyebrow at the antics on the dance floor.

Once Sophia and Sallie Mae are safely out the door, I turn and fist my hands on my hips.

"Time for drinks!" Ev announces and heads straight for the bar. "I'll bring you back something."

JD sees me on my own and instantly makes his way toward me. He sways as he does so, and I know he is already three sheets to the wind.

"Why helloooo, pretty lady. Ready for your bachelorette party?"

"Ready as I'll ever be, JD."

"I'll be honest – I think you may have fallen off of your horse one too many times, Devon, but if you're saying yes to marrying McKennon, I'll support you," JD slurs, shooting another shot.

"Thanks for being a good friend, JD."

He teeters back on the heels of his boots, and then asks, "Where's your drink?"

I start to open my mouth to let him know Ev is getting me one, but he lumbers off before I have the chance.

"You need a drink," he says over his shoulder as he wanders away.

"Who is that?" Ev asks, coming up to me from behind and sticking a Cosmo in my hand. "He's just the prettiest boy in this bar."

"And the drunkest," I snort, taking a sip from my glass.

"Introduce me, would you?" Ev begs, facing me.

"That's not going to be a problem," I say as JD makes his way back over to me, sloshing two shots all over himself and the floor.

"I got the bachelorette another mind eraser," JD announces triumphantly. "Here." He juts the drink toward me. The liquid spills over the side and just misses Ev's new boots.

"Excuse me, cowboy. These were expensive," she barks, tapping the toe of her cowgirl boot at him. He looks at her blankly and blinks a few times. Ev takes the shot meant for me and sends it down the hatch.

"I love mind erasers," she purrs. When JD continues to stand in front of us like a statue. Ev turns to me. "Does he speak?"

"Usually I can't get him to shut up," I tease and shrug my shoulders.

"Pardon. Little drunk over here," JD proclaims, swaying from side to side.

"I'm the one who is supposed to be tipsy. It's *my* bachelorette party," I remind him. Ev wags a finger at JD, and his eyes cross.

"Good grief, JD. How much have you had to drink? If you are going to be the drunk one at my party, you are going to have to dress the part." I wade across the dance floor over to the cowgirls and their goods to pick out a party favor or two. I walk back to JD and plunk a pink party hat on his head. One of the buckle bunnies follows suit and places a feathery boa around his neck, giggling the entire time. Another one of them hands him a cellophane-wrapped package containing a huge inflatable penis.

"Blow this up for us, would you? Please," she coos, batting her lashes. Ev gives her a dirty look, and the buckle bunny gives her a sour look right back, but still backs up two steps.

"Hang out here for a second, Ev. I'll be right back." I manhandle JD into a booth.

"Hey, I want to dance," he protests. "Don't leave. I did this for you."

"Just sit down for a few minutes. I'm not leaving, I promise. Come find me on the dance floor once you've sobered up a bit. OK, JD?"

"OK, Devon." His eyes are bleary then he lifts the inflatable penis to his lips and begins to blow it up.

I shake my head and roll my eyes as I turn to head back over to Ev.

How on earth did he get that drunk so fast?

"I think he's blacked out," I tell Ev.

"Who cares? Just looking at him makes me want to misbehave, Devon. His face is pretty enough for framing."

"Ev! He's in no condition."

"Those arms, those distractingly green eyes," she continues, ignoring me. "Shall I go on?"

I look over at my friend slumped back in the booth, still blowing into the penis. I tilt my head and focus on JD. I can sort of see what Ev is seeing.

I guess.

JD is young, twenty-something years young, with moves smoother than silk – when he isn't wasted, that is. He has a gleaming white, rock star smile, featuring all too perfect straight teeth, and alluring, big green eyes that pierce right through you. His eyes have just enough naughty glinting in them to serve as a warning that any smart woman should beware. JD only stays put for mere seconds before he's back up on his boots and approaching us.

"I sat out for eight seconds. I can always sit for eight seconds. Beyond eight seconds, well ..."

"JD, do I have to call McKennon to come get you?" I warn, interrupting him.

"I did what you asked, Devon, but no more sitting and no more big sister stuff from you. This is what I call a bootie rich environment," JD whispers in my ear from behind.

"You live your life between your legs, JD."

"Indeed, I do." JD tips his hat to Ev with a smirk and hands her the big pink penis. She strokes it seductively, and he raises an eyebrow before heading clumsily toward the mechanical bull.

"Growl. I want some of that!" Ev announces.

"Ev," I start, but she's already abandoned me, following JD.

Oh, boy.

I follow her, following him.

This is going to be interesting.

6

"Sssstart 'em up, Earl," JD calls to the fellow manning the mechanical bull.

"You sure about that, JD?" he replies.

"I'm sssh ...sure," JD slurs from the side of the ring, draining another beer.

"You look a little too loopy to be taking on the best mechanical bull operator this side of the Mississippi," Earl razes.

"Wanna place a wager on my ride?" JD asks, taking a moment to perform some stumbling stretches for his adoring buckle bunnies. I roll my eyes, taking note that Ev is one of them.

"I bet 'cha $500 bucks you can't make the eight," Earl taunts.

"You're on," JD hollers, pumping his arm and stepping into the red, white, and blue inflatable cushioned ring. He mounts the bull, adjusts his seat, lowers his hat over his brow, and raises a hand in the air. "Ready when you are, Earl!"

Ev races from the other side of the ring and joins me.

"This is going to be good," she hoots.

"I just hope he doesn't get hurt," I groan.

"Oh, stop being such a party-pooper. Here," Ev admonishes,

shoving her unfinished long-neck into my palm. I take it as the LED light on the scoreboard above the dance floor is set to zero.

Earl licks his lips and settles in behind the control console. He turns on the power, takes hold of the joystick and starts the bull out slow. JD bobs up and down in total control. He has his left hand fisted around the woven rein attached to the front of the headless, hide-covered bull, and he waves the other over his head.

"Piece of cake," JD shouts as his adoring fans hop up and down outside of the inflatable ring.

Earl licks his lips again. He is clearly enjoying the view of the buckle bunnies jumping around the outside of the ring in their glittering tube tops, bodacious breasts bouncing about.

"I was just gettin' warmed up," Earl shouts back as he sends the bull into a fast and furious series of bucks, rolls, and spins. JD clutches tighter with his inner thighs and grips his spurred heels into the side of the bull. The bicep of his riding arm reflects the work he has undertaken by bulging beneath his rolled-up flannel sleeve.

It is an epic battle of will between JD and Earl. Left, right, left, spin. Earl is cranking the controls hard. It bewilders me that JD can even ride the thing in his drunken state. All the girls swoon over JD as his hips swivel in time with the bull, determination set in his jaw.

"Look at those hips! Hang on, hot stuff," Ev shouts, pumping her fist in the air. JD ebbs and flows over the mechanical bull. The eight seconds feel like forever.

"I can't imagine what he would look like on a real one," Ev squeals beside me. It seems she is fairly drunk herself.

Suddenly, I shudder thinking how dangerous his real-life career actually is. Earl continues increasing speed. The fake bull spins and turns faster and faster. JD continuously corrects his position and stays on.

"I'm going to take him back to my hotel tonight, Devon."

"Ev." I raise my eyebrows at her, but before I can respond, the buckle bunnies cheering JD on start counting down the final three seconds of his ride. It looks as though he is going to make the eight and win the money. With one final spin, the clock buzzes, and JD wins the bet.

He dismounts the bull and lifts his hat from his head. All bravado and cockiness, he takes a bow, and Earl shifts the joystick in the control booth. The bull spins to the right and wallops JD right out of the ring. Before I can catch her, Ev races to JD's side. I am powerless and follow behind.

"Are you OK?" Ev asks. She's really playing up her concern.

"Nothin' a cig, another shot of whiskey, and a lie down won't cure," JD drawls, rubbing the back of his head, which clearly connected with the floor. He pinches a pack of smokes in his shirt pocket and brings it to his lips.

Earl walks over, lights JD's cigarette, and tosses a bunch of bills on his chest.

"Don't get so cocky next time, and maybe I'll let you walk outta my ring rather than knocking you out of it," Earl huffs.

JD just nods, and Earl stomps back to his booth. Although Ev was the first to come to his aid, a gaggle of girls fall to their knees around JD.

"I'm going home with him," says one with pouty lips. "You OK, boo-boo?"

JD turns his attention to her and away from Ev.

"No. I'm going home with him," says a bodacious brunette in a tube top. "You all right, sweet cheeks?"

JD's head rolls toward her.

"I've got your hat, honey pie," says a big-breasted blonde as she runs her fingers through JD's hair. When she puts JD's hat on her head, Ev pipes up. She's clearly had enough of JD's groupies.

"Shut the hell up, the lot of you! There'll be no more fighting over him, ladies. I'm the one going home with him. You can go home with a piece of Devon's cake, or you can continue the fight over the inflatable penis. It's your choice," Ev barks, showing her big-city toughness.

I can hardly contain my laugh as buckle bunny mouths fall open all around me.

"Here you go," I say, offering the giant inflatable extremity to the one wearing JD's cowboy hat. She glares at me.

"Off you go now. Shoo," Ev commands with a wave of her hand, plucking JD's hat from the pretty blonde's head.

"Seems like you've got it all figured out," the girl hisses. "What's your name, anyway?"

"Ev."

"Do you always get what you want, Ev? Do you always tell everyone what to do?" the girl snaps. In response, Ev puts a finger to her lips, pops a hip, and thinks for a moment.

"Not always. Well ... yeah. Actually, I do." Ev eventually replies with a smirk. "Now if you don't mind, I have an injured cowboy to attend to." Ev flips her red hair, sending it flying over her shoulder, and bends down next to JD. He's still laid out flat on the floor of the bar.

When the manager comes over to make sure everything is all right, Ev orders JD a shot. I just stand by watching the whole debacle.

"Your shot is on the way, cowboy. Now about that lie down. Is that alone or with company?" she purrs.

"I'll have you know – I ride bulls, and I'm hung like one," JD slurs. I palm my face and groan.

"Promise?" she asks, helping him to his feet and into a booth. When Ev orders another round of shots, I wander off, help myself to a piece of cake, and watch the events unfold from a not-too-distant barstool.

I can't wait to tell McKennon about this one.

Later, I join them in the booth and sip a glass of water while Ev orders several more drinks for herself and JD. They are both properly plastered. JD licks his lips and raises an eyebrow.

"You know, you didn't have to order all those drinks," he slurs, slamming a fist on our table.

"Whyyyy?" Ev slurs right back.

"I was ready to go home with you after you saved me from that big bad mechanical bull and its mean operator back there."

"Now you tell me," she chastises. "I am going to have a freaking headache tomorrow."

JD leans in and kisses her lips. He stands up wobbly, then takes her hand and tugs her up out of her seat. He points toward the exit.

"Don't say a word," Ev whispers to me as JD tugs at her hand. She tugs him back, and he falls back into the booth. I can smell the alcohol hot on her breath when she continues to speak. "Whether or not I get to bed him, he's a star in the making. They don't make men like this one in the city. He's so pretty, but all man at the same time. I'm going to make him a star."

Make him a star? What in the hell does that mean?

All I can do is give her a disapproving look. It's Ev. Ev does what she wants, when she wants. She wouldn't be the head of her own company in New York City of all places if she weren't that way. She puts a hand on my shoulder in response to my frown and pouts her lower lip.

She sure is sauced.

I roll my eyes and make a "zipping up my lips" gesture. She squeezes my shoulder when I throw an imaginary key over it.

"That's my girl," Ev laughs and lets her head fall back. Her beautiful ruby hair streams behind her, and JD puts his lips to her neck. He gets himself upright again, lifts her out of the booth by her hands, and they stare into each other eyes. I feel faintly like I might be sick. McKennon's comments on JD return to my mind, 'Be careful with that one. Good kid. Young. Kinda stupid, but with potential, I suppose.'

Ev has got her work cut out for her.

Laughing, they nod to each other.

"You all right to get home on your own, Devon?" Ev asks.

"Not a problem," I assure.

I can't wait to get home to McKennon and out of this crazy situation.

I wait to leave and watch JD attempt to maneuver Ev across the dance floor and past the icy eyes of his groupies. Wobbly, they finally reach the exit, and the bouncer holds the door open. I see JD stumble, then signal for a taxi with Ev tucked beneath his beefy arm just before the bar door swings shut.

7

JD

My mind is blank, and the ache in my head is blazing. I just rolled off of yet another woman whose name I don't know. I can't even remember if I found my release in this drunken haze. I am motionless for a while. I wait to make sure the body beside is asleep, so I can make my escape. I need to get the hell out of here.

Wherever I am.

As I lie here in the dark on the eve before Devon's wedding, I wish for the first time that there were more to my life, more than my eight-second thrill rides on raging bulls and momentary ecstasy with nameless women. I envy McKennon for being a one-woman man. Thinking of Devon and their impending wedding, I drag a hand over my face. I vaguely remember crashing Devon's bachelorette dinner.

I must be with someone from the bar.

It's still dark, and I look around, careful not to stir the woman next to me. I'm in a hotel room.

I think.

I see the digital numbers on the clock on the nightstand.

3:01 a.m.

The body next to me has its back turned, and I'm relieved. The goodbyes are always awkward when they know I want to leave. I can't remember her face, her name, or how I got here.

I. Can't. Remember. Anything.

I wait. It seems like forever before the breathing from the body becomes deep and rhythmic next to me. Once I am sure she is completely asleep, I hold my breath and sneak out of the bed. I slip back into my clothing, secure my cowboy hat on my head, grab my boots, and scoot out the door. Once it clicks softly behind me, I exhale.

Thank heaven I got out of there unnoticed.

I squint in the hallway light and rest my shoulder on the door-jamb for a moment, trying to get my bearing. I expected to be in one of the usual generic hotels I frequent with my conquests, but this place is nice. I mean, really nice. I note the chandeliers down the hallway and button my open shirt at lightning speed. I pull my boots on and take the stairs to street level. I want to avoid being stuck in an elevator with anyone. Even guys don't like to be caught doing the walk of shame. Halfway down, I feel like I've already taken a million steps and think the woman's room was on the top floor. Once I'm out on the street, I hail a cab back to Green Briar.

I step out of the taxi, glad to be back on familiar ground. I unlock my truck and plant myself face down across the bench seat, ready to sleep off another hangover, another night, and another woman I don't remember.

8

DEVON

Tradition is what Sophia called it. I initially resisted it, but eventually obliged her insistence that McKennon and I spend the evening before our wedding day separately.

Now I'm glad that I did because I wake up refreshed, having slept in one of Green Briar's giant bedrooms. I missed McKennon in the moments before I drifted off but feel refreshed now that I've opened my eyes. I'm grateful I didn't have too much to drink last night. My stomach flutters as I think of what today will bring.

I can't wait to see McKennon and slip the wedding ring on his finger.

When my phone chirps, I stretch and reach for it, hoping it might be my future husband, but it isn't. I'm not surprised when Ev informs me that she has a beast of a headache and is running behind, noting she still has to pack up her room and check out. I'm thrilled that she's accepted the invitation to stay at Green Briar tonight. I don't bother asking for the dirty details on JD. I know I'll get those later, even if I don't want them. I flip my phone onto the bed and pad to the shower to begin preparations for the day.

"Something old, something new, something borrowed, something blue," Sophia chimes as she scurries around her bedroom.

Sophia has turned her quarters into the perfect dressing room for a bride. The air is fragrant from the dozen vases of white roses strategically placed around the space and the caterers she hired have laid out a light spread of fruit, pastries, tea, coffee, and champagne.

"I am happy that it is just you and me right now," I say as Sophia hands me a flute of bubbly, the hair and makeup consultants having already come and gone.

"Me too, darling," she replies, opting for a cup of hot tea for herself. "You've really learned how to take fate in your own hands and not let circumstance drag you down. I'm proud of who you've become since coming to Green Briar. Oh, this wedding is just icing on the cake!"

"I didn't get to this place alone, Sophia. You told me it would be a waiting game with McKennon. You told me to be patient, and he'd choose to come back to me, back to us. I took that advice. Now, I'm getting my happily ever after."

"Indeed, you are, my dear. Indeed, you are," Sophia responds thoughtfully, removing the bag from her china cup and blowing over her hot tea. I take another sip from my flute and smile.

"Shall we?" Sophia asks, setting her tea on a table. I nod and walk up to the full-length mirror in the room's corner where my wedding dress is waiting. I step into the gown, and Sophia busies herself with fastening me into it.

"This dress is your something old," she murmurs, once she has me buttoned up. Then she pads to her dresser and opens a velvet box. "And this is your something borrowed." Sophia holds up a necklace and crosses the room to me.

I gently lift the dangling tresses that are intentionally hanging from my up-do, so she can adjust a single strand of pearls around my neck.

"Sophia, they are beautiful," I coo.

"Andrew gave them to me as my something new on our wedding day."

"Sophia, you are too good to me. My heart couldn't be happier right now. I'm honored to wear these," I reply, touching the gems around my neck.

"McKennon is like a son to me. And you are like a daughter." She catches my hand and gives it a squeeze. My breath hitches, and I start to tear up. "Ah! No crying yet. We've got a whole wedding to get through, dear." Sophia scurries over to the table, pulls the champagne from the ice bucket, and promptly fills my glass.

She's trying to distract me.

I can't help but laugh.

"Don't get me too drunk now, Sophia. I want to remember my wedding day," I tease as the tears ease.

"Just a little to take the nerves off," she replies with a wink.

What would I do without Sophia?

"Now, what are we going to do about something new and something blue?" Sophia asks.

"Oh, Ev handled the something new! She gave me a new pair of cowgirl boots to wear under my dress."

"And I've got the something blue covered, too," Ev says, boldly entering the bedroom and bee-lining it straight to the champagne bottle Sophia just returned to the ice. She pours herself a flute, drinks the whole thing down, and then refills the glass.

"Rough night?" I ask with a lift of my eyebrow.

"Fabulous night, but a hell of a hangover," she responds with a sinister grin. "You look beautiful, by the way."

"Tisk, tisk," Sophia clucks to Ev. "A lady shouldn't drink like a cowhand."

"Sophia, that dress certainly is one-of-a-kind, just like you," Ev says, kissing Sophia on the cheek. Ev brushes off Sophia's disapproval like a champ.

"Thank you, dear," Sophia replies with a sigh. "I'll allow a little cowhand in a woman now and then, I suppose."

They both giggle and embrace. Sophia and Ev had really hit it off at my bachelorette dinner last night. They exchanged stories about New York City, and Sophia's great romance story with Andrew during The National Horse Show totally enthralled Ev.

"Here," Ev says, jamming a box into my hand. "It's your something blue."

I pull the satin ribbon and unwrap the silver paper from the small box. When I open the lid and peer inside, I see a saucy blue, lacy garter with a silver horse pendant on it.

"Oh, Ev. It's perfect!" I gush.

"Let me help you get it on before you slip into those new cowgirl boots I gifted you yesterday."

As I take a seat on the edge of the bed, Ev stretches the garter suggestively. I shake my head and raise a leg so she can slide it on for me. I bite my lip as she buries herself under my wedding gown like a hungry bachelor and tugs the lacy item up my leg until it is secure around my thigh. Sophia and I giggle like schoolgirls over Ev's over-the-top theatrics.

Once Ev removes herself from under my skirt, I look at myself in the mirror then give my dress a spin.

"I feel like a princess," I say.

"You look like a princess," Ev assures.

"One of the greatest joys of a woman's life is her wedding day," Sophia whispers. "Be sure to enjoy it. Stay in the moment, my dear."

I step to the window and look out over Green Briar's sprawling front lawn. It's full of guests milling about. It wouldn't surprise me if Sophia invited the whole darn town to the wedding. I'm sure she did it to make up for my and McKennon's sparse guest list.

"It's time, dear," Sophia murmurs, acknowledging the wedding planner who just knocked at the door and gave her the nod. Ev takes a moment to give my nose a final powder, then hands me my bouquet of red roses and baby's breath. I take in a deep breath of the floral arrangement.

Here goes nothing.

Ev lowers my veil over my face, grabs one last flute of champagne, and then lifts the train of my gown with her free hand. We follow Sophia down the staircase and out onto the porch. Waiting for me in the drive is a horse-drawn carriage, manned by a driver wearing a top hat, long dress coat, dark pants, tall shiny boots, and white gloves. He bows at the waist when he sees me.

"Your carriage awaits," he says with a smile, opening the glossy black door for me.

"Oh, Sophia! It's a wonderful surprise," I rave. "Thank you. This is so special."

"Think nothing of it, my dear," Sophia replies. "Go now. Get in. The man of your dreams is waiting for you."

"Yeah! Break a leg, cowgirl," Ev adds, draining the glass of champagne she brought down with her. I climb aboard and am happy to be in boots rather than heels.

"Be sure to enjoy your wedding day, my dear," Sophia reminds me.

I will.

I watch Ev and Sophia step into a four-wheeler. In the driver's seat is the head wedding planner, the clipboard in her lap. All three of them wave to me, then whiz off toward the ceremony.

"Are you settled, miss?" the carriage driver asks.

When I nod, he hollers 'giddy up' to his team of horses. With a snap of his whip, they begin their short *clip-clop* toward my future. The sun is warm on my skin, and I feel my breath hitch as my eyes survey the land. Acres of long viridian grasses billow on the breeze around the horses out to pasture. The beauty of Green Briar is overwhelming, and another wave of happiness washes over me.

What feels like moments later, I hear the carriage driver call, "Whoa there, boys." At his command, the big draft horses slow, then stop.

I gasp.

Green Briar has been transformed into a wedding wonderland. I didn't think the farm could be any more beautiful than it already is, but Sophia's vision for our day is dazzling me. White lights are strung through the limbs of the tree where I first met Sophia and then McKennon. They twinkle like a million little shining stars. The trellis where McKennon is waiting for me is covered in greenery and white roses. It is positioned at the top of the hill where I write, where I overlook McKennon training horses in the riding arena below, where

Sophia and I talk, and where Faith grazes. It is my most favorite view of Green Briar.

I comb back through my memories — all we've been through and where we are today. Our business is growing. I have my buckle. Faith made a full recovery. Willa will give us Star's baby. McKennon has healed from the loss of his first wife.

The driver takes my hand as I step down from the carriage. When I look up, McKennon flashes me his beautiful 'I'm right here, cowgirl' smile from the end of the aisle, and I am overwhelmed with joy, full of calm.

Rows of chairs full of bodies face my cowboy, but they turn at once when they see him light up at the sight of me. A white runner down the aisle invites me to walk into my future.

It's like slow motion as I walk toward him in Sophia's incredible wedding dress. A smile crosses each face as I pass by.

Remember this day.

I meet everyone's eyes and smile back. They are impressed with the scenery.

So am I.

9

We say 'I do' in front of everyone we know, everyone Sophia knows. My heart skips a beat as McKennon slips the wedding band on my finger, and I slip one on his.

"I now pronounce you man and wife. McKennon, you may kiss your bride," the minister announces.

"I love you," I whisper with tears in my eyes.

"I love you, too," McKennon murmurs, removing his black cowboy hat. He kisses me lovingly and then looks deeply into my eyes. Our happy smiles curve upward, and then we turn to face our guests who clap enthusiastically. I hear whistles, raucous yeehaws, and slap after slap land on McKennon's back as we make our way down the aisle, followed by our maid of honor and best man.

"This just might be better than winning a buckle," I say to McKennon as we are ushered back into the horse-drawn carriage.

"I'd say," Ev adds as she climbs up behind us. JD trails behind her.

"It's even better that our man of honor behaved himself during the ceremony," McKennon chuckles.

"Shot gun," JD hollers and leaps up next to the surprised carriage driver.

"Guessin' I spoke too soon," McKennon murmurs, raising my knuckles to his lips for a quick kiss.

"Not often that I have company up here," the driver says with an edge of disapproval as JD settles in next to him. I shake my head, but smile. Nothing can ruin my mood today.

"Giddy up," JD barks at the team of horses, ignoring the driver's comment.

The carriage driver shakes his top-hatted head, then clucks the team forward. McKennon, JD, Ev, and I are whisked away for photographs in Green Briar's lush back pastures. After the photo session, we are delivered to the main lawn in front of Sophia's farmhouse. Our reception is hosted beneath a big-top white tent. The party is a buzzing hive of activity. The wedding guests are clearly already enjoying Sophia's southern hospitality, not to mention the cocktails.

"Announcing Mr. and Mrs. Kelly!" the DJ declares as we stride hand in hand across the temporary dance floor. We take our seats at the head table in front of all the guests. My eyes scan the crowd looking for my family as the servers circle tables, pouring bubbly into flutes for the toast.

I wonder if they are here.

"Ladies and gentlemen, let's hoist a glass to Devon and McKennon," JD trumpets into a handheld microphone. JD really does look handsome all cleaned up. I've never seen him in a suit coat before, but I'm glad that both he and McKennon wore their black hats, dark jeans, and boots to the wedding. I steal a glance at my maid of honor. Clearly, Ev thinks JD looks handsome, too. She watches him intently with a faraway look in her eyes. The conversation under the big-top simmers down, and JD continues, "I wish you all the happiness and love a lifetime will allow. May your happily ever after begin right now. It's time for these two to saddle up and settle down, y'all. Cheers!"

There is an orchestra of clinking glasses, a few hoots, a couple hollers, and an over-the-top yeehaw from somewhere in the crowd. It gives us all a good chuckle, then the silverware chimes on the glassware, signaling McKennon and me to kiss. At their command, we gaze into each other's eyes, and our lips meet happily.

I aim to be fully present like Sophia had told me to, but I can't help feeling like the evening is speeding by. I don't want to miss a moment of my wedding day. Sophia has made everything about it immaculate. I am overwhelmed with emotion considering everything: the caterers bustling about, the perfect white roses in the table centerpieces, the Western-themed menu, the carriage pulled by those gleaming ponies carrying me to my favorite place on the farm, and the trellis atop the hill.

I touch my hair, the earrings in my ears, then the pearls hanging around my neck, and settle my gaze on my left ring finger. I vow to remember the way my hair is swept up off of my shoulders. The feel of Sophia's lucky diamonds in my ears and her pearls around my neck. The look on McKennon's handsome face as he waited for me at the end of the aisle, and then how he lovingly, gently slipped on the ring that now wraps around my left finger.

I will never forget.

McKennon stands and clears his throat, bringing me out of my movie reel mind.

"I ... uh ... I have somethin' I want to say." My cowboy pulls out a crumpled piece of paper from inside his suit coat and then rubs the back of his neck. He looks into my eyes. It's the same look that was in his eyes as he said, 'I do.'

Love.

After a pause, his lips finally move. "I've been workin' on this for a long while now, Devon. Think I finally got it right, so here it goes."

I smile up at my handsome husband standing over me in front of everyone we know.

It doesn't get much better than this.

"Devon. You are the ultimate expression of beauty. Each layer flows like the ocean. Your arrival at Green Briar changed all my plans. You helped me find the way back to my love of horses *and* humans. Like a tree recovering from a tough winter, I've grown branches because you watered me with your love. Today we start our life, right here, right now, and in this very moment, the past disappears. You listen to me like I am the only one around. You help me to see the light when the room is dark. Together, we've learned that not striving for perfection is perfect. With your help, I face my fears and overcome obstacles. When I am with you, nothing is wrong, and peace is all around. You make me the man I am. Together we can simply be. From now until the day I take my last breath, I pledge, I promise, and I declare you are my one and only. I am you, and you are me, now and forever."

And I am breathless.

Finished, he folds the paper and hands it to me. A single tear slips down my cheek, and he wipes it away with his thumb. The white tent is silent, and as we look out upon our guests, there isn't a dry eye in the place. Pretty much everyone here knows McKennon's history. Women sniff and dab their eyes with tissues. Men clear their throats and quickly finish their drinks. A soft smile spreads across Sophia's luminescent face as she lays her beautiful eyes on McKennon, and then on me. JD stands and slaps McKennon on the shoulder.

"Didn't know you could get so sentimental," JD chuckles, glancing at Ev. "Thanks for ruining future wedding speeches for every single man in this room, McKennon."

"A man's word is his bond. I'm putting my whole heart in this marriage, and I wanted to make sure my wife knows that," McKennon responds, meeting my gaze.

Swoon.

After McKennon and I share our first dance, we sit down to a meal in true southern fashion. Our plates are piled with heaps of brisket, sausage, ribs, and pulled pork with all the traditional accompaniments. The meat is slathered in McKennon's barbecue sauce. It's always laced with the perfect amount of heat and sweet. A glint appears in Sophia's eye when he asks if she had provided his recipe to the catering team. McKennon rises from his seat, steps behind Sophia's chair beside me, and takes a knee between us.

"Thank you for everything, Sophia," he says. "Thank you for believing in me, for saving me when I thought I had lost everything, for giving me a home here at Green Briar, for embracing Devon, and for seeing what I could not for so long. Most of all, thank you for giving us the most beautiful day."

"I couldn't agree with my husband more," I whisper. "Thank you for everything you've done for us, Sophia."

I reminisce back to my first day at Green Briar and the mystery woman I first met here. My throat tightens and my eyes water overwhelmed by the mother-figure Sophia is to me today.

"Quick, use this to dab your eyes, dear. We can't have you ruining your make-up," Sophia says with a smile, tucking a handkerchief in my palm.

"Thank heaven for you, Sophia," I murmur, wiping my tears.

"I'm so proud of both of you," Sophia continues. "It was a great honor to host your wedding."

"It was perfection. It is perfection," McKennon drawls, waving a hand around at the reception.

"Now a word of wisdom for you both." A slip of a smile spreads across Sophia's peach lips.

McKennon and I lean in closer to hear what she has to say. I recognize the mischievous look in her sapphire eyes.

"Go on," I encourage with a grin of my own.

"Well, Andrew and I snuck off from the festivities on our wedding night."

"Sophia, you dirty dog," McKennon chuckles.

"We just couldn't wait to be alone together," Sophia giggles.

"I reckon I understand that feelin'," McKennon murmurs, looking deeply into my eyes and taking my hand. I feel the usual heat rise to my cheeks.

"I remember what it was like to be young and in love. I want you to know that it won't hurt my feelings one bit if you feel inclined to do the same," Sophia continues. "Lovebirds, it's your day. Do as you please."

"Thank you, Sophia," I whisper. "Thank you so much."

After dinner, we wander among our guests to thank them for attending. We are sure to chat up our business partners, people we are selling Star's foals to, and the owners of horses we have in train-ing, even Sterling is there.

"I see you took my advice," Sterling comments as he shakes McKennon's hand. He grins at me and bends the brim of his hat.

"Indeed," McKennon responds, wrapping an arm across my bare shoulders. "Like you said, a man sure is lucky to find love twice in a lifetime. I'm holding onto this woman here, Sterling."

"Good. Congratulations, son. If you'll excuse me, I was on my way to find me a refill of whiskey. Sophia brought in the good stuff." Ster-ling lifts his empty glass and gives the remaining ice cubes in it a whirl.

McKennon nods as Sterling steps away. As we scan the area for whom to speak to next, I tense as a woman makes eye contact with me from across the dance floor.

She's here. She actually came.

"Everything OK?" McKennon asks, concern touching his brow. He drops his arm from across my back and takes my hand. I don't have time to respond because she's suddenly standing in front of me with an expectant expression on her face. I bite my lip because *he's* right behind her.

Breathe, Devon.

"Mom, this is McKennon," I murmur.

"Ma'am, it's a pleasure," McKennon drawls, removing his hat with his free hand. "You have a mighty fine daughter here."

Always the gentlemen.

"So, you're the cowboy who's just married my daughter," she says, looking him up and down.

I am pretty sure I am crushing McKennon's hand.

10

MCKENNON

I am pretty sure my knuckles are going white.

What's with Devon's death grip? It's just her mother. Is that her father bringing up the rear?

I'm still never sure what I am going to get with Devon. I figure right now I better play it safe and not get too emotional over actually meeting one or both of her parents for the first time. I know nothing about Devon's family. She doesn't talk about them much, if ever. If I bring up family, she always changes the subject, so I leave it alone. If she doesn't want me to know about them, I figure I don't need to know so long as we are happy. And we are. Now here I am, meeting them for the first time. To say her parents seem stiff is an understatement.

"Devon," the man says through a tight jaw. He puts a hand on her mother's shoulder protectively, as if holding her back. "Congratulations."

"Is this your father?" I ask.

He's intense.

"Stepfather," Devon murmurs.

"We're just glad to have even gotten an invitation to this affair,"

Devon's mother pipes up. "I'm Olivia, and this is my husband, Richard."

"Olivia. Richard." I nod to them both. "Glad you could be here with us on our special day." I go on to tell them how much I look forward to getting to know them both better. It's the truth, too, even though my wife looks pained as I say it. I make a note to get the down low about her obviously tense family history as soon as possible.

"Well, we just wanted to say hello and give you our congratulations. Enjoy your day, Devon," her mother mutters, ending the dialogue. She gives her daughter a hesitant hug. They both keep distance between their bodies and lightly tap the other's shoulder blades.

"Thanks for coming, Mom," Devon manages. With a quick smile, a nod, and a flip of her brown bobbed hair, Olivia tugs her husband away toward the bar.

Strange. Thinkin' I need a drink now, too, after that exchange.

"Hold on, Mom," Devon calls after Olivia. "Are you and Richard staying at Green Briar tonight?"

Olivia turns back toward us and nods.

"Will you be at the breakfast tomorrow morning?"

"We will. Yes," Olivia offers, looking to Richard. Richard nods.

"Let's talk more then. OK?"

"I'd like that, Devon. I'd like that very much," Olivia replies with a weak smile.

Devon bites her lip and nods. With that strange exchange complete, I see Olivia sneak a tissue from her pocket and dab her eyes as Richard leads her away.

"That's my cowgirl," I assure and squeeze my wife's hand. "That's a good thing you did just there."

"To say we had a tumultuous mother-daughter relationship is an understatement," Devon whispers, watching her mother and Richard wander away.

"At least you've got a mom. I never knew mine," I console, feeling a little downtrodden. "At least I have Sophia."

Thank heaven for Sophia.

"We are both so lucky to have Sophia. Part of me wishes I'd never met mine, too," Devon drones.

"That's the thing about family, Devon. When you're little, they are there to take care of you. It's their job to make sure you go to bed, get out of bed, brush your teeth, have good manners, get good grades, all that stuff. Then you grow up. When you grow up, you get to choose the family you want for yourself. It doesn't have to be biological. You don't have to subscribe to the ideals of others. When you are an adult, you earn the right to do what's right for you. It doesn't matter what anyone else thinks. And you don't have to suffer other people's choices or mistakes, either. You've made your own family here at Green Briar. We are your family now."

"My husband gives the best advice in the world," Devon whispers, leaning her head on my chest.

"I aim to please, miss. Now come on. Let's sit down for a moment, and you can give me the cliff notes on your family, so I know what I've gotten myself into here," I say, shifting my wedding band and giving her a one-cornered smile. "Need to be sure I'm not up to my neck in too much hot water."

Devon gives me that heavenly smile of hers, and I can tell she's considering it.

I already know my new wife so well. I can't wait to know her even better.

"All right, cowboy. I'll tell you, but we are keeping this conversation high level. There will be no pity parties on our wedding day, especially from the bride. The past is the past. I'm more interested in the present and my future with you."

"Good, but I reckon this new knowledge will help me understand what makes you tick better. Lord knows I need all the help I can get in that department, woman," I tease.

I like getting a rise out of her from time to time, especially when the topic is heavy for her.

Devon shakes her head, slugs me lightly in the shoulder, and takes me by the hand in search of a place to chat. We have a seat at an empty table on the fringe of the reception tent. Most of the guests are doing the boot scootin' boogie on the dance floor or are mingling at the bar chatting over cocktails.

"OK. I'm going to make this quick because it is the past, and I'm leaving the past in the past. The future is where I am focused. Got it?"

I nod but keep my lips zipped. I want to hear what she has to say.

"Here it goes. My mom and dad fought all the time when I was a kid. It wasn't pretty. A lot of harsh words were shared. My mom ended up having an affair and then filed for divorce soon after. It sent my father into a deep depression. He still wanted to work things out. Mom wouldn't budge," Devon sighs, takes a deep breath. I reckon the tough part is coming from the contorted expression on her face.

"Go on," I coax. "I've got you."

"He committed suicide before the ink was even dry on the paperwork. My mom married her lover and didn't even mourn my father. That guy she is with. Richard. That's him. That's the man who broke up my family. As soon as I was old enough to leave, I left, and I never looked back. My biological dad is dead. I blame my mother. That's why I don't talk about my family."

Suddenly, it all makes sense.

"Is that why you wanted to walk down the aisle by yourself? Why you wouldn't let Sterling escort you?" I ask.

"Yes. Walking down the aisle alone was my silent tribute to my father." Devon looks down at her hands clasped in her lap.

I am stunned. Devon has been through so much. She knows what loss feels like, too. Maybe that's why she had the will to wait while I figured myself out. I reach out and touch her cheek.

"I didn't know all that," I whisper. "Thank you for sharing that painful experience with me."

"You're not the only one with secrets and a dark past, McKennon Kelly. I owe the truth about my past to you though," she murmurs. "You're my husband now. I don't want to talk about it anymore though. Case closed?"

"Case closed," I assure, but I can't help but worry a little.

Case closed until tomorrow when she speaks with her mother again at our breakfast celebration.

11

DEVON

"Here comes trouble," McKennon teases as Ev approaches our table.

"What's going on over here? It's your wedding, for heaven's sake. Why do you two look so somber?" Ev asks, taking a seat.

"I just introduced McKennon to my mother," I groan.

"And Richard?" Ev asks with a raise of an eyebrow.

"Yep," I sigh.

"That would explain it. It was a very gracious thing for you to do, Devon. Inviting them to your wedding after you haven't spoken in so long. Very gracious." Ev puts a reassuring palm on my shoulder.

"Thanks, Ev. It was more Sophia's doing then mine. She sort of coerced me into giving her their address. Someone once told me that when you grow up, you get to choose the family you want for yourself. That's what I am doing here with McKennon at Green Briar." McKennon squeezes my hand. I squeeze back.

"Those are some pretty wise words. I completely agree," Ev responds.

"Courtesy of my cowboy philosopher here."

"Why, McKennon, you are one smart cowboy, aren't you?" Ev

teases.

"I aim to please, miss," McKennon drawls with a tip of his brim. Ev's eyes sparkle like emeralds at the gesture.

"I'm liking this cowboy stuff, Devon. I can see how a girl could get into this. Speaking of cowboys ... that JD is one handsome devil and is one heck of a ride in the sack."

McKennon's eyes go wide at the commentary. Studying me for a moment, he clears his throat and takes a swing of his whiskey.

"Too much information there," he mutters.

"Oh, look! There he is at the bar," Ev continues. "Oh my, he's bending over to pick up the napkin he just dropped." She tilts her head to the side and examines JD's rear.

"Ev! Wasn't once enough for you?" I remark, slipping a glance at McKennon. He sticks a finger in his shirt collar and gives it a tug.

"Truth is, I fear the boy doesn't even remember me," she sighs.

"What? How is that possible? You were all over each other last night. You two left together, didn't you?" I probe.

"Yes, I took him back to my hotel, but the kid was really snook-ered. It was my fault. I bought him an awful lot of whiskey. I'm amazed he could even perform last night. Actually, that he's even standing right now. When I woke up, he was gone. I was making eyes at him the whole ceremony, but he looked confused."

"How do you not remember being intimate with someone?" McKennon asks, but then shakes his head. "Oh, never mind. It's JD. Anything is possible with that kid."

"Well, I'm going to make sure he remembers me now," Ev declares. "I'm off to get some more of that JD-magic. Just watch, I'll reel him in all over again."

"That pairing is a train wreck waitin' to happen," McKennon muses as Ev struts off to take a seat at the bar. She crosses, then uncrosses her legs, crosses them again, flips her hair, fanning out like a flame, and boosts her cleavage.

"Lady sure knows how to make herself available, huh?" McKennon murmurs near my ear.

Indeed.

12

JD

"Hi." I sit down at the table, uninvited. "Pretty fancy digs here, ain't they?" I wave a hand above my head, addressing the big white tent, all gloriously lit and decorated for the wedding.

"It's quite the production," the woman admits, not meeting my eyes.

"I reckon maybe you and me might find our way down the aisle one day," I lie, laying it on thick, hoping to land her in bed. If that line doesn't snag her, I'll adjust my belt buckle when I'm sure she's watching.

"Well, look at you," she replies, looking me up and down.

"Can I offer you a drink, miss?" I ask, tipping my hat and slipping a whiskey in front of her.

"Sorry, cowboy. You're awfully cute, but I don't do country, and I don't drink whiskey," she responds coolly, rummaging through her purse and then reapplying her lipstick.

"Thinkin' you just haven't had the right type of doin' by a country boy," I say, slyly scooting my seat a little closer to her. She snaps her compact shut, rolls her lipstick down slowly, and presses her ruby red lips together as she returns the items to her tiny clutch.

"Ah. You must be the hunky and very young, JD. I've gotten the scoop on you, young man."

"Oh yeah? What'd ya hear?" I ask, scooting even closer.

"I've heard through the grapevine that you always go for the low-hanging fruit, so to speak. Do I look like low-hanging fruit to you?" she asks, fanning her left hand in front of my face.

"Apologies, miss," I drawl when I see the wedding ring.

Not sure how I missed the rock on her hand, but what the hell? She didn't have to be such a bitch about it.

I glance around and resolve to hightail it away from her before the husband decides to appear. I'm not looking for a pop in the nose this evening. So what if this one slipped through my fingers, there are plenty of others to choose from.

Leaving the table in search of an easier mark, I spot the redhead from the ceremony perched on a leather barstool at the bar. I take a seat next to her and order another whiskey.

This one sure smells nice.

"Is that woman you were talking to over there your hot date?" the redhead asks. She scrunches up her nose in disapproval. I can't help but notice the faint dusting of strawberry freckles across it. They are pretty dang cute, a youthful touch on a beautifully mature face.

"Nah, weddings are lame. I wouldn't bring a date to somethin' like this, not with so many already drunk women ripe for the taking right here waiting for me to show up." I flash her my pearly whites.

"Uh. That's interesting," she replies. She furrows her brows, flips her flaming hair over her shoulder and puts a hand on her slender neck.

I like the looks of this one.

"I'm not drunk yet, just trying to nurse a hangover," she continues after an awkward pause.

"I can help with hangovers."

"Is that so?"

"Yep. I gotta know your name first though before I can get to fixin' ya up."

She gives me a strange look, just like she did during the ceremony and all throughout the photo session that followed.

Am I supposed to know her name? Have I met her before?

"Well, in that case, my name is Ev."

"Ev?" I ask. I feel my eyebrows drawing together.

Strange name.

"Yes, Ev."

"What kind of name is Ev? Haven't heard that particular name before."

"Ev — as in the letters 'E' and 'V'. It's short for Everly."

"Ah, I see. Well, Ev. Seems we've both got us two-letter names. I'm JD. Short for two names that I didn't give to myself, and I'd rather not divulge. Ever."

"Now I'm curious. What are those two names then? I won't tell. It'll be our secret. Promise."

"Sorry. Can't do it," I reply, shaking my head.

"Aw, come on, cowboy," she pleas.

"You'll have to get me awfully hammered to tell you my birth name, miss."

"Deal. I'll buy you a drink – make that drinks." Ev flashes a mischievous smile.

"It's a wedding. Ain't the drinks free?" I quip.

"It's a metaphor, cowboy. Come on. Let's do this," she commands, signaling for the bartender.

"What can I get you?" the bartender asks.

"Whiskey?" Ev inquires with a lift of her crimson eyebrow and a twist of her matching-stained lips.

"Whiskey'll work," I reply.

I dig this chick. Fiery. Just like her hair.

"How would you like that whiskey, miss?" the bartender asks impatiently, eyeballing the lineup of wedding guests at the far end of the full bar.

"Bring the bottle and two shot glasses," she orders, slipping him a large bill. He takes her tip with a nod and hurries away. Five seconds later, he obliges and leaves a bottle of whiskey. It's the good stuff, too.

"Where are you from?"

"New York City."

"I figured it was something like that. Is that how you get things done there?" I ask, filling our shot glasses to the tippy top.

"Why, yes, it is, cowboy. Got a problem with that?" she retorts.

"Fine by me," I say with a shrug. I suck my drink down, and she follows suit. I pour us another and then another.

"OK, cowboy. Let's take a breather. That's three shots in a row."

"Your wish is my command, miss. I was just gettin' loosened up for the guessin' game I figure we are about to start playin'."

"Oh, are you ready to play already? I like games."

"And I like that sass you're showin' me. Go on then. Give it a guess."

"Let me think. JD? JD. What could JD stand for?" Ev puts a polished nail to her pouted, kissable lips.

"Here we go," I sigh, pouring myself another whiskey.

I really hate this game. Played it often enough, but if it will lead to bedding a redhead tonight, then I plan to suffer through it.

"I've got it. It's Jimmy Dean. Isn't it?"

"Like the sausage links?" I grunt. "Nah. Try again."

"How about Jethro Derrick?" she asks, obviously trying not to laugh.

"Jethro Derrick? Come on." I shake my head no. "You're never gonna guess."

"Can I keep trying? This is fun," she chirps, taking a sip from her shot glass.

I wag a finger at her.

"Ah-ah, now. Shot glasses aren't for sipping."

"Right," she laughs and tosses the rest down her throat. "Now can I keep guessing your name?"

"I suppose if it amuses you that much," I reply, refilling her glass. "Go on then. What else you got?"

"All right. Hmm. Let me think." She squints and tilts her head, pondering me. "How about Jeffery Richard? You look like a Jeffery Richard."

"As in Jeff Dick? That's clever, but nope," I chuckle. "Although I have been called a dick once or twice in my lifetime."

"Yes. That, I figured. OK then, what about Jerry Dylan?"

"You've got quite the imagination, but no," I affirm, shaking my head and running a hand over my face. "Try again."

"Jonathan Daniel?"

"Uh-uh," I groan.

"Jimmy David?"

"No. There's not a chance you're guessin' this one. I'll give you a hint. My first name is not Jimmy."

"Fine," she hoots, slapping her slender thigh. "Let me keep trying."

"Glad you find tryin' to figure out my name so amusing. You have two more guesses then I'm ending this game."

"Justin Dustin?"

"Seriously? That's one of your last guesses?" I raise my eyebrows and finish another shot.

"Well, it's gotta be something terrible if you only go by JD. Is it Jeb Donald?"

"OK. Enough. This is too painful," I say. She is laughing hysterically, and it's probably the sexiest laugh I think I've ever heard. It isn't high pitched like the girls I usually bed. It is authentically adult.

"Come on, please tell me?" she begs.

"Not sure I want to tell you now because your laughing like a hyena has got me pretty entertained. Anyone ever tell you that you've gotta sexy giggle?"

"You think a hyena laugh is sexy?"

"Sure do."

"Well, that's a first. Come on, cowboy. Please tell me. I'll buy you another drink if you do."

"I reckon we probably don't need any more drinks. How's about a dance instead?" I ask, eyeing the bottle of whiskey we've been draining. It's nearly empty. I know if I'm going to take this woman home, I need to pace things. I want her good and coherent for the things I'm planning on doing to her. Plus, I'm not looking for a repeat of last night. I hate waking up next to a stranger.

I'm turning a new leaf today.

"You tell me your name, and you'll get your dance."

"Deal."

"Out with it then," she presses.

"Fine," I sigh. "Reckon I need a pinky swear out of you first though. If my real name gets out, my reputation will be ruined."

Ev laughs, puts an elbow on the bar, and extends her pinky. I shoot another whiskey, give her the eye, and then wrap my pinky finger around hers.

"Mums the word, ya hear?" I tighten the hold I have on her finger. Ev nods, and I look over each of my shoulders to ensure no one else is within earshot. I lean forward and whisper near her ear, "JD is short for Jackson Drake, and make a note that JD is spelled with the letters 'J' and 'D' only. I think those dots people like put between abbreviated names are a waste of time. Plain and simple, it's JD McCall."

"Noted on the periods, but Drake?" she whispers back, raising an eyebrow.

"Yes, Drake. I've been told my mom read a lot of cowboy romance novels when she was pregnant with me. A lot. Remember mum's the word, ya hear?"

"My lips are zipped, cowboy," Ev replies.

"They better be."

"So, here's a question for you," she says, changing the subject abruptly. "What's the first thing you thought when you saw me? Be honest. I like to make adjustments based on what people's first impressions of me are. It's good for business."

"That's a mighty straightforward and strange question after the name game."

"Just tell me. I'm a city girl. We are direct."

"I see that. Well, when I first saw ya standing up there at the wedding, I thought I'd like to have sex with the likes of her."

"Be serious!"

"I am. You interested? I reckon you're worth a ride around the arena."

"Maybe," she replies. That strange look crosses her face again for the tick of the clock, and then it's gone. "Think you can stay on?"

"Trust me. I can stay on," I say, dragging a finger over her knee.

"What do you know about pleasing an older woman?" she asks.

"You aren't an older woman to me. You're a show pony. This look of yours is all show. All dressed up and lookin' pretty, but I reckon no one's been in that saddle for an awfully long time."

"And how do you know that? It should offend me you would talk to me that way."

"Don't take offense. You know you're all show, lady. Let me show you a thing or two about ridin' a cowboy," I press, opting for a sip of water over whiskey.

"That's your read on me?" she asks, finger circling the rim of her glass.

"Yes, ma'am, but if you'd like to stop being a show pony, I could show you how to loosen up. I could get you back in that saddle."

"You can't just say whatever you want to me, you know, you youngster!" That strange look crosses her face again but is erased and replaced with a glint of amusement.

"And why not?" I whisper, swiping her sleek, red hair to the side and kissing her neck gently. When I pull away, I look into her slivered green eyes. I know her knees went weak at the move because I felt the tension go out of her body for just a moment. My experience tells me she isn't quite ready to let me know that I've gotten under her skin though.

All in due time.

"I've been around the block a time or two, young man," she says, pressing a palm to my chest. "Your slick moves won't work on this seasoned mare like it might with the fillies."

"I'll change your mind. Give me a little time."

"Is that so?"

"Sure is. I know how to work a lady *and* a room. I always start with the ladies, but now I best be makin' the rounds, start shaking some hands. There might be a sponsorship out there among the guests waiting for a bull rider like me." I wink at her.

"So you want a sponsorship?" she asks.

"I reckon I'd like to be a superstar," I tease. "I'd also like that dance you promised me." I stand up, tip my hat, and strut off toward the dance floor.

That should leave her wanting more of what I have to offer.

"Interesting," she says, loud enough for me to hear.

13

DEVON

"Isn't he a little young for you?" I whisper, sneaking up behind Ev, still seated at the bar, eyes trailing after JD.

"Isn't McKennon a little old for you?" Ev asks, turning around and putting her hands on her hips.

"Fair enough. Just remember, JD's been around the block. Wild hearts can't be tamed. And JD's a wild one."

"Who said anything about taming anyone? I like a little wild in my life, Devon."

"There are a lot more women than men in the horse business," I caution. "JD is known for thinking below the belt, rather than with his brain. There are a lot of women for the picking for one hot guy in the rodeo realm."

"Well then, more men should be cowboys," Ev replies, admiring her manicure. "Plus, he's cute, and I'm not finished with him yet."

"JD usually goes for the low-hanging fruit."

"Are you suggesting that I am low-hanging fruit?"

"You were last night."

"And I intend to be again. There'll be room in my bed tonight. I'm happy to roll the dice."

"Not tonight, Ev! You are staying at the main house. My mother is staying at the main house. You'll give Sophia a heart attack if you take JD to your room! The hotel was one thing, but here at Green Briar? I don't know about this, Ev."

"But Devon. He's so handsome. Look at those hips move. Good lord. If he's dancing and riding bulls with hips like that, what do you think he does in the bedroom? It was amazing. It's funny, I don't even mind that he seems to not remember anything about our sheet-twisting last night. I intend to do that with him again, but this time, he'll remember. I promise you that. I can't believe you never gave him a whirl."

"Oh no, you didn't. I can't believe you just said that." I look out on the dance floor where JD is grinding on the woman who interviewed me for the YouTube video at Congress. "JD? Gross. He's my friend. Seriously, what are you going to do with all that? Him? He's nuts, just look at him."

"Don't know yet, but another trial run shouldn't hurt in deciding. I'm thinking of taking him back to the city with me. Perhaps I'll make him a star."

What the heck is she talking about?

"A star? I can't even wrap my head around what you mean by that, Ev. A one-night stand is one thing. JD is very good at those, but I can't see him hanging out in Manhattan. He's pure country."

"Hell, Dev. That's what I like about him. How about you let me take an uncalculated risk with a younger, sexy cowboy? It was seriously the best sex of my life."

"That you claim he doesn't remember," I groan.

"He'll remember it this time. Come on, Devon. Let me have some fun."

"All right," I say, raising my palms in surrender. "Never say that I didn't warn you, and keep the noise down in the house tonight, for heaven's sake."

"Thanks for the lecture. Now, I'm going to get my grind on." Ev raises a sassy eyebrow at me. I shake my head as she strides to middle of the dance floor to sandwich herself between JD and a bodacious blonde he's moved on to.

I sigh.

McKennon walks up and trails a hand down the satin at the back of my dress. "Well, isn't that an interesting looking threesome?"

I roll my eyes. I want Ev to have fun, but fun with JD can get a woman's heart broken.

"Help me," I groan.

"That's what I came over here for, my bride. Enough watchin' other people gettin' it on. I'm lookin' for some action myself. From my wife. How's about we take Sophia's advice and sneak back to our house, so I can get you out of this dress."

"Cowboy, take me away, PAH-Leease," I giggle, pressing my lips to his neck. He smells so nice. "I can't wait to get you out of those clothes myself."

"Well, off we go then, wifey."

With that, McKennon scoops me up and drifts out of the big white tent, nodding goodbye to lingering guests as we make our exit. I wrap my arms around his neck and rest my head on his strong shoulder. He sets me on my boots once we are a good distance away and takes my hand. He lifts it, kisses my knuckles.

"I love you, wife," McKennon whispers as we wander out onto Sophia's land, leaving the reception and the dancing threesome behind us.

Once we are on the porch of our perfect little house, McKennon lifts me again to carry me over the threshold. He kicks the front door closed behind us and heads straight for our bedroom. Wordlessly, he tosses me down on our wedding bed. I bounce on the soft mattress.

"Take this off of me now!" I demand, tugging at the fastenings down the back of my bodice.

"Only if you return the favor, miss," he drawls, gesturing a hand toward his own clothing.

When I notice that his manhood has already stirred, my cheeks heat in their usual way. As he crosses the room, butterflies zip in my stomach. McKennon sits behind me on the bed and begins loosening the satin-covered buttons from their holes. He kisses my neck, taking an excruciatingly long time to release me from the top of my dress. Once the bodice is freed, I stand and let the dress slip down around my legs. McKennon releases a long slow whistle, as I stand before him in my wedding-night white under things and my cowgirl boots.

"I think we forgot to remove somethin'," he chuckles, rising to kiss my mouth. He trails his lips to my neck, along my collarbone, up over the mound of my breasts, drags them down my stomach, over my panties, brushes the inside of my thighs, then takes the forgotten blue garter between his teeth. He slips it down my leg to the top of my boots, pulls it out with his index finger and lets the elastic snap back to my calf.

"Ouch," I tease as my heart pounds against my chest. He just gazes up at me with those sultry sapphire eyes, a sinister smile of his own tugging at the corner of his lip. McKennon stands to remove his suit coat and then unbuttons his shirt slowly.

He then returns to me, gently lifting each of my legs to remove my cowgirl boots. He tosses them one at a time to the corner of the room. We exchange smiles as each one lands with a *thunk*. It takes everything I have not to attack him and get things moving faster, but I wait. McKennon likes to take his time with these things. He revisits the garter, drags it the rest of the way down and off over my polished toenails.

"Someone's gonna be awful sad we didn't toss that bouquet of yours or this here garter," he drawls tossing it over his shoulder. It lands on the lampshade, and we both have a chuckle.

"Knowing our luck, JD and Ev would have been the recipients. Good lord, can you imagine?"

"Not somethin' I'm interested in thinkin' about right about now, miss. Don't go muckin' up my mind. I've got things in store for you just now," McKennon murmurs, dragging his lips up my body.

Once he's kissed every part of me, he stands and dips a finger into the cup of my delicate bra and sneaks a peek inside. Then returns to kissing my mouth.

"I can't wait," I breathe, tearing from his kiss. I fumble to the front of his pants, tug his belt loose, pop the button, unzip the zipper, and in one fell swoop, drag them to his ankles.

"Daring Devon," he croons, sweeping me into his arms and tossing me onto the bed again.

14

MCKENNON

I love this woman.

In the bed, in the dark, Devon lets out a whispery, happy moan. It's a sound that always pleases me in the best sort of way.

Means I'm doin' things right by her.

The sound of her lost in pleasure always arouses me, spurs me on to quicken my pace. But tonight, I'm takin' a little extra time. I want our wedding night love-making to go on forever.

I love the look of her as she rides me, the way her hair has fallen out of that swept up hair do, streaming down over her shoulders, so lush, so shiny. I can see flickers of ecstasy overcome her face as she loses herself in the motion of our bodies joined. She tosses her head back, all of that hair flowing, and wraps herself around me like a cloak, clinging to me all arms and legs, so I can devour her neck with my mouth. No matter how many times I've been like this with her, I will always want more.

"I want you on top of me," Devon pants, delirious with lust and love.

Switching roles, I flip her over as requested and settle in above her. That lovely, breathy moan comes again. I am filled with delight. I am pleasing my wife, and I am proud. I feel her give and tighten before her teeth nip at my shoulder. I'm setting the pace now, trying to lasso myself back into control. I've been at the brink more than once while she was gliding above me.

Hang on, cowboy. Hang in there.

Pausing, I take deep, steadying inhales. I hover above her in awe. She takes my breath away with that hair splayed out around her angelic face on the pillow. I brace my arms on either side of her and move again, watching the gloriousness of her satisfied eyes as she pulls my hips toward her again and again.

"I want to make you happy, Devon." I lower my lips near hers. "Every day of your life."

"Oh, McKennon," she breathes. Her beautiful brown doe eyes pierce mine. "You do. You are."

My pace is slow, patient as her mouth moves against mine again. Our bodies sway, and I can't help gradually deepening my thrusts. When she fists her hands in my hair, her breath heaving, I quicken the rhythm more. I watch her eyes, wild, desperate, and I know what she wants. Release.

Lord only knows, I am ready.

My hands grip her hips. I suck in a breath as her body arches back. Devon knows what to expect now. We are both on the brink of exploding in pleasure. When it comes for us, we welcome it in unison. Earth-shattering unison.

"McKennon," Devon purrs. "I am the happiest woman on earth." She draws me down to her. We lie together trembling, limbs intertwined, spent flesh to spent flesh.

"I aim to please, wife. I'll aim to please always," I murmur, pressing my lips to her temple. "I was waiting for this moment all night."

"Same here, husband," she breathes, beautifully relaxed.

I stroke her hair for a long while, appreciating the moment, appreciating her, reflecting over our wedding day in my mind, and before I know it, my wife has drifted off to sleep.

15

As the bar gives the last call and the DJ plays the last song, the redheaded vixen and I are among the few wedding guests still lingering. McKennon and Devon have long since made their departure. I got my dance and then some with Ev, but I have had enough of the dancing. I'm ready to move on. I'm ready for some moving between the sheets with this wily one.

"How's about we take a walk?" I suggest. "I'll show you around the place, miss. Seems this gig is on its last legs, anyway." I take note that the lights are coming up, and a few guests are still wobbling drunkenly about the dance floor. "I'd like to show you some other things, too. Maybe slip you out of that dress here soon."

"How old are you?" Ev snips. The question surprises me. I figured she'd be a sure thing tonight.

Can't go having her get second thoughts now, not after I've put in this much effort.

"Does it matter? We are both adults, aren't we?"

"I guess it doesn't. And yes, we are."

"Well then, what'll it be?" I ask, offering her my arm.

"Let's take that walk of yours, JD."

Ev smiles as she tucks her hand into the crook of my elbow. I smile, too, as I lead her out of the tent and into the night. The moon is full, hanging low in the sky, and casts a yellow light on the path leading to the barn.

"This is where I come to think about things. I come back to Green Briar to get quiet."

"You? Quiet? I can't imagine," Ev teases.

We meander over Green Briar's acres, listening to the chirps of crickets in the distance.

"It is beautiful here, but perhaps a little too quiet for the likes of me. I grew up surrounded by concrete. The city is loud. Noise is in my blood."

"New York City. That place is a little too loud for me. Sirens, horns, all those people. A country boy can only handle that sort of stuff for a little while. I only set foot in big cities when I am out on tour."

"So, you come here to get quiet? Why?" Ev probes, changing the subject.

"Bull ridin' is a crazy business," I reply, pulling open the doors to the main horse barn.

"Bull riding. That's an interesting profession. Why ride bulls?" Ev asks, stepping inside. The horses stir in their stalls and a serenade of whinnies greets us when I flip on the aisle lights.

"It's always what I've wanted to do. I grew up with the rodeo. It's in my blood, like the city is in yours. My father was a stock contractor. When I was a boy, he raised the winning bucking bulls I wanted to ride one day. I learned the bull ridin' ropes from my uncle, though." I pause for a moment in honor of his memory.

I clear my throat and continue on before Ev can ask questions. "My sister had a barrel pony, too. We all went on tour together and lived in a luxury RV with huge living quarters out on different fairgrounds all year long. My mama loved to cook and made our food during the events. In the evenings, we would all gather around a bonfire, and my uncle would play the guitar. Those were the good days. I rode my first sheep when I was about five years old."

"You rode sheep?" Ev asks, furrowing her brow.

That's what they start youngsters on. It's called mutton bustin'.""

"Mutton busting? This country thing is going to take some getting used to. What happens after you ride the sheep?"

"You upgrade to steers."

"Of course. Why didn't I think of that?"

"I imagine it's hard for a city slicker to wrap her head around, but after I graduated from sheep, I was riding steers by the fourth grade. I never wanted to be anything other than a bull rider like my uncle. Come on," I say, tipping my head toward the horses. I take Ev's hand and lead her to meet Faith and Willa.

The ladies always like the horses.

"These are Devon's horses. The white and brown spotted one is Faith. I'm sure you've heard lots about her."

Ev nods and hesitates before giving Faith a quick pat on her outstretched muzzle. Willa puts her head over the open top portion of her stall door and nickers.

"This must be Willa. She's a pretty one," Ev hums.

"Yeah, she sure is. Willa is the one who brought back the Green Briar empire. She won us a big show with a big purse last year. It's been booming around here ever since then. Went from ghost town to the place to be overnight. She's in foal right now," I say, stroking beneath Willa's white mane. "You're gonna be a momma soon, girl." I coo, but catch myself and quickly snap my mouth shut.

Stop acting like a softy. You're trying to get laid, not make this redhead fall in love with you.

"You know them all intimately, don't you?"

Darn. She noticed.

"I guess," I huff, shrugging my shoulders. "Just horses."

"So you work here?" Ev asks.

"Yeah, they cut me a check every now and again. I help with the day-to-day when I'm not out on tour and go on the road with them to horse shows from time to time. I have a lot of freedom between my bull ridin' gigs, so I pick up work here at Green Briar. McKennon has been good to me. I've danced at his weddings. I'll sing at his funeral. Sophia, too. They're my family."

"And Devon?" Ev inquires with a raise of a thin eyebrow.

"What about her?" I ask.

"You were interested in more than her horse at one point, weren't you? You don't hide your affinity for her very well."

"Maybe, but then I realized Devon couldn't handle a cowboy that is hung like a bull, moreover, one that can thrust like a bull. That woman doesn't take any bull," I chuckle.

"I think there might be more to the story, cowboy. You were interested in her once, weren't you?"

"Yes. No. I don't know. Not really. No, not Devon." I hesitate for a moment and rub the back of my neck. "Well, not exactly. OK, fine. Maybe. She sorta reminds me of someone is all, but I always knew she was better suited for a guy like McKennon. It didn't really stop me from tryin' from time to time, though. I like a challenge."

"Was it the challenge or was it the woman?" Ev presses.

"I don't really know to be honest, but when a nice, normal girl like her walked onto Green Briar, it got me thinkin' maybe I'd like a little somethin' like that. You know, somethin' longer term." I clear my throat, realizing I'd just gone soft again.

"So you *are* interested in love? Aren't you, JD?"

"Not sure I'm capable of commitment. There has been a lot of loss in my life. It's a long story," I admit.

"I'm interested. Do tell." Ev encourages.

"It's not one I care too much to dive into, but I'll give you the short version." I brace myself. "I have big aspirations for my career. My dream has always been to ride bulls, just like my uncle did, and I'm doin' it. Doin' it pretty dang well, in fact. It's my way of payin' tribute to my uncle. He was killed when one of my daddy's bulls stepped on his chest during a rodeo event. I was just a boy when I lost the family member I felt closest to. Losing his brother turned my father cold. He wasn't all that pleased about having to shoot one of his prized bucking bulls after it happened either. He just got plain mean. My dad started slappin' my mama around. Not too long after I lost my uncle, my mother ended up running off with a roper. To say my sister's and my relationship with our father was strained is an understatement. Anyway, my sister ended up running off with a cowboy herself."

"McKennon?" Ev asks.

"Reckon Devon told you about all that?" Ev nods, and I continue, "Yeah, my father did not approve. Not long after Madison married him, she was crushed when a horse that McKennon had trained fell on her at a horse show. She died, too. I was there. It set off a whole horrible chain of events. Years later, Devon showed up here. We became friends, but she fell for McKennon who ended up takin' off on her. Devon waited for him though."

"You may not have inserted all the details, but that sure isn't a short story, JD. I'm sorry to hear you've been through all that. I know a thing or two about losing people, too. It's awful. It can ruin you if you aren't careful."

"Yeah, well. There's more, but honestly, it's too much for my brain. Thinking about it all makes me feel scrambled, you know?" I like that she nods. "All that emotion. The bulls and the ladies keep my mind off of it. I'm hopin' that you'll be tonight's lucky lady. Haven't had me many redheads."

"You are naughty," she replies, shaking her head.

"Darn right, I am," I assure and conjure up the crumpled newspaper clipping from my wallet. I hand it over to Ev. "It's a newspaper story about my uncle's big break into the rodeo scene. I keep it on me to remind myself that we come into this world alone, and we go out alone. After all that loss, I decided it wise to go out on my own, so I wouldn't get hurt again or hurt anyone else."

I think I hear her mutter 'sounds familiar,' but I just keep right on talking. "I figure I might as well just work on being alone, except for the occasional night or two with a beautiful lady, of course."

"So what's your type then, cowboy?" she inquires, handing the article back to me.

"Hmm. I like secretaries, bartenders, waitresses, dancers, and bull riding groupies," I say, tucking the yellowed piece of paper back in my wallet. "I like women I meet at wedding receptions. I like women I meet on the *National Bull Riders* tour, in elevators, and sitting next to me on bar stools. I pretty much like all women. Right now, I'm likin' the looks of you. I have one rule, though. I don't sleep with women who are my friends."

"Like Devon?"

"That's right, like Devon. At least I have the good taste not to do somethin' like that. The Devon part of my story, well, it doesn't matter now. She's made her choice. She's McKennon's wife. I'm not a bad guy, you know."

"I didn't suggest you were. Men, their insecurities, and all the things they do to keep love away, I can see through all that because I understand it. I know that's why you have the reputation you do. Your weakness is you *can* fall in love, but you've decided not to. That's why you never settle, keep being with woman after woman, and stay out on the road. It's a smart plan, if you ask me."

I like the way this woman thinks.

Ev faces me, strings her arms around my neck, and runs her fingertips through the hair at the base of my neck.

"You've got me all figured out, don't 'cha? As far as weakness goes, did I mention that I have a weakness for women I meet at wedding receptions?"

"I may have caught that. I might need more information first."

"Aw, come on, and give me a try. I'm like a good steak. I just melt in your mouth."

"Tell me why you are such a playboy first. Don't you believe you might have a soul mate out there somewhere?"

"I don't believe in the soul mate thing. We are animals, and we are here to mate, you know, spread the seed. Only thing is we think differently than animals do. We think there is a thing out there called love. Hogwash, I tell you. Either you are attracted or you're not. That's the only thing there really is. So if I'm attracted to it, I go for it, spend the night or maybe a few. Some people want to take it further than that and try a relationship, but relationships don't last. I've always been the 'go for it' kinda guy."

"So you don't get hurt?" Ev asks.

"Like I said, my philosophy is that you come into this world alone, and you go out alone, so I figure I might as well just work on being alone. I gotta have some fun along the way though, and that requires the opposite sex." I avoid her question perfectly. "I like to keep it light, unattached."

So no one gets hurt. Particularly me.

"I'll only hurt you if you let me," Ev says, as if reading my mind.

"Ditto," I respond. "I'm in a truthful mood from the whiskey, so here it is — my mother left, my sister died, my dad was a monster. I definitely don't want to end up like him, although he's a bit better now that he's aged and set things right with McKennon. I just — I don't know — shut down. I hide behind my humor and sexuality. I never have wanted anything real, anything that involved love or family for fear of losing them. So I sleep around. I have a good time. I don't get hurt."

"Like I said, sounds like a smart decision," Ev replies.

"Never told anyone that before. I don't enjoy thinking about that stuff. There was this girl once. She was the first and the last I hung my heart on the line for. Devon kinda reminded me of her. Watching Devon walk down the aisle today kinda felt like losing her all over again. Can't say why exactly. I think there is always one thing. The one thing, the one person, the one situation that ruins you for anyone else."

"I could help you forget," Ev whispers.

Now this is more like it.

"That'd be mighty nice of you, miss."

"Do you remember me?" Ev asks.

"What do you mean?"

"We've met before."

"Believe me. If we'd met before, I know I'd remember you."

"I'm not so sure about that, cowboy."

"What's that supposed to mean?"

"We only had the best sex I've had in years after Devon's bachelorette party," she explains. She's wearing a pained expression now.

"With all due respect, I don't have any idea what you are talking about." I take a step back and rub my palms, now sweaty, on the front of my jeans.

"I can tell by the look on your face that, in fact, you don't remember me. It's probably my fault you don't remember last night. I did get you even more drunk than you already were, which was very drunk, when I laid my eyes on you. Why don't you come back to my room, and I'll remind you? Wanna mess up my bed with me, JD?"

I regain my composure.

"I would like that very much, but at the main house with all the guests? Sophia will have our hides!"

"Ah yes, Devon warned me not to make any noise at the main house," Ev replies with a sulk.

"How's about we take a roll in the hay here. Nobody's gonna come down here until sunrise," I say, suggestively. "Unless that's too country for the likes of you."

Ev raises an eyebrow and tucks a polished nail between her lips.

She's thinkin' on it. That's good. I'll help her make up her mind.

I swiftly take her up in my arms and kiss her deeply. I guide her backwards into an empty stall used for storing hay. I move my hands over her body. I am captivated with her curvy hips, full breasts, and, good lord, her soft lips.

"You taste good, Ev," I mumble into her mouth. I lower myself to a seated position on a hay bale and pull her down with me. She immediately goes to work, stripping me of my suit jacket, and then unbuttons the front of my dress shirt deftly. When she drags her fingers down my bare chest, I tip my head back in pleasure and close my eyes. I sense she's hiking up her dress. Before I know what's hit me, she positions one long leg after the other to my sides, settles down to straddle me, and moves on my lap. The moment is electric, and every part of me is charged. I need to rein things in though, so I'm back in control.

This woman has experience.

"Stand up," I order, opening my eyes. "Take your dress off. Do it slowly."

As Ev complies, I know I'm grinning like a clown. I watch perhaps the best striptease I've ever seen. I loosen my belt and let my big silver buckle hang to one side. I like how Ev's big emerald eyes go wide at my antics. For a moment, I think about what our children's eyes would look like. I crease my brow and shove the thought right out of my stupid head. I silently admonish myself and get back to the task at hand. I unbutton my Wranglers and lower the zipper gradually, deliberately.

Ev struts toward me, unclasping her thin, lacy black bra, removing it bit by bit. She tosses it on the stall floor. My eyes wander eagerly over her body. She stops in front of me, leisurely running her hands over my chest again. She pushes my dress shirt over my shoulders while looking deeply into my eyes. I rise from the bale of hay, kiss her hard, and then break it off to retrieve my suit jacket. I spread it over the top of the bale and instruct Ev to sit on it. A sinister smile twists across her lips as she complies with my demands once again.

Standing above her, my heart hammers in my chest. I slowly slip my leather belt from the loops of my unbuttoned jeans. Ev's breath hitches as I lace the leather around her arms and tighten her elbows behind her back. After securing her arms, I crouch on the tips of my boots and run my hands up her legs. When I reach her hips, I hook my fingers on the panties she left on and pull them toward the floor greedily.

"Do you remember me yet?" she breathes.

"Reckon, this is gonna be something I'll never forget," I reply.

16

DEVON

I walk to the farmhouse, anxious about talking with my mother. It's been years, after all. As the overnight wedding guests mingle and help themselves to the breakfast buffet, I spot her seated at a white-linen covered table sipping her coffee. When she lifts her head, our eyes meet. I wave, and she nods. I make my way toward her with a knot in my stomach and a lump in my throat.

"Where's Richard?" I ask.

"He's still up in the room. He wanted to give us some space to talk." She turns her delicate coffee cup around on its floral saucer. Sophia has pulled out all the stops again. I'm sure it thrilled her to have the occasion to use her fine china.

"That was thoughtful of him," I mumble.

"I want you to know that I forgive you, Devon."

"Forgive me for what?" It slips out of my mouth before I can take the edge off of it. I can't help my defensive tone.

"Do you need me to list it out for you?" she asks, curtly.

"Have at it," I sigh.

"For disappearing. For not staying in touch with your family. I'm your mother, for heaven's sakes, Devon. For not telling me who you've been spending your time with or where." She waves a hand around the room.

This will not be easy.

Unsure of what to say, I put my elbows on the table and massage my temples.

Ev and JD enter the room, boisterously, hand in hand. My mother raises an eyebrow, and I watch JD lead an obviously smitten Ev to the stack of plates at the end of the long buffet table. He hands her one, then focuses on loading his plate high with bacon. He picks up a piece with his fingers and waves it in front of Ev's lips. She makes a growling sound and rips a bite off with her teeth. I've never seen Ev act with such abandon. I continue rubbing my temples and shake my head.

Good grief. I hope they kept it down last night.

"Do you know how upsetting it was for me to receive an invitation to my daughter's wedding written in handwriting that wasn't your own?" my mother continues. "Whatever happened with that Michael fellow? Last I heard, you were supposed to marry him, and then to find out you were marrying a ranch hand. I raised you to be more than this!"

I bristle at her choice of words.

Hackles are definitely up now.

She sips from her coffee, pinky finger raised. The regal gesture irritates me. We weren't rich. We were average or less than. In my mother's imagination, our life is always grander than it really was.

"Mom —," I begin.

"You just don't think about it when your child is small," my mother interrupts. "You don't think about how it will be when your child grows up. Things ended up differently then I imagined they would. Where did all that time go? Why has my child decided not to include me in her life?"

"Mom. It's not like that. I just needed ... I just needed space." I swallow hard. "When Dad died, I just couldn't reach out. It hurt too much. You moved on so fast. We didn't have a chance to grieve together. I needed to grieve."

"You always preferred him to me. You were always your father's daughter. Weren't you?" She hurls the words at me. The comment stings.

"Mom, I'm sorry I've been distant. I'm sorry I wasn't the one to tell you I was getting married to McKennon. I know you tried your best. Sometimes parents just don't know how to do the things their children really need. I know you want to be part of my life. I know deep down you want what's best for me."

"I do," she responds.

"What's best for me is McKennon. He's not some ranch hand. He's an incredible horse trainer, and he's helped me earn my dreams. He's good for me. He treats me the way a man should. He keeps his promises. Please don't worry about me."

"That's what mothers are supposed to do."

"Mothers are also supposed to let their grown children make their own decisions and mistakes. I've made my fair share of mistakes, but marrying McKennon isn't one of them. I will do better, Mom. From here on out, I'll stay in touch."

"I'd like that, Devon," my mother dabs the corner of her eye with the cloth napkin from her lap.

"I miss you, Mom. Please know that. I'd like to start over. I'd like you to know the real me. The grown-up me." I reach over and rest my hand on her forearm. "I'd like to know the real you, too."

"Oh, Devon," she sighs. "I'm so sorry your father and I fought all the time. No child should have to grow up with that. I was just so unhappy. I felt like he didn't see me. I felt like it didn't matter that I was the mother of his child. I just felt invisible in our home. I'm glad you've found a man who treats you right. I guess that is all a mother can ask for. I didn't mean to have an affair, but Richard ... well ... I guess he treated me the way I wished your father had. I knew what I had done was wrong. That's why I filed for divorce soon after I met Richard. I never thought your father would care. I certainly never expected him to end his life over it."

"Mom—"

"Please let me finish. Devon. I want you to know that I grieved your father. I grieved the loss of the love we had every day toward the end of our marriage. I blame myself for his death to this day. What my actions did to him. Did to you. I suppose I can understand why as soon as you were old enough to leave, you left and never looked back. If I could take it all back and could've figured out a way to make it work with your father, I would. I lost you in the entire process. I never got to say any of this to you. You never gave me the chance to tell you I'm sorry. So here it is, I'm sorry."

Tears are streaming down her face now. The perfectly applied makeup ruined and staining her cheeks. My heart softens.

This is my mother. I love her. I want her in my life.

If McKennon can put his painful past behind him, I can, too. I want to move forward. This is an opportunity for a new beginning.

"Mom, I'm sorry, too," I whisper. "I have missed you. Thank you for coming to my wedding. We would have missed out on this opportunity to clear the air if you hadn't."

"If only we could have had this talk beforehand. Look at me, I'm a mess," she sniffs, blotting her face with a fresh napkin from the empty place setting beside her.

"I'm glad we had this talk, Mom. I really am." I take her hand and give it a squeeze.

"Me, too, Devon," she says with a smile. My heart swells when she squeezes my hand in return. "I'm going to hold you to that promise to stay in touch."

"You can count on me to hold her accountable, too," McKennon adds, nodding to my mother, then kissing me on the cheek. I eye him as he settles into a chair beside me with a cup of coffee.

"How long have you been eavesdropping on us, husband?" I ask.

"Oh, just caught that tail end there. That's all."

Always keeping an eye on me.

"Will you please excuse me," my mother says, standing up. "I'm going to go freshen up and check on Richard."

"Mom," I whisper, rising to meet her. "I love you." Before I know it, we are embracing.

"I love you, too, honey," she whispers back, giving me another squeeze before turning on her heels and hightailing it for her room.

"How'd that go?" McKennon asks when I return to my seat.

"Actually, not that bad. I'm going to call her more. We worked a few things out. We'll work out more, but we are talking again."

"That's good, Devon. Real good. I'm pretty dang proud of my wife right now. You can choose your friends, your husband, your horses, but you can't choose your biological family. You just gotta love 'em anyway," he drawls.

My cowboy philosopher.

After breakfast finishes, the remaining wedding guests gather out in front of the main house on the sprawling lawn. Sophia arranged a rose petal trail leading out to the awaiting limousine. She insisted we packed for our honeymoon before the wedding festivities, and I know someone already tucked away our suitcases in the trunk. Sophia has thought of everything. Everyone cheers as McKennon and I bound down the front porch steps to the door of the car held open by the driver. My mother is waiting near the limo separated from the other guests. Her eyes are still red from crying, but her makeup is touched up.

"Go on, Devon," McKennon encourages.

I walk to my mother feeling lighter. Something has shifted between us in a good way.

"Mom, I love you. Let's leave the past in the past now, OK?"

"OK, Devon. I love you, too." She dabs a tissue to her eye. "Oh, go on now. Have fun on your honeymoon."

"I will. Thanks, Mom. I'll call you when I get back and tell you all about it."

She smiles and gives me a quick hug.

"That's all a mother ever really wants. Go."

"Thank you for coming to my wedding, Mom. It means a lot that you and Richard were here for the happiest day of my life," I whisper near her ear, and I mean it. Relief floods me at having completed something that had been haunting me for so long. I've cleared a path for a relationship with my mother, wiped the slate clean, and it feels refreshing. If only my father could have been here.

If only.

As I rejoin McKennon, Sophia steps out from the crowd.

"Thank you for everything, Sophia. Thank you for making our wedding day perfect," I gush.

"My pleasure, dear."

At that moment, Ev gallops up to me with JD on her heels.

"Wishing you lots of good honeymoon sex!" Ev exclaims, wrapping her arms around JD's waist.

McKennon groans, I roll my eyes, and my mother covers her ears. I feel the usual heat rise to my cheeks.

"Heck yes! I second that good sex part," JD hoots, slapping McKennon on the back. "Congratulations again, brother."

"I'll be in touch when you get back, Devon. We have a manuscript to discuss," Ev says, releasing JD and giving me a hug. "I hope that honeymoon sex is as good as the sex I've been having," she whispers near my ear.

"You are so naughty," I whisper back.

"You know it. Now get out of here," she giggles.

"I'll get this fire engine out of your hair," JD announces as he swoops Ev up into his muscled arms. "Happy for you, Devon," he says with a wink as he turns on his boots and lopes off up the steps to the main house with Ev laughing wildly in his grasp.

"Happy for you, too," I call after him.

I think.

"I'll see to it that your editor friend gets back to the city in one piece, but from the sound of things last night, I can't promise whether it will be with or without JD," Sophia interjects, watching the pair's theatrics.

"Oh, my goodness, Sophia. I told Ev to behave herself! I am so sorry if they made a scene last night."

"That kid," McKennon groans, palming his face.

"I think they started off in the barn," Sophia giggles. "I saw them sneak into the house late last night, coming from that direction. I'm sure they thought everyone was asleep, but I was still up having my nightcap. I was too excited about the wedding to shut my eyes."

"Sophia, I am so sorry," I reply.

"Don't be! With all the racket those two were making, I found myself wishing I had a little of that for myself."

"Sophia!" McKennon and I gasp in unison.

"One is never too old to yearn, my dears," Sophia says with a mischievous smile and another giggle. "Besides, I have another one of my feelings about those two."

"Oh, you do, do you? What kind of feeling?" McKennon inquires, rubbing his strong chin.

"Something similar to how I felt about you and Devon the day she showed up to Green Briar."

My jaw drops.

"JD and Ev? JD? Impossible," I blurt.

Sophia shrugs her shoulders and gives me one of her signature peach luminescent smiles.

"You are a wily one, Sophia," McKennon drawls.

"I am indeed. Have fun, you two. Off you go now."

Sophia never ceases to amaze me.

17

JD

I roll over and toss an arm over Ev after tangling up in the sheets with her again.

"How's about we go for a ride?" I ask.

"I thought we just did," she murmurs, tracing a finger over my bicep.

"And a dang good ride it was, but I was thinking we'd take a couple horses out. Go for that kind of ride. Would you like that?"

"When in the country, I suppose I can do what the country folks do."

"You are a strange woman, Ev."

"Why would you say that?"

"Most women jump at the chance to ride a horse with the likes of me, but you don't seem all that impressed with horses."

"I can take them or leave them. You, on the other hand, I could ride all day," she replies, rising from her position on the bed to straddle me.

"I like the way you think," I say. Her hair tumbles around her shoulders. I reach up and run a hand through her mane and pull her to me for a tongue-twisting kiss ...

Who am I to deny a woman her needs?

After a second roll in the hay, I force myself to get out of bed.

"Go freshen up, miss. I'm takin' you out for that ride, like it or not. It's a beautiful day for ridin'."

"Oh, all right," Ev grumbles. She lifts herself from the bed and struts naked to the bathroom. My eyes can't help but follow. She knows I'm watching.

Confident. I like that.

"Be right back, cowboy," she says with a sly smile, turning to give me a full-frontal view as she slides the door closed slowly on its track.

Damn.

I can't help smiling as I pull on my boxer briefs and jeans and lace the belt that was around Ev's arms last night through the loops. I pull on my boots and shrug into my shirt. I button it slowly, thinking over the night before.

"Ready?" Ev asks, stepping from the bathroom. She is fresh faced without a trace of makeup, and her fiery hair is swept into a low ponytail. She looks glorious, younger. She's wearing skinny jeans tucked into the pair of cowboy boots she wore to the wedding and a tight T-shirt. I can tell the boots are a recent purchase, not a scuff or ding in the leather, no sign telling of work on a ranch, but they suit her just fine.

"You look lovely," I breathe.

"I don't get a chance to go out like this much."

"I like the look of you not all made up."

"Thanks," she replies, looking like a much softer version of herself.

"Come on. Let's head down to the barn."

Down in the barn, I pull two trusted mounts from their stalls.

"This here is Cash," I say, snapping my sister's old show mount into the crossties. "He's retired from the show pen. He'll take good care of you out on the trails."

Ev nods. She seems a little timid for a moment, but then wanders over to the grooming kit I set in the aisle. She selects a body brush and starts to work on Cash's coat.

"For a city gal, you sure look like you know what you're doing around a horse," I say as she brushes Cash with vigor.

"I have some experience," Ev replies, but she doesn't embellish any.

Interesting.

"Whom are you riding?" she asks.

"This here is Studly. He's in training with McKennon. Coming along nicely. He'll appreciate a day out on the trails."

"Suiting name for the horse you plan to ride," Ev chuckles, retrieving a hoof pick and picking up Cash's foreleg.

I watch her move around Cash, easily lifting each leg and removing debris before I start in on grooming my mount.

"I reckon you are impressin' me around the horses, miss."

"I've got some tricks up my sleeve," she replies. "I didn't know you ride horses. I thought you only rode bulls."

"It's my little secret. I used to ride with my sister a lot when we were kids. My old horse, Bell, is over at my dad's. I go see her now and then. Take her out for a ride, but that's our little secret now."

"Why don't you want anyone to know you ride horses?" Ev asks, tossing a saddle pad over Cash's withers and then his saddle.

She can tack up, too? This woman keeps surprising me.

"Makes the girls go all gaga. Don't want them to know I'm good around horses. Might make them want to make a keeper out of me." I watch her tighten the girth for a moment before saddling Studly, waiting for her response.

"Why would you share this little secret with me then?" she probes, taking Cash's bridle off a peg, slipping the bit into his mouth, and then lifting the headstall over his ears.

"Don't know. Figured you earned it," I say, saddling my horse.

"Earned it? How's that?"

"You're just different is all."

"Hmm. Interesting," she says with a lift of her eyebrow. "Are we doing this or what?"

"We are," I slide my bridle on and lead Studly down the aisle. "Come on."

Ev takes Cash's reins and falls in behind me. Outside the barn, I motion for Ev to lead her horse up next to me.

"Here, let me help you get on." I position myself next to Ev and loop my mount's reins over my shoulder. Studly stands patiently, and I start to lift her toward the saddle.

"Let me go, cowboy," she barks. "I know how to mount a horse."

And how to give orders.

"Oh, you do now, do you?"

"Yes, I do. I went to preparatory school. I learned how to jump them even. It's been a while since I've ridden, though. A long while."

Surprise, surprise.

"Well, that explains a lot. I was wondering how you knew what to do back there. Also, explains why you seem a little timid around them. You'll be back to expert in no time. It's like riding a bike."

"Riding these beasts was part of the program. Mandatory. As in, I had to. Speaking of mandatory, come to think of it, I need you to get me a helmet."

"A helmet?" I chuckle. "What kind of helmet do you want? One of those fancy velvet hunt seat caps? Don't know if we keep any of those around here."

"It's not about being fancy. It's about safety first, JD. I have a lot of good ideas in this head of mine, and I want to protect them."

"All right, all right. Let me see what I can find. Here, hold Studly for me." I hand over his reins and retreat to the tack room. I rummage around for a bit before producing an old English riding helmet. I trot back out of the barn and hand it over to Ev. A one cornered smile creeps to my mouth as she blows a puff of dust off of it.

"This thing looks ancient," Ev says, dusting the cap some more before fitting it to her head and snapping the chinstrap.

"I reckon it was Sophia's. She was an Olympic jumping candidate at one point."

"Is that so? Well, thank heaven for Sophia. Now I can protect my brain."

"A lot of people say that about Sophia," I reply as Ev tucks her boot in the stirrup and lifts herself into the saddle with ease. I mount my horse and take note of her excellent equitation as she walks Cash in a couple warm-up circles in the drive. Her heels are down, her chin is up, her back is straight, her alignment is spot on – all the things a rich girl would learn at a school that makes horseback riding mandatory.

"One thing you should know about Cash is that he is spur trained. You don't need spurs to cue him, though. He knows the drill. Most important part is that when you want to stop him, just squeeze with both your heels. Don't bother pulling back on the reins," I instruct.

Ev gives the cue a whirl, and Cash immediately puts on the brakes.

"Nice," Ev chimes. I like the smile that's crept onto her unpainted mouth.

Girls. They always like the horses, even if they pretend they don't.

"Come on," I say as I lead Ev out toward the well-worn bridle path around the perimeter of Green Briar. As we ride side by side through Sophia's sprawling acres, my eyes survey the land, blades of long grass billowing in the breeze like waves of the tide.

I love it here.

We are silent for a long while. I notice a peaceful, slight smile across Ev's pink lips. I can't remember ever sharing silence with someone and being this comfortable, this calm.

"So where are we heading?" Ev asks, shifting in the saddle and facing me. Her breasts catch my attention. They look perfect in her form-hugging top.

"Checkin' on the yearlings for McKennon. He's got a good bunch this year," I say, dragging my attention from her chest and meeting her emerald eyes with my own.

Ev laughs, tossing her head back, ponytail trailing her spine. My eyes widen, and I give her a sideways tilt of my head.

"What's so funny?" I ask.

"Hmm, nothing," she answers.

"Come now," I probe. "I'm intrigued by that outburst."

"Well," she purrs. "I was just thinking that if I hadn't gotten you so drunk at Devon's bachelorette party, if you can call it that, you would have remembered me at the wedding. I can't stop thinking about the way you looked at me. You were so confused."

My mind tries to fight through the haze of that particular evening, wanting to remember being with Ev badly, but all I can remember is waking up in that hotel room and galloping down from the top floor as fast as I could.

"Suppose I owe you an apology for not remembering our first night together."

"Apology accepted. I was waiting for you to say that. I remember enough for the both of us, though. That happen to you a lot, cowboy?"

More than I like to admit, but I'm not going to tell her that.

"I rarely spend more than one night with a woman," I confess.

Well. Just one. Buckle bunny Brittany, but I'm not going to tell her that either.

"What about that girlfriend? The one who broke your heart?"

"I'm not in the mood for sad stories, Ev. My life circumstances turned me off long-term relationships long ago. My career doesn't allow for it either."

"What if I want you for more than the two nights I've had you? One of which you don't remember."

What's she getting at?

"I'm listening."

"Come with me to the city. I'll introduce you to people. You could be the next big thing. You are the most handsome, rugged man I've laid eyes on. They'll eat you up at the modeling agencies. JD McCall. That name of yours, it just rolls off the tongue."

"What are you proposin' here, Ev?" I furrow my brow, but I'm taken with her compliments.

"Pretend I'm a fat cat rodeo promoter, and I'm fixing to cut you a big check," she says.

"The city? Ah, I don't know," I say, rubbing the back of my neck and scanning the fence line to the yearling pasture, looking for any signs it needs fixing.

"Just consider it. With me, you'll never have to worry about money again. I'll make sure you make plenty of it."

I like the sound of that.

"What do you mean?" Ev has my attention now.

"I'm going to make you a star, cowboy. Remember those ideas I'm protecting with this helmet? I'm going to build you an actual career. You'll have to get over that 'rarely spend more than one night with a woman' thing, though. I hope you aren't threatened by a powerful, older woman taking the reins for you?"

"Nah. As long as I get to take the reins when I'm riding you."

"Occasionally ... if you are lucky. Come back to New York with me, JD."

"I'm a fly by the seat of my pants kinda guy. Suppose I'll try anything once, especially if I get a little more of that sugar you gave me last night. Truth is, I have to be there anyway for an upcoming bull riding event. As fate would have it, my next tour stop is in New York City next weekend."

"Well, I'll be darned if this isn't perfect timing! I'll have to work fast. I imagine I'll only have a few days and a few nights with you?" she asks.

"That's right, but I'm more interested in those nights," I drawl. "Count me in."

"Excellent." Ev seems pleased.

Heck, if there is money to be made, I'm in.

I still need to get my trailer finished up. I fantasize about a new paint job and getting the electrical installed.

"Are you ready to sign a cowboy contract?" I ask, cueing Studly into a side pass until I'm right alongside of Cash. My leg bumps Ev's.

"Sounds intriguing. What's a cowboy contract?" she asks.

I extend my hand out for her to shake. She takes it and gives it a firm pump, like a true businesswoman.

"And, just like that, A Star Is Born," she says with a smile. "I've already booked our flight. I had a feeling you might say yes to my proposal."

"You do move fast," I reply.

"Like lightning," Ev laughs. "You have seen nothing yet, JD. Speaking of moving fast, can we do something other than walk on this ride of ours?"

"You want to move up a bit, do you?"

"Yes," she commands, heeling Cash into the trot. She posts in her Western saddle, but quickly realizes her mount is only going to jog ... slowly.

"Used to ridin' English, huh?"

"They sure didn't have any of these saddles with horns at the school I went to," she scowls. "It's a pretty comfortable saddle though."

"Well, at least you have the right cap, even if the saddle under your fine ass doesn't match," I tease, cueing Studly into a lope. Ev transitions to the faster speed with ease as we cross Green Briar's acres toward the far pasture.

18

A yellow moon floats in the denim sky outside my window. I'm still plenty surprised to not be sitting in coach. I twist the champagne flute on my tray table, wishing it were a bottle of beer, and look out over squares of farmland and perfectly engineered neighborhoods. I can't help but think about how much humans have created boxes for themselves, parceled off, private, separating yours from mine, a fence here, a brick wall there. That's something I have a hard time buying into. It's why I ride bulls, why I choose to live untethered. I don't believe in boundaries and need to run with herds as wild as I am. I wonder what will happen in New York City. I ponder agreeing to follow this crazy plan Ev has in mind.

Whatever it is.

I was already heading to New York. It made saying yes to her proposal easy. I reckon I've got nothing to lose. I'll try anything just to see where it goes, especially when there's a sultry redhead involved promising me potential stardom.

But ...

I glance over at Ev. She's hammering away at her laptop. I hardly know the woman. Although, it sure is nice knowing I'll have a steady lay for the few days I'll be spending in the city. I have no intentions of sticking around for long though, for whatever it is she thinks she's gonna do with me. I'm gonna land, get off this airplane, stay at her pad, get my lovin' on, ride my bulls, collect my check for making the eight, and then hightail it back to the country.

"So you're pretty successful, right?" Ev asks, interrupting my train of thought.

"I don't know if successful is the word for what I do. I sure work hard. I mean, I have things in my life that I appreciate," I reply.

"Like what?" She leans in.

"Well, for one thing, I appreciate this upgrade to first class. I appreciate the beautiful lady sitting next to me."

"Enough with the flattery, cowboy." She waves me off and sips from her glass. "What do you really appreciate?"

"Well, I reckon I appreciate freedom. I appreciate clean air and the open road. I appreciate wide-open spaces and trying to tame something that's untamable by hanging on to the rankest bulls on earth for eight seconds."

"Have you ever thought beyond eight seconds?" Ev asks.

"Nah, don't need to. I wake up bull riding. I eat bull riding. I dream bull riding. It's not just something I do. It's who I am. If you want to be great, you have to keep getting on the back of the bull. There's no time to think about it. I just do it. I appreciate the freedom being able to ride bulls provides me. For example, it is the reason I can be sitting here next to you. I'm untethered. No freakin' offices, no desks inside of cubicles, no making money for someone else."

Ev nods and her fingers fly across her keyboard. A smile creeps across her lips. She's interested in what I have to say.

"You have an event coming up in New York. Tell me about it."

"So, you wanna watch me straddle one?"

"Yes, I suppose I do."

"Well, the National Bull Rider events differ from your typical rodeo. You have to climb up the ranks from the lower pro circuits to earn the right to get on the NBR tour. Only the top 35 bull riders in the world get to compete against the rankest bucking bulls on the planet. My upcoming event is at Madison Square Garden."

"Rankest?"

"A rank bull is an elite athlete. They are built like freight trains and can weigh up to 2,200 pounds. A rank bull regularly scores big points. They are nearly impossible to ride. Nine times out of 10, a cowboy won't ride a rank bull. I'm one of the lucky 35 that have the strength and moves to stick to them for a full eight seconds."

"Go on," Ev's fingertips click across her keyboard. "How does the judging work on these rank bulls? How do you win?"

I could talk about this all day long.

"Well, a qualified ride is worth up to 100 points. That is, 50 points for the rider, and 50 points for the bull. The rider has to stay on top of the bull for eight seconds and has to ride with one hand free. A cowboy is disqualified if he touches himself or the bull with his free arm. Any ride that is scored 90 points or higher is deemed exceptional. As a matter of fact, I have a few of those under my belt. At the end of each event, the top 15 riders compete in the Championship Round. It's called the short round or short go."

"So, the rider with the highest point total from the entire event becomes the winner?" Ev asks, draining her champagne as the flight attendant moves around our cabin refilling glasses. Ev and I both extend our flutes when she reaches our seats. I decide to hold my tongue about wanting a beer.

When in first class ...

Ev sips her drink, minimizes her document, and pulls up her web browser.

"It says here that riders compete in over 300 televised events around the world, and every bull rider's dream is to qualify for the NBR World Finals. Is that true?"

"That's right. The World Finals champion gets a million bucks on top of his winnings over the course of the year. The most important part though is that $20,000 belt buckle. I've got my eyes set on that beauty. I've got me plenty of buckles, but that's the one I aim for."

"I look forward to you earning that buckle," Ev whispers near my ear. "When you do, I'll let you tie me up again with whatever belt of yours it'll be hanging from."

My mind flickers back to our lusty evening in the barn. I shift in my seat, feeling myself stir down below.

"This is all great intel," Ev says, turning back to her laptop and reopening her document. As she types furiously, I try to bet a gander at what she is working on, but she tips a shoulder to me and turns the computer screen. I shrug, turn to the window, and go back to sipping my champagne. I can't help wishing it were a beer again.

The airplane speaker clicks on, and the attendant informs us that the crew is preparing for landing. Ev waves her glass in the air, signaling for a final refill. A thin blonde shimmies over to top us off.

"You'll need to finish this quickly. Tray tables and seat backs up. Laptop away, too," she instructs with a sweet smile. She's cute, but I don't acknowledge her lingering look in my direction.

Unusual.

19

"So, you were always planning on coming to New York then? Are you sure this trip isn't about you and me?" Ev asks as she steps out of our limo.

"Nope. Sorry. I'm fixin' to have a lot of fun with you while I am here though," I drawl, slipping out from the leather seat after her.

Gotta keep this light.

"Good ... That's *real* good," she replies.

I furrow my brow at Ev's odd response but choose to busy myself with a gander up at the high-rise in front of us.

"Welcome home, Ms. Mitchell," a man in uniform says, trotting up to the car. He retrieves our luggage and pauses when he spots my dusty rigging bag next to Ev's designer luggage. "This one too?"

"Yes, that one, too," Ev tells him.

"I'll have these brought up right away," he answers, scratching his head.

"Thank you, Henry. It's good to be home," Ev replies, slipping him a bill.

She has a doorman? Classy.

I whistle as I step inside the lobby.

"Nice place."

"If you like this, wait until you see my apartment." Ev tips her red head toward the empty elevator. I follow her in, and once the doors are shut, I pin her in the corner and devour her mouth. When we reach her floor, Ev breaks from my lips, teeters for a second on her heels, and then composes herself. I smirk as Ev's fingers tremble, trying to get her key in the lock.

I love knocking women off their rockers.

"This is home." Ev swings the door open and steps to the side. I eye her leaning against the doorjamb. She looks properly disheveled from my grope in the elevator. She adjusts her blouse that's fallen off her shoulder, secures the buttons that have popped open, and smooths her pencil skirt back to its proper position.

I step into her apartment, toss my gear bag in the corner of the hallway entrance, and toe out of my boots, figuring she'd appreciate me not mucking up her floors.

"You sure pack light, cowboy," she says, eyeing my dusty bag on her pristine marble floor in the same way the doorman had.

How'd he get up here with our stuff so quickly?

"All I need for a good go-around is a clean pair of jeans, a shirt, those boots I just took off, this hat on my head, some workout clothes, and my ridin' gear. If I need anything else, I'll hit a laundromat or a convenience store. All I've ever needed fits in that bag there just fine."

"What do you sleep in?" she asks.

"The nude." I feel the corner of my lip turn up. She is surprised for just a moment, but recovers quickly.

"Go ahead and take a look around. I'm going to freshen up. Help yourself to a beer from the refrigerator. I'll be out shortly."

Beer! Finally.

"Yes, ma'am," I reply. I see her eyeball me for the briefest of seconds before what I assume is the bedroom door clicks behind her.

In my socks, I move deeper into her dark apartment. I make out an enormous state-of-the-art kitchen and fish a beer out of the equally enormous fridge. I check out the bottle's label in the light from the appliance. It's some fancy import that I've never heard of before, and I make a mental note to stock her with something more domestic.

When I get a chance, I'll pick up a 30 pack of somethin' light.

I twist the top and take a proper swig as I search for some light switches. I find a dial on the wall and crank it. Suddenly, floor-to-ceiling motorized shades along the perimeter of the room rise, and the lights of New York City glow through windows around the room. I am dazzled. I step to the glass and look down. I'm pretty sure we are on the top floor. I finish my beer and ponder what I'll do with my time here. Winning a buckle is on the agenda, and some very good sex with the woman in the other room makes my short list, too.

I hear another light flick on behind me, and I tear my gaze from the window. Ev is in the kitchen of the full floor, single-level warehouse apartment, twisting the cork out of a bottle of red wine. I like the look of her in the silky satin robe tied at the waist.

"Come have a seat, cowboy," she instructs, gliding toward the white wraparound leather couch in the center of the room I'm standing in. Ev sets a second glass and the open bottle on a glass-top table. She settles in on the big white couch, tucks her bare feet beneath her, and takes a sip of wine while watching me intently. Her eyes sweep my body as I make my way across the room. I up the ante by giving her my best cowboy sway of the hips.

"Nice place you got here," I say, knowing full well that whatever she is paying in rent is likely astronomical. The space suits her perfectly, though. It is quietly elegant. Black. White. Gray. Her red hair is the only shock of color in the whole place. Even though it lacks color, Ev's apartment is strangely welcoming and comfortable, but still feels very rich. It works. Just like my father, Ev seems to have a refined taste and the money to indulge it.

Yep. I pegged her correctly that first time I saw her.

She's likely a well-off divorcee. They always come with a sad story. I should know. I have bedded a few of them in my day. I'll find out her story later, if ever. I rarely stick around long enough to give them a shoulder to cry on. I'm just here for the sex and the place to stay while I am in town for my event.

Then it will be Háštá la vista, baby.

If she wants to tell me her sad story while I'm hanging 'round, I'll listen, but I'm not lookin' to pry it out of her anytime soon.

"I guarantee that once I get you on a magazine cover, it will sell a million copies, and you'll be able to afford a place like this for yourself," Ev ponders, interrupting my thoughts.

"And what the heck makes you think you can get me on a magazine cover?" I ask, heading to the kitchen for another beer, ignoring the extra wineglass on the table.

"Because I am Everly Mitchell. That's why. I am a powerful promoter and agent. I've built a business by trusting my instinct. I know what I see."

"And what do you see, Everly Mitchell?"

"I see a stunning cowboy who hasn't even begun to build a career for himself."

"Why this cowboy?"

"Because I would be the first one in line to buy a magazine with you on the cover. That's why."

Huh.

I return to the couch. I take a sip from my beer and set it down. Ev lifts my bottle from the glass-top table and slips a coaster beneath it. As she leans over, I whisper near her ear, "Is that so?"

"It is," she breathes.

I take that as an invitation. I shift from beside her to hover above her and untie the satin ribbon at the front of her robe. She gasps when I run a hand over her firm female body and lower my mouth to hers. She is reserved with her kiss, and I pause to look at her.

Strange.

"You were much more eager last night *and* this morning, come to think of it. Somethin' on your mind?"

"It's just — I'm expecting someone."

Just as I think we were about to launch into something sultry, she drops this bomb on me?

"Expecting someone? Now?" I ask, irritated at the situation in my pants.

Before Ev can answer, there is a knock at the door.

"Oh! Right on time!" Ev exclaims, slipping out from under me and off the sofa. She tightens the robe that I just untied around her as she pads to answer the front door. I straighten myself on the couch and attempt to pay attention to the conversation in the foyer, rather than on the ache in my nether region. I take a long swig of beer to numb the pain. I shake my watch down my wrist and look at its face. It's almost midnight.

"Estefan, you are right on time! I can always count on you, darling."

Estefan? Darling? Who the heck is at the door? I'm not into sharing if she thinks that's what's going to happen. Oh, hell no.

"JD, this is Estefan," Ev says breezily as she comes back into the living room. "He'll be shooting you tonight."

"What?" I jump up from the couch. "Shooting?"

"Taking your pictures. Estefan will be taking your pictures, JD."

"Pictures?"

"He certainly is handsome," Estefan comments. "You didn't mention he was slow though. Are people from the south slow? Or is it just cowboys?"

I clench my fists.

"Stop teasing him, Estefan. I haven't had a chance to explain this to him yet." Ev pops him in his shoulder. He mouths 'ouch', rubs his arm, and sets his black shoulder bag down on the floor with a *thunk*. I look at Ev expectantly.

What on earth is going on here?

"JD, Estefan has come over to take some photos of you tonight. In order to get your modeling career off the ground, we need a digital portfolio of you pronto."

"Pictures, huh?" I huff. I settle back into the sofa and chug the rest of my beer.

This is not what I was expecting.

"Estefan, why don't you go get set up in the studio? I'll prep JD."

Estefan nods and heads down a hallway. Clearly, he's familiar with Ev's apartment.

"You have a studio?" I inquire.

"Of course," she chirps. "Listen, I've already made some calls. Representatives from Stampede Automotive and Lariat Jean Company are in town. They were planning on being here for that bull riding event of yours anyway, but I've asked them to come early to meet with us. They agreed. There is always business to be done in Manhattan, and they've adjusted their schedules. I've set appointments to meet with both of them tomorrow."

"You work awfully fast."

"When I set my mind to something, it happens. You'll learn that soon enough," she says, heading toward the kitchen. She pops the top on another beer, strolls back to me sitting like a stone on her couch, and hands it to me.

"Come on. Let's go. Estefan should be ready for you by now."

"Yes, ma'am." I stand and take a pull from the beer bottle.

"Oh, and JD?"

"Yes?"

"Lose the shirt."

I shrug and do as I'm told. I peel off my snap-button shirt and then strip off my undershirt.

"Much better," she hums, and I follow her down the hallway, eyes glued to her ass swaying beneath that dang satin robe.

20

The photo session wasn't all that bad. I felt a little bit like a piece of meat, but I seemed to follow directions to Estefan and Ev's approval. At least, she seems pleased right now. I am drinking my fifth beer, watching her fingers tap away at that laptop. She is perched on a barstool at the kitchen island. Estefan has his huge digital camera plugged into the computer as she reviews the photos of me and selects her favorites.

"Oh, this one is just gorgeous!" she exclaims. Estefan nods beside her.

"Do you want to see them, JD?" she asks.

"No. Not right now," I reply. I don't know if I'm ready to see myself photographed as man meat yet. I'm still processing some of the positions they put me in – particularly, the one in my undies pretending I'm riding an imaginary bull. I shake the thought of it out of my head.

"You are quite a good model, having never done this before," Estefan adds.

"Thanks. I think," I mumble under my breath.

I drain my longneck and wander into the kitchen, still shirtless. I put the empty in the recycling bin where I noticed Ev's put the others and stand at the island facing her. I like watching her. She wears a sexy, satisfied smile.

After I've finished yet another beer, she slaps the computer shut. She kisses Estefan enthusiastically on the cheek.

"You've done it again, Estefan! You are a photographic genius. I've just sent off some of the most amazing pictures I've seen in my career ... of a bull rider of all things."

"Pleased to have pleased you, Ev. Now can I go home? You do realize my hourly fees are quite hefty. Not to mention, you are in the after-hour price zone."

I check my watch. He's been here for at least three hours taking pictures of me, then helping Ev select the best ones.

"Yes, yes. Just bill my office. You are worth every penny!" she exclaims, leading him to the door. "Good night, my genius friend."

"Good night, Everly. JD." I nod at Estefan, and he disappears through the door.

"Great work tonight, Mr. Cowboy," Ev says as she comes back into the kitchen.

"That's Mr. Bull Rider to you."

"OK then, Mr. Bull Rider ... follow me."

Curious, I leave my post in the kitchen and follow her down the long hall. She pushes open a door to a room I haven't been in yet. I'm hoping it's her bedroom. I'm ready to get some action after that fiasco.

"You can sleep here in my guest room tonight."

"I'm not sleeping with you?" I ask suggestively, stringing my arm across the doorjamb, and flexing just the right amount to lure a woman. It's a move I've practiced plenty of times before. To my surprise, she shoves me into the room.

"No, you aren't sleeping with me tonight. I need you rested. You have a big day tomorrow."

"But it's already three something in the morning," I whine.

"Exactly. Goodnight. Rest well. I'll see you in the morning." With that, she shuts the door on me.

That's just great.

Ev is acting like a very different woman from the one I conquered at Green Briar. She's all business. I hope she drops the 'no messing around' game and gets back between the sheets with me soon. I wander around the guest room. I bounce on the bed.

Soft.

I go into the attached bathroom and gander at the miniature-sized shampoo, conditioner, soap, and lotions lined up along the edge of the sink. I pop the top on one and take a whiff.

Smells fancy.

I examine the little plastic bottles and can't help but wonder if Ev does this often. It's then that I notice the travel-sized toothbrush and toothpaste.

What have I gotten myself into?

21

I awake to the drone of city sounds. I rub my eyes as horns honk and sirens scream at street level. I turn my head and look at the clock on the nightstand.

5:01 a.m.

Always the early riser from years of caring for livestock, I stretch and am shocked at how well-rested I feel.

Must be the bed upgrade.

I strut to the bathroom in the buff and start the shower. I need to get a workout in. I've got to do something with the pent-up frustration from not sleeping in Ev's room last night. I slide open the glass door and step into the steam.

Fresh out of the shower, I tighten a towel around my waist, flex my muscles in front of the mirror, give myself a smirk, and slick back my wet hair. I smell coffee and head down the hall to the kitchen.

Ev is sitting on a barstool at the island. A long leg is seductively peeking out beneath that robe I liked so much last night. She shifts in her seat and props that same leg up on the seat next to her. Her hair is piled on top of her head in a messy bun, and she is focused on a newspaper.

"Coffee's on. Mugs are above the pot. Help yourself," she says, not looking up.

I pour myself a cup, lean back against the marble countertop, and take a sip. I angle myself just right. I know it won't be long before she'll check out my bod. It's taking longer than I want for her to notice me, and I get impatient.

"You got a gym around here?" I ask.

"There's one in the building," she says. Her eyes finally take a walk all over me, and I am satisfied. "In fact, I'll be heading there shortly for a workout of my own."

"I like a woman who takes care of herself," I reply, taking a slurp from my mug. I see her jawline clench at my noise, so I do it again.

Pay attention to me, darn it!

"Why don't you go get changed? I'll show you to the gym in 15 minutes. Don't forget we have a full day today. We need to be at my office in midtown by 8 o'clock."

I do as instructed and reappear in the kitchen in my workout gear. Ev is already there and changed herself. She hands me a bottle of water and a pair of white earbuds and heads for the front door. I swat her rear as she walks by. I can't help myself. Her ass looks miraculous in that tight athleisure wear, but she jumps and shoots me a glare.

Unexpected.

"Aren't we the youngster?" she snips, but a slow smile eventually comes, and I am relieved.

We take the elevator down several floors, and the doors part to reveal a state of-the-art gym. I head straight for the treadmills over-looking the expansive city in front of them. Ev is playing it cool with me, and I need to run off my frustration. I need to get some action soon or I'm going to explode. I plug the earbuds into the machine, blast some heavy metal, and run for a good long while until the sweat pours.

I'll need another shower.

I join Ev in front of the free weights. Sweat glistens above her brow, and her hair damp with sweat has turned a dark maroon. She lifts barbells above her head, and then in front of her in different repetitions. I marvel at the toned triceps on her upper arms. I have to drag my eyes away from her breasts as they press forward in her sports bra with the effort of lifting the 20-pounders. When she rests the weights beside her and drops into a downward dog, waving her tight rear in my face, it is almost too much. I retrieve the heaviest set of barbells I can find. I furiously pump them, mixing in sets of burpees.

An hour and a half later, we've showered. Ev had sent out my clothes to be laundered sometime in the night. They were hanging inside a sleeve of plastic on the back of my bathroom door when I came up for my second shower after the gym. I've never had my jeans pressed before. I think it looks weird. I give myself a gander in the mirror and nod. I smooth my plaid western button down across my chest and shake my head at the ironed seams at the front of my jeans. I do a couple squats to loosen them up from the washing and then head down the hall. Ev is waiting for me.

"You ready, cowboy?" she asks, tipping her ruby red head toward the door.

"Hang on a sec," I say, and lope back to the guest room. I grab my ball cap and secure it backwards on my head.

"JD, would you mind wearing your cowboy hat instead?" she asks, eyeing my cap.

"Sure." I shrug my shoulders, take off the ball cap, and retrieve my Stetson from the kitchen counter where I had left it last night.

"Now you look the part," Ev affirms. She hands me a plastic container holding what looks like green slime as we step out the door.

"What's this?" I ask, making a face.

"Breakfast to go." I raise an eyebrow, and Ev continues, "It's a green smoothie. You'll get more than your daily serving of fruits and veggies in that single drink."

I swirl the green goo in the container and take a tentative sip.

"Wow, that actually tastes pretty dang good," I admit as we head toward the elevator.

"Gotta keep my next big thing in good health," Ev adds, punching the button to the lobby.

Outside of the building, I pause for a moment on the sidewalk to pat a passing pup. I nod and tip my brim to its owner before slipping into the town car behind Ev. Moments later, we are being driven to Ev's office in midtown.

In the backseat, she is serious, scanning an open file folder in her lap. She looks sharp in her black fitted business suit. Her blazer tucks perfectly at her hips, the crisp white shirt beneath it is open just enough to make a man curious about the breasts it covers, and her pencil skirt hovers just above her knees, which are pinched together, leaning off to the side. The position of her legs reveals the red bottoms of her high heel shoes.

Classy.

After exiting the car, Ev nods to her driver in thanks, and then weaves between the pedestrians on the sidewalk scurrying to their own jobs. She has the hustle of a true city dweller. I follow her, but bump into a few shoulders trying to keep up.

"Yeehaw!" A man in a suit hollers at me. The other suits flanking him laugh. One man slaps the one who yelled the comment on the shoulder. Ev stops in her tracks at the front of the building and glares at the men. They hush up and hurry on down the sidewalk.

"Sorry about that," Ev says. "They look like someone's stupid interns. How tasteless."

"Don't bother me none," I reply with a broad smile. "I've seen more freedom in my lifetime than they'll ever know. I'm proud to be a cowboy. I don't expect city folk to understand. Takes more than a 'yeehaw' to get under my skin."

"Well, yeehaw then," Ev says with a look of relief and a smile. "Come on, JD."

To be honest, if it were any other place, at any other time, with any other person, that guy would have gotten what was coming to him, but right now, right here, I best behave and play along with Ev's little game.

She breezes into her office building, and I follow. Coming out of the revolving doors, I am in awe of the towering front lobby.

"I'll need to get you a guest badge," she says, pointing to the security desk. "Good morning, Ben. I need a guest badge for my friend JD here."

Friend?

"Identification, please," Ben states as he rises from his seat behind the desk. He looks me up and down. I momentarily wonder if I should wear a suit like everyone else. Then I shove off the thought. I hate how city folk can spur on a moment of feeling less than. I hand over my driver's license, shove my hands in my pockets, and chew my cheek.

"Jackson Drake from Texas," Ben says flatly. I cringe when he says my actual name out loud.

"Just put JD McCall on the badge, Ben," Ev instructs, eyeing him.

"Yes, Ms. Mitchell. Figured he wasn't from around here is all," Ben mutters.

He takes my picture with a little camera on his computer, hands my I.D. back to me, and passes over a little plastic card he's printed from a machine. I clip it to my shirt pocket.

"Thank you, Ben. This way, JD," Ev says with a nod.

We step into another elevator, and Ev presses the button to another top floor of another building. When the doors peel open, a team of women rush Ev.

"Good morning, Ms. Mitchell," one says, handing her a latte.

"Your morning report is on your desk. Mr. Flanagan called already. Your first meeting is at ...," clucks another.

I tune out the rest of it as I follow the fast-paced bustle of women down the hall to another lobby-type room with deep mahogany leather couches and windows overlooking Times Square.

"JD, would you wait here, please? I need to prep for our meetings this morning."

"Sure," I say lazily, plopping down on one of the couches. I already find the pace of the city and Ev's life exhausting.

"I'll send someone to retrieve you shortly."

"No problem," I reply as Ev struts off to her office across the way. I let my eyes linger on the sway of her hips in that tight black skirt before she shuts the door behind her. I look out the window and bide my time with daydreaming about the bulls I'll be riding soon at Madison Square Garden.

22

I spend most of the dang day on that couch, and I'm bored stupid. I watch men and women filter in and out of Ev's office. As they leave, they pump hands and say their niceties. It all seems like a bunch of bullshit to me.

Phony.

I am only invited into each meeting briefly. All the suits sit around a conference table in the room connected to Ev's office. This particular group asks me to turn around. I oblige. When I face them again, they nod to each other in agreement, on what exactly I can't be sure, and ask me to tell them about myself. They continue to look at each other with slight nods as I talk about my bull riding successes, and then after a few minutes standing at the front of the room like man meat, I am ushered out of the room by Ev's assistant and told to sit back on the couch outside her office.

"Can I offer you anything?" she asks me again. The last few times, I just shook my head, annoyed.

"Got any beer?" I ask this time.

Her eyes widen, then her eyebrows furrow.

"I can offer you coffee, tea, soda, or water," she snips, settling back behind her own desk with a frown.

God, she's uptight.

She could use someone messing up that pulled-together package.

Ain't going to be me, though. I don't dig her vibe.

"Water'll do," I say, wandering over and leaning on her desk. I tip my head side to side, looking her over. It's an attempt to amuse myself and make her uneasy. She nods, rises, assures her blouse is buttoned up and her skirt is straight, and then hurries away.

Uncomfortable. Good.

I put my fist in the candy bowl on her desk. I stuff the handful in my pocket, then unwrap a piece, toss it in my mouth, and leave the wrapper on her keyboard.

Why are big city chicks so snooty?

After what feels like eternity and four glasses of water later, Ev finally emerges from behind her office door.

"Are you ready to get out of here, cowboy?" Ev asks.

"Am I ever," I assure.

"Well, first, you need to change."

"Change into what?"

"Just a little something to spruce you up for a night on the town. I had some fresh clothes brought in for you."

"They are hanging in the bathroom in your office, Ms. Mitchell," the snooty assistant chirps.

"Thank you, Beth. Go on into my office, and get changed, JD," Ev instructs.

"If changin' gets me out of this place and in the fresh air, your command is my wish," I reply, shrugging my shoulders.

Beth gives me a look. I imagine it's because I sounded disrespectful to her boss. I ignore her. Ev laughs and touches me on the cheek. It feels more motherly than loving.

"Thank you for being patient with me today, JD."

"Ah, no problem," I say, rubbing the back of my neck. "See ya, Beth."

The assistant I've been messing with all day nods, turns on her heels with a flip of her hair, and sighs audibly.

I reckon she's happy to be getting rid of me and my antics. I head into Ev's big office, spot the bathroom door open, and spy the clothes hanging in there. I'm dreading what might wait for me. I step in, close the door, and strip the plastic from the hanger, revealing a crisp white button-down shirt, black suit jacket, and fresh Lariat jeans. It's reminiscent of what I had recently worn to the wedding.

Not bad. I can wear this.

I dress in the fresh clothes, pull my belt and buckle through the loops of the new jeans, slip back into my black boots, and adjust my cowboy hat. I crunch up the plaid shirt and jeans I had been wearing, shove them under my arm, and step out into the lobby area I'd been sitting in all day. Ev has slipped out of her suit coat and applied a little extra face paint. She went from day to night in an instant.

"So where are we headin'?" I ask in the elevator on the way down.

"I want you to meet some more people."

Vague.

"My first New York City evening outing with you," I drawl.

At street level, Ev's driver is waiting with a door open. Ev slides onto the leather seat, and I follow.

"I just need to catch up on a few emails while we drive," Ev says, engrossed in the screen of her phone. I raise an eyebrow but keep quiet.

The woman is a workaholic.

After some painful stop-and-go through Times Square, the traffic eases as we drive uptown along Central Park.

Finally, something green to look at.

We pull up along another curb on another street in the city and exit the car.

"Here we are." Ev takes my elbow. I open the establishment's door for her, and an astonishingly beautiful woman instantly greets us.

"Welcome to Chez Pierre, Ms. Mitchell. Right this way."

"You certainly are well known in these parts, miss," I murmur next to Ev's ear.

"It's true. We come here often for business. I'm a regular, but the truth is, this city loves me," Ev replies with a laugh.

The city loves money, and it's clear Ev has a lot of it.

I watch the woman's hips sway as she leads us through the dimly-lit restaurant. Ev puts a finger below my chin and lifts it. With a smile and a raised eyebrow, she wags a finger at me.

"I don't blame you for looking. She has a spectacular ass," Ev says. "However, while you are keeping my company, I would appreciate it if you tried to be a little more discreet in your admiration of other women. I have a reputation to uphold."

"And what's that?" I ask.

"That I can have anything I want. And you, JD McCall, are what I happen to want at the moment."

News to me after the night I spent alone in her guest room and the day I spent sitting on a couch in her office. But I'll play along.

"I only have eyes for you," I drawl.

"That's better," she purrs.

We reach an enormous circular table and seated at it are some of the most beautiful women I've ever seen. I pause to take in the scenery and hook my thumbs in my belt loops. My eyes wander over the bodacious blondes, saucy red heads, and athletic brunettes. I am careful though not to gaze too long at any one of them. I plan to keep Ev happy, but boy, could a guy get used to this. An older man rises from his chair, and Ev slides up to him. He opens his arms, and they embrace.

"JD, this is Martin Bloomberg. He and I have done business together for ages. Haven't we, Martin?"

"Indeed, we have. You've brought me some of the best talent in the city, Ev. It's a beautiful partnership we have."

I scan the table, and everyone is looking at Ev and this man like they are the king and queen of New York.

Maybe they are.

"Martin owns MBFC."

"MBFC? What's that?" I ask, a little too loudly, and the entire table gasps.

"Ladies and gentlemen, we have ourselves a bona fide cowboy here. He's from a small town in Texas. We can't possibly expect him to know anything about the fashion industry, can we?" Ev replies, covering for me.

Martin expectantly nods to the table. On cue, all the guests shake their heads from left to right, and a few chime, "No," and "Of course not."

"JD, my boy," Martin begins with a slap to my shoulder. "Let me explain. The fashion industry is a teeny-tiny, insular cosmos. Although fashion plays a major role on the world stage, just a handful of companies dominate the industry. My company, MBFC, that's short for Martin Bloomberg Fashion Conglomerate, happens to be one of them. Ev tells me you are going to the be next big thing." He extends a hand to me. I take it.

I like the sound of this.

"Pleasure to meet you, sir," I say, pumping his hand.

"Call me Martin."

"All right. It's a pleasure to meet you, Martin."

"Everly, would you see that our server brings the reserved wine list, while I introduce JD to my girls?"

His girls?

"Have fun, JD, but not too much fun. Remember our little talk?" Ev says with a wink over her shoulder, walking in the direction of the bar. I like the sway of her hips even better than the woman who brought us to the table, but I'll keep that little tidbit to myself.

For now. Gotta keep her guessin' if I'm gonna get into her bedroom. Jealousy is a mighty strong card to hold.

"I also happen to own this fine restaurant," Martin continues. "The women who don't quite cut it for our modeling department often find working here agreeable while they pursue their acting careers or other endeavors. I feel offering them a position here is the least I can do after they don't make the cut."

"That's generous of you," I mumble.

"New York is a tough city, my boy, but don't worry, you've already made the cut. I've seen your photographs. Ev has fine taste in her young men," Martin comments, assessing me and rubbing his chin.

Her young men?

"JD, these are the top models from around the world," Martin says proudly, extending a hand palm up toward the table. "You'll be working with some of them very soon. Let me introduce you."

I gander at Ev conversing across the room with another woman at the mammoth mahogany bar for a moment, then trail Martin around the table meeting beautiful woman after beautiful woman.

This is getting good.

23

EVERLY

As I make my way over to retrieve the wine list, my niece, Melissa, is standing behind the bar with a broad smile and wide eyes. She nods her head enthusiastically in JD's direction and bites her knuckles.

Melissa, nickname Missy, is my twenty-something niece, but she is more like my younger sister. She is an aspiring fashion designer. She's working at Martin's restaurant in her free time to develop contacts with potential investors. Her designs are excellent, and I promised my brother I'd look out for her when she came to live in the city. I recommended the gig at Chez Pierre while she establishes her line. Having built my own empire, I know what the girl needs to develop the grit it requires to give the fashion world a go. She's talented, but she needs experience, contacts, and work ethic.

I smile, signal to Missy to cool it, and sneak a glance in JD's direction to make sure he can't see her display. I am relieved to find his focus is on Martin, who is introducing his gaggle of models. As I expected, the women around the table are also responding to him, their expressions, cheeks blushing, eyes averting, lashes fluttering, and smiles rising, only cements what I already know. JD has star power. An odd feeling settles over me. It's a strange sense of pride.

"Ahem, Everly Mitchell! What are you doing with that?" Missy squeals, grabbing a hold of my arm across the top of the bar.

"Shhh. You are going to blow my cover as a cool cucumber. What's wrong with having a brief fling with a cowboy?" I ask, shooting her a mischievous grin.

"Absolutely nothing! He's even better looking than your usual projects," she whispers.

"You're right there. He certainly isn't a buttoned-up suit-and-tie type."

"You certainly checked the box on the young and good-looking part though."

"Indeed, I did," I reply with a grin.

"You should go down South more often."

"You know I care little for leaving the city, Missy," I remind her.

"I know, I know, but he's so different from the others. I just want to know *what* exactly you are doing with all of that. Details, please!" Missy blurts, suggestively swirling her hips.

"Later!" I swat her with a giggle. "Come on, Martin wants the reserve list."

"On it," Missy replies. She disappears for a moment, then returns with the thick menu. She hands it over. "Don't you dare think that I am going to forget getting the scoop on the cowboy from you."

"I always give you the scoop, and I'll do it later," I say with a wink, gliding back over to the table with Martin's prized wine list in my possession.

He never wants the sommelier to come over to the table. Martin is far too proud. He likes to think he knows it all when it comes to wine, amongst a plethora of other things. I roll my eyes at the pretense that my job sometimes requires. To take my mind off of Martin and his appreciation for the finer things in life, I search out JD. I find him seated at the table and head toward the open chair next to him. I can't help but smile. JD looks like a fish out of water in his cowboy hat, surrounded by Martin and his models.

"I own the clothing makers that service the stores your kind shops in," I hear Martin say as I hand over the leather-bound list to him, settle into my chair, and place my napkin in my lap.

"My kind?" JD asks, furrowing his brow. I see JD's jaw clench and drop my gaze to note his hands are fisted in his lap.

"Country folk, they —," Martin begins.

"Yes, that's right," I interrupt before JD thinks about lunging across the table and punching Martin in the face. I put my palm to JD's hands, wringing now beneath the table. "In fact, Martin, we've already met with Lariat Jeans, Big Outdoors Athletic, and Banner Boot Company, which are all under your umbrella."

"Oh, good. Good," Martin replies, pleased.

"On a side note, we also spoke with the truck arm of Stampede Automotive and Rocket Energy Drink."

"We did?" JD whispers.

I nod enthusiastically and can see an electric spark in JD's emerald eyes.

"Wow," JD says, chewing his cheek then smiling. His hands relax beneath my palm.

"Come, come. Let's have ourselves a drink then," Martin coaxes.

JD and I exchange a lingering look. Martin hums at the head of the table and engrosses himself in the special wine list. It's a binder reserved for him and a few choice Chez Pierre clientele only. I fish around in my laptop bag for a moment and pull out a large envelope. I set in on JD's plate.

"What's this?" he asks.

"Something that will please you," I whisper in his ear. I slip my hand between JD's legs under the table, and he grins, reaching for the packet. He slips the paperwork from the manila envelope. He studies the various pages for some time, and then his eyes go wide.

"That's a number followed by whole lot of zeros, Ev," he murmurs.

"It is indeed. It's what you can expect now that I'm your manager." I slip the manager part in hoping it will slide right by, but he eyes me the moment the word leaves my lips.

"Never had a manager. Don't need one," JD says, visibly tensing at the thought.

"You do now, cowboy," I reply, removing my hand from his crotch to dig into my bag again. "You can call me your agent, if you'd rather. Just sign here." I point to the dotted line and offer him a pen. He takes it but doesn't sign the documents.

"Perhaps these might help you make your decision," I say, pulling a smaller envelope from my bag. "We'll get these added to your bull riding vest right away." I spread a slew of sponsorship patches across the tablecloth, and JD's eyes grow wide again, transforming from slits to just about popping from his eye sockets.

"How'd you know where they go?' he asks.

"Quick internet search. It does the trick every time. As your manager, it's my job to know what to ask of your sponsors."

"Why are you doing all of this for me, Ev?"

"I'm good at seeing the potential in things, in people. And I know how to hustle when I see possibility."

"When did you have the time to make this happen?"

"I was already penning proposals in my mind before we left Green Briar."

"Is this what you were working on so intensely on your laptop during our flight to NYC?"

I nod, and JD rubs a finger lovingly across the patches, twirls the pen for a moment, and then signs the documents. I feel the satisfied smile of a good deal closed spread across my lips.

I always get what I aim for.

Happy hour has everyone more relaxed. Martin's top two buttons are popped, and his tie is loose. The models don't sit up quite as straight as they once did and have actually begun talking amongst each other.

"Cowboy boots, jeans, pickup trucks, and ... supermodels! That is going to be the next phase of MBFC. Thanks to Ev's genius ideas, our business continues to expand!" Martin exclaims. He raises a glass and nods to our servers. On cue, they hustle about the table refilling everyone with what might be the nineteenth and twentieth bottle of very expensive wine.

"I want a cowboy," one of the tipsy models croons, lifting her glass above her head for a refill.

"He certainly is easy on the eyes," says another model. The rest of the girls giggle and hoist their glasses as well.

I know how to pick them.

"Here's to JD!" Martin exclaims before sipping from his glass.

I sip from my wineglass and glance at JD. He drinks beer rather than wine. He is all smiles and clearly very satisfied with himself. I'm certain JD feels valued and a little drunk himself.

That is the point of all of this, after all.

Our steak entrees are delivered, while luscious platters of side dishes to pass are settled in the center of the table. Missy sets my plate down and raises an eyebrow. I follow her gaze to find JD snagging a scallop from a dish in the center of the table with his fingertips. As he shoves it in his mouth, I notice the silverware still wrapped in his napkin. The butter sauce drips down his chin.

"Yum!" he announces, smacking his lips and reaching across the table for another one.

"I'm still working on his manners," I whisper to Missy, who presses her lips together. The glint in her eye tells me she wants to laugh, but she remains composed knowing her boss is seated at the head of the table. Martin has his wait staff go through extensive etiquette training, and he has eyes like a hawk. Martin is giving JD a pass in that department because he knows I'll take care of those details, but he won't stand for one of his servers having an outburst in his restaurant. I know Missy isn't willing to get fired over JD's uncultured shenanigans.

"JD, tell us about this bull you mentioned earlier tonight. Tell us about Jackhammer," Martin inquires. He leans forward with interest and swirls his wine glass.

"I'd be happy to, Martin," JD replies, licking his fingers and dragging his palm across the tablecloth. I shake my head and offer him my linen napkin.

Lord, his manners are atrocious.

It doesn't seem to matter though. The table guests of New York's elite models are entranced as JD animatedly begins to tell his bull riding story.

"Ah, Jackhammer. Some guys called 'im 'The Hammer.' He was a beast! Best score I ever had on a bull, I tell ya. That ride was right here in New York," JD says, leaning forward and putting his elbows on the table. He selects a breadstick from the basket in front of him and points it at Martin.

"Do go on," Martin encourages.

"It all started with me grippin' the end of my rope tight and pushin' my heels down. I was ready for the ride. I hollered, 'Let's ride!' and the gatekeepers let my bull go. The gate of the bucking chute swung open, and Jackhammer exploded, I tell ya. He was a furious twist of angst and strength. That ride was happenin' in slow motion to me. My job was stayin' on the bull for eight seconds without touching him with my free hand."

Excitedly, JD bounces out of his chair, turns it around with one hand, straddles it backwards, starts grinding in his seat, and circles his breadstick above his head. The legs of the chair screech on the marble floor and everyone at the table leans forward, enthralled.

"He was unridden back then, and I reminded myself that the first buck is always the most violent and the most important one. Grittin' my teeth, I squeezed my thighs with all my strength. We were just gruntin', whirlin', spinnin', jumpin', you know? I told myself if I could make it through Jackhammer's first buck, then I could last the next seven seconds."

JD pauses to bite into the breadstick that he's just dragged through the lemony sauce pooled on the scallop platter. Martin stiffens and gives me a glance.

"I'll take care of it," I mouth. Martin nods. I squirm a bit in my seat as JD stuffs the entire thing in his mouth, folding it in like an accordion with his index finger. Martin examines his wine, and the models look away as JD chews appreciatively, his cheeks bulging like a chipmunk. It feels like an eternity before he finally swallows and then swishes his mouth with a swig of beer. I quickly pass the scallop platter and the breadbasket to the woman next to me. She passes them on down the table and out of JD's reach. Reenacting his bull ride in his chair, JD lifts the front legs off the ground and slams them back to the floor. I clench my teeth.

"I remember that ride like it was yesterday. The dirt arena whirled and became a blur," JD continues. "I used all the strength I could muster to find any sort of rhythm with Jackhammer's bucking motion. I strapped my right hand in tight to the rope secured around the bull's body. My free hand waved above my head, and I dug my spurs into his sides. I was hangin' on to that bull's hide for dear life. I still remember how my muscles burned with each countermove."

I notice everyone in the room is hanging on every word coming out of JD's mouth, including my niece.

He's got charisma. That's good.

I've got a full schedule of interviews lined up for him already. Glad to see he can entertain an audience.

"The Hammer and I had become one. I felt the win in my gut, but it was definitely one of my toughest runs. The bull was giving his all, but so was I. Finally, the buzzer sounded. *Bzzzzt*. It was sweet music to my ears. I leapt from Jackhammer's back as a pick-up rider galloped up alongside us. I smiled to myself as that horse and rider loped me away to safety." JD pauses for a moment and looks around. "Hey! Where'd those breadsticks go? They are dang good in the sauce that those squishy things come in."

"I'll retrieve more from the kitchen," one of our servers assures, and then drifts off toward the kitchen. I shake my head.

"I could eat a hundred of those things, Martin. Good place you got here."

"I'm glad you are finding the establishment enjoyable, JD. I'm on the edge of my seat here. Please continue."

"All right, where was I? Oh yeah. At that point, The Hammer was still bucking up a storm in the center of the arena like a maniac. He was mad. Nobody ever rode him before. Getting rode makes the really rank ones good and angry, but it was good for me because I could tell from all that pissed off twistin', whirlin', and buckin' he would earn me more than his fair share of points. Took the wranglers a long while to get him back behind the shoots."

"A 'rank' bull is considered an elite athlete," I add, noting the confused expressions around the table. "A qualified ride in a bull riding event is worth up to 100 points: 50 for the rider and 50 for the bull. The rider has to stay on top of the bull for eight seconds and has to ride with one free hand. A cowboy is disqualified if he touches himself or the bull with his free arm. Any ride that is scored 90 or higher is deemed exceptional."

"That's right. This one here learns quick," JD hoots, hooking his arm around my neck and giving my head a rub. "Gave you a lesson on the airplane, didn't I?"

"Between JD and the internet, I am learning a thing or two about the bull riding business," I add, tapping JD's arm. When he removes it, I hastily adjust my hair. "What really got my attention about working in this new niche, though, is the National Bull Riders Organization has a 95% sponsor renewal rate. The NBR has done an excellent job of aligning itself with corporate partners like MBFC. It says something about your company, Martin, that you are willing to be associated with a growing sport that's on the verge of going mainstream."

"And where the possibility of severe bodily injury weighs heavily over every moment," JD drawls. I elbow him gently in the side, and he hushes up. I don't want to scare Martin off. I want to hook him on the opportunity of investing in JD, investing more heavily in my business.

"Do tell me more, Ev." Martin loves statistics, and I have more where that came from.

"Martin, their sponsorship metrics are off the charts: 54% of NBR fans are more likely to recognize a sponsor than the average American adult, while 12% of fans made a purchase specifically because a company was a NBR sponsor. Not to mention, the NBR tour is televised weekly around the globe. Their television broadcasts reach half a billion households in 120 territories around the world."

"I'm growing more and more impressed with this opportunity, Ev. Good work." Martin strokes his chin and grins.

I know how to hook executives and pull in talent.

"Yeah, well, let me tell ya," JD begins again. "With each of us rated on a scale of 0-50, like Ev said, I needed a combined 87 points to move into the lead at this particular event. In bull riding, scores in the 80s are very good, but I was hoping to break into the 90s. Like Ev said, that would be exceptional."

"And what score did you earn, JD?" Martin asks, still smiling at me.

"Well, Martin, I tell ya, the crowd went dang wild when the score came in. I'm the only man who rode Jackhammer before he was retired. He and I earned a 98. It's one of the few 98s ever earned between bull and rider on the tour. I'm pretty darn proud of that ride."

"Fantastic!" Martin exclaims, slapping the table. "Tell me another of your cowboy tales, JD."

"Well, Martin, this one bull, Merciless ... he almost castrated me," JD begins. A few models gasp, putting their hands over their mouths. I'm certain that after my slew of NBR statistics and hearing about JD's heroic ride, Martin is seeing dollar signs now, so I did my job for the evening. I take the moment to excuse myself and squeeze JD's shoulder before heading to the ladies' room. Missy takes notice from her position near the corner of the room and trails in after me.

"That body!" she squeals.

"I know."

"Those green eyes."

"I know."

"That cowboy butt wrapped up in Wranglers."

"I know."

"That swagger."

"I know."

"The manners, though. Good grief." Missy examines herself in the mirror.

"*I know*," I sigh, leaning a hip against the bathroom counter and folding my arms across my chest.

"Did you see him stuff that whole mini shrimp skewer in his mouth and pop all the shrimp off at once?" she asks. "And that breadstick! Yikes."

"I missed the skewer. I saw the breadstick." I roll my eyes and palm my face. "He needs training in the manners department."

"Ev, you are a miracle. He is exactly what New York City needs!"

"He will be once we get those manners in order," I say with a smile. "Hey, can you do me a favor?"

24

JD

Having said our goodbyes to Martin and his models, I follow Ev out to the street where her driver is waiting to whisk us home.

Ev is incredible. I seriously can't believe my luck. I gain a slew of sponsors, have a belly full of beer, chowed down on unusual and expensive food, met some hot babes, told a bunch of my favorite bull riding stories that folks actually wanted to hear, and have a hot redhead to go home with. I expect to have earned some hanky-panky tonight.

I notice a big Husky dragging a teenage boy down the sidewalk. The teen is attempting to type away on his cell phone, and I chuckle. The dog drags the retractable leash out to the end of its line and tugs his way toward me for a sniff.

"Hi ya, boy," I say, crouching down to stroke his head.

"Come on, Rex. Don't bug that guy," the kid says, looking up from his cell phone and tilting his head at the sight of my cowboy hat. "Sorry about him," he adds when Rex licks my face with his warm tongue.

"Aw, it's all right," I assure, rising from the dog.

"My parents make me walk him every night," the kid grumbles.

"Fresh air will do you good. Thanks for letting me pet your dog." I glance over at Ev, and she is watching our interaction from inside the car with interest.

The kid nods and drags Rex on. He is obviously more interested in getting back to tapping on his cell screen than conversing with the likes of me.

"See ya," I call after him and join Ev in the backseat.

"What a night," I announce as I settle in. I open the little bar in the back of the car and rummage around in it. I locate a whiskey and twist the top. I swig right from the little bottle.

"We have glasses for that in here, JD," Ev admonishes.

"Uh-oh. Why are you snarling at me? What did I do wrong?"

"I'm not snarling, and you did nothing wrong," Ev responds in a lighter tone. "Everyone loved you today, JD, but we are going to have to work on those manners of yours a bit. Not everyone will be as relaxed as our company was tonight about seeing you shove a whole shrimp skewer in your mouth or enjoy watching you touch everything on the table with your fingers."

"Where to, Ms. Mitchell?" the driver asks.

"Give us a moment," Ev replies. "We are waiting on one more person. Thank you."

"Manners are for stiffs," I mutter.

"You just signed a contract with a lot of zeros, JD. You will have to make a few adjustments for your sponsors. Representing them appropriately will require a little lesson in manners."

"What if I don't wanna?"

"What if I want you to?" Ev asks, unbuttoning two buttons of her silky blouse.

"You've got my attention ..." I eye the lace of her bra peeking out at me.

"I've made arrangements for you to sit in on the etiquette class the servers are required to take before their employment at Martin's restaurant. You'll learn about putting your napkin in your lap, how to use cutlery, select wine, as well as basic table manners."

"What do I get out of this deal?"

"I think you've already gotten quite a lot, JD. I'm certain your bank account has never looked better with the sponsorships I've negotiated for you."

"The money's nice for sure, but what about you and me? I want more in that department. That's what I'm getting at. What do I get out of the deal?"

"Unfortunately, chivalry seems to be going out of style these days," Ev sighs. "It's a pity, really. Good manners and common courtesy have become a rarity rather than a common standard. The gentleman is a dying breed, but we are going to remedy that for you."

"I agree with you that my table manners may need a little work, but don't tell me I don't know how to be a gentleman. That's in my blood. It's the cowboy way. Despite being a little light with my tongue from time to time and a bit of a womanizer, I do have the innate sense of chivalry that men from the South possess. I am all 'yes ma'am', bendin' of the brim, openin' doors, and whirlin' women around dance floors, miss."

"All right, I'll give you that, cowboy. As far as those table manners go though, here comes your teacher," Ev nods toward the window, and, to my disappointment, swiftly buttons her blouse back up. One of our servers from dinner tonight is galloping up to the car.

"Threesome?" I ask, wiggling my eyebrows. Ev shakes her head and frowns.

"Hi," the server says, climbing into the car.

She's pretty cute. She'll do.

"JD, this is my *niece*, Melissa," Ev advises.

Dang. No threesome for me.

"Oh, hi," I say to her. I feel a bit defeated. I eye the big black binder she has tucked under her arm. It's been non-stop work with Ev since I got to New York. I'm still hoping I'll get some action tonight, even though I'm feeling tired now.

"I hear you need some etiquette lessons, cowboy. I do all the etiquette training at Chez Pierre, so Auntie Ev is paying me a little extra under the table to teach you. Honestly, I can use all the cash I can get."

"Pleased to make your introduction, Melissa," I say, trying on some manners.

"You can just call me Missy."

"All right. Nice to meet you, Missy," I say, settling back in my seat after pouring another pint-size whiskey into the glass Ev provided.

Ev instructs our driver to take us to her apartment. Ev and Missy chat about my sponsorships during the drive, and I'm feeling mighty excited about having those patches added to my vest. I'm not so excited about the upcoming lesson in manners from Missy. Thank goodness I've got plenty of alcohol in my gullet to get me through this.

Once we are back in the high rise, Ev instructs me to take a seat at her glass top dining table.

It's gonna be another late night.

I drag a hand across my face, grab a brew from the refrigerator, and then sit across from Missy with a sulk. She has the binder spread out in front of her. Ev makes multiple trips to where I'm sitting, bringing a box full of silverware, place settings, glassware, and such. She stacks everything at the end of the table, and I eye the pile with contempt.

"This should get you started, Missy. JD, you be nice to her now and behave yourself. She's family. I'm going to take care of some business in the studio while you two have your lesson," Ev says.

"Sounds good," Missy chirps as Ev disappears down the hall. I watch her walk away and feel slighted.

"I like the Ev I met back at Green Briar, the carefree lady I met at the wedding there," I mutter. "This woman is completely different. She is all business, all the time. It's not much fun."

"That's Ev for sure," Missy adds, arranging a place setting in front of me. "She's all about her business and closing deals. Get her out of the city — if you can, and she's a different person. Maybe you can encourage her to take a vacation again sometime. She'll loosen up then. Ev could use more frequent vacations."

"Does she do this often?" I probe.

"What? Have me teach manners to a cowboy at her dinner table after I've finished a long shift at the restaurant? No, I can't say she does," Missy teases.

"That's not what I mean. I just can't help the feeling that I'm some kind of project or somethin'. I'm feelin' a little like man meat, not that I've been bothered by being used before or doin' the using, but this just feels different. I don't know ... it's like an act or somethin'."

Missy eyes me and bites her lip.

"That's a better question for Ev. I'm not touching that one." I grimace at her response. "OK, ready to get started?" she asks, skirting the subject and situating the manual in front of me on a stand.

"Ready as I'll ever be," I drone, propping an elbow on the table and taking a swig from my brew.

"All right, JD. Just try to make this fun. Let's start with basic table manners. First, elbows off the table, sit up straight, say 'please' and 'thank you'."

"Yes, ma'am," I sigh and oblige, reluctantly removing my elbows and straightening in my chair.

"See, you're getting the hang of it already," she chuckles. "Take a look at this diagram here. Table settings are always arranged for right-handed people. In a clockwise direction, you'll find the following: wine and water glasses, spoons, knives, chargers, and dinner plates with the napkin placed on top, dinner forks, bread plate, and butter knife, and ending with the dessert spoon and dessert fork. You always put your napkin in your lap when you sit down, even if food hasn't been served yet. At a restaurant like Chez Pierre, your server will put your napkin in your lap for you. If you should excuse yourself from the table, neatly place your napkin next to your plate. The server may refold your napkin while you are away. When you return, place the napkin back in your lap."

"All that effort over a napkin? This is exhausting," I groan, scrutinizing the graphic in Missy's book and finishing my beer.

"There may be additional pieces such as cups and saucers, or specialty utensils like seafood forks," Missy continues, paying my complaint no mind. She glides across the kitchen, retrieves two beers from the fridge, pops the tops, sets one in front of me, and takes a sip from hers. "Ah, that's good. There's nothing more satisfying than a cold beer after a long shift."

"Or a long day," I add as my mind travels back over everything I've been through in the short time I've been here: a late-night photo shoot last night, an early morning workout, a bunch of meetings, a lot of sitting on a couch in Ev's office, the dinner, and now this.

"That's how Ev rolls. When she sees talent, she puts him or her through the paces. She's doing that for me with my fashion line. You've got it made with her. Just hang in there and do what she asks of you. It'll all work out. Actually, it seems like it is working out already."

"She certainly works magic, and fast. Still can't put a finger on why she's doin' all this for me, though."

"She likes you. That's why. She's probably back there making more magic for you right now."

"I can think of a few magic things she could do right now to prove that she likes me. She could —"

"Come on, let's focus," Missy interrupts, changing the subject. "Where were we? Ah yes, back to your place setting. You may see up to four beverage glasses for one person's place setting. Glasses are arranged in a diagonal or square pattern to the right of the dinner plate, and are composed of glasses for water, white wine, red wine, and a champagne flute for occasions that require a toast."

"What about a glass for the beer?" I ask.

"That, your server would bring separately when you order it."

Blah, blah, blah.

Missy's lesson goes on and on until I am on the fairly drunk side and can hardly keep my eyes open. Sleep has never sounded so good. I expect I'm going to be sleeping alone again tonight. It's fine though, I haven't got the energy for banging anyone, anyway.

"And that's it!" Missy exclaims as she flips the last page of her training manual and closes the binder.

"Thank heaven," I grunt, pushing aside my plate and dropping my heavy head on my arms.

"And what do we say?" Missy asks.

"Thank you, Missy," I grumble into the crook of my arm.

"You're welcome, JD. I'll see you tomorrow. I'm off to the guest bedroom."

"What?"

Where am I going to sleep?

"It's couch city for you, big guy," Missy adds as if reading my mind. "Didn't Ev tell you I'm spending the night?"

"News to me."

"Well, good night," she says cheerfully. "Hopefully, for Ev's sake, and your own, you'll retain some of what you learned tonight."

I'm tempted to ask if she wants company, but I rule it out. There's too much at stake, too much risk if I pursue her now.

"Good night," I mutter as she gallops down the hall.

I rise from the table, arch my aching back for a stretch, and eyeball the leather couch. Once Missy shuts the door to the guest room, I pad down the hallway and notice the light is off in the studio. I head back the way I came, stop, and knock on Ev's bedroom door.

Nothing.

I turn the knob and poke my head in. She's fast asleep in her clothes with a file folder open on her lap. I wander into the room and examine her. Even though this all-business Ev is foreign to me, I still like the looks of her.

"What are you all about?" I wonder aloud. "Still not sure why you are doing all this for me."

I notice my modeling pictures spread out next to her. I gather them up, retrieve the folder from her lap, tuck them inside, close it, and put the folder on her nightstand. I turn off the little lamp at her side, brush a hand across her satin cheek, and cover her with a blanket from the edge of the bed. I close the door gently behind me.

I make my way down the hall again and out into the great room. I sigh at the couch, shrug my shoulders, strip off my clothes, and drop onto the leather. Naked, I drag a throw off of the back of the sofa, and I am asleep before I know it.

25

I startle awake to the whir of a blender blasting in the background.

"Rise and shine, cowboy!" Ev announces over the grind of the appliance.

The shades rise all around me. The morning light is blinding, and I jump off the couch at the racket coming from the kitchen. The blanket that was once covering me slips to the floor. I rub my eyes and attempt to get my bearings as the blender grates on my eardrums.

What a brutal way to wake up from a surprisingly peaceful slumber.

My eyes finally focus, and I see that Missy's have gone wide at the sight of me.

"Now I know what you are doing with *that!*" Missy exclaims, ogling me below the waist, and taking a sip from a green smoothie with a wicked smile. I grab a throw pillow lickity-split and cover myself. Normally, I'd let her look, but it is Ev's niece doing the looking, and it doesn't feel right.

"Missy was just about to head home." Ev elbows Missy with a shake of her head and wanders over to me with a second smoothie.

"We'll be seeing her a little later, though. She's got the day off and is going to tag along with us. She wants to see you in action."

"See me in action?" I ask with a smirk. My mind heads in a naughty direction, and I consider letting the pillow go.

"Why don't you put your workout clothes on? We'll hit the gym then go over the plans for the day, JD," Ev says, handing over the glass of slime.

Still holding the throw cushion over my privates, I accept it and take a sip. I eye Missy over the lip of the glass. She wiggles her eyebrows, but before I do something I'll likely regret, I hightail it toward the guest room in search of my gear bag.

"Nice tushie!" Missy hollers after me, and I feel my face cheeks warm.

A run and some heavy weights will do me good.

Down in the gym, Ev and I warm up side by side on the treadmills.

"So what do you have in store for me today?" I ask. I'm feeling sour, and I don't really want to hear the answer because I'm understanding that her plans don't include anything horizontal between us.

"We are going to stir up some JD McCall fans for your bull riding event this weekend. We're going to lure them in from New Jersey."

"How?"

"You'll see," she replies, putting in her earbuds and cranking her machine to high.

"Full of surprises, aren't we, Ev?" I grumble, knowing she can't hear me, and punch my own button to full speed. After our workout, I shower and dress, but I still feel antsy waiting for Ev in the kitchen.

"Will you go meet Missy downstairs?" she asks as she breezes into the kitchen. She is dressed down in a button up blouse, jeans, and the boots she wore at Green Briar. Her hair is up in a ponytail. I like the looks of her like this. I am hoping to get a glimpse of the woman I met back in the country today.

"She should be here any minute. I'll be down in a moment. I just have to make a quick call to confirm our location with the audio-visual team," she adds.

"I'll see you down there then," I reply, saddened to realize that, despite her attire, she's still in her all-business mode. I pat my shirt pocket and head for the door. Whatever Ev is planning has me stressing out. This adventure isn't turning out how I thought it would.

I need a smoke.

When I get to street level, I streak out the front door and breathe a sigh of relief that Missy isn't standing on the curb waiting for me. I need a moment to myself. I flick the lighter and bring the flame to the cigarette between my lips. I take a deep drag, happy that I had a few stashed in my gear bag. The cigarette is old and tastes stale, but it's taking the edge off. I finish the smoke in a few puffs and contemplate having another as I crush the filter on the sidewalk under my boot tip.

"You'll have to quit smoking. It doesn't settle well these days when you are in the public eye," Ev says, strutting up to me as she puts her sunglasses on.

Now she wants me to quit smoking?

"Oh, come on. I only do it every now and then," I say, putting a second cigarette between my lips in protest. "There's nothing like a good smoke after a romp in the hay or a night on the town drinking with the boys."

"I mean it, cowboy. Your body is your greatest asset. It's time to take care of it." Before I can get a flame to the tip, Ev takes the cigarette dangling from my lips and flicks it into the street. "This city is basically no smoking, anyway."

"Fine, no skin off my knee," I mutter, crushing the box with the ones I still have left in my fist. I can go two more days. I just have to last two more days with Ev, and then my life will go back to normal. My event starts on Saturday. I'm certain I'll make the short go on Sunday. On Monday, I'll be getting the hell out of New York and be heading back to the country. At least I got a load of money and solid sponsorships out of this deal. A couple days without nicotine and some loving from this lady won't kill me.

I hope.

"Thank you," Ev says with a smile and kisses me on the cheek.

The touch isn't much, but it gets me thinking that maybe she'll at least eventually come around on the intimacy part.

"Let's get this show on the road!" Missy exclaims, stepping out of a taxi. Ev's driver pulls up, we pile into the car, and at once, we are off to the next thing.

Whatever it is.

We cross the city and make our way to New Jersey. As we come out on the other side of the Lincoln Tunnel, I sulk and stare out the window. I'm not having much fun. What I thought was going to be a few days of great sex has turned into galloping around, shaking hands, posing for pictures, and feeling pretty darn confused. I try to lighten my mood by focusing on the upcoming bull riding event tomorrow and the freedom that will come with it.

26

EVERLY

We are on the Jersey shore. The waves are crashing in the background and the salty air whirls my hair around my face. My team has a portion of the beach roped off. Inside it is a metal round pen and today's sponsor, Lariat, has brought in a real live bull for the photo shoot.

"Interesting choice for his attire," Missy says, watching JD wander along the beach.

"I didn't dress him," I reply. "He insisted on the outfit."

"Well, I think it is exquisitely simple."

"As a fashion designer, I thought it would appall you."

"No, no, on the contrary. He is a vision. It really is the simplicity that does it for me." I glance at Missy. She touches her temple. "In fact, I'm having visions for my new line right now just looking at him."

"Visions for next year's line?" I laugh.

"You should know that he asked me last night if you've done this before," Missy adds.

"Done what?" I ask.

Missy raises an eyebrow at my response. "He thinks he's a project, Ev."

"Oh." I feel a little guilty. "I suppose he's smarter than I pegged him for."

"Also, he prefers the version of you he met at that Green Briar place."

A distance away, JD leaves the hard packed sand at the water's edge and strolls toward the roped off area of the beach. He tips his brim to us, and we both wave.

"He said that?"

"Yep. Like I said, this one seems different from your usual experiments." Missy runs a hand through her windblown hair and looks toward the set. "I'm going to wander around a bit and play with these ideas in my head."

"OK."

As Missy heads off, I turn my attention from her back to look JD up and down. He is chatting easily with the camera crew, the creative director from Lariat jeans, and the model who will accompany him today. JD appeared sullen the entire ride here, but with an audience and a job to do, he comes to life. That's a quality tough to come by in the talent I seek. The man seems oddly in place, especially after all I've put him through in the past couple of days.

I can't help but notice how his biceps bulge with every handshake and his back muscles ripple like a current beneath his thin black V-neck T-shirt. I don't know what I like more, the megawatt smile he keeps flashing or the Lariat jeans that are molded to his butt. Today, he insisted on wearing a ball cap, rather than the cowboy hat I prefer. The bits of blonde peeking out through the hole above the adjustable band actually make my heart swell a little.

Odd.

This is going to be a memorable ad campaign for Lariat. My eyes search out my niece. She has her sketchbook out, feverishly moving a pencil, pausing only every once in a while to consider JD.

I've given the creative director the reins on this project, which leaves me free to watch events unfold as she moves people into position.

"All right, everyone. Take your places," she instructs through a megaphone.

JD struts into the center of the round pen and strips off his shirt. He's wearing the brand's jeans, holds a lasso, and has replaced the cap he left the apartment in with a logoed Lariat baseball cap.

I guess the creative team liked the looks of him in a ball cap, too.

My heart pings in my chest as JD turns the hat backwards. The move reveals his bright green eyes and tanned face, held together by a perfect, straight nose. The golden skin of his torso glistens in the sun, and my pulse quickens at the sight of him. His dedication to gaining a physique that allows him to ride bulls is clear.

For a moment, I ponder his bare arms, and then I allow my eyes to sweep over his rippled stomach and across his lean hips where a silver belt buckle hangs at his waist.

Why haven't I taken advantage of him since we've been in the city?

"Because he's a project, Ev," I remind myself in a whisper.

My job is to find the talent, reel it in any way I can, and then, once the ink on the contract is dry, turn that talent loose to make money for my company. My job isn't for the faint of heart. It isn't about love. It's about power. I've done this plenty of times before, and I admonish myself for being momentarily affected by JD's looks. I consider the belt around JD's waist again. My mind flits back to the night in the barn when that belt and buckle was secured around my arms. It was so unlike me to hand over control to him that night.

I shake the thought from my head and focus on the action around the set. As I expected, beach goers are lining the edge of the temporary round pen we've set up in the sand. We obviously attracted them to our lights, camera, and soon-to-be action.

"Bring in the girl!" the director shouts. It's clear she has determined the size of the on-looking audience is acceptable. Dominique, one of Martin's models, receives a final dusting from the make-up artist and steps into the pen with JD. I move in closer to watch, mostly to listen.

"You ever smelled a bull or a barn before?" JD asks Dominique. She wears a quizzical expression.

"No," she answers, coyly. He winks and reveals his rock star grin.

"Well, it's my favorite smell in the world," JD says, signaling for the bull to be released. Apparently, it's a docile bull, not one of the rank bulls that JD is accustomed to riding. It's more prop than anything.

"Hold on to your hats, ladies and gentlemen. It's about to get western up in here!" JD shouts, running full speed toward the bull and swinging himself onto its back. I expect an explosion, but the bull stands in the center of the ring like a petting zoo animal. The cameramen take their places around the perimeter of the ring, already snapping shots and rolling footage.

"Lose the robe," the director calls.

Dominique gracefully waltzes into the center of the arena and strips off the garment. She is wearing a silver sequined bikini, cowboy boots with spurs, and a straw cowboy hat.

"You're gonna have to earn those spurs you're wearing, cowgirl!" JD announces before releasing a long, low whistle. He tosses his lasso around Dominique and drags her toward him. I bite my lip.

That wasn't part of the script.

The crowd claps, laughs, hoots, and hollers. They love JD. I look over at my team and the creative director. They have smiles plastered to their faces, and the camera shutters flick a million times a second. I know JD just delivered Lariat a money shot, yet I feel a wave of jealousy come over me. I'm not accustomed to feeling much of anything for my male projects.

This isn't good.

A few hours later, I am sitting on a barstool at the Musty Crab Saloon sipping a margarita by myself. Missy is well on her way back to the city, wanting to get her inspirations from the day into her design program. I'm still on the clock, though. We hired street teams to walk the beach and the boardwalk passing out postcards with JD's photos. The copy on them promises an open bar meet-and-greet with the NBR bull riding star where they could win a chance to attend the big event tomorrow. It's working like a charm.

I take a sip from my drink and watch JD lay it on thick with the women who are eagerly moving through the line at his signing table. He has ditched his ball-capped boyish look for his full-on bull rider persona. Women in bikini tops and short shorts surround him. I can't help but assess JD in action.

It's my job to assess my clients after all.

It is clear that he has the ladies enthralled. While his lips move, his eyes survey their plunging necklines, and they are hanging on his every word. They may want the free tickets to tomorrow's event that we've been dangling in front of them, but I'm sure they'd enjoy a free ride with JD, too. JD's grin is sinister when he tosses the ladies waiting to meet him little plush bulls with the NBR logo embroidered on them. When he's out of those, he tosses tokens to ride the mechanical bull. As the crowd attempts to grab the prizes, I hear squeals and can't unsee the breasts bouncing all around JD. I roll my eyes, but something about the way these women react to him stirs something in me.

Is it desire? Is it jealousy?

I admire the cowboy from afar, and I promise myself that I will not fall for a client. The next moment, though, I find myself daydreaming about how good he is between the sheets. Perhaps I don't want anyone else to know that while he's on my watch.

That's it. That's what this feeling is.

I ponder JD some more as I suck back my third margarita, desperately wanting the event to be over.

Maybe tonight I'll let him in my bed?

I always keep my distance and keep it business once I have my projects secured, hook, line, and sinker, but something about JD is needling at me. I decide that I'll break my own rules tonight.

Just for the fun of it.

27

Once the promotional event is over, and we're back in the car, I breathe a sigh of relief. The photo shoot and following meet-and-greet were great successes, but the more time I spend around JD, the more unease I feel. Cowboys emanate a rugged charm, but also seem to carry a layer of danger with them. I can't help noticing that women make fools of themselves over them. I don't want to be one of them.

I will not be one of them.

Still, I look at JD and drink him in. He is settled in the seat's leather, his head is resting back, and he is looking up out of the sunroof. His black V-neck T-shirt is molded across his chest, his hands are relaxed on his thighs, and his legs are open. I peek at his package framed nicely in his new Lariat jeans.

"That was a long day," I say, breaking our silence.

JD lifts his head, a one-cornered smile across his fine lips, and stares at me openly. The look is disturbing. He has a way of watching me that makes my body tingle, and he's doing it right now. I shift in my seat and quickly gain my composure. I raise an eyebrow and trail my eyes over his lean, fit body – those close-fitting jeans, the black shirt that shows off the breadth of his chest, the muscles of his upper arms, and the glint in his green eyes.

He raises an eyebrow of his own, smiles fully, and shifts down deeper in the car's seat. He widens his legs and adjusts the big buckle at his waist, but he doesn't say a word. He certainly is one of my most devastatingly well-put together accomplishments. I move my eyes from lingering on his crotch and trail them back up his body to that chiseled face with that oh-so-straight nose and the blonde hair that fringes his face. I press my lips together and look right into his eyes.

"You're staring," JD drawls.

"So are you," I shoot back.

"Like what you see?" he asks.

"Yes," I murmur.

We hold each other's gaze until his eyes narrow and glide over my body like hungry fingers. It's just the two of us in the dimly lit car whizzing back to the city, and my professional world feels very far away.

"S'pose I told you, I liked you better when I met you at Green Briar," he says, intently.

"Missy may have mentioned that you feel that way," I reply.

JD sits up, leans toward me with his forearms on his knees, and presses his fine lips together. I find myself longing to kiss them.

"I'm over here wonderin' if that woman I met was real or if it was all an act. The Ev sittin' in front of me right now is a lot more serious, a little less youthful, and definitely not as interested in foolin' around," he accuses.

I don't speak at once. I am struggling with things I don't know how to put into words. I can't admit that I had planned this all along.

"You're probably not the only person who thinks that way," I say. I shake my head. "It's pretty common gossip, really. This. You and me. It's just business."

JD swears softly under his breath, and he runs his hands through his golden locks. He retrieves the ball cap from the seat next to him and twists the brim in his hands. He settles it back on his head, pulls the brim low over his eyes, and leans forward.

"I like to fool around, Ev, but I don't much like being played for a fool. You're an excellent actress, and you've made me a good amount of money, I'll give you that, but I thought we actually had a connection. It doesn't settle well that I'm being used."

"What do you care? You use women all the time," I answer, glaring at him.

"Yeah, maybe I do, but what happens between the sheets — well, that's always real for me."

"Who says it wasn't real for me?"

"It's easy to tell the difference. You haven't touched me since I've been in your damn apartment. You've been all business since we got to this forsaken city. It wasn't hard to figure out that I'm just the business part now. Hearin' you say it only confirms what I was thinkin'. I feel like a game piece, not a lover."

I scowl at him as he stares at me with angry eyes. He settles back in his seat again, crosses his arms across his chest, and looks out the window.

"I'll be leavin' as soon as my bull ridin' event is over. Thanks for what you have done for me. I do appreciate the sponsorships, and I'll keep up with the responsibilities that come with them, but you and me? This is over," he concludes through a tight jaw.

He actually sounds a little resentful. I bristle at the fact that he is dismissing *me*.

"This is not the way we play my game. I say when it's over. This is not over," I growl. Before he can reply, I lunge at him from across the car and straddle his lap. The look in his eyes is dark and quiet.

"Where's this coming from, Ev?"

"You still want me. You think that doesn't show?"

"It's flattering when women throw themselves at me," JD says, wrapping his arms around my waist. "Sometimes I think I'd like to find one that makes me want to be different, better."

"Yeah, right," I huff.

"I don't know. Maybe it's you?" He sounds sincere and pulls me tight to his chest. I push away from him and glare down into his eyes.

"I am not capable of more than I've already given you."

"That right there is your act, Ev. I don't want an act. I want the real you. Who the hell are you? Really?" he demands.

Before I can respond, JD grips me by the back of the neck and devours my mouth with his own. Our tongues twist in a furious battle. My hands remove his baseball hat to tangle in his hair. His hands are under my blouse, fumbling for my breasts. We hear the motor of the window separating us from the driver and break feverishly from our kiss.

"Uh, Ms. Mitchell? We've arrived," the driver advises. He clears his throat and immediately drives the tinted glass pane divider back up.

I swiftly remove myself from JD's lap and wipe my swollen lips. JD adjusts himself in his jeans. I smooth my shirt, tighten my ponytail, and retrieve my bag. I thank heaven my driver gives us a moment to gather ourselves before he opens the door. I nod to him, strut from the town car, and hightail it to my apartment, leaving JD in the street to fend for himself. Once I am in the elevator, I breathe and tip my head against the wall.

What am I doing?

I clench my jaw in frustration and search the bottom of my bag for my keys. When the doors part, I hurry out into the hallway with them in hand to find JD standing in front of my door. He's breathing heavily.

"How did you get up here?" I ask in shock.

"Galloped up all those damn stairs for you, miss," he drawls.

"I'm impressed."

"I'm in shape," he says with a grin. "Take me inside, Ev."

I step to the door, turn the lock, and nod for him to go inside. I follow him into the dark apartment and tentatively close the door behind me. I leave my hand on the doorknob and drop my forehead against the cool exterior.

Am I going to do this?

JD steps up behind me, and I feel the heat of his hard body at my back. He kisses my neck, and I tip my head, so he can have easy access to more of it. His tongue glides up my skin and finds my ear.

He teases my earlobe as his hands wander over my backside, up my hips, under my shirt.

I am going to do this.

"You need a proper lover, Ev," he whispers near my ear.

I turn to face him and search his darkened eyes.

"I know," I admit.

JD draws in a long breath and holds my eyes.

"I want a woman tonight. Considering our situation, you are the only woman available."

Silenced, I just stand here, rigid, unmoving, my heart beating in my chest at his proximity. JD's eyes fall to my chest.

"I want you right now. For real, Ev," he says huskily.

I hesitate, not because I don't want this, but because I'm afraid to let anything become too real between us. I can't lose control. I can't give away my power. I can't break my own rules.

JD notices. His green eyes soften and study my face. I've never experienced him this way. He's almost thoughtful, but just as abruptly, he shifts gears.

"You know you want it," he growls, pressing his hips into mine. I am pinned against the door. His mouth covers mine, and his hands explore my body hungrily. I give in.

"Come with me," I manage into his mouth. I lead him down the hallway into my bedroom. I ache to have him touch me, kiss me, take me. "I might regret this later," I whisper.

"No, you won't. Neither will I. I guarantee it. I want to make an impression. This will be the last time we do this before I leave for the country. Let's make it memorable."

I tense up. I don't understand the emotions whirling around inside of me. I'm suddenly not sure I like the idea of what he's saying, but I don't say a word. I just go to work on his clothing. I lift his shirt over my head and bury my face in his chest, peppering kisses every-where. I work toward his navel, and then expertly release the buckle at his waist. My fingertips fumble to pop the button of his jeans. JD groans and loosens the hair from my ponytail. Moments later, I am undressed, and we tumble to my mattress. He is slow and tender with me. His lips toy with mine gently. In breathless silence, JD positions himself above me.

"Don't forget protection," I breathe.

"Never do, miss," he hums, taking care of the deed.

I am all too aware that his steely body is about to press against me. I feel the warmth of his hands. He operates his lips on me with expert sensuality. JD means business, and it shows. The times we've already spent like this fade compared to what is happening between us right now. I snake my arms around his neck and lift myself to his kisses with abandon. Lightning is striking. JD smiles slowly at the look of me.

"You like?" he murmurs, grazing his lips over my neck.

"Yes," I groan, digging my fingertips into the thick muscles of his upper arms.

JD's experienced touch sends my mind reeling. My body is completely under his control. I arch up to him and move restlessly, wanting pleasure. My stomach flips at the thought of the glorious release that comes later. I feel the crush of his hips, open my mouth to his devouring kisses, and want him even more. I am lost in hopeless delight without a care in the world as he glides above me. I take note that I'm hearing the faint sounds of flesh against flesh. JD is behaving more intimately than I thought possible for a playboy like him.

I like it.

As his mouth lingers on mine, his hands move to beneath my hips and cradle them. I part my lips so his tongue can slip through and probe mine. Our breathing is hurried and intermingled.

"You are wonderful," I breathe against his neck. My hands explore the powerful muscles of his back and pull him toward me again and again. JD thrusts harder.

"I'm on fire for you," JD groans.

I shiver below him, enjoying every powerful grind of his hips. I am moving frantically with him now. It's even better than when we were at Green Briar. I can't get enough.

"Don't stop," I say, clenching my teeth.

"As if I could," he gasps, pumping harder.

I am mindless, frantic. Suddenly, I am there, right there. As JD drives us to fulfillment, my headboard bangs noisily against the wall. I hear his harsh, ragged pants. I feel the rigor with which he is working our bodies. Blinding light explodes behind my closed eyes, and I can't contain my sob of ecstasy.

JD doesn't stop moving, even as my body goes limp in complete satisfaction. His skin is damp from the effort. His breathing is ragged. He groans in pleasure. I feel him tense, swell, and then find his own release seconds later. He falls to the side, and I cradle him heavy in my arms. We quiver together in the sweet aftermath. JD draws in a long, shuddering breath and presses his lips against my temple.

"I'll be sleeping in here tonight," he drawls. "Screw your guest room."

"You can stay," I say.

He releases a satisfied sigh. I smile against his shoulder. I'll think about what I've done tomorrow. Tangled together, we slide naked into sleep almost at once.

28

I wake up and stretch. I've never felt this rested before. JD has given me the best sleep I've ever had. A smile tickles to my lips, and butterflies flit in my stomach at the thought of our love-making last night. That's definitely what it felt like.

JD and I made love.

I shake the thought of it out of my head.

I'm not capable of love.

I stretch an arm over the sheets next to me. They are cold. He's not here. I sit up, still naked, and rub my eyes. I glance at the clock on my nightstand and go stiff.

"10:30 a.m.!" I shout. "I never sleep this late." I scurry from the bed and slip into my satin robe. I wander down the hallway to the kitchen. JD is perched on one of the barstools, slouched over a coffee mug in his workout clothes.

"Mornin'," he drawls with a lazy smile.

"Why did you let me sleep so late?" I ask.

"Reckon, you needed the rest, Ev. You are one hardworkin' lady. Not to mention, I worked you over pretty dang hard last night." His eyes walk all over me, and I instinctively tighten the belt of my robe. He narrows his lids at my response and turns back to his coffee.

"Have you already been down to the gym?" I ask.

"Yep. Made coffee, too. Though the pot turned off a while ago. Should be warm still."

I head straight for a caffeine fix. I pour a measure into a mug and join him at the counter.

"My event starts today," JD says, looking at me again. "Will you be joining me?"

"Of course." I sip my coffee and contemplate his handsome face through my lashes. "I've set up an interview for you before the event. We need to be to the Garden by noon."

"More business stuff, huh?" he mutters, losing the glint in his green eyes.

"I wouldn't miss seeing you ride today, JD," I offer, understanding I hurt him during our conversation in the car. He's still feeling like a project.

And he is.

I can't lie to him about that, so I say nothing more on the topic.

"Oh, I have something for you. It's important."

I leave my coffee cup on the counter and head back down the hall. I return from my studio with a hanging garment bag.

"What's this?" JD asks.

"Unzip it." I give the bag on the hanger a little shake with a grin.

JD drags the zipper down the front of it, tucks a hand inside, and the glitter returns to his emerald eyes.

"My vest," he concludes.

"With the patches in all the right places," I add, removing it from the hanger and holding it open for him to shrug into. JD rises from his seat and puts one arm, then the other, through the Kevlar protective vest he'll wear today. He steps into the foyer and admires himself in the mirror with softened eyes. Pride swells inside of me as he gently runs a fingertip around his newly adhered sponsorship patches.

I did that for him. My connections did that for him.

He turns from the mirror and struts toward me with purpose. My eyes search his handsome face.

"Thank you for doing this for me, Ev," he murmurs.

"Thank you for doing this for me, JD," I reply. "We are both earning quite the payday from this partnership."

"Your project," he quips. I simply nod. "I see last night hasn't changed anything."

"No, it hasn't," I say softly, even though I sense I might be lying just a little. I tap my wrist where a watch will be shortly. Time is my excuse to avoid any further conversation about the status of our relationship. "I have to hurry and get ready. We don't want to be late for that interview. We've got those sponsors on your vest to please." I turn on my heels as fast as I can and leave JD standing alone in his vest.

An hour and a half later, JD and I walk into Madison Square Garden. He has an interview to complete, and then he'll warm up with the other cowboys before the event starts at 2 o'clock.

"Here, this is for you," JD mumbles, thrusting a white envelope into my hand.

I smile at him and accept it. It's the first time he's spoken to me since I gave him the vest in the apartment. As I reviewed his talking points on the ride over, he simply nodded along with his eyes adverted out the window. I open the envelope and pull out a single ticket for the event this afternoon.

"Don't think too much of it. All the riders on tour get free tickets to the events when we want 'em. Since you said you wanted to see me ride, I figured."

"Thank you," I reply, ushering him to the Pro-Bull Radio table for his interview. "Break a leg, JD."

"There'll be no breaking of anything today, miss," he says with a bend of his brim.

He shakes hands with the radio host and takes a seat at the table. As they settle in to conduct the interview, an assistant adjusts a lavaliere microphone under his western shirt and attaches it to his collar. I prop myself up against the cement block wall behind them to listen in.

"Ladies and gentlemen, I'm Wyatt Williams, and you're listening to Pro-Bull Radio. Today, I'm smack in the middle of New York City at

Madison Square Garden where denim-and-leather-adorned bull riders from America's heartland are rubbing shoulders with suit-and-tie-clad Wall Street bankers. Later today, there'll be a cowboy-crazy crowd cheering as chiseled men desperately cling onto 2,000 pounds of testosterone-filled bovine rage. I'm here with JD McCall. He'll be one of the riders going for the buckle at today's event. Welcome, JD."

"Glad to be here, Wyatt," JD drawls.

"JD, the NBR is gritty and exciting, and oozes sexiness. In fact, you are one dazzling cowboy. I reckon the ladies are going to like the look of you in the new Lariat Jeans campaign you've been shooting this week."

"That's the goal, sir. My agent, Everly Mitchell, has worked some major miracles in a very short time. In addition to the Lariat Jeans campaign, you'll be seein' me work with Stampede Truck, Rocket Energy Drink, Big Outdoors Athletic, and Banner Boot Company. They are all very generous supporters of my bull ridin' career."

JD looks over and winks. I beam at him like a proud parent. He is working the talking points perfectly. I guess he actually was listening to me in the car after all. He's making me look good. It's always better when they make my job easy. The sponsors will be pleased. The man sure can turn on the charm when it's show time.

"NBR cowboys are among the most authentic, real athletes in sports. You don't take a sponsorship unless you believe in the brand behind the money. Isn't that right, JD?" Wyatt asks.

One of our sponsorship providers idles up. She leans on the wall next to me, folding her arms across her chest, and propping up a boot.

"Everly," she says, tipping her head with a smile. I tip mine in return.

JD sees our interaction from the corner of his eye. He straightens in the chair like an experienced business executive.

Good boy.

"So, this is the superman you wrangled us into backing. He looks even better in person," she adds.

"Yes, Gemma. That's JD McCall. I think he has an excellent shot at winning this event. He knows how to interview, too."

"Well, let me get a listen then," Gemma says, turning her attention to the interview. I hold my breath.

"That's right, Wyatt. For Rocket, the company's entire branding platform is based around action-sports, and NBR is the best action sport on dirt. Speakin' of authenticity, I'm wearing what I represent right now. In fact, I've only ever ridden my bulls in Big Outdoors Athletic shirts, Lariat Jeans, and Banner Boots. I support the companies I believe in and use. The only spin I know how to handle is on top of a bull. Later this year, you'll see me in Stampede Truck's behind-the-scenes series covering the NBR's cowboys, the bulls, and their stories as we aim for makin' the NBR finals in Las Vegas. Stampede Trucks are tough and the only trucks I drive," JD shares.

Thank heaven.

"You are quite the busy cowboy, JD," Wyatt responds.

"Yes, sir. I reckon I am. Bein' busy keeps me outta trouble."

Both men chuckle.

"All right, JD. Next question. Rumor has it you are making all the girls in the horse world crazy. A handsome bull rider who knows his way around horses seems to make them all swoon —"

"Uh," JD interrupts, rubbing the back of his neck. "The 'knows his way around horses' part is supposed to be a secret."

"Well, it's no secret in the horse world that you had a hand in Devon Brooke's Quarter Horse Congress win that the marriage proposal of all horse world proposals followed," Wyatt persists. "We even covered it on Pro-Bull Radio. We got word during the NBR event that runs in tandem with Congress. That video got millions of views."

"Yep. I was there. I helped M&D Kelly Quarter Horses with Willa and helped McKennon with his plans to ask Devon to marry him. McKennon's a good man. He's a top-notch horse trainer, and he's fantastic with horses. Devon supports that. I support that, too. We are kin. We all work together, so McKennon can take a good horse and make it a great horse, and then we sell it for great money rather than good money. That's all a part of how we make our living at Green Briar. I work there when I'm not on tour."

"So you admit you *do* know a thing or two about horses then?" Wyatt presses.

"Yeah, I reckon I do," he murmurs, shooting me a green-eyed glare.

I may have left that part out while I reviewed his talking points with him. When I scheduled this interview, I leaked that little tidbit of news to the radio programmer. He liked that he could hook both the rodeo fans and the horse show enthusiasts with that particular angle during the interview. Everyone in that world knows about McKennon Kelly's history. I figured it could help feed the fire of desire for JD just a smidge more if they knew he could handle horses and bulls and had a relationship with the mysterious McKennon Kelly.

"Now tell us about you, Mr. Bull Rider. Are you the best at what you do?" Wyatt asks, shifting gears.

"Well, I've won a lot of buckles in my time on tour. I'm certainly not the best in the world, but I'm not the worst either. I've got my sights set on being the best, though. You can count on that."

"Well, JD, I'm sure all our listeners here at Pro-Bull Radio will be rooting for you this weekend. Good Luck."

"Thanks, Wyatt. It's been a real pleasure."

As the two men shake hands over the table, the assistant scurries back to JD. She removes the microphone from his collar, and he nods his thanks. Wyatt and JD banter back and forth like old friends for a moment. Perhaps they are. My eyes wander over the man that had ravaged me so thoroughly last night, and I feel weak in the knees. I glance at our sponsor to make sure I haven't given my desire for JD away, but she is nodding to herself and biting her lower lip. I let out a quiet sigh. She sees it, too.

Star material. Heartbreakers make for great ad campaigns and brand recognition.

"He's a looker, that's for sure, Everly. I'm thinking he'll look real nice behind one of our steering wheels, on the front of our promotional materials, and perhaps modeling at next season's auto shows. With a win here at the Garden, we could really do something special and add in his title."

"He already drives a Stampede Truck back home," I note.

"He'll be needing the newest model," she replies.

I can't help it, a smile sneaks across my face. My heart pounds at the thought of some big-time cash being infused into my business. I am the woman making JD's dream a reality. Not to mention, I'm getting richer doing it, too.

JD is my meal ticket, and I'm his.

JD wraps things up with Wyatt and struts toward us waiting for him in the wings. He reaches Gemma and flashes her his perfect rock star grin. When he puts his arm around my shoulders in front of our sponsorship partner, my stomach swoops.

Why is my body responding to him like I'm a teenager?

"JD McCall, meet Gemma Fallon from Stampede Trucks," I state, trying to ignore the warmth of JD's arm.

"Pleasure to meet you, Miss Fallon," JD drawls with a nod.

"Great interview, Mr. McCall," Gemma says. "Everly has shared with us your PR plan. It looks like you're on the verge of being a mighty famous young man. We'd like to see you behind the wheel of one of our new trucks."

Gemma holds out a pair of keys, jingles them, and points to the custom lime green quad cab, three-quarter ton, chromed out dually with the full tow package parked in the center of the bull riding ring.

"After the event, it's yours. Enjoy, fella," she continues.

As he takes the keys, JD's face washes over with gratitude and awe.

"That truck is a dang statement if I've ever seen one," he replies, letting out a long low whistle.

"We had it painted up in the NBR's brand colors," Gemma replies. "I'm glad you can handle it. I find it mighty loud."

"I like loud. I can do loud," JD answers. "I like all that bright green mighty fine."

"Well, that makes me happy to hear," Gemma says. "You'll look terrific behind the wheel, JD. You'll be like a physical billboard for NBR and Stampede Trucks."

"I like the sound of that," I insert.

"Thought you would, Everly," Gemma adds with a wink.

"I'm mighty grateful for the truck, Gemma. Give my gratitude to the folks on the Stampede team. It's been a pleasure, ladies, but I best be getting back to the locker room. I've got a bull riding event to win," JD concludes, removing his arm from around me. Heat flares through my body, across my shoulders where his warm arm had been, and bleeds out toward my cheeks, down my neck. Lower. To all the places that he had affected last night. I swallow hard and take a deep breath.

Maintain composure.

"Good luck, JD," Gemma and I say in unison.

"Everly," JD murmurs. He takes my hand and kisses the back of it gently. "I expect to see you in the stands. I'm bettin' on you being my lucky charm up in that seat I reserved for you."

"I'll be there," I breathe.

"Good," he says, releasing my hand, tipping his brim, and turning on his heels for the locker room. My heart hammers after him.

"Swoon," Gemma says with a wicked grin, fanning herself with a NBR program.

"Where can I get one of those?" I ask of the program, well aware that the flush JD brought to my cheeks is clear to anyone within six feet of me.

It has been a long time since I've felt this kind of quickening of the heart, and since it can't be ignored, I determine it must be fought.

I will not fall for my client.

29

I f anyone had told me I would spend a night at the side of a stinking bullpen, watching spit, snot, and dirt flying in all directions and actually enjoy every minute of it, I would have asked them to call a psychologist pronto, but that's exactly where I am.

For the second night in a row.

I find my seat as the bull riding event begins with its opening of pyrotechnics, explosions, and flames. I now know that the night will continue on with enough thrills and spills to keep me glued to the edge of my seat. Bull riding is strangely beautiful to watch with all the twisting, rolling, and changing of directions. It's as if man and bull are angry dance partners performing countermove after countermove in an attempt to best the other. I am utterly enthralled watching 160-pound men compete against 2,000-pound beasts. The danger of it makes my heart pound, and my head tells me to get out of this while I still can.

Why have I always been attracted to men with dangerous professions?

The Garden is filled to capacity, and behind the chutes, there are signs and banners lining the arena wall. I smile knowing that, because of me, half a dozen of the brands advertised on them now sponsor JD.

I'm sitting above the arena where the announcers sit. It's roped off to most people and reserved for the media, VIPs, stock contractors, and event sponsors. I notice some of the bull riders' wives occupy the space, a few of them with youngsters on their hips. I can't imagine bringing a child here or having one with a bull rider.

Ever.

Yesterday, I used the ticket that JD gave me, one of the free seats complimentary to the bull riders. It wasn't a bad seat really, but for today's event, I've gotten myself behind the chutes. I want a closer look since I'm learning the ropes of this bull riding thing. I want to be in earshot of the goings on down there where the cowboys are. It wasn't really hard to get back here. I pulled the manager card and used my looks to win over the security guard behind the velvet rope.

Last night, JD rode his bull for a score of 84. It wasn't enough for him to make the top two, but it was a good enough ride to put him in contention to win the event. Today, he has to ride his second bull to get a shot at riding a third in the final short go round.

I look down at the cowgirl boots I bought on the shopping trip with Devon before the bachelorette party. The ones I thought I would never have reason to wear again in New York City. I grin, knowing JD approves of me fashioned like a cowgirl.

My pulse spikes when the announcer calls his name. I see him hook a boot in the fence and climb over the rail to settle onto a bull's back. His brows are pinched together in concentration, and his jaw is clenched. My eyes light up, not with lust, but appreciation, and my world suddenly compresses at the sight of him.

What is happening?

Last night, I went home to an empty apartment. I didn't like it much, not after the night I had spent prior messing up my bed with JD. He texted me after the event wrapped for the evening to let me know he was going out drinking with the guys. His plan was to spend the night at the hotel where all the riders were staying.

I couldn't help but wonder if he was out looking for another conquest now that our time together is coming to an end. I felt relieved though when he added a text that said, 'Be there tomorrow?'

I replied with a simple 'yes.' It's satisfying to know that he wants me here today. He just as easily could have dismissed seeing me again before he leaves, but here I am.

I never intended for JD to be anything more than a boy-toy for a few nights. Nothing more, but getting to know him little by little, the way we made love two nights ago, working with him side by side on his career, and finding myself rooting for him fills me with an odd longing. It's not my style, but I am getting soft over this one.

I can't have that, can I?

The announcer cuts off my line of thinking, and I tune into his words.

"JD McCall has finished in the top third overall in the NBR world standings three years in a row. He is considered one of the best bull riders in the world, folks."

I watch JD adjust the wrap around his hand, while other cowboys try to tighten the rope around the bull's hulking body. He pounds on his fist, then squeezes his legs, and adjusts the position of his seat again. JD appears calm, but I can't deny my own nerves. This is a very dangerous sport.

I've felt this uneasiness before.

"This round, McCall is riding Tornado. He's a good bull, and if JD can stay on, he's assured a position in the short go, ladies and gentlemen," the announcer twangs.

The sponsors are going to be pleased. JD has grown strangely still, but the pause lasts for a mere moment. I watch him nod his head in quick jerks, showing he is ready for the ride. The gate swings open, and the roar of the crowd is deafening. Tornado lunges forward with a ferocious buck, his head down, and his hind legs reaching for the stadium's ceiling. As I watch him, a familiar wave of anxiety crashes over me.

JD holds his free arm up and out, working on staying centered over the massive beast. Tornado lurches into a spin to the right. JD stays right with him, almost as if he expected the bull's move. The bull bucks again before suddenly shifting in the opposite direction. This move sends JD off-center. I gasp, thinking the bull is going to rocket out from underneath him at any moment, but JD corrects himself. He turns, swivels his hips, and waves his free hand, searching for the correct balance beneath him. He looks so different. He looks like a different person. Those green eyes are wide and paying attention to everything other than me.

Of course, everything other than me. He's trying to stay alive, for heaven's sake.

I suddenly have a creeping fear he might not come back from this ride if the bull puts him in the dirt and tramples him. I never thought I'd have these feelings of dread again. I have insulated my life from ever feeling that kind of pain again.

Why is this young cowboy stirring dread in me?

This is only supposed to be a good time, another project. He isn't supposed to mean more than that, but it's feeling like that thing I've designed my life to avoid ever feeling again. I know what I want. I have faith in my business acumen and myself. I have an unwavering faith in my independence. I will never depend on someone and then lose them completely.

Never again.

Death was a rebirth for me. I'm standing on my own two feet now. I can't let them get swept out from under me again. I'd rather return to a padded room than give love a chance again.

I clutch the railing, stand, and yell encouragement to JD. I doubt he can hear me, but I do it anyway. A ping awakens in my chest, and I wish he were wearing a helmet, rather than that black cowboy hat.

JD's forearm is bound to the bull and strains with effort. Somehow, he finds the strength to right himself. Tornado bucks again and spins faster. To my relief, the buzzer sounds, and JD reaches for the wrap on his hand. He frees himself and instantly leaps from Tornado's broad back. He lands on his hands and knees, but he scurries quickly to his feet. He lopes toward the arena fence and jumps up out of harm's way. As JD takes a seat on the rail and wipes his brow, I release the breath that I didn't even realize I was holding. The bullfighters steer Tornado out of the arena, and the adrenaline slowly drains from my system.

JD's score comes in strong, and the crowd roars. He will select his third bull shortly and then move into the final round. I sit back in my seat hard and drag my hands through my hair. I know it isn't wise to let the past come whirling back to strangle me, but in moments like this, I'm not free from it, not completely. I put my elbows on my knees and bury my face in my hands.

He's alive.

30

JD

I trudge into the arena to the roar of the crowd, blare of rock music, and explosions of pyrotechnics. I line up with the other finalists for the last draw of the day.

This is it. The short go. I made it to the final round.

One by one, I hear bulls being assigned to the other riders. I sneak a peek at Ev up in the announcer's space above the chutes. I know she worked some of that Ev-magic to get into the VIP area, and something about that move makes me tingle inside.

Maybe she likes bull riding. Maybe she liked watching me ride. Maybe she wants to get closer to the action.

She looks like the Ev I met at Green Briar. She's dressed in a tight white V-neck shirt, tucked into her jeans, a plain brown belt circles her lean waist, and those pristine, unscuffed cowgirl boots are on her feet. That flaming hair is pulled away from her fresh face in a ponytail. Those green eyes blaze down on me in the center of the ring. A smile sits on her pretty mouth.

I'm happy she's here. Wasn't sure she would come.

I toss her a gallant smile and salute her with a tip of my hat. When the announcer steps to me, I reach my hand into the golden chalice to pull my bull. I raise my chip. It's Cork Screw.

Good bull. Mean bull. Really mean. Should get me the points I need to cinch this thing though.

I didn't mean to drink so much last night. The plan was to just take the edge off. I'm battling an empty feeling in my gut. I reckon it's because I won't be returning to Ev's apartment again. Trying to drink that feeling away didn't work in the slightest. In my beer-soaked state, I ended up sending her that unplanned text, and now I'm hungover.

Be there tomorrow? What a lame text.

She simply replied, 'yes,' and that was good enough. It made me feel better. My head pulses with a dull ache, and I hope it doesn't disturb my concentration. I barely made it through the last ride on Tornado.

I'll need all of my focus to make the eight on Cork Screw. I've studied his tapes. He's a contender for NBR's Bull of the Year, and he's slammed more cowboys into the dirt than I care to count.

I don't aim to be one of them.

I can't think about being one of them. I slept on the dang floor of my buddy's hotel room, and I didn't get the good night's rest I should have. I'm a little pissed at myself, but I've ridden in worse shape than this before. I press the heel of my hand to my pounding forehead and draw in a long breath. I make my way to the chutes, stomping across the hard packed dirt, and gaze upward at Ev. Every bull rider knows it isn't a question of if a bull rider will get injured, but when and how badly. A wave of nerves rocks me, but I steel myself as I drop my gaze and move to assume my position.

Not today. Not in front of her.

My head is thrumming between my ears. I try to tune out the vibration, the sound of the crowd, and the announcer. Instead, I focus on helping the rider ahead of me get ready. I am scheduled to ride second and need to concentrate on something else, anything else. I need to calm myself before my ride in roughly 15 minutes. I start in on tightening the bull rope behind the shoulders of the bull in the chute below me. I know helping my buddy, who drew the first position, get centered on his bull will take my mind off of things. Wade works the tail of his rosin-stained rope and then wraps it around his gloved hand. I put a boot on the bull's hard back to keep him from leaning on Wade's leg.

"You picked Cork Screw? You're gonna have one crazy ride. That bull sure can kick you in the pockets," Wade says, through a clenched jaw as his bull bucks in the shoot.

"Looks like you got a crazy one under you, too," I reply, grimacing as I put an arm out across his chest to keep his head from slamming into the railing in front of him.

"Yeah," Wade mutters, shoving his cowboy hat down over his brow. He rocks his hips from side to side, making sure his seat placement feels right.

"Make the eight, man," I say, looking into the bull's angry dark eyes before shifting my gaze to meet Wade's determined ones.

Wade nods and flashes me a smile.

"Let's go!" he hollers, and the gate swings open. I step back, cross my arms, and watch the ride. Something is in the air tonight. I can't quite put my finger on it, but I know I don't like it.

Not at all.

Wade's bull is a tank. Snot swings from his nostrils before he even clears the metal gate. I take a step back to avoid the spray, and he thunders away from the chute, kicking up a storm of dust.

I chew my cheek as he gallops off to the edge of the arena, circles to the left, and into Wade's riding hand. That's usually a good thing, but before Wade can get set, the bull reverses wildly and rounds to the right. I clench my jaw as Wade's body slides off center with the direction reversal.

My eyes flash to the countdown clock. There are five more seconds to go –that is, if Wade can regain his center of gravity. Wade slips further to one side. Sensing his rider is off balance, the beast rears up. Wade slides even further out of position.

This doesn't look good at all.

The bull drops back to the dirt, drives his front hooves down, and releases a ferocious buck. I bite my lip. The bull's body is nearly vertical, and with that, I watch Wade lose the battle. He is launched through the air, and a surge of panic overcomes me.

Wade lands face down in the dirt beneath the bull. That's when it gets ugly. The beast bears down on him and drives his horns into Wade's near-lifeless body.

"Get out of there, brother!" I yell, even though it's unlikely he can hear me.

Wade doesn't move, and hooves come crashing down on his legs. I hear the crowd gasp. The bullfighters flail about, trying to distract the bull enough to get him away from the wounded cowboy.

Finally, a horse and rider team charge in, rope the enraged bull, drag his twisting bulk out of the arena, and disappear back behind the stands. Knowing what comes next, I clutch the railing in front of me and bow my head. The medics rush in and hover above Wade. Moments later, they have his neck in a brace and carry him out of the arena on a stretcher. He's likely unconscious. The fans are deathly silent. It's sobering. Nobody likes to see a bull rider get hurt, ever, but it happens. This is bull riding. Every time one of us gets on the back of a bull, we are tempting death. I don't have time to rush to the locker room to get an update on my friend. I am up next.

The show must go on.

I am rattled. Seeing Wade go down before me brings back memories of my uncle. I grit my teeth, needling on the danger my bull riding career constantly puts me in. It's the first time I've ever really thought this way, and it surprises me. It's always been live or die, now or never. Thinking beyond the next eight seconds is not something I do.

Until now.

I think of Ev up in the stands and find myself concerned with how she might be feeling right about now. I wonder if she's scared having seen that accident.

Why am I thinking about all of this now? Why am I thinking about her? Maybe I have more to live for than I thought I did.

I push this newfound uncertainty aside and say a silent prayer for Wade. I force my legs over the chute and onto the back of Cork Screw. The bull is full of energy beneath me. I have to calm my own nerves. I know I'm transferring my anxiety to the animal.

If only my head would stop pounding, and my gut wasn't twisted up with dread.

I sense an explosion on the horizon. My face drips with sweat, knowing the bull will become a missile underneath me at any moment. I see the wide, concerned eyes of my comrades around me. They know I'm shaken, but keep working the ropes and readying my bull, anyway. I'm paying attention to everything other than my ride. I remind myself to trust the men that help me in the chute. They are keeping the bull in place, helping me tighten my rigging. My job is to find my balance, anticipate where the bull is going, and then neutralize his moves with mine. I feel a strong palm on my shoulder. I'm getting a gesture of reassurance from another bull rider, but it doesn't keep the thought from coming.

When is something really bad going to happen to me?

31

DEVON

We've just returned from our honeymoon after spending a wonderful, low-key week in Jackson Hole, Wyoming, or cowboy country, as McKennon calls it. We've finished dinner and shared all of our adventures with Sophia. McKennon has flipped on the television so we can tune into JD's bull riding event in New York City.

"JD's lookin' really good. If he can pull off his next ride, I reckon he'll bring home that buckle," McKennon drawls.

"JD *is* looking good," I agree. "I wonder how Ev's been holding up, having had him under her feet for the last week. I haven't had a chance to check in yet."

"She's a grown woman. I'm certain the two of them have been getting along just fine," Sophia chirps.

McKennon and I exchange a look indicating we both feel differently. We turn our attention back to the event as Wade Masterson is stomped beneath a bull. McKennon's face twists as the announcer asks viewers to say a prayer for the fallen bull rider. McKennon closes his eyes and pinches the bridge of his nose. He's not able to watch the cowboy being carried out of the arena on a stretcher. I idle up next to him and put a reassuring palm to his shoulder. He stops touching his nose, places his hand on mine, and looks up into my eyes with his blazing blue ones.

"I hope that doesn't rattle, JD. He and Wade are friends. JD's riding second in this go," McKennon murmurs.

"He'll be OK," I reply, trying to sound confident. I'm anything but. I know this type of thing can rattle even the toughest cowboys. They know their life is on the line every time they ride, but they don't like being reminded of it so blatantly.

"Would you like some sweet tea, my dears?" Sophia asks, reappearing from the kitchen, carrying a tray with three tall glasses and a pitcher of sun tea. I listen to the jingle of the ice cubes.

"That would be nice," I answer. McKennon nods and a soft grin spreads across his lips. Sophia always lightens his mood.

"Come sit," Sophia instructs, setting the beverages on the coffee table. She motions me toward the sofa. "What did I miss?"

"Nothing," McKennon and I say in unison.

I leave my position at McKennon's recliner to join Sophia on the couch, and she looks from McKennon to me quizzically. Leaving it be, Sophia hands me my glass as JD's name pops up on the television screen. In anticipation, we all lean forward in our seats, recognizing JD in the chute on top of the bull. The cameras are angled on him from somewhere above to give viewers at home a behind-the-gate view of the preparations taking place in the chute.

JD's protective vest is littered with new sponsorship patches. I know they are Ev's doing. The woman has connections. I'm a benefactor of them. Evidently, JD is now, too.

JD adjusts himself on the back of his bull, wrapping, and then re-wrapping his gloved riding hand, as other cowboys tighten the rope around the animal's belly. The announcers talk over the action in gunshot fashion, listing JD's stats and that of his bull.

I take a sip of my tea and sneak a glance at my husband. He is strangely still. He looks worried. I turn back to the television. JD shoves his hat down low over his eyes with his free hand and nods feverishly that he's ready for the ride. The gate swings open, and the bull explodes out of his containment. He bucks hard, rear hooves pointing toward the overhead camera. The bull's head is low, and as the camera zooms in, it's clear he's angry. I can see it in his dark eyes. Cork Screw spins faster, faster, and then even faster. Sophia gasps beside me as JD slips to one side. I put my fingers to my lips when his seat slips. He's literally riding the side of the bull, rather than his back, and he's hanging on to his bull rope for dear life. My shoulders drop in relief when Cork Screw slows his spin.

"All right, JD, now's your chance! Right yourself, brother!" McKennon yells at the screen.

The camera zooms in, and I can see the expression on JD's face. Only five seconds have gone by, and he looks delirious, but the determination is clear as he attempts to drag himself vertical again. The muscles and veins in his riding arm are strained with effort. He nearly gets back into position, but the bull leaps beneath him. As all four of his legs leave the ground, his front-end twists left, and his rear end twists right. On the television, bull and cowboy look suspended in mid-air, and in that instant, the bull jerks forward. His head pitches low to the arena floor, and it takes an unbalanced JD with him. JD is flung forward, and his unprotected head connects with one of the bull's horns.

"Oh, my goodness," Sophia murmurs, covering her eyes with her fragile hands. McKennon and I are frozen in time watching the accident unfold; neither of us can look away.

JD slumps and slips down the side of the bull. The bull isn't finished with him, though, and sets into another breakneck spin. JD's body whirls like a rag doll beside the bull he's still tethered to.

The bullfighters are frantically trying to free JD's hand. Cork Screw won't be distracted, and he won't stop spinning. I'm horrified by the runaway freight train JD is attached to. The bull swings his horns violently at the multiple men furiously waving their hands around him.

Finally, the horse and rider team are able to lasso the tornado. The horse digs his heels deep in the dirt arena, so the cowboy can pull the rope taut and wrap it around his saddle horn. At the rider's cue, the horse backs up, tugging the bull with him. The rope goes tight around Cork Screw's neck as his eyes bulge wide and his tongue rolls out to the side.

"Good! Choke that bastard!" I scream, clutching the arm of the couch.

"Come on, guys! Get him out of there!" McKennon hollers.

Sophia squeaks, peeks out from between fingers, and then covers her eyes again quickly.

With the bull out of the spin, a brave bullfighter runs up, jumps on Cork Screw, and can hold on long enough to loosen JD's wrap from around his hand. Once set free, JD takes an unconscious nose-dive straight into the dirt. He lays face down, unmoving, as the bull-fighter drags JD by the boots out of the path of the bull's enormous hooves.

"Get the medics in there now! He's hurt!" the television announcers yell.

The camera pans from JD's slumped body in the center of the ring to the cowboy on his horse. The team is dragging Cork Screw toward the exit gate. The bullfighters flank the bull from the sides, yelling for him to 'git'. Finally, the bull's massive body disappears into the depth of the stadium. The television station immediately goes to commercial.

"Damn it to hell! That damn McCall curse!" McKennon roars. He is instantly up on his feet, pacing the room, scrubbing his face. No doubt memories of his late wife, JD's sister, are pulsing through his mind.

I snap up my phone and make the call. I feel numb.

"Ev!" I cry into the phone.

McKennon suddenly stops pacing when he realizes we actually have boots on the ground. He and Sophia approach me, worry etched in their faces.

"She's with him," I tell them.

"Thank heaven," Sophia breathes, working her hands in concern.

I push the speaker button.

"Ev, I'm here with McKennon and Sophia. We were watching the event on TV. We saw JD go down, but then they went straight to commercial. What's going on?"

"JD's hurt badly," Ev says. I hear people talking urgently in the background, but their words are muffled. "He's alive though."

"Thank heaven," McKennon mutters, running a hand through his hair. He paces the room again. Sophia's silence is a clear indication of her concern.

"We are heading to the hospital now," Ev explains. "I will call as soon as I know something."

"Thank you, Ev. I'm so glad you are there with him."

"Me too," she replies. "I have to go. I'll call you soon."

"Promise?"

"I promise."

The phone goes dead. Sophia's and McKennon's faces have lost all color. I imagine mine has, too. We wordlessly move toward each other and collapse in a three-way hug.

"Please let JD be OK," I whisper to my family, hoping my prayer will reach the big guy in the sky.

Sophia and McKennon won't make it through another loss. Neither will I.

32

EVERLY

I n front of my eyes, the horns of a 2,000-pound freight train collide with JD's head. I release a blood-curdling scream. The dark recesses of my memory burst alive. I see fire. I see smoke. I see twisted metal. I sense death as I run from the stands and force myself out into the arena.

It's happening again.

"Let me through! I'm his girlfriend! Damn it!" I shriek into the face of some gruff cowboy who's attempting to hold me back.

"Take it easy, miss," he drones, trying to restrain my flailing.

Another man in an NBR vest makes his way toward where we are struggling. He looks official. His eyes meet mine.

"What's goin' on here?" he asks, placing a hand on the cowboy's shoulder, as I continue to squirm in his grasp.

"Says she's McCall's girl," the cowboy alleges.

The official turns and looks out into the arena where JD's crumpled body lays, then back to me.

"Please," I beg. "I'm all he's got right now."

"Let her through, Bennett," the man instructs.

"You stay out of the way of the medics," the stern cowboy growls, loosening his grip.

I swallow hard and nod. He holds my eyes for a moment, then releases me.

"Thank you," I murmur to the official, ignoring the cowboy, and race toward JD. The medical staff surrounds him, and I collapse on my knees in the dirt beside them. JD groans when they carefully flip him over so he's on his back. His eyes are closed, and his head is bleeding near his hairline. I just hover as they feel his arms, legs, head, and stomach. They press here, they press there, assessing him. I'm biting my lip so hard that I taste blood, and then his eyes flutter open.

He's alive. He's alive. Thank heaven.

"Get me outta the arena. These people didn't come here to watch me lie in the dirt," JD wheezes.

Noting JD's consciousness, a serious older man in scrubs directs a series of questions at him: "Are you OK? Where does it hurt? Do you know where you are? Can you feel this?"

JD doesn't answer his rapid fire. He groans, tips his head to the side, and closes his eyes again. I keep my focus on JD's beautiful face, trying to ignore the gush of blood running from his head wound. I wring my hands while the older man places him in a neck brace. The others lift him carefully, and then strap him down to a backboard. They hoist JD into the air and start heading for the exit of the hushed arena. In a haze, I follow the men carrying JD. I can hear the wail of an ambulance approaching.

"Wait," calls a voice. I pause and see the cowboy who was restraining me earlier hustle in my direction. I grit my teeth.

What does he want now?

"Here," he says, extending a cowboy hat toward me.

"What's this?" I ask. My brows knit together as I look at the black hat he's holding out.

"It's McCall's. He'll be wanting it back," he says.

"Oh, yes. Thank you," I whisper, taking the hat from him.

I shake my cloudy head and race up next to the stretcher the medical team just placed JD's backboard on. I take JD's hand in mine. I run along with the men wheeling him toward the street level exit of the building. JD's eyes flicker open again. He seems to notice that I am there. I squeeze his clammy hand. I think I see a faint attempt at a smile before his eyes close and his face goes slack.

I gallop along with the hustling paramedics in a state of familiarity. They fling open the rear doors of the ambulance, and I release JD's hand. They gently lift the stretcher and guide my broken cowboy into the back. I climb into the ambulance and am stopped by the driver.

"Who are you to this man?" he asks, impatiently.

"I'm his ... agent," I hiss, shoving him aside. I put JD's hat on my head and climb aboard, positioning myself on the bench beside JD. I reach for his hand again. My phone vibrates in my pocket. I fumble for it with my free hand, still clutching JD's hand in my other. I look at the screen and instantly know I need to channel calm for this conversation. The medics work around me, and I can't process anything they are saying at the moment.

"Devon. I'm with him," I manage. She's with McKennon and Sophia. I am on speakerphone. I swallow hard, holding back the memories and the tears, as I try to console JD's friends, his family.

The back doors swing shut, the siren flips on, and I briefly lose my balance as the vehicle lurches forward, rushing us to the hospital.

33

The medical team bursts through the emergency room doors, and I race behind them into the hospital. JD's hat is a little too big for my head and slips over my eyes. As I push the brim up, a strong palm lands on my shoulder.

"This is far as you go, ma'am," one medic orders.

I heed his instruction and stop in a daze. As they hurry JD away, I'm left standing like a stone in the halogen lights of the hospital lobby. Terror coils around my heart and threatens to squeeze it dry. My mind relives the ambulance ride: the EMTs cutting JD's protective vest, ripping his shirt open to expose his chest, jamming a tube down his throat, and squeezing air into his lungs with a manual resuscitator.

I can't do this again.

I feel like I'm going to be sick. I take JD's hat from my head and hastily dust the arena dirt off of it. A nurse rises from behind the reception desk and approaches me.

"Hello. I'm Glenda. You don't look so well, dear. Will you let me help you?"

I nod. Glenda takes my icy hand in her warm one and guides me to a chair in the waiting area. Shakily, I put JD's hat on an empty seat. I sit, and Glenda settles in beside me. She pats my trembling hand.

"What's your name, dear?" Glenda probes.

"Everly Mitchell," I mumble.

"Everly, can I get you something to drink?" she asks.

"Water, please," I strain. My throat is tight and dry. Glenda nods and scurries away. She returns swiftly and hands me a small plastic cup. I take a sip of the lukewarm water and force a smile.

"Thank you."

"Everly, who did you come in with just now?" Glenda asks, looking from me to the cowboy hat in the chair beside me.

"McCall. JD McCall. He's a bull rider," I manage. If I say much more, I'll break wide open.

"Are you family, Everly?" she probes.

"I'm ... I'm ..."

What am I to him?

"I'm his agent. I've been in touch with his family by phone. I'll be responsible for reporting back to them. He's from out of state," I croak.

"I see. I'll do my best to get an update for you as soon as I am able." The phone rings, and she glances over her shoulder. "I'll just be over there at the reception desk. You let me know if you need anything at all."

"I will. Thank you, Glenda."

Heat and pressure build behind my eyes. I am grateful to be left alone, and that she didn't rattle off any bullshit about needing to be a family member or patient privacy.

I expect an update. I'll get an update.

I let out a long, shaky sigh and close my eyes. I feel the tears brim over. Hot and silent, they slip down my face. I don't know how much time has passed when I feel a touch on my shoulder. Glenda hovers over me.

"Mr. McCall has been in and out of consciousness, Everly. They are waiting for a radiologist to do a CAT scan."

"A CAT scan?" I gasp. Alarm bells are going off in my head.

"I'm sure it's just a precaution," she assures. "I'll keep you advised with what I can."

I force myself to breathe.

"Thank you for your kindness, Glenda."

"You hang in there, Everly," she whispers and drifts back toward her perch behind the desk.

My past and present are colliding. I have to be careful. Dark memories are firing up in my mind. JD's injury is the hot poker igniting them. I learned the hard way that falling for someone with a dangerous profession is a road to agony. I don't want to go through that again.

But here I am.

I jump when my phone vibrates in my pocket. I pull it out and glance at the text on the screen. It's Devon asking if there is any news. I'm not ready to speak to her yet, so I text back he is semi-conscious, waiting for a CAT scan as a precaution, and I'll call as soon as I know more. She replies with a 'thanks,' and I start to pocket the phone again, but decide instead to distract myself with email.

Work. Work always takes my mind off of things.

I click on the message with the subject line 'Approval Needed: McCall Media' and open the attached files. The photos Estefan took in the studio of my apartment on JD's first night in New York unnerve me. There he is – alive, vibrant, physically able, staring at me from the glossy pages of a magazine layout. I hadn't had a chance to tell him I secured the piece yet. I swallow hard, knowing he is broken down somewhere in this building. I don't know what he will look like when I see him again.

If I see him again.

My heart wrenches realizing that no matter which way this goes, he certainly won't look like he does in these photographs. I move on to the next attachment and see the billboard spreads. I approve them all and tell my team to start immediately implementing the campaign in a daze, then tuck my phone away. I drop my head in my hands and just sit silently as the ongoing ER whirls around me.

"Ms. Mitchell?" a male voice asks.

I lift my head and wipe my eyes. A man in scrubs with a stethoscope looped around his neck stands above me. Glenda hovers to his right.

"Ms. Mitchell. I'm Dr. Ryan. I've been tending to JD McCall. I understand you are his agent, and you are here on behalf of his family. Is that correct?"

"Yes," I assure, sitting up straight in my chair. "Is he all right? What can you tell me, Dr. Ryan? I'd like to relay any information I can about his condition to his family right away."

"Mr. McCall is out of harm's way for now. He is stable, but he has suffered a concussion, and has a separated shoulder and several rib fractures. He will need to remain in the hospital for observation for a few days, but I expect he will make a full recovery."

Thank heaven.

"And his bull riding career?" I ask. I'm his agent, and I better act like it right now.

"Dangerous business," he decrees, nodding to the cowboy hat in the chair next to me. "I wouldn't recommend anyone return to that sport after I've seen what can happen, but I expect he will have to be out of competition for a minimum of three months."

I squeeze my eyes shut and curse.

JD will not like this.

"Thank you for the update, Dr. Ryan. Am I able to see him?"

"He's resting now, but I'll find out if he's up for a visitor when he wakes."

"I'll come get you right away," Glenda adds.

"Yes, please do that. I'm not going anywhere until I see him. I'll need to inform the family now."

Dr. Ryan nods and heads back through the swinging doors. Glenda gives me a hopeful smile and resumes her position behind the desk. I press my mouth into a tight line, fighting to keep all the emotion whirling through me bottled up tight. I fish my phone out of my pocket and make the call. The other side picks up on the first ring.

"Devon, I have news," I assert into the receiver.

34

DEVON

Sophia, McKennon, and I have been sitting anxiously in silence for what seems like an eternity when my cell phone lights up on the coffee table. I immediately answer. On the other side, Ev sounds tired. Sad. Scared.

"Ev? How is he?" I blurt. "I've got you on speaker."

McKennon moves closer to me on the couch and wraps an arm around my shoulders. Sophia wrings her hands in her lap.

"JD is stable. He has a concussion, a separated shoulder, and rib fractures. The doctor just advised that he is going to remain in the hospital for observation. He's resting right now, but I should be able to go in and see him sometime tonight."

"That's a relief," McKennon sighs. "It's bad, but it's not that serious."

"Good grief, McKennon. What are you talking about? JD's injuries are serious!" I bleat.

"Not in terms of the rodeo business, they aren't," McKennon replies with a grimace.

How can he even say that right now?

Disgusted with his comments, I squeeze my eyes shut, trying not to think about JD hanging limp off the side, riding arm still tethered to the bull, being whipped around like a rag doll, but I can't keep the visions from my mind.

"A separated shoulder means a lot of recuperation before he will be able to ride again," McKennon adds. "He will be off tour longer than he'd like, dropping in the standings, and likely not making it back in time to qualify for the finals."

"Unfortunately, that's right, McKennon. According to his doctor, he will have to be out of competition for at least three months," Ev asserts.

"Did they say when JD could come back to Green Briar?" I ask.

"I'm sure the doctor is going to advise against travel right now, Devon. I think it's best if he stays at my apartment for a while. I can get him what he needs. Whatever he needs. A nurse, physical therapy, anything."

"Ev. Are you sure? Taking care of an injured bull rider won't be easy. That's a lot for us to ask of you."

"I want to help him get through this, Devon. JD is going to survive this. I think it's best for now."

"I'm so glad you are there with him, Ev," I reply into the phone. "I can't imagine this happening, and he not having someone he knows there to be with him. Thank you for being there."

"It's terrible timing for him to have suffered an injury given that his PR campaign is about to start rolling, but I guess it's a good thing. It will keep money in his pocket while he is recovering," Ev continues.

"I knew that was coming," McKennon groans, rolling his eyes.

"It's just like you, Ev, to think of the business side of things. It's important, too. Thank you," I say to smooth over McKennon's comment.

"I'm sorry I can't help it," she croaks.

"I know," I reassure.

"I think he needs his Green Briar family, though. Can any of you come here?" Ev asks.

I am not particularly interested in going back to the city, but my friend needs me. JD needs us. The feeling of being rested and happy from marrying McKennon and our unbelievably romantic honey-moon dissipated the moment we saw JD go down on the television.

"You should go," Sophia whispers. A haunted look overtakes her face. I look to McKennon, and he nods.

"McKennon and I will be on the first flight we can book," I reply.

"A separated shoulder, a couple busted ribs, and a concussion — those kinds of injuries come with the territory, but it's his mind I'm most worried about. Getting something that means a lot to you took away can really screw up your head." McKennon pauses for a moment with a faraway look in his eyes. "That McCall curse makes my stomach turn."

He touches his heart and points at the sky. I swallow hard.

He's thinking of Madison.

"If it helps any, I have some big news for you about your book. I'm demanding it be shared in person this time though," Ev inserts, slicing my tension with her words.

"Using our business relationship as bait, are we?" I tease, trying to lighten my mood.

"Yes, as a matter of fact, I am."

"Well, in that case, are you also picking up the tab on our travel expenses?"

"Fine," Ev sighs. "If it gets you to New York faster, consider it done. I'll have my assistant make the arrangements."

"Thank you, Ev. Take care of him until we get there. Stay strong, my friend."

"I'm trying," Ev whispers. "See you soon, Devon."

I hang up the phone and turn to McKennon. He embraces me and kisses the top of my head.

"I'm glad you are going to be with him," Sophia says.

"Me too," McKennon mutters. "I'll call Sterling. Give him the news about his son and ask him to stay on to look after you and Green Briar a while longer, Sophia."

"Thank you, McKennon. I'll be all right here. Just keep me informed of what is going on with JD," Sophia replies.

"We need to go pack ... again," I add.

We bid our goodbyes to Sophia and head back to our little house. Once inside, I stand at the kitchen counter and watch McKennon pace the front porch. He holds his phone with a death grip and wears a dark expression as he talks to Sterling about his son. Feeling dark myself, I tear my eyes from my husband and pad into our bedroom to repack.

Knowing Ev, we will fly out on the first flight in the morning. My instincts prove accurate when my phone pings 25 minutes later with an email from Ev's assistant outlining our travel itinerary. McKennon wanders into the bedroom and kisses my forehead. I blow out a breath and plop onto the corner of our bed.

"When are we leaving?" he asks.

"First thing in the morning," I answer. "How did your conversation with Sterling go?"

"It's the rodeo biz," McKennon replies with a shrug. "Went as good as it could, I reckon. Sterling knows how things can go. He's worried about his son, but he knows JD's in good hands with us. He's going to stay on here to keep an eye on the business, the horses, and Sophia."

"That's a relief," I sigh. "McKennon, I am so worried about JD."

"We are going to make sure that brother of mine is going to be all right. JD is always on the road for bull riding events, and he's gotten through worse. He's tough, but our support is going to make a difference whether or not that knuckle head admits it."

"Thank you for coming with me," I reply.

"I aim to please, miss. I'm a little concerned about what happens after we leave though. Ev ... that's where I am not so sure. He's been through injuries in the past, but he's never been under the spell of a red-headed vixen before."

"You're worried about Ev?" I ask, confused.

"Maybe," McKennon drawls.

"I think it is Ev that should be worried about JD," I counter.

"Those two seem cut from the same cloth. Someone's gonna get hurt."

"Someone is already hurt, McKennon," I respond, even though I know he's speaking about matters of the heart.

McKennon eyes my suitcase open on the bed, holds up a high heel by its strap on his index finger, and raises an eyebrow.

"Can take the girl out of the city, but can't take the city out of the girl, I see," he chuckles, expertly changing the subject.

This really is no time for humor, but I laugh with my husband despite it all.

G lenda, the kind nurse, nudges me awake from where I am slumped in the waiting area.

"He's asking to see you," she whispers with a soft smile. "That's a good sign, dear."

I sit up straight, rub the sleep from my eyes, and check my watch. It's after midnight. I collect JD's cowboy hat, scramble from the chair, and onto my feet.

"Thank you, Glenda. Please take me to him."

"Follow me. It seems he's in the clear, dear. They have transferred him from the ER to the observation room he'll be in for the rest of his stay here."

She leads me through the swinging doors to the elevator, and in silence, we ride up to his floor. Glenda steps out when the doors part, and I follow her down a quiet hallway to his room. My eyes sweep over JD lying in a partially reclined hospital bed. Once larger than life, he looks small. His eyes are closed. His head is wrapped in gauze. IV lines are taped into his arm. Machines are monitoring his wrecked body.

"Not too long," Glenda murmurs as she steps out of the room.

I hover in the doorway. This moment is all too real. I've done this before, but I remind myself this is not like it was before.

He is going to live.

According to the doctor, JD is going to survive this. I will myself to move, set the cowboy hat on the windowsill, and take a seat next to the bed.

"I'm here, JD," I whisper. He opens his eyes and stares at me without focus, trying to comprehend.

"You've been in a bull riding accident, JD." He moves his hand slightly toward me, and on instinct, I reach out and take it.

"My head," JD moans.

"I know. I'm here, JD," I say. "Devon and McKennon will be here soon, too."

His green-eyed gaze finally focuses on mine. I can see the glaze in them, an effect of the drugs he's been given.

"I ... I think I love ..." he struggles.

"Shhh," I interrupt.

I gently stroke his hair, and he closes his fingers around mine. His eyes flutter shut. Through a blur of tears, I feel like my insides are being torn out. The past I've buried deep is being dug up, sitting here in a room like this. I am reliving the most painful part of my life. I slump over the edge of JD's bed and sob into the sheets until I'm spent. After some time, I feel a hand touch my shoulder.

Glenda.

"It's time to go," she whispers. I rise from the chair, and JD turns his head against the pillow with a groan. My heart clenches in my chest as I force myself to turn away and follow Glenda out of the room. With one last glance back at JD, I start down the corridor to the waiting area.

The emotion churning in my gut is too much to handle — uncertainty, guilt, nausea, and a hefty dose of leftover terror. A jumble of images from the past and the present rumble around in my mind, starting with today's accident in the arena, but worst of all are the memories I thought I'd buried from the racetrack. I can't stop them from playing over and over in my head. I run down the hall and beeline for the ladies' room. I push open the door, kick in a stall, and promptly throw up.

36

DEVON

"Wake up," McKennon whispers, squeezing my hand. I rub my eyes, realizing I slept through our early morning flight.

"Enjoy your stay in New York City. Thank you for flying ..." I hear a cheery flight attendant chirp through the overhead speaker.

I'm not feeling cheery at all.

Moments later, we are standing in New York's busy airport. I look around with a sense of disorientation. It's been a while since I've been around this kind of hustle and bustle.

I don't miss it one bit.

Heading toward the baggage claim, we are surrounded by men in suits with laptop bags swinging from their shoulders and women fully made up, dressed to the nines in the latest designer fashion. I resent the sound of their high heels clicking on the concourse next to me. I am a different breed now, but I was once one of these people. I know McKennon and I look out of place in our jeans and cowboy boots.

After snagging our suitcases from the conveyer belt, we stroll toward the airport exit. I smile when I see a man in a dark suit and driver's cap holding up a sign with my name on it. I knew from the itinerary a car was sent to retrieve us. We follow him out to the curb, slide into the back seat, and while the driver puts our luggage in the trunk, I text Sophia that we arrived safely and will call her later. When the driver returns and slips behind the steering wheel, I ask him to take us straight to the hospital.

Dragging our suitcases, we enter the hospital through automatic doors. Noting Ev is not in the waiting area, I head for the reception desk. McKennon stands stoically beside me. He doesn't like New York City, traveling, or hospitals. The pleasant-enough woman at the counter gives me JD's room number, and at once, we are rushing toward the elevators. When the doors part, we stroll down the hallway, find the room, and hesitate at the door. McKennon's blue eyes lock on mine. Neither of us is sure what we'll see when we enter the room. I take a deep breath and knock tentatively.

"Devon? McKennon, is that you? Get in here!" JD hollers.

I knit my brows together at the unexpected enthusiasm in his voice. We step inside to find JD upright and alert in his hospital bed. He has a tray of food in front of him. His head is bandaged, and his arm is in a sling. He doesn't look all that bad, considering.

Ev, on the other hand, looks like hell. She is slumped in a chair in the corner of the room. Her eyes are red. Her hair is on top of her head in a messy bun. Her eye makeup is smeared. She looks like she hasn't slept in days.

"JD! I'm so relieved to see you. How are you feeling?" I ask, rushing to his bedside.

"I feel pretty dang good, Devon. Whatever they are giving me is making me feel kinda loopy and hungry!"

I look at his breakfast of rubbery scrambled eggs, a dry pancake, pale fruit in a cup, and orange juice.

That wouldn't make me feel hungry at all.

JD folds the pancake in half and stuffs the whole thing in his mouth. I smile and shake my head.

"Some things never change," McKennon drawls, stepping forward and putting a palm to JD's uninjured shoulder.

"Ev? How are you?" My eyes meet her tired ones. "Have you been here all night?"

"I have, but I'm fine. You arrived at a good time. JD has just come back from some tests. This is the first time he's really been talking since he's been here."

"He certainly is alert," McKennon adds with a chuckle.

"They've got him on some serious pain meds," Ev notes.

"I see," I reply, as JD slurps the fruit chunks out of the tiny plastic cup, forgoing the spoon next to it. Juice dribbles down his chin, but he doesn't seem to notice. I touch JD's hand, give it a squeeze, and hand him the napkin next to his tray. He stares at it for a moment, sways a bit, and then lifts it to his mouth. He misses his lips the first time and then manages to drag it across his face. JD's gaze turns to McKennon.

"Did I make the eight?" he asks.

Just like JD to wonder how he scored the night before rather than worry he's in the freaking hospital.

"As a matter of fact, I checked the event standings this morning. You scored 88 points. You won the event by three points," McKennon replies with a soft smile.

"Yes! If only I'd stuck the dismount, though," JD chuckles, then groans and touches the wrapping around his head.

I guess the pain meds aren't that good.

"That's not funny, JD. You scared the hell out of us," I mutter.

"I'll be fine. Been through worse. I'm a little pissed off I'll have to be off tour, but that's part of playing the game, I guess. Still sucks, though. I expect you talked McKennon into coming, huh?"

"You are in the hospital, for heaven's sake, JD. Of course, we'd come. You are family. No one had to talk me into anything," McKennon assures.

"I wish you hadn't come. You don't need to see me all banged up. I reckon seeing me like this is conjuring up some memories. That can't be good for you. You've seen enough McCall wreckage to last a lifetime."

McKennon's throat works for a moment.

"Don't you be worryin' 'bout that, brother," he finally says. "I've been around this lifestyle long enough to know you're not on your deathbed right now."

"I'm banged up real good is all. Thanks for being here. Both of you. Means a lot to me," JD says softly. "Hey, what about my buddy Wade? Is he all right? He went down just before I did. It's coming back to me now."

"Wade has a broken leg. He's been treated and released," Ev answers.

"What about my truck?" JD asks.

"What truck? Your truck is at Green Briar," McKennon replies with a hint of confusion.

"Are you sure you're OK? Are you having memory loss?" I ask.

"I've taken care of it," Ev inserts. "It's already parked in the garage at my building. One of JD's sponsors gifted him a new Stampede Truck."

"That's impressive," McKennon drawls, lifting an eyebrow.

"It's all Ev's doing. She's really gotten me the rock star treatment out here. Now I've gone and messed it all up by getting hurt." JD drops his head in his hands.

His emotions are certainly all over the place.

Ev rises from her seat and crosses the room.

"That's simply not true, JD," Ev assures. "You may not be out riding on the circuit for the next few months, but you haven't messed anything up. In fact, it will be easier on your sponsors to have you stay here. There will be interviews for you to do. I'll keep your profile high. I've just approved your media campaign. It's going up all over the city as we speak. No one's going to forget about you. Not with a face like that and me behind you."

"Stay? Here? In New York City? I want to go home," JD grumbles.

"The doctor advises against any travel in the near future, JD," Ev continues. "You'll need to be monitored to make sure the concussion doesn't have any additional affects to your brain, you'll need physical therapy for your shoulder, and your ribs need rest to heal. I'll take care of everything, including your career. You'll be staying with me at my apartment."

"I have to stay in New York?" JD mutters, gloomily. "I need the country."

Cowboys never like to be told what to do.

"When you are healthy. When you are ready, you'll come home to Green Briar," McKennon replies.

"It's not forever, JD. You'll be in good hands with Ev," I interject.

JD takes a scoop of his eggs, shovels them in his mouth, and chews them with anger.

"Is anyone here interested in a visit from a special guest?" a woman asks from the hallway. A small bark follows. Ev, McKennon, and I turn. A puppy with a big red bow around its neck trots into the room and leaps up onto the bed with JD.

"Hi ya, fella!" JD declares, nudging his food tray away to tuck the pup under his uninjured arm. "Thank you, miss. I just love dogs." The puppy licks JD's face as his tail wags a thousand miles a second. JD instantly brightens as he strokes the soft golden fur.

"I'm a volunteer with Manhattan's Paws for Patients program," the woman tells us, nodding to JD with a grin. "We are just making the rounds and cheering up the patients."

I take Ev to the side.

"Why don't you go home, freshen up, and get some rest. You look like you could use it. McKennon and I will stay here with JD until visiting hours are over. JD seems like he's handling this fairly well."

"Except for the staying in the city with me part," Ev adds.

"I'll talk to him. He'll come around. He knows it's in his best interest, even if he's not ready to admit it. Are you sure this is all OK?"

"Yes. I'm up for it. I've already got plans for what he'll be doing in his downtime."

"Is that all this is? Business?" I ask, remembering Ev's antics at my wedding.

"Just business," she replies, but she won't look me in the eye.

"You are one heck of a businesswoman, Ev. That's all I can say."

Ev crosses the room back to JD and strokes the puppy.

"Isn't he somethin'?" JD gushes.

"He's cute all right. You are a softie, JD McCall," Ev answers.

"Don't you go tellin' anyone now, Ev," he says through his smile.

"How much pain medication are they pumpin' into you?" McKennon asks with a roll of his eyes, but he smiles and moves in to give the pup a scratch behind the ears.

"I'll be back soon," Ev says to JD. "Devon and McKennon are going to stay with you while I go home. I need a shower and some sleep."

She runs a hand over his cheek. He catches it and kisses her palm. I notice McKennon's eyes sliver just the slightest at their interaction. Ev retrieves her purse and the cowboy hat from beside the chair she was sitting in. She places the hat on JD's bedside table.

"I rescued this from the arena for you. Can't be a cowboy without your hat, can you?"

"It ain't the hat that makes the cowboy. It's the cowboy that makes the hat," McKennon drawls.

I can't quite put my finger on it, but I sense my husband isn't a big fan of what is going down between JD and Ev. Now isn't the time to pry that out of him. I make a mental note to save my interrogation on the topic for another time.

"I would have preferred it was a helmet, but I suppose JD wearing this hat brought him a win and that buckle," Ev says, ignoring McKennon's comment. "JD, when you get back into that ring, I want you protecting that head of yours. Deal?"

"Now that's a darn good point. It's not uncommon nowadays. It used to be looked down upon, not cowboy-tough to wear a helmet, but JD, from now on, I think you better get with the times and protect what brains you do have," McKennon teases.

It eases the tension in the room, and we all have a chuckle.

"It's a deal. Thank you for everything, Ev. Really," JD mumbles.

"You're welcome, JD," she breathes, turning her attention to me.

"I hope you enjoy the hotel room I've set you up in, Devon. We'll have that meeting I mentioned soon."

"I second the helmet plan and also what JD just said. Thank you for everything, Ev," I reply.

"It's my job. It's what I do," she responds with a shrug of her shoulders.

Ev moves toward the door and hesitates to glance back at JD. He's fallen asleep. The little dog has wiggled out from under his arm and is standing at the end of the bed wagging his tail. The volunteer scoops up the pup with a smile.

"Mission accomplished. Buster and I are off to spread joy to the next patient."

"Thank you," Ev, McKennon, and I say at once.

After Ev leaves, I settle in with a book, McKennon with a newspaper. JD sleeps the rest of the time we are there, but we stay with him until visiting hours are over.

37

MCKENNON

Everything about New York City makes my skin crawl. Times Square is too loud, too dirty, too crowded, and there's too much concrete. I reach across the backseat of the cab and catch Devon's hand. My beautiful wife wears the concerned expression I've learned so well since she's come to Green Briar.

"JD is going to be OK," I assure, giving her a squeeze. "As far as bull riding accidents go, he seems to be in pretty good shape. It could have been much worse. Men tempt death every time they get in the chute."

"I know," Devon whispers. She turns toward the window but grips my hand.

I can't help but wonder if she's thinking about JD or if she's reflecting on the life she once lived here. It appalls me that my wife could have ever called this place home. She seems so well-suited for, and comfortable with, country living. I try to imagine her cramped in a tiny apartment, squeezing between people for a seat on the subway, walking home from work alone at night in these streets, and I shudder. I want to take her back to Green Briar immediately, but I hold my tongue.

The taxi pulls up along the curb, and I hand over bills to pay our fare. I run a hand over my chin and take a gander at our hotel from the sidewalk. I don't doubt for a second that Ev has put us up in a nice place. It is then that I see the first of many posters of JD McCall in New York City. I stop in my tracks. His image is plastered on the side of a bus stop shelter.

"What are you looking at?" Devon asks, idling up to me with both of our rolling luggage bags.

I shake my head and point ahead of me at the advertisement. Devon's mouth drops open. I take my bag and follow my wife as she wheels hers closer to the life-size image of JD in front of us. I am lost for words as I observe the image of a man I've known most of my life. In the picture, JD is naked, except for a pair of underwear and the cowboy hat on his head. His arm is raised in the air, and he's riding a huge, superimposed energy drink can as if it were a bull.

"Bull rider JD McCall does it all for the kick," Devon reads the lines emblazoned across the insinuating ad.

"This is what your friend had JD doing the past week?" I ask, aghast.

"I guess so," Devon replies with a shrug of her shoulders.

"Like I've said before, good kid, just kinda stupid," I huff. Disgusted, I turn my back on the bus shelter and head for the hotel lobby.

Once we check in, Devon retreats to the bathroom of our fancy hotel room in Times Square. She's asked me to call Sophia to fill her in while she takes a bath. Seeing JD all banged up and then plastered on that ad has left me uneasy. I pace the room for some time thinking on it, but I can't settle down. I dial the number into my cell. Sophia answers on the first ring.

"Hello, Sophia," I drawl.

"How's JD?" she asks, instantly.

"He's banged up pretty darn good, but he'll be back on his boots in a few months. Glad I got to see him for myself."

"I'm sure it provided some relief to see him with your own eyes and hear that he'll recover. I don't know how this family would manage another loss. I can't bear to think of it."

"Let's not then," I coax.

"So, what do you think of New York?" Sophia asks, taking my cue.

"Crazy," I mumble, standing in front of a huge window watching lights, buildings, cars, and people whirling about below me. "I think that's the best way to describe it."

"Tell me more," she hums.

"I can't believe Devon used to live here. It's too crowded, too noisy, too dirty, but exciting, too. I guess. Seems like everyone is goin' a million miles an hour here – tryin' to get noticed, goin' broke, gettin' rich, or hopin' to get famous. Speaking of famous. You won't believe whose face someone apparently plastered all over the city."

"Whose?" Sophia asks.

"JD. Ev works her magic fast."

"I had a feeling," Sophia replies.

"That attention is going to go straight to his head," I mutter. "Kid doesn't think clearly when his head is all jumbled with dollar signs and attention."

"What exactly has Ev done for him?" Sophia probes.

"I'll get the full report when I see him tomorrow. He was pretty out of it today. Had him on some pretty powerful drugs."

"I see. You do that, McKennon." I can hear the concern and curiosity in her voice.

Sophia really loves JD. We all do.

"And you?" I ask. "What were you up to today, Sophia?"

"The best thing on earth. Tagged along with Sterling while he looked after the horses. He's good at keeping our pregnant mares happy and tending to my land."

"Sounds heavenly," I reply.

I miss Green Briar terribly. I've been away from what I know best and the land I love most for weeks now, except for the brief stop home just before JD's injury had us heading for New York. Our honeymoon was pure bliss, but my roots will forever be at Green Briar. It's like a magnet. I can't stay away long without feeling a little lost nowadays.

"Willa and Faith told me to tell you and Devon to hurry back soon."

"With bells on, Sophia."

"Give JD my love. Adieu," she chimes and hangs up on me before I can reply.

Shortly after, Devon emerges from her bath wrapped in a fluffy white robe and promptly orders room service. In companionable silence, we devour the tray of food splayed out on our bedspread. The television hums in the background, but we aren't paying attention to it. There's far too much to process from today's events.

"You promise JD is going to recover?" Devon asks, removing our empty food tray from the bed, then perching next to me on the mattress.

"I promise," I murmur and stroke her cheek. "What do you say we relive a little of that leftover honeymoon magic in this big bed here?"

A smile finally replaces the worried look she's been wearing all day.

My mission is accomplished.

"Yes, please," Devon whispers.

Without hesitation, I tug the belt of her robe loose. An hour later, we pass out in each other's arms, exhausted and sated.

38

DEVON

I 'm startled awake by the rasp of knuckles on our hotel room door. I peek my head out from beneath the covers and open my eyes enough to see a note card slip beneath the door. I slither out from under McKennon's arm and pad across the floor barefoot to retrieve the message.

It reads, 'Figured the lovebirds might need to sleep in. I'm at the hospital. Meet me there. Ev.'

"Wake up, sleepyhead," I whisper, kissing my husband's temple. "Ev is already at the hospital. She's asked us to meet her there. Join me in the shower?"

I smile when McKennon groans with pleasure and, at my request, tosses the bedding to the side. In one fell swoop, his feet are on the floor, and I'm in his arms.

"I love that I never have to ask twice," I murmur near his ear.

"I aim to please, miss," he says, setting me on the marble counter next to the sink to turn the shower on. He tests the water and steps in.

"Come on in. It's just your temperature. I'll wash your back."

I leap off the counter and into the shower with him.

"I love that I never have to ask twice," he echoes.

"I aim to please, cowboy. Now, are you only washing my back, or can we discuss other places?" I tease, raising my hands in the air, waiting to be lathered. McKennon chuckles, and I watch impatiently as he turns the soap over in his hands.

After a blissful shower, I am squeaky clean. McKennon didn't miss an inch of my skin. We stop off in the lobby for a quick cup of coffee and a pastry and then step out into the commotion of the city to hail a cab. As we whiz across town, our jaws drop repeatedly. There are JD posters everywhere — at the bus stops, on billboards, on sides of buses, on buildings.

"Damn, that kid is everywhere," McKennon comments.

"Ev is very good at what she does, McKennon," I add.

"If her job is to paste pictures of my naked brother-in-law all over this forsaken city, I suppose she is."

"You don't like Ev much, do you?" I probe.

"Can't put a finger on her is all. I don't want to see JD get hurt."

"JD? Hurt?" I laugh. "I don't want to see Ev hurt! JD is the playboy here, McKennon."

"I reckon you're right there, but I have an inkling something is going on between the two of them."

"Of course there is! They are having sex. Lots of it, I'm sure. It's what JD does!"

"I agree, but I saw somethin' in his eyes. It wasn't the drugs. Maybe a little fear from his bull riding accident has crept in, but I don't think that's it. I think he might have feelings for your redheaded friend. Feelings I'm not so sure she's interested in returning."

"No way," I chuckle. "JD doesn't have feelings."

"We'll see," McKennon replies.

We pull up to the hospital, pay the driver, and slip out of the cab. As we pass through the revolving doors, up the elevator, and down the hall to JD's room, I am overwhelmed by the scent of disinfectant and feel my usual distaste for anything medical creeping up on me. McKennon knocks on the open door, and we wander into the room. Ev is perched next to JD's bed, holding his hand.

"McKennon, get me out of here!" JD wails, thrusting the back of his head into the pillow.

"Soon enough, brother. Just hang in there."

"Easy, JD," Ev says. "The doctor is coming in shortly to give us an update on when you will be released."

"Not soon enough," JD groans. "I feel like I'm in jail."

"Aren't we in a grumpy mood today?" I tease and hand JD a cookie I swiped from the hotel. "To take your mind off of things."

"Thanks, Devon," he says, ripping into the wrapper and shoving half the oversized treat into his mouth.

"I have to get back to the office to sign off on a few contracts. Devon, I'd like to have that meeting with you, too. McKennon, would you be so kind as to stay here with JD and get the update from his doctors?"

"I'm happy to stay here with JD, ladies," McKennon says with a tip of his hat.

"Thank you, husband," I say, pressing my lips to his. "JD, you be nice to him."

"I will if you sneak me another one of these cookies," JD replies, finishing off the rest.

"You got it," I say with a smile.

I am happy to leave McKennon and JD to themselves for a while and accompany Ev to her office. Also, not to mention, free my nostrils of the hospital smells. Ev's driver is waiting at the curb and whisks us uptown to the building where I've met Ev so many times before. We enter the building, pass through security, and I clip the guest badge to my blouse. We ride a crowded elevator up 40 floors, and I feel relief when I settle into a leather chair in front of Ev's desk. I have forgotten how exhausting and cramped New York is.

I prefer wide-open spaces these days.

"I've got big news for you, Devon," Ev says from behind her huge desk. Ev shifts a stack of paper toward me.

"My manuscript," I say, touching the pages.

"This! This is fantastic!" she exclaims, tapping the papers with her fingernail. She opens a drawer with a smile and slips another piece of paper across the desk.

"What's this?" I ask.

"This is your contract and advance for the final book. I've made some markups in the margins where I think there is room for improvement."

I skip over the contract and go straight for the check. My eyes widen.

"Ev! That's a lot of zeros!" I exclaim, covering my mouth.

"Told you I can make anyone a star," she says with a grin. "I got him a lot of zeros, too." She points out the window. JD is plastered shirtless on a billboard slapped on the side of the building across the street.

In the middle of Times Square.

"That'll take some getting used to," I say.

"I think this is the best view in Manhattan. I had to pull a few extra strings to make that happen. Wait until you see the Lariat Jeans spread I got him. It's going to be featured in all the magazines you cowgirls read. His ad will curl toes in the ladies' boots for sure!" Ev spins in her oversized chair like a giddy teenager.

"I hear you could have had either one of them. JD mentioned he had an eye for you at one point. I think McKennon suits you, though. I'm pleased you chose him. It left JD wide open for me to play with."

"So, JD does pillow talk?" I ask, raising an eyebrow.

"He's told me a few things," Ev replies.

"Are you just playing with him? Or do you really care about him?" I ask, thinking of the conversation I had with my husband this morning in the taxi.

"Care about him?" Ev responds, thinking it over for a moment. "No, just business, but it sure is fun to play with a cowboy."

"That's how things start, Ev. Wild hearts can't be tamed. I know you don't intend to care, but —"

"Devon, I've taken on projects before. Don't forget I'm not just your editor, dear. I'm your publicist, too. Which means I'm qualified to mold him into a star if I want to."

"I know, but JD is, um, different."

"Nothing I can't handle. Trust me. He's in good hands."

"It's not your hands I'm worried about, Ev."

"Well," Ev sighs. "I can tell you this. I sure like the looks of that boy on my arm out there. I'm going to make him a star."

"I think you already have," I say, nodding to the billboard.

Ev stares out the window at the image of JD for a beat and then slaps her palms on the desk.

"On to other business. Let's go over your contract and the time-line. I can't wait for you to have a book in the world."

"All right," I say, scooting the chair closer to her desk. She flattens the paperwork and begins dissecting the clauses. My head is spinning slightly. I don't know if it is because my book is heading toward publication or if I am feeling the same unease my husband does about the nature of Ev and JD's relationship.

39

Ev and I arrive back at the hospital with two large pizzas. Giggling like high school girls skipping class, we sneak them past the receptionist desk, into the elevator, and gallop down the hall once we are on the right floor. JD and McKennon are quietly playing cards when we enter the room.

"Where did you get those?" I ask, setting the pizza boxes and the bag of accompaniments down on the windowsill.

"Gift shop. Where'd you get that?" McKennon asks, hungrily eyeing the pies Ev and I delivered.

"Ray's Pizza. It's my favorite pizza place in NYC. My mouth has been watering the entire way here," I reply, serving up huge, hot slices onto paper plates and passing them around the room.

"There are, like, a million Ray's Pizzas. They all claim to be the original. But the real one's on 11th, I think. I made sure you country boys got the real deal while you are visiting my city. You'll need these. It's pretty greasy," Ev adds, following me around the room with a stack of napkins.

"There's only one topping, and it's my favorite, so no complaining. I just love their chicken finger pizza! JD, I know I promised you another cookie, but this is way better. I guarantee it," I say, passing him a plate with four slices piled on it.

McKennon takes a bite and groans.

"Good, right?" I ask with a smile.

"Now that's a slice of pizza," he comments with a heavenly smile of his own.

"What do you think, JD?" Ev asks, accepting her serving from me and blotting the grease on top of the cheese with at least five napkins.

"Mmm," JD responds. He's just shoved an entire slice of pizza in his mouth. I don't blame him. It has to beat what they've been serving him here.

"What made you decide to play cards?" I ask, pouring soda into plastic cups.

"I had to get JD's mind off of getting out of here. His belly aching is driving me mad," McKennon says as I sit and take my first divine bite of Ray's pizza.

"Oh, my goodness. Now this is pizza. This is one thing I do miss about the city. Nothing like a good New York slice," I gush.

"Has the doctor been by with an update?" Ev asks.

JD nods enthusiastically but has stuffed the third of his four slices into his mouth.

"You eat, brother. I'll fill them in." McKennon rolls his eyes and flashes an easy grin.

"Well, what did he say?" I ask. "Good news, I hope."

"It's good news all right. JD has the all clear. He's got his hall pass outta here first thing tomorrow. Of course, he still has to take it easy, but he has the green light to recover somewhere other than the hospital. According to the doc's tests, apparently JD's brain isn't any more scrambled than it was before his accident," McKennon teases and gently knuckles JD in his good shoulder.

"Oh, JD! You can come home," Ev blurts.

"Home?" McKennon asks, with a raise of his eyebrow.

"I mean, back to my apartment for a while," Ev remarks, a slight blush reaching her cheeks.

"Don't worry, man. She makes me sleep in her guest room," JD mutters. "It's all business between us, but I appreciate the place to be laid up until I can get back to Green Briar."

"Happy to help," Ev replies, turning her attention back to soaking the grease up from her pizza.

"Hey, are there any slices left?" JD asks, holding up his empty plate.

"There sure are," I reply, setting mine to the side and filling his again. I eye Ev as I cross the room. She looks vacant, sad almost, but not quite. I can't register her expression. Whatever this is, it's very different from the Ev I talked to not long ago in her office.

"We appreciate everything you are doing, Ev," I insert. I feel like I can't say it enough. McKennon nods.

"Like I've said before, it's my job," Ev murmurs, glancing at JD who is busy stuffing more pizza in his face.

"How'd your meeting go?" McKennon asks, changing the subject stealthily.

"Guess who is going to have her very own book published next fall?" I bleat.

"I'm so proud of you!" McKennon exclaims, setting down his food. He crosses the room to where I'm standing. Before I know it, he's swept me off my feet and spins me around the room. I can't help but giggle until I notice Ev watching us. I think I notice a flash of envy.

"It's all thanks to Ev. She is a miracle worker," I add quickly as McKennon sets me down.

"So, it's good news all around then," McKennon drawls, retrieving his plate.

"Good news all around," I agree.

I wander over to Ev and squeeze her shoulder. She looks up from her barely eaten pizza and gives me a weak smile. This is definitely not the same Ev who said her relationship with JD was strictly business merely a few hours ago.

Something really is going on between them.

40

Over the pizza, we plan JD's extraction from the hospital for the next morning. Satisfied, JD falls asleep. Ev heads back to her office. McKennon and I return to the hotel. Ev has invited us to a dinner party this evening, but I'm confident I'll be attending on my own. I know my husband. As expected, McKennon opts for downtime in our room.

My cowboy just isn't cut out for city living.

"Are you sure you don't want to come out and explore the city with me?" I ask after freshening up. I slip out of my bathrobe and into my favorite little black dress.

"I'm mighty tempted given that dress, miss, but I'm thinkin' this bed is awfully comfortable right about now," McKennon says with a yawn.

"Not one for the nightlife, huh?" I tease, tugging a high heel onto one foot.

"I'm a country boy through and through. Don't know nothin' about being a city slicker. Old men like me rise early and find a good night's sleep more agreeable to the nightlife."

"That may be the case now, but I'm sure you whooped it up back in your heyday," I reply.

"Maybe," McKennon drawls with a one-cornered smile. "However, now I'm a happily married man. I don't need to look at any merchandise. I've got everything I want in the woman in front of me."

Swoon.

"Ditto, husband. I'm only doing this for Ev's sake. She put us up, is taking JD in until he's back on his feet, and got me my book deal. I feel like it would be rude if I didn't accept her invitation."

"Makes sense. Just don't stay out too late on me. I don't sleep so well these days without you tucked under my arm. Deal?"

"Deal," I smile.

"Come here," McKennon requests.

I wander over to his shirtless body sprawled on the bed and trace my tongue from above the button on his jeans up to his mouth. As our lips meet, he groans and sweeps us into a desperate kiss. I'm tempted to stay and take my husband for a roll in the hay, but I pull away.

"Don't stop," McKennon objects. He catches me by the wrist and gently tugs me back toward the bed. He has my lipstick all over his face, and I shake my head.

"You are so tempting, handsome husband of mine. I'd much rather stay here and ravage you, but I need to go get to the bottom of what's going on with JD and Ev. I think you may be onto something. Ev was acting weird today." I pull a tissue from the box on the nightstand and wipe McKennon's lips.

"Good idea. I'd sure like to know what Ev's intentions are with my brother-in-law," McKennon agrees, leaning into the tissue. "I guess we've got the rest of our lives to do the dirty, but if I'm still awake when you get back, you're going to get it."

"I'll hold you to that, cowboy."

"One request though," he adds.

"Which is?" I ask.

"Lose the face paint first," he chuckles, eyeing the tissue in my hand.

"Deal," I answer. I give McKennon a shimmy and head to the bathroom to retouch my lipstick before I head out.

An hour later, I am downtown in a swanky Manhattan club. I should have known Ev's dinner party would be more party than dinner. The DJ clutches his headphones and thrashes to the thrumming beat of the record he's spinning. I can't take my eyes off of his bushy pelt of chest hair. His sequined vest glinting in the overhead lights curtains it. The music he's creating is loud, and dancers undulate on the floor in front of him. The liquor is clearly flowing. I swallow hard and think of my husband back in the hotel room.

McKennon would absolutely hate this.

Glad that McKennon opted to stay behind, I follow Ev through the dense crowd. When we finally arrive at the bar, Ev is instantly served.

As usual.

While we wait for our cocktails, Ev is swarmed by a group of very handsome, very young men. I expect they are male models or want to be. They obviously know of Ev and her reputation for building careers, but she seems unusually aloof. She takes their business cards, waves them off with a flick of her wrist, and promises to follow up with them another time. These are the business opportunities the Ev I know scoops up in a butterfly net. The queen of networking is at a party and not actually networking.

Odd.

After our drinks arrive, Ev floats away from the bar, and I follow. She locates a table in a quieter sitting room away from the pulsating dance floor. As I slide into the red velvet booth, I can still feel the vibration of the bass through my body.

"I am excited about your book," Ev says. "I think it is very promising. I'm really breaking through in the Western media genre. I think it is a channel that I might really enjoy expanding into."

"Ev, are you going country?" I ask with a sly smile.

"Maybe," she says with a shrug. "Honestly, it wasn't a market I ever considered, being based in New York City, but the success I'm having with you and now JD, well, it's interesting. I didn't know that the country had a little of what I was missing until I actually trekked out there for your wedding. Much finer looking men than here in the city, that's for certain. I like the ruggedness of it all. McKennon and JD are so unrefined. I love it. So do my photographers and clients."

"They are certainly different from the city dwellers," I reply, sipping my martini and looking around.

"More men should be cowboys. Maybe I'll even work on getting that husband of yours some modeling deals. He is a fine specimen, too," Ev continues.

I almost spit my drink on the table.

"I don't think McKennon would like that, Ev. He's been approached by a million companies after that video of our engagement went viral, and he's turned them all down."

"That's insane, Devon. Do you know how lucrative those endorsements can be? He doesn't know what he's missing."

"We are doing just fine without them, Ev. Trust me. That kind of stuff is more JD's style, anyway. I'd leave McKennon out of your negotiations."

"Fine," Ev huffs with a roll of her eyes. "That husband of yours can be quite the wet blanket."

"I've heard that one before," I laugh, remembering JD uttering those same words a world ago at my train wreck first horse show with Faith.

"JD has embraced the lifestyle quite well," Ev assures.

"Speaking of JD, love never looked so good on you," I say.

"Love?" Ev asks with a horrified look on her face.

"I've known you for a long time, Ev. I've never seen you blaze through a room filled with male specimens and not stop to at least discover your next project. Something is happening between JD and you, isn't it?"

Ev sighs, presses her lips together, and takes a long sip of her own martini. She won't meet my eyes. I wait. I've baited her. I want to see what she'll say next.

"Maybe at the moment, I'm a little taken with JD, but love? That's not in the equation for me. I want to remind you of the secret, Devon," Ev finally says.

"The secret?" I ask.

This is not the response I expected.

"The secret to being a powerful woman, of course."

"Go on," I encourage.

"Here it is. Stay hungry. I know you met the cowboy of your dreams, but you can't let your life get boring. Stay hungry."

"Is this about you or me, Ev?" I inquire.

"It's about both of us. It's about all women. It's my philosophy. I am only as old as I feel I am, as I think I am. I have flings with hotties like JD to remind myself that I still have it. That I'll always have it."

"Have what?" I ask, furrowing my brows.

"Stop crunching up your eyebrows like that. Your face will thank you. All I am saying is young, old, supposed to, not supposed to, just do whatever it takes for you to stay young, free, alive."

"Like you?"

"Like me, but in your own way."

"I think I understand what you're saying, Ev, but I think you are side stepping my question."

"Maybe I am."

Feelings for Ev can be tricky, so I change tacks.

"So, what are you planning to do with him?" I ask.

"Continue as planned. I've got a mountain of media lined up for him. Once he's feeling up to it, that is. He can do phone interviews from my apartment until he's finished up his physical therapy. From there, I don't know. I guess it depends on how long I can keep a country boy in the city."

"I know you've got the business side on lockdown. I'm asking about the emotional side, Ev. McKennon and I have both noticed a certain electricity between you and JD. Want to discuss that?"

"Oh, Devon. You are always so concerned with my wellbeing. I know what I'm doing. It's just physical."

"I don't know who's playing with who in this relationship, Ev. I don't want to see anyone get hurt. I don't want our relationship to be strained if things go south with JD. We have a book to pull together."

"Nothing is going to change our relationship, Devon, and JD won't hurt me so long as I'm careful and don't get attached. Besides, I don't get attached. Ever." Ev finishes her drink in one gulp and flags a server for another.

While she places the order, I contemplate her carefully. I don't believe Ev. I see it. McKennon sees it. The question is who is going to hurt whom.

Is JD going to hurt Ev? Or is Ev going to hurt JD?

The whole relationship is confusing. I could probe a little further, but Ev is being coy. She won't tell me anything that she doesn't want me to know.

I dutifully sit through another round of cocktails as Ev rattles off a series of next steps for my book and JD's career, but I stop her before she can order another round.

"I think I've had enough, Ev."

"Are you leaving already? What's up with you?"

"I miss home. I miss McKennon. I'm not comfortable in the city anymore," I confess, waving a hand around the dark lounge attached to the nightclub.

"All right, then. We'll go, Devon. We have an early morning picking JD from the hospital, anyway. I'll walk you out and help you hail a cab."

"Thanks, Ev."

"This is my world. It's not yours anymore. It's clear as day, and I don't mind that one bit."

On the way out of the club, sweaty people keep bumping into me, and I detest the cramped, dirty feeling the city gives me now. I still can't believe I used to live here, that I used to spend time on the club scene. It feels like eons ago. I'm glad I left.

I'm the country's girl now.

Once we are outside, I take a deep breath as Ev hails my cab. One instantly appears at the curb, and Ev holds the door open. I smile wearily and climb inside.

"Remember what I said, Devon. Do whatever it takes for you to stay young, free, and alive. If it's going back to your husband, so be it, but hold on to your fire. Don't lose that flame. Trust me, loving someone more than you love yourself can drive you mad."

"What?" I ask. "Is there something you aren't telling me here?"

"Never mind. It's just my past sneaking up on me." Ev shakes her redhead and flicks her wrist. "It's all in the past. I'm keeping it there."

"Ev, are you OK?"

"See you tomorrow, sleepyhead," she replies, slamming the door in my face.

As my cab drifts onto the street, I watch Ev out the back window. She climbs into her town car, and it pulls away in the opposite direction. I am more confused than ever. The Ev I know would have turned on her heels and stomped straight back into that club, with a wingman or not.

Interesting.

On the way back to the hotel, I mull over what Ev said, and I can't quite put a finger on what she is trying to tell me.

Is it a warning about losing myself in my marriage?

Is it her way of telling me she doesn't believe in love?

Or is it simply to embrace all that I am and disregard what people want me to be?

I'm too tired to try and solve Ev's puzzle. Back at the hotel, I race to the elevator and fly down the hall to my room in hopes my cowboy is still awake. At the door, I check my wristwatch.

1:30 a.m. Not likely.

I slip my card in the lock, open the door, and let it click quietly behind me. The soft glow of the TV is illuminating McKennon's beautiful face. He's sitting up, but his head is slumped to the side, eyes closed, mouth slightly ajar. His breathing is rhythmic. I know he's asleep. I'm too tired to wash up appropriately. All I want to do is to be in his arms. I wiggle out of my shoes, my dress, my undergarments, and slide under the soft sheets beside him.

McKennon snuggles up beside me, strings an arm over my waist, and kisses between my shoulder blades.

"I'm so glad you're back," he whispers.

"Me too," I breathe in return. I scoot closer to him and feel impossibly safe.

I'll think more about Ev and JD tomorrow.

41

"Aw, heck no. I'm not getting into that. I can walk just fine. It's my arm that ain't working, not my legs," JD barks, staring down the nurse who has just pushed a wheelchair through the door.

"I'm sorry, Mr. McCall. It's hospital policy," the nurse retorts, unshaken by our prideful bull rider's outburst.

"Come on, JD. Lighten up. This is your ticket outta here. Get in the chair," McKennon orders, bending his brim to the unaffected nurse. "Apologies, miss."

"This isn't my first rodeo," she chirps to McKennon. He gives her a smile and a wink. His charm makes my stomach do a backflip. "Now get in!" the nurse barks back at JD.

"Come now, JD," Ev coos. "Let's get you out of here and back to my place."

"Fine," JD sniffs, scratching the arm strapped to his body in a sling.

Ev and I start to help him out of his bed, but he's in no mood to be assisted.

"Let me do it," JD grumbles, scooting to the end of his bed.

He stands and strides to the chair in the corner where Ev has stacked a fresh change of clothes for him. We all cover our mouths and try to hold back our laughter when we notice his hospital gown has come untied up the back. JD gives us a full moon as he retrieves his boxers and bends to pull them on. The nurse turns her head and blushes. Ev looks happily entranced by his behind. McKennon and I exchange a glance.

It's then that McKennon clears his throat. "Let's let the man dress in private. JD, we'll wait for you in the hall."

"Mighty decent of you, McKennon. Don't mind givin' the ladies a show though," JD guffaws. The blushing nurse bolts out the door, pushing the wheelchair at breakneck speed. As she whizzes by, I feel heat rise to my cheeks, too.

"You will not be showing my wife anything," McKennon replies, steering me by the shoulders toward the door.

"All right then, brother. Someone's gonna have to help me get my shirt on though. My shoulder's hurting something fierce."

"I can help with that, if you'd like," I hear Ev say as McKennon directs me out into the hallway.

She sounds so unlike herself. As if she is asking permission. Ev doesn't ask permission of anyone.

"He's ready," Ev says a few minutes later, peering out of the hospital room. The nurse wheels the chair back into the room with McKennon and me behind.

"Sit," she orders.

"Fine," JD grumbles, lowering his cowboy hat over his eyes and plopping into the wheelchair. "Let's get this over with."

"Good man," McKennon assures, placing a palm to JD's good shoulder.

"I'm only in this thing to get the hell outta here," JD huffs.

At that, the nurse whisks JD out the door and down the hallway. Once we are in the elevator, I notice Ev position herself next to JD's chair. He looks up at her and slips his hand into hers. I squeeze my husband's hand and nod in their direction. McKennon presses his lips together and gives them a curious glance.

JD and Ev's hands remain entwined as we exit the elevator and he is rolled through the automatic doors out to the curb. Ev's driver is waiting for us there and, rather than the usual town car, he's driving a SUV big enough to take us all at the same time.

Ev doesn't miss a beat.

As McKennon and the driver position themselves to help JD out of the wheelchair and into the backseat, Ev reluctantly releases his hand. Once we are all piled in and are being whisked uptown to Ev's apartment, it's only moments before JD falls asleep against Ev's shoulder, thanks to the dose of pain medicine administered before leaving his hospital room.

Despite the wheelchair debacle and his shoulder being in pain, JD seems in good spirits when we wake him. At Ev's door, he pushes his way into the apartment, retrieves a soda from the refrigerator, and settles into the couch.

"He acts likes he lives here," McKennon puzzles.

"He kind of does," I reply.

"For now," Ev adds. I note a hint of sadness in her voice. "Shall I open a bottle of wine, Devon? I know it's early afternoon, but what the hell?"

"Let's," I agree.

"McKennon, can I get you anything?" Ev asks.

"I'll have a glass of water. Thanks." He sets his hat on its crown next to JD's on the counter. He wanders over to join his brother-in-law on the sofa, and Ev lifts an eyebrow at his back.

"Water?" Ev asks me, pouring a glass and popping the cork on a bottle of white.

"He's a special occasion drinker these days."

"OK, then," Ev muses as we move into the room to join the men on the couch.

"So, what do we need to do to get you settled in here, JD?" McKennon asks.

"Not much," JD says with a shrug. "Got everything I need in my rigging bag from the event. Plus, I've been staying here for a while now. I know the ropes." He turns to address Ev. "I assume the guest room is still available while I heal up?"

"It's all yours," Ev replies with a smile and then sips her Sauvignon Blanc.

"All right then," McKennon replies.

He reaches for the glass on the table, but his phone rings in his pocket before he can take a drink of water. McKennon fumbles to his jeans, attempting to shimmy his hand into the tight front pocket. With little success, he readjusts himself and leans back on the couch for a more appropriate angle. My eyes widen as his jeans tighten just enough that I glimpse my husband's well-endowed package.

Oh my!

I blush, nibble my lower lip, and hold my breath. Ev turns her head to look out the side window.

"Excuse me. I have to get this. Anywhere I can go to take this call?"

"Guest room," JD commands, waving his hand. "First door on the right, down that way."

McKennon nods, answers the phone, and struts down the hall.

"Nice package," Ev quips with a bump to my shoulder.

"Um, thanks," I murmur, looking over at JD. He takes a long drink from his can of soda and unhappily stares Ev down.

"Thank goodness it's just your shoulder that needs recovering," Ev says, turning her attention back to JD. "We would have been screwed if you had broken anything more on that beautiful body."

"Are you just using me for my looks, Ev?" JD growls.

"Maybe," she muses. She leans over, pecks JD on the cheek, and smooths the hair off the bandage on his forehead.

"Careful. That hurts, too," JD advises.

"See what I mean about a helmet being mandatory," Ev says, touching the covered cut and bruises above his brow. It looks more like a motherly gesture than the touch of a lover. It weirds me out a little.

Thankfully, McKennon comes back into the room.

"Who was it?" I ask.

"Sophia. Willa is about to pop," McKennon drawls, running a hand through his dark hair. "I reckon we best be gettin' back to Green Briar."

"Oh, my gosh!" I exclaim. "I can't believe it's time already. She is going to have the most beautiful foal."

"You gotta keep the wheels turning at Green Briar," JD says. "There's a lot of good going on there right now."

"Are you going to be all right now? Here?" McKennon asks, motioning toward Ev.

"I'll be fine, McKennon. Just a few bumps and bruises aren't gonna keep me down. You've already been away from the ranch too long with the honeymoon, and now this. I'm a tough cowboy. I'm gonna get through this. Besides, I don't want you leaving everything we've built up at Green Briar for too long on account of my bull riding injury."

"I know you, kid, all too well. I expected you wouldn't want me jeopardizing the business." McKennon extends his hand, and JD takes it.

"Oh, and another thing." JD digs into his shirt pocket and gives Ev a prescription bottle. She turns the bottle over in her hand, reads the label, and looks to him. "Pain pills. Only give those to me if I really need one. I've seen too many bull riders get hooked on those things. I won't be one of them."

"Good man," McKennon says, softly slapping JD on the back.

"But JD ..." Ev begins to protest.

"Bull riders are pure bravery. I'm all testosterone with a high pain threshold. I don't need those damn pills. Up on those bulls' backs, I have to push it. It's my job. This is the consequence of my profession," JD says, gesturing to the sling on his arm.

"What if I could find you a better job?" Ev whispers.

"After this injury, I might consider it. But then again, the way time passes on the back of a bull is unlike anything else in this world. That's why I keep riding, year after year, injury after injury. I want to keep feeling that rush. There's nothing like experiencing those eight seconds. Besides, it drives the ladies wild. Isn't that right, Ev?" JD asks, flashing her his rock star smile.

"They say the broken cowboys are the ones who choose the bulls. The smart ones ride a bull once, and then switch to bronc riding," I interject.

"Like McKennon," Ev asks.

"Like McKennon," JD replies. "McKennon. Devon. Can I have a word?"

McKennon nods, and we follow JD as he makes his way slowly down the hall. I glance back at Ev. She pours herself another glass of wine, settles back into the couch, and inspects JD's little bottle of pills.

"Not a bad place to recover," McKennon says, taking a tour of JD's guest room. I take a seat on the bed and wait to hear what JD has to say.

"I clearly was too loopy to say so at the hospital, but it means a whole lot to me you both came here."

"Of course we would, JD. You're family," I say.

"Having familiar faces at the hospital really helped me face that place and the pain. Thank you from the bottom of my heart, brother and sister," JD murmurs.

McKennon, JD, and I lock in an embrace.

"Family," McKennon whispers. "That's what life is all about."

"So, when are you heading back?" JD asks, stepping away from us. His eyes are misty, but he doesn't shed a tear.

"I'd like to book a flight out for tomorrow morning. Now that we know you are settled in here and out of harm's way, I gotta get back to my duties. Sterling has been holding things together for far too long. Devon, is that all right with you?" McKennon asks.

"Of course. As long as JD feels strong enough for us to go."

"I don't want you guys to miss the birth of Willa's first foal," JD chuckles. "I'm expecting pictures of that little one. I sure hope the baby is golden like her ma."

"Me too," I chime in with a smile. "And be careful what you ask for. I might overload your phone with millions of baby Willa pictures!"

McKennon clears his throat. JD and I stop teasing each other and stand at attention. We both know that sound means business.

"Are you sure you are in good hands here with Ev?" McKennon asks.

"I'll be fine," JD replies, but he runs a hand through his hair, chews his cheek, and adverts his eyes from our faces.

"Not very convincing, brother," McKennon replies. "I'm a little concerned after seeing your half-naked body plastered on posters all over Manhattan."

Stunned, JD's mouth falls open, and his face turns ashen.

He doesn't know about the posters. Or the buildings. Or the buses. Or their shelters.

After a moment, JD regroups himself and storms out of the guest room.

"Ev!" he hollers down the hall. "What's this about my naked body on posters all over this forsaken city?"

McKennon and I exchange an "uh-oh" glance as we try to interpret their muffled voices. I wait to hear tables turning and glass breaking, but suddenly my ears fill with the sound of Ev's and JD's laughter.

"What on earth?" I say, towing McKennon out into the hall with me. When we reach the couch, JD and Ev are embracing, still laughing.

"I am quite pleased with myself right now," JD chuckles to McKennon and me. "Have a look at this!"

Ev flips *In Touch* magazine open on the table. In it is an article titled, '*Forget the City, Let's Country. Meet Bull Riding's Hottest Cowboy.*' I look at my husband. His eyes are wide. There, in front of us, are the pictures we've seen plastered around the city, plus a few more, surrounded by more words than in a *New York Times* article.

"Look at that, will you?" Ev taps the glossy photos with the back of her hand.

"I'm a superstar," JD says with a gleam in his eye. "Thanks to Ev that is. Things are all good here, McKennon. Book that ticket home."

JD plants a kiss on Ev's cheek, tucks her under his good arm, and swings his feet up onto the coffee table. I notice his eyes don't once leave the magazine, though.

42

The next morning, McKennon and I speak a little as we pack our belongings for the return trip to Green Briar. Ev's assistant has secured us a late morning flight out of LaGuardia Airport.

"Here, don't forget to pack this." I toss the *In Touch* Magazine filled with JD's semi-celebrity photos into McKennon's suitcase. "I don't think JD will forgive you if he hears Sophia doesn't see that."

"I don't quite care if I never see this again," McKennon grumbles, shoving the magazine into the front pocket of the case. "Those two read us that article more times than I care to count last night."

"Are you all right leaving JD behind with Ev?"

"He seems quite satisfied with what she's made of him. He's a grown man. If he wants half-naked photos of him in publications and plastered on the sides of buildings, billboards, and buses, so be it. Besides, the doctor doesn't want him traveling right now. I can't argue with that."

"Are you still concerned about Ev's intentions?"

"Of course, I am. Haven't quite seen JD like this. Can't put a finger on what it is though."

"Smitten?" I ask.

"Smitten with what is the real question. Is it Ev or the fame?"

"Maybe it's a little of both ... for both of them."

"Thing is, I don't know if JD is capable of anything that lasts beyond eight seconds. The rodeo has a way of doing that to a fellow," McKennon says with a grimace.

"Funny. I don't think Ev is capable of anything that lasts more than a New York minute. Manhattan can do that to a lady. They just might be perfect for each other," I respond.

As he zips his suitcase, McKennon only nods and presses his fine lips together.

"So," I say, shifting the subject. "We have a few hours before we have to be at the airport. What do you say I show you where I used to live and treat you to breakfast at my favorite old spot? It's on the way to the airport."

"Is this the place you lived with Michael?" McKennon asks, sapphire eyes searching my face. "Don't quite want to know much more about that gent, especially where he once laid with my wife."

"I would never take you there, McKennon." I swallow hard and pause for a moment to regain my composure. His comment has taken me aback.

Was that a flash of jealousy?

"I want to show you the building where my first apartment in the city was. I lived there *alone*, and I was proud of it once."

"By all means, let's go then," he says with a fresh smile. "I want to hear all about it and this restaurant of yours. Is it good?"

"The best!" I exclaim. I'm happy that my cowboy is interested in learning more about my past.

A past that doesn't include my ex-fiancé.

Our taxi snails its way to the Upper East Side, and we get out on yet another corner with a poster of JD plastered to a bus shelter. McKennon doesn't address it, but I can sense his discomfort at the sight of it. His jawline clenches ever so slightly. I take his elbow and tug my bag along, feeling relieved that we packed light.

"Let's walk," I suggest. "My old building is just around the block."

The sidewalks are quiet with most city goers settled in their offices now. We pass my once often-frequented neighborhood bodega. I stop to admire the bouquets of flowers overflowing into the street in front of the store. I pick up a plastic-wrapped package of yellow tulips and inhale deeply.

"I used to buy a bouquet of tulips every Friday night on my way home," I say with a smile to my husband. "They always made me happy."

"I'll plant you a garden full of tulips when we get back to Green Briar. Will that make you happy, Devon?"

"Yes," I breathe as my heart turns over in my chest. I replace the flowers and wrap my arms around his neck. "I could not possibly love you more, McKennon Kelly."

"I aim to please, miss," he drawls, before planting an oh-so gentle kiss on my lips. "Now, where's this apartment of yours?"

I thread my fingers through his and lead him another block up.

"There," I say, pointing to a window at the tippy top of a pre-war building. The building was built before elevators were invented, and my legs ache reflecting on the five-flight walk up I used to make several times a day.

"Which one?" McKennon shades his eyes from the sun and looks up.

"The third window over across the top. It was the first apartment I could afford on my own in Manhattan. It was small, but it was all mine. I lived in New Jersey with a roommate before I moved here. Hell of a commute over to the city every day. It was exhausting, so I signed the lease here when I met Ev and my writing career started to take off," I say. A swell of pride rushes through me at the memory.

"Looks like you had a nice view. Pretty, full-grown trees lining this street," McKennon replies.

"I used to sit out on that fire escape right there and watch the birds in those very trees," I whisper.

"Figured you might," McKennon murmurs, brushing a finger along my cheek. "I can just imagine you sitting up there thinking about your future."

"How do you know me so well?"

"Just do," he hums. "Now about that brunch. Shall we?"

"Yes, yes! They have the best pancakes. They are huge, and you can have them filled with anything you can think of!"

"Sounds interesting. Lead the way."

A few blocks later, we are sitting at a sunny two-top facing each other. The warm light pours through the ceiling to floor windows and the pale yellow walls of the diner only add to the glow. Fresh flowers adorn the tables and New York memorabilia lines the walls. I don't recognize any of the servers or cooks, but I'm not sure why I should expect to. Everything turns over fast in New York City. A server arrives, delivers coffee, and takes our order.

"It hasn't changed a bit. I've written many articles here," I say, taking a sip of my coffee.

"I can see why it appeals to you, Mrs. Kelly. It is very cheery in here," McKennon replies, taking a sip from his mug.

"Exactly. Did you know that the color yellow is known as the most energetic of the warm colors and is associated with laughter, hope, and sunshine?"

"Didn't know that. Learn somethin' new from you every day," McKennon drawls with a smile, but it suddenly fades away.

"What? What's wrong?" I ask.

McKennon ponders me for a moment, rubbing his strong chin between his forefinger and thumb, then casts his eyes into his coffee cup.

"Do you miss this? This city? This place? Your own apartment? Your old life?" he asks, quietly.

The sunlight pouring in the window illuminates his down-turned face. I examine its smooth contour, the rigid jaw line, the perfectly dished nose, the slight stubble of a day-old shave prickling from a square chin. His hair is dark beneath his cowboy hat and showing the signs of an overdue haircut, twisting into slight curls at the base of his skull. The blue eyes that look like weather flick up to my face. He is so alarmingly well-proportioned. It is still heart-stopping.

My husband is the most beautiful man I've ever laid my eyes on.

Ev is right. My husband could do justice to any magazine spread she might pitch him for, although he'd never agree to something like an advertisement or a billboard. McKennon's aversion to using his looks for such things doesn't bother me one bit. It means his body, his face, his soul are all for me.

Nobody else. Just me.

"When I left New York, I thought I was running away. Little did I know I was running toward exactly what I need."

"And what do you need, miss?"

"You."

"Me?" he asks, pointing a finger toward his chest.

"You. It's that simple," I murmur with a grin.

He gazes into my eyes for a long moment, and my heart swells when the confident smile returns to his face.

"I couldn't be happier with where my life has taken me, McKennon," I assure, catching his hand, touching his wedding band, and then kissing his knuckles.

"Music to my ears, Mrs. Kelly. Music to my ears."

After sharing a healthy plate of buttermilk pancakes bursting with fresh blueberries and homemade syrup, McKennon and I bid my old life goodbye and head for the airport. All I want to do is go home.

Green Briar is home now.

43

"Hurry, you two," I hear Sterling bark as McKennon and I retrieve our bags from the airport conveyer belt. "You're gonna miss it!"

"What's going on, Sterling?" McKennon asks as we hustle up to him.

"Now that you got that son of mine settled, you have another matter to deal with! Sophia sent me to the airport to fetch you. Willa's in labor."

"Right now?" I gasp.

"Right now," Sterling affirms.

"Goodness! Let's get going then," I yelp with excitement.

"Truck's right outside," Sterling replies. "Let's go."

My heart is pumping as McKennon hurls our suitcases into Sterling's truck bed. I can't wait to see the first M&D Kelly Quarter Horse foal come into this world.

"Sophia's with the vet right now," Sterling tells McKennon as he slips into the driver's seat and shifts into gear. McKennon nods and reaches a hand back into the quad cab to take mine. As Sterling speeds off toward Green Briar, my husband gives my fingers a squeeze and tosses me a heavenly smile over his shoulder.

I can't wait to get home.

"You two have a good eye together," Sterling says, waltzing into the barn. "M&D Quarter Horses is showing a lot of promise."

"Means a lot, Sterling," McKennon replies.

"Oh, my dears! You're here. You're finally home!" Sophia chirps, flowing down the aisle to greet us.

She kisses McKennon on the cheek and gives me a gentle hug.

"How was New York? How is JD?"

"New York was, er, interesting. JD seems to be getting along just fine. We'll give you the full scoop over dinner, Sophia. The question right now is how's Willa doing?"

"It's a healthy baby boy," Dr. Hamilton says before Sophia can answer. He slides the stall door closed behind him and wipes his hands on a towel.

McKennon and I look at each other with wide eyes.

"We missed it!" I cry as my heart plummets in my chest.

"Plenty more foals comin', Devon," McKennon assures with a smile.

"But it was Willa. It was Willa's first baby. I wanted to be here for her," I murmur.

"I know you are disappointed, but it looks like Doc and Sophia handled everything perfectly in our absence. Plus, you're here now," McKennon says softly.

"Thank you, Dr. Hamilton," I insert, trying to mask my discontent at missing the birth.

"My pleasure. The colt is up on his feet and walking around. I don't expect any issues," Dr. Hamilton says. "Willa had as good a birth as I've ever seen. McKennon knows the drill with foals, but if any of you have any questions, call my office."

"Will do," McKennon replies, shaking our vet's hand.

"I'll be back in a few days for a routine check in on mama and baby," Dr. Hamilton adds before tipping his hat and heading for his truck.

"Come on. Let's go see our first foal," McKennon instructs, nudging me toward Willa's stall.

My disappointment disappears when I peek between the bars on the door. I purse my lips and tilt my head slightly in an examination of the brand-new colt.

McKennon saunters up behind me and stands close enough that I can feel his heat radiate against me. When he puts his hands on my hips, butterflies swoop in my stomach like they always do, and I smile. Our tiny foal is quivering in the corner behind Willa's bulging belly. I make a kissing noise with my mouth, and Willa whinnies to me.

"You did a good job, Willa," I coo. "Your baby is so handsome."

"He's the spitting image of his mama," McKennon asserts with pride. "When he grows up, we'll have a Palomino stallion to add to our breeding program."

"We are so lucky," I say, tipping my head back on McKennon's chest.

"Indeed, we are," McKennon murmurs, kissing the top of my head.

"Green Briar's never been so full of life. Welcome to the world, golden boy," Sophia chimes, looking at the tiny Palomino colt, all legs and lashes, blinking up at her from behind Willa.

"The future's so bright, you're gonna have to invest in some shades," Sterling chuckles, giving McKennon a slap on the back. "Congratulations, son."

"Thanks for all of your help around here while we've been gone."

"Thanks for looking after that bull riding son of mine," Sterling replies. "He's in a tough business. I know injury is part of the game, but it sure soothed my nerves knowing you two were out there checking up on him and reporting back to us."

"Speaking of reports, I expect a full update on JD's condition this evening. Dinner will be served at 7 p.m. sharp. Please join us tonight, Sterling." Sophia adds.

"I'll be there. I'm looking forward to getting the full scoop. Although I feel awfully relieved just knowing JD is going to recover. I was having some awful flashbacks of my brother and ..." Sterling's voice trails off.

"I know," McKennon whispers, putting a hand on his heart and pointing at the ceiling.

Sterling's expression is stoic. He's clearly thinking of his daughter's passing. He offers McKennon his open palm. As they pump hands and share a moment, I wander away to Faith's stall.

"You're an auntie, Faith," I whisper to my mare. I kiss her velvet nose, trying to put thoughts of Madison out of my mind.

After bidding Sophia and Sterling goodbye until dinner, McKennon struts down the aisle toward me. He looks so handsome in the tight red and black plaid shirt that is sculpted to his torso, sleeves rolled up to the elbow, cowboy hat tipped low and over his brow accentuating his alluring eyes.

"Come," he instructs, holding his hand out to me. I take it, and he leads me down the aisle. He is quiet, and I fear he is lost in some kind of memory of his late wife. He opens Willa's stall door with a squeak.

The colt takes flight and races a circle around the stall, kicking bedding into the air. McKennon ignores the fearful actions of the young equine and escorts me to the opposite corner of the stall. He motions toward the ground with a jut of his chin. Silently, we sit down in the deep bedding. After our golden boy settles back next to his mother, we chuckle to each other. I smile at McKennon, and the moment stretches. He bends the brim of his cowboy hat before shifting toward me in the bedding. I bite my lower lip.

"I love you, wife," McKennon breathes, sapphire eyes locked on my face.

My heart sets to racing.

McKennon Kelly loves me.

"I never tire of hearing you say that, husband. I love you, too."

"Count on hearing it several times a day for the rest of your life," McKennon assures, touching my cheek.

Unable to resist, I remove his cowboy hat and run my fingers through his hair. I lean in and kiss his mouth gently. McKennon returns my kiss with equal gentleness. Wordlessly, I lift my shirt up my back.

We don't need words.

I toss my shirt aside and turn my attention to his. I unbutton it slowly and plant little kisses as I go. Once it's open, my hands trail his bare chest, fingertips grazing his pectoral muscles, over his belly button, down his happy trail to the button at the front of his jeans. When I pop it open, McKennon groans and boosts my body onto his hips. I sling my arms around his neck.

"He might be too young to see this, Devon," McKennon chuckles. The colt is hiding beneath Willa's tail, peeking at us from behind his lashes.

"Willa, cover his eyes," I giggle, moving toward McKennon's mouth again. When McKennon's hands travel over my body, I sigh at his touch. He lays me down in the freshly bedded stall. The shavings are prickly on my skin, but the sensation is nothing compared to the overwhelming tidal wave of desire I feel for my husband right now.

Cowboy, take me away.

It isn't until we sit down to dinner, and are facing Sophia and Sterling's expectant stares as they wait for our debrief of New York, that I realize I can't remember when I last took my birth control pill. My mind retraces the whirlwind of the wedding, the honeymoon, JD's injury, and the resulting trip to Manhattan.

I don't have a clue.

44

JD

I'm still not sure how I got roped into all of this. That's how I feel – *roped* like a steer at the end of a cowboy's lasso. I feel like a raging bovine, twisting, turning, and wanting to run away, but held in place by the line tied around the saddle horn.

I'm trying not to think of the circuit and all the bull riding events I'll be missing during my recovery, but I just can't help it. I feel sick knowing the World Champion title and that cool million has slipped through my fingers. I wish I were on the road with the cowboys heading for the next tour stop.

My accident has helped me understand why a man would want revenge on an animal. I think about the bull that killed my uncle. I think about Charming crushing my sister. I get why my father has a bull's blood on his hands, and why McKennon almost had Charming's. I have a mind to track down Cork Screw. He put me in this position. That bull is responsible for the misery I'm experiencing right now. My mind is racing all right, and I follow the thoughts as they travel in a different direction.

McKennon and Devon are back at Green Briar, and it makes my gut clench. Thoughts of home bubble up and part of me wishes I were there, too. Yet, another part of me is excited about the career Ev has designed for me. It's always been my dream to see my name in lights, and I have while on the bull riding circuit, but this thing Ev has done for me is something else entirely.

Worst of all, though, are these unfamiliar feelings I have for Ev. They are simply unexplainable. My head is a whirl as I hobble from room to room, following Ev as she hustles around the apartment.

As usual, I can't keep my eyes off her body. That wave of fire-engine hair tumbles around her shoulders as she works, and I wonder if I'll ever have the chance to bed her again.

"There," Ev says, breaking me from my chain of thoughts. She stands in the hallway between the guest room and what was once her office. "I hope this is suitable."

"It's awful kind of you to do this for me, Ev," I reply, shifting my gaze from my room to the space she's transformed for me to work in with my physical therapist. "I'm feeling a little guilty about taking over your office."

There is softness in her eyes when I say it. It's unlike her. She steps to me and kisses my cheek. There's a hesitation on her part for just a moment, as if she'd like me to take her in my arms. I don't though. I'm not sure I have any right to. Wouldn't mind it in the least. I've been ogling her for a while now, but I don't go there.

"Nothing but the best for my star client." She steps away, composes herself, and gets back into business mode. "I need you back on your feet because your modeling career is taking off."

"That so?" I think about tomorrow's physical therapy appointment, rub my shoulder, and wince.

"JD, are you in pain? Do you want me to get your prescription?" Ev asks, concerned.

"Nah. I'll get through it. How's about we take a break from all of this?" I reply. Abandoning my shoulder, I massage my temple. I'm tired of thinking.

"We can do that," she says with a smile.

"That'll do," I add with a nod and a wink. I do not trust my smile so much these days, so I don't offer her one. After a beat, I add,

"Thank you for everything you are doin' for me ... everything you *have* done for me, Ev."

I'm afraid she's going to admonish me for saying it so much, but a sudden ease washes over her face. She nods, turns, and starts down the hall.

I follow her into the kitchen, and she dials a number.

"Who are you calling?"

"I'm ordering dinner."

About 45 minutes later, I am sitting in the living room cross-legged at her coffee table on the fluffy rug.

"Still can't believe you can get any darn thing you want delivered to your door in this city," I say as Ev pads into the living room with two white bags of Chinese food that's just been brought to her door.

"There are some advantages to living in the city," she replies with a wink.

"Dang amazing, I tell you," I say, poking around in the bags and pulling out cartons as Ev wanders back into the kitchen. She returns with a beer, an uncorked bottle of wine, and a glass. She hands me the brew, sits on the opposite side of me, and pours her wine.

"Plates?" I ask.

"I like to eat out of the carton," she replies, taking a sip of from her glass.

"Nice." I give her a smile. I like her best when she's willing to let some slack out of the rope that's got her so wound tight.

She opens her carton and expertly pops a piece of broccoli in her lovely mouth with chopsticks.

"I ain't using those wooden sticks. Not when fingers work just fine." I grab a spring roll between two fingers and slather it in sauce. I shove the whole thing in my mouth.

"I hear you there, cowboy. I suppose fingers are way less complicated." She still scrunches her little nose at my antics, though. I watch as she dunks her own roll in the sauce and bites it perfectly in half from her chopsticks. "I do like to use my manners though," she adds after she's finished chewing.

"Hell with manners," I chuckle, shoving another sauce-laden roll in my mouth. "This stuff is good!"

She opens her laptop and turns it to me. I read the opening article on the National Bull Riders Association website. It reads, *"NBR: Fans rally around fan-favorite JD McCall after Madison Square Garden event injury. In the championship round, JD McCall was hung up in his bull rope following his 88-point ride. Paramedics examined McCall in the arena before sending him to the hospital. McCall suffered a concussion, a separated shoulder, and rib fractures. McCall remained in the hospital for several days and will be out of competition for at least three months."*

I shift my eyes from the screen, and my stomach turns.

"Didn't need to read that," I grumble. "I'd rather enjoy this food here." I'm not really hungry anymore though.

"This is good news, JD!" Ev chirps. "Your sponsors love that the fans are with you. It's going to keep your campaign alive because of the support you are getting, even if you will be out of the arena recovering for a while. Sponsors are all about the fans, and if they are sticking with you, well then, the sponsorships will stick, too."

I find a way to conjure up my appetite, and we eat companionably for a while. I take a swig of my beer and mull over what Ev said. I feel something like gratitude well up in my chest.

The fans and the sponsors are sticking with me. No doubt, Ev has something to do with both things.

"So, what exactly is it you do again, Ev?" I ask.

"I'm your agent," she replies with a smirk.

"I mean —," I huff. "I don't really know what you do all day at your office. You aren't here much. Enlighten me?" I raise my eyebrows.

"Mitchell Media Group is part agency, part publishing house, and part public relations firm. My company is a hybrid of the things I do best. I came into some money a while back. I don't like being told what to do, so I built a business where I do the telling. I like being the boss."

"And you are darn good at what you do, Everly Mitchell. You got

New York City to plaster pictures of this country cowboy all over it. That's sheer power," I chuckle.

"Stop teasing me," Ev murmurs. A hint of blush has reached her cheeks. This isn't like her at all. She's showing vulnerability. She looks down and stirs inside her nearly empty carton with her chopsticks. Something swells in me every time Ev reveals this softer side of herself. It's rare, and I feel inspired to act. I start to get up, and she watches me with those lovely eyes of hers.

Green, like mine, and a bit sad and a bit curious.

It takes something to rise from my seated position on the floor because my ribs ache, my shoulder pulses, and my head still rings occasionally. It's ringing right now. I make my way to her side of the table and gently take her chin with my fingertips.

"You are an extraordinary woman, Ev. I would never tease you about something like that. You built a business. A very successful business. You can make something out of nothing with the magic you possess. Look what you've done for me. I'm on freaking billboards. I'm in a celebrity gossip magazine. Look what you've done for Devon. You got her a book deal. You are simply amazing to me."

I can't help it. I'm telling her the truth. I want to tell her the truth. I sense she hasn't been complimented nearly enough in her lifetime, especially not by me. Ev takes my hand from her chin and kisses my palm.

"Thank you, JD," she whispers. I do a double-take when I think I've spotted a tear. She sniffs and rubs her eye with the back of her hand.

I tuck my hands in my pockets, chew my cheek, and bob from toe to heel. The moment feels heavy, and I don't know what to do with myself. Emotions aren't my strong suit. Neither is honesty, but I'm waist-deep in both right now. I start to clear the coffee table, but grunt at the lightning bolt of pain that shoots through my shoulder.

"Here, I'll help you," Ev offers, clamoring to her feet.

Together, we clean up the place. I feel exhausted.

"Well, goodnight, then," I drawl at Ev's back. She's stacking what is left of our takeout in the refrigerator.

When she doesn't reply, I start toward the guest room, but Ev unexpectedly catches me by the elbow.

"Why don't you sleep in my room tonight? Let me take care of you. How much pain are you in right now, cowboy?"

"Gotta be honest, I'm in pretty rough shape."

"I'll be gentle, I promise," she whispers near my ear. When she nibbles my lobe, my eyebrows immediately shoot up, but it's hard to argue the point about my condition since all the blood just drained from my head into my groin.

This should be interesting.

45

When Ev pulls away to look at my face, her offer lingers between us. It's glimmering there in her emerald eyes, a question waiting for my answer. I nod, and she leads me by the hand to her bedroom.

Once inside, she pushes me gently to the edge of the bed and undresses me. My lips clip up as she slowly undresses herself. A bolt of pride shoots through me when I discover I am already rising to the occasion. I thank my lucky stars I resisted the temptation to take those painkillers the doctor prescribed. They would have made this moment impossible. I'm still praying my body can get through this though. I am determined to focus on the moment. I act casual, mask my pain, and scoot up the bed so I can rest my torso against the headboard. I focus on appreciating the view of my redheaded vixen at last, only in her birthday suit.

To my relief, Ev appears to want to make things easy on me. She slips beneath the soft sheets, straddles me, and smiles at the realization that I'm clearly ready in the best of ways. I can't wait for this. I've wanted this opportunity to be with her again for too long.

Ev presses her hands to my hips and skims them up my side. Her feather light touches set my skin ablaze, and my heart hammers as her glossy red hair falls around her shoulders. She traces my shoulder blades with her fingertips, leaving hot trails on my skin. She pulls back, and my eyes sweep over her perfect breasts.

"Do you like what you see?" Ev inquires.

"Very much," I reply.

"We are going to take this slowly, cowboy. We don't want to do any more damage to what's already been done, do we?"

"No, ma'am," I breathe, reaching to meet her mouth with mine.

As we exchange whisper-soft kisses, I'm grateful she isn't expecting a rumble tumble affair. We've certainly had those, but my body isn't at full strength.

My face feels hot. Blood is pumping behind my eyes. Ev parts her lips slightly and sighs when I lightly tangle my tongue with hers. This has the makings of a different kind of interaction between us. It's a battle to contain myself, with Ev straddling me.

God, she's beautiful.

I lift my hips in angst. Ev's green eyes turn sinister when I buck beneath her.

She presses her lips to my forehead and trails them to the tip of my nose. She kisses my cheek, nibbles an earlobe, and then takes her tongue to travel the length of my neck. I press a kiss to her chest, linger a moment on each breast. Her mouth continues to travel my body. I feel sweet agony as she moves to my stomach. Her tongue circles my belly button, makes its way toward my thighs, and momentarily finds me there. I let my head fall back, and my fingers find their way to tangle in her hair. Just as I am about to break, she shifts gears and begins retracing the route her mouth had taken. I am still, so still. I can barely wait for her next move.

When her eyes settle on my mouth, I can't wait for her to kiss it. Ev softly takes my lower lip between her teeth. Finally, she kisses my mouth deeply, and we both unleash the hunger we've been holding back. I can feel her shiver when I run my fingers up her spine.

Has her skin always been this soft?

"It's been too long since we've done this," she confides.

"I have to have you, Ev," I utter. "I can't wait any longer."

"Your wish is my command," she murmurs, unwrapping a package from the nightstand and expertly outfitting me with it. Gently, she positions above my hips and lowers herself down.

A rush comes over me. In a tidal wave of pleasure, my mouth collapses on her neck. She sighs into the top of my head as we start to move together. I ache everywhere, not in pain, but the good kind of ache. Every part of me is energized, turned on. It's the first time I've felt good since that damn bull tore me up in the arena.

Ev lovingly takes her time, and we rock in sweet union. Her mouth is warm as she finds mine. Our matching green eyes meet in pure pleasure. It suddenly occurs to me that this is the best love making of my life.

Love making? I'm losing my mind. I don't make love.

I've been with plenty of women before, but this feels *different*.

Stop thinking!

I shove thoughts of love out of my mind and work on grinding harder without injuring myself. I push us both to the edge, and at last, it comes for both of us.

Ev cries out one last time, and we crash against each other, panting. I clench my eyes and lie back with a sigh, realizing I am fully satisfied for the first time.

There's something lingering, though. It's a soft ache in my heart. It's a new feeling, something I can't quite put a finger on. For the longest while, I needle over this unfamiliar sensation as we simply lie in each other's arms, bodies buzzing, me stroking her hair, and listening to the noisy sounds of the city below us.

Love?

46

After a while, Ev rolls to her side and props up on an elbow. When our eyes meet, I feel my heart turn over inside my chest. She is a vision with all that red hair framing her face. I find her utterly arresting, and I'm quite certain we just made love. I didn't know I had it in me.

Until now.

"Tell me about your sister," Ev muses, tracing a fingertip along my jaw.

"Aw, hell."

She's trying to get me to open up.

I roll over to fish the secret pack of smokes from my jeans bunched up on the floor beside the bed. I've been sneaking smokes out on the balcony while Ev is at the office. I tap one out of the package and put it between my lips.

Ev plucks it out of my mouth.

"Hey now!" I holler.

Unfazed, she snaps it in two, tosses the pieces over her shoulder, then resumes her position with interest.

"Tell me about your sister, please."

"Madi," I sigh. "She was a good one. Good horsewoman, great in the show pen, but she liked chasing cans best. Really pissed off our daddy."

"Chasing cans? As in men?"

I chuckle.

"Nah, nothing like that. She certainly had her share of cowboys calling, but she was always looking for the one. That one was McKennon. I reckon you read all about that in Devon's book." Ev nods. "Barrel racing is what I mean by chasing cans. It's what us bull riders call the barrel racing girls on the rodeo circuit."

"Do you miss her?"

"Every single day."

"I know the feeling," she whispers.

"What do you mean?" I probe.

A look of alarm suddenly crosses her face.

"I changed my mind. Let's not tell our sad stories. Tell me about the bull riding circuit instead."

Indeed, it is a much easier topic, so I'm willing to oblige the shift in conversation. Although, I make a mental note that Ev seems to have some skeletons in her closet. Not surprising really, but I wouldn't mind knowing more about her.

The real her.

"Well, you've seen the worst that can happen. Every bull rider has an accident coming for him. Mine happened to be tangled up alongside 2,000 pounds of mean with my hand caught in my bull rope. Bull riding is a game of inches that's going a hundred miles an hour."

"I thought we were going to discuss brighter things? It was terribly hard to see you like that. I was afraid I was going to lose you." Ev is silent for the tick of a clock. Her eyes are soft, but I can tell from her expression that she is far away. Her mind is clearly somewhere else.

"Hey, hey now. You aren't going to lose me. Where'd you go just then?" I ask, reaching up to stroke her cheek.

"It's nothing. It's just that I was really worried about you." Ev sniffs and tosses her hair over her shoulder. "Enough of that. What was your best ride?"

"Well, there was this red beauty, I tell ya. Older than my usual rides, but so smooth, yet at the same time, all twisty with plenty of buck."

"Where was this ride?" Ev asks.

"After a wedding, in a barn, best dang ride of my life."

"Come on. Be serious," Ev scolds.

"I am serious. You're the best ride I've ever had. Top-notch," I murmur, running my fingers through her hair. I lift my mouth toward hers. There is a moment of hesitation on her part, but then our lips meet.

"You don't believe me?" I ask when I pull away.

"Oh, you're good, cowboy," she laughs. "I'm sure that line has worked millions of times before."

I know she doesn't believe me. Hell, if I were Ev, I wouldn't believe me either, but I really am speaking the truth.

"Why do you ride bulls, JD?"

I shrug my shoulders, ego a bit bruised, and contemplate the answer to her question.

Why do I ride bulls?

"I guess for the rush. I don't know. Being able to make the eight kinda makes you feel like you'll be young forever, but mainly it's redeeming my uncle. He was aiming for that cool million. I want to win that buckle for him."

"Oh, your uncle. How do we keep winding up on dark subjects?" Her face gets pale and that faraway look washes through her eyes again.

"Shh. Enough talking for now," I whisper, nibbling her neck. She sighs, and it sounds happy despite her expression.

"You know what makes me feel young, provides a similar rush, and hopefully lasts longer than eight seconds?" she asks, tossing the sheets off our bodies.

I instantly understand what she is getting at. I arch an eyebrow, grin, and crush my lips to hers. We meet in the middle, where no words are necessary.

After we do the deed for the second time, we lie together in the afterglow. I feel worlds away from my injury on Cork Screw, from my thoughts of Green Briar, and worry about missing out on the rest the tour. Ev traces gentle circles on my bare chest. Her head rests on my shoulder. I play with her hair.

"Tell me about the girl," Ev says, interrupting the silence.

"What girl?" I ask.

"Right, there's been so many," she teases. "Tell me about the one that reminds you of Devon. The one that put you off lasting relationships."

This is unexpected.

"Well, uh, long story short, I had my big great love in my teens, and ... well, she died," I grumble, clenching my teeth.

"What happened?" Ev asks, gently.

I don't want to talk about this.

"I haven't thought about this in a long while," I say, shaking my head.

"I'm sorry. I shouldn't pry."

"No, it's all right," I reply with a sigh. "It was an accident at her family's farm. She was tossing bales out of the hayloft. That girl was tough. She was a damn good cowgirl. The teenage-me thought I was going to marry that girl."

Ev slips her hand into mine, and I take a deep breath.

"Anyway, she was out in the barn alone, feeding the horses. There wasn't anything unusual about that. She threw bales down from up near the rafters all of her life, but somehow, on that particular day, she lost her balance. The assumption is that her hand caught in the baling twine, and she went tumbling from the loft to the concrete floor below. When she didn't come in for dinner, her parents finally found her and called an ambulance. She was unconscious ... she never woke up."

"I'm so sorry," Ev croaks.

"I held her hand when her parents decided to take her off life support. I swore off ever lovin' someone after that. It hurt so dang much."

Ev gasps and covers her mouth. She looks ashen. I can't read her expression.

Is it recognition?

"Are you all right, Ev?"

"Don't worry about me. This is about your loss, JD. Please just continue."

"That girl was the first death in my life," I carry on, although I'm not sure why I do. "Unfortunately, not the last. I stopped racking my brain for reasons it happened, but when Devon turned up at Green Briar, I thought I saw a ghost. She looks an awful lot like Carrie."

"Does Devon know any of this?" Ev asks.

"No. Devon doesn't know. McKennon doesn't know about it either. It's a story I've buried deep. Now and then, though, I'll look at Devon and the memories will sneak up on me. I figure that's why I feel so compelled to look after Devon. Maybe at one point, I felt romantically toward her, but not anymore. She's my sister," I continue. "I don't know why I'm telling you this."

I drag a palm over my face. This is too much truthfulness for me to handle. I shift in the bed, uneasy with retelling the past, and attempt to regain my balance. My emotions are all over the place right about now. Ev hit a nerve, and I intend to return the favor.

"Oh, JD. I didn't mean to get us back on that line of talk. I just ... I just wanted to hear about who you were before us."

Us?

"Your turn, Ev. I've told you some of my secrets. Let's hear some of yours. Tell me why *you* don't get involved?"

Ev looks like a deer in headlights. She's clearly reminiscing about a past I don't know anything about.

"I won't," she replies. "I refuse. Please ask me anything else."

At my question, the tough, accomplished woman unravels in the bed beside me. I can't help but soften as tears begin to trickle down her cheeks. I hand her the box of tissues from the bedside table, and she grabs one and dabs her eyes.

"Fine. How old are you? Is that safe territory?"

"I'll never tell," she replies with a slight smile.

"I'm fresh outta questions then. Tell me something, anything about yourself, Ev. I want to know you. I really do."

She sighs.

"I wanted kids once. I did believe in love."

"Now you don't?" I inquire. "You're young enough for love and children, I reckon."

"Life in the fast lane and at the helm of a successful company doesn't really support that," Ev says with a sniff.

"Just because you are older now doesn't mean that you can't have children one day." I stroke her cheek, and she waves me off.

"This is a silly conversation for me to be having with a playboy cowboy."

"I have the feeling you've lost something important to you ... someone, most likely. I know that look. I've been in those shoes."

Too many times.

"Maybe you're right, JD."

"I reckon you aren't gonna tell me, are you?"

She shakes her head and blows her nose into a tissue.

"Well, if you ever want to get that boulder off your chest, I can be a pretty darn good listener when I try. Ask Devon."

"I enjoyed having McKennon and Devon here," Ev says after a while. "It's obvious how much they love you, JD, and how much they love each other."

"Yeah, I have to admit those two are a darn good match. I might be ready to put the past behind me and have a little of what they have in my life," I reply, taking Ev's hand and kissing her knuckles.

Ev stiffens and pulls her hand away. I didn't mean to upset her with the comment. It's been relieving to talk to a woman about emotions and the past. This is unfamiliar territory for me. This is tricky. I take her hand again and hold it to my heart. I want to keep her in bed, keep her talking, understand her, but she wiggles her way out of my hold and slides out of bed, taking the duvet with her. She looks messy and wrecked.

Like my insides.

"I think it's time for you to go to the guest room now," she says, slipping into the bathroom and closing the door behind her.

47

B esides Ev and Erwin, my physical therapist, I haven't seen another soul in weeks. I've been cooped up in this luxury, sky rise apartment for so long that it's beginning to feel like a jail cell. Don't even get me started on being stuck in New York City. While I appreciate the phone calls from McKennon, Devon, Sophia, and my father, talking to them is making me miss the country and Green Briar even more fiercely, but at least there's money coming in because of my blooming modeling career.

I've become a freaking ping pong ball. Ev's apartment is the table, and she's holding the paddle. One minute she invites me into her bedroom, gets my emotions involved, and makes me think she wants to know me. The next minute, she's shutting me down and sending me back to the guest bedroom.

Ev changes things up so quickly, she might as well be a bull. Being with her is like when I'm in the ring and know I will not make the eight. The ride is slipping through my fingers. I can't read her, and I'm getting sick of it. Sick to death of the whole situation. I just want to feel normal, and be up and on my boots again, but I'm taking the rest of the season off from bull riding. It's not because I want to, I have to abide by the doctor's orders. At least that's what I tell myself.

And so, we've fallen into a strange routine. Sometimes we sleep together, and sometimes we don't. Ev goes to work, and I do my physical therapy. Ev clearly put in a request for a male therapist, and he scares the chaps off of me. Erwin is a giant. The man is ripped with muscles and wears bright, too-tight spandex outfits that make me cringe. He is never a second late for our sessions and barks orders at me incessantly.

I'm feeling edgy. Most days my only glimpse of Ev is of her heading out the door. We are in one of our dry spells, and she's not giving me any action. I can't stop wishing my therapist was female, but I reckon Ev wouldn't trust that. It's just that it would be nice to have another woman around, even if she were only my physical therapist.

I know Ev wouldn't want me getting it on with someone else under her roof. Yet, it would be nice to see if my smile might still make a lady swoon. Lord knows, I've tried it on Ev, but she's so single-minded about building my career that I think she's hardly noticed my smile at all. It's been the guest room for me for days now, and it irks me.

The frustration of sleeping separately, my damn injury, and being cooped up in this dang apartment with only Erwin as company is taking its toll on my masculinity. Rather than dive headlong into self-loathing, though, I cowboy up and attack my physical therapy like I once attacked the back of bulls. My only mission is to recover and recover fast.

Today, Ev has me set up at the kitchen counter to do another phone interview. I've done so many of them since I've been laid up that I can't even keep count. Ev wants me to keep the fans loyal by showing them I'm country tough, but also accessible. I've got my messaging points memorized. I figure the least I can do is keep my sponsors happy while I'm sitting the rest of the tour out. They seem to like the stats Ev sends over, analyzing the growth of my fan base and how regularly they tune in to hear me yack.

Thank heaven for my fans.

As she heads out the door for the office, Ev gives me a nod. She's good at making herself scarce. It doesn't matter. I know what to do. I pick up the headset, put it over my ears, and push the button to join the call. I get a briefing from the radio station's assistant. As usual, I am put on hold and wait in queue for a few minutes. I take a sip from the green smoothie Ev left for me on the counter.

"All right, Mr. McCall. I'm putting you through to the live line for your interview," the assistant chirps.

I clear my throat and wait for the show's host to introduce me.

"Welcome to Sports Factor. Our guest today is JD McCall. He is considered one of the elite riders on the National Bull Riders Tour — otherwise known as the major league of rodeo. Thank you for joining us today, JD."

"Glad to be here. Thank you for having me."

"Your injury report is long," the host continues. "You know what it feels like to tear a shoulder muscle, fracture a rib, and wrangle with a concussion. If you had pursued any other kind of athletic endeavor, your career might be in peril. But that's the beauty of bull riding, isn't it?"

"That's right. In bull riding, the risks are high, and that's in the back of your mind, but there's always an opportunity for another ride. Mentally and physically, it's tough going through an injury like this, but I'm working on rehabilitating my shoulder while my ribs heal, then I'll be back, ready to make the eight again."

I think.

"Even though fans won't be seeing you ride for the rest of the season, you've found another way to give them a glimpse of what you're up to. Isn't that right?"

"Yes, I feel blessed to have amazing fans and sponsors who are giving me something else to focus on while I'm off tour."

"You've been doing quite a bit of modeling during this time."

"That's right. It certainly helps to have a decent mug when the rest of me isn't working at full strength," I chuckle. The radio announcer does, too.

"You're living the dream," the host encourages. "You're featured in magazines representing the best brands in your sport. You have loyal fans rooting for you during your recovery, and you know that eventually you'll be back out there riding bulls."

"Yeah. I'm one lucky cowboy. Ever since I was knee high to a grasshopper, this is what I've wanted to do. I believe if you have a dream, you just have to keep working at it and not forget where you came from."

I complete the rest of the interview in a fog. I can't get the thought of that bull using me as a welcome mat out of my mind. I'm tired of talking about how Cork Screw wiped his hooves all over me and then stomped on me for good measure. I've had hundreds of rides in my career where nothing happened except that glorious moment of hearing the buzzer signaling a completed ride.

How did things get so out of hand?

Don't get me wrong, I've been thrown. I've been banged up really good, but I've never suffered a serious injury like this before. It's getting to my mind. All it took was one ride to throw my entire life off course. A simple slip of my bull rope, and here I am. Doing phoners in Ev's kitchen while the National Bull Riders Tour goes on without me.

I've been stuck in this void going on two months. I'm living with something unsettling. Something I don't want to admit to myself or anyone else. The truth is, I'm afraid I've lost my nerve for bull riding.

Furious, I slap my face at the thought of it and vow never to think it again.

48

Despite my concerns about the future, it's been a good week. I've been in Ev's bedroom more than I've been in the guest room, and that feels like a small victory. She hasn't gone dashing out the door near as much since I stopped asking her personal questions. I'm still struggling with the knowing of Everly Mitchell, but I've resigned myself to giving her sex if sex is all she wants. I'm not interested in anymore dry spells in that department.

I'll get the information I want out of her, eventually. I hope.

"Where are you going?" I ask.

"It's two in the afternoon, cowboy," Ev says, slipping out from under the sheets and wrapping up in her robe. "I can't stay in bed with you all day."

"How come?"

"Because this is becoming a nasty habit. I have work to do, JD."

"Don't tell me you don't enjoy lounging around in bed with me," I tease, propping up on an elbow and slipping her my megawatt smile.

"I never said that. And stop smiling like that at me," Ev barks, putting her fists on her hips.

"Come back to bed, Everly." I flip the sheet off of my naked body and give her a good look at what she's about to leave behind.

"I will not. Cover yourself up, JD."

She's playing hard to get, but I can see the longing in her eyes as they walk all over my exposed body.

"Please." I pat the mattress beside me.

"I really need to make an appearance at the office. My employees are probably playing solitaire on their desktops and neglecting the clients."

"Why crack the whip at work, when you can do it right here with a ready and willing cowboy?"

Ev's eyes become slits, and one corner of her mouth turns up wickedly.

"That's a very tempting offer. I'd like to whip some sense into you right now, but I really need to get some work done."

"Later then?" I ask. "I'm sure I can get that whip delivered before you get home."

"You're impossible."

Ev stomps off into her walk-in closet, and I lie back in the bed. I'm not able to keep the smirk off my face as I listen to her rustle around, covering up that perfect body of hers.

She reappears a time later, standing in front of me in a pencil skirt, fitted blouse, blazer, and high heels. Her face is freshly painted, and all that red hair is pulled back in a sleek bun. She's stunning. It's impossible not to stare at her, but she looks like she has a rod bolted to her spine. I sigh, knowing Ev is in work mode. I prefer her properly disheveled to this uptight, all-business version.

"I'll miss you while you're gone," I say.

"Good," she replies and slips out of the bedroom door.

After my late-day therapy session, I sit down in front of the television and prop my feet up. I'm feeling pretty dang proud of myself. I got the all clear from Erwin. I've regained full mobility in my shoulder. I'm pleased that my body is bouncing back better than expected, and my head doesn't ache like it used to. It's sweet relief. When I hear the key in the door, I put my feet on the floor and click off the set. I wasn't really watching, anyway. Just biding the time. My stomach flips the instant Ev comes in.

"Welcome home, honey. How was your day?" I ask, testing the waters. I know by now that Ev runs hot and cold. Some days, she is hard and sharp-edged, others, she's softer. I'm certain it has something to do with the fact that I've been housebound, and she is taking care of me. I imagine it isn't easy having someone like me in her home all the time. I was supposed to be a project, a pit-stop, not someone she comes home to, but this thing between us is starting to feel like a relationship.

Sort of.

"It was exhilarating." Ev breezes into the kitchen, tosses her blazer on the counter, and begins fishing around in the refrigerator.

"Wow, that good, huh?" I raise my eyebrows.

She's in a good mood.

I watch with interest as she retrieves two glasses, a bottle of champagne, and then dumps the contents of the icemaker bin into a silver bucket. She sweeps toward me and hands over the bottle, setting her laptop bag along with the glasses and ice bucket thing on the coffee table.

"I am quite pleased with myself right now," Ev says. The grin on her face has me grinning, too. "Let's celebrate. Pop the top on that, would you?"

"I have something to celebrate, too. I got a thumbs-up from Erwin today. I'm no longer a couch potato. Now that I have a clear brain scan and full mobility in my shoulder, I can get out of the apartment."

"JD, that is excellent news! I'm happy for you."

"So, what are you celebrating?" I ask, tearing away the foil and uncoiling the wire cage from the bottle. Ev slips her hand into her bag and pulls out a file folder.

"I've got some big plans for you."

Uh-oh.

"What do you have up your sleeve now, Ev?"

"I've been looking at additional revenue streams and ways to continue building your career while you are off tour," Ev says, spreading papers out on the table around me. "Modeling has been an excellent source of income, but I have my eyes on even bigger things for you. Have a look at this."

I smile when I see my headshot clipped inside one of the open folders.

"It's still amusing to see my mug all Hollywood like that," I reply.

"Hollywood is exactly it." She slaps the glossy photo with the back of her hand and points to what looks like a contract.

"What have you gotten me into?" I ask, tentatively.

"This is huge. I've just secured you a minor role in a movie, shooting right here in New York."

"What?" I cannot work my trembling fingers on the cork. "I'm not an actor!"

"It's a just small role. You won't have many lines. You just have to look handsome. You can do that easily," Ev assures.

"Aren't I supposed to audition for something like that?"

"Not when I represent you, you don't." Ev is pleased.

I am freaking out.

"Ev, this is too much," I murmur, setting the unopened bottle on the table. I rub my jaw.

"That's right. Too much. Too much money, that is. Let's review the contract, shall we?"

I swallow hard.

Acting? Staring at a camera during all these photo shoots is one thing, but a movie?

I know I told Ev I'd like to be a superstar at the wedding, but this is too much. I'm suddenly feeling untethered. My entire life has changed in the blink of an eye. Meeting Ev, coming to New York City, living in her place, the modeling, the sponsorships, the billboards, the bull riding accident, my recovery, being off tour, falling for Ev. I didn't intend for any of this.

How did I get here?

I feel like a rank bull just rocketed me to outer space. I see stars. I can hear Ev talking. She's excitedly flipping through the stack of paper on the table in front of me. She wags a pen in my general direction and points to a dotted line. My vision blurs. The room starts spinning. I feel myself falling forward, and then everything goes dark.

49

A cool, wet washcloth is on my forehead. My eyes flutter open, and Ev looks down at me from her perch on the edge of the couch. I groan and pinch the bridge of my nose.

"JD? Are you all right?"

"What happened?" I ask, tugging the cloth from my brow.

"I think you fainted."

"Fainted? Cowboys don't faint. I reckon I got lightheaded is all. Probably has something to do with that concussion Cork Screw gave me," I lie. I know it has nothing to do with the concussion. The doctor has already cleared my head.

"I see," Ev says. She reaches out and touches the newly healed scar at my hairline. "I was worried you would split this open again. You smacked your noggin good on the coffee table."

"Nothing a couple aspirin and a good night's sleep won't remedy," I murmur.

Now I'm fainting. What has become of me? I have to regain my dignity.

"You have dirty in your eyes," I drawl, shifting us into safer territory. Sex is always easier.

"And you have dirty in your eyes, too," Ev replies.

"Let's get dirty right here, right now," I suggest.

"I'm not doing dirty with you anymore."

"What?"

Hot, cold, hot, cold.

"I had a temporary lapse of judgment over the last few weeks. I have to ask you to sleep in the guest room from now on."

"This again? Come on, Ev. Aren't we passed this? I care about you. I think you care about me, too."

"I am not the sort of woman you want, JD." I take the lift of her brow as a subtle challenge to prove her wrong.

"I'll be the judge of that," I answer roughly.

"I can't, JD. I can't do this with you. I'm sorry. I can't get involved with my clients."

"For heaven's sake, Ev. We are already involved. I'm not your freakin' client either. *You* brought *me* here. You did all of this *to* me. I did this because you wanted me to."

"That may be so, but I represent you."

"That's it?"

"That's it," she says, rising from the couch. "I'm going to bed."

Is she kidding me right now?

"You're giving me whiplash, woman," I reply, aiming to hit a nerve. "Has anyone diagnosed you as bipolar?"

Ev stiffens, and her face goes blank. I brace myself for the back-lash. Astonished, I watch her quietly put the unopened champagne back in the refrigerator.

"You can sign the contract tomorrow," she says icily from the kitchen. "Also, now that you've got the all clear, we have an event to attend together this weekend. I expect you to be on your best behavior. Good night, JD."

I run my hand over my face, shift on the sofa, and stare at Ev's back as she walks down the hall. I want Ev. The puzzle of it is, the less I try to care about her, the more I do.

When the bedroom door clicks behind her, a wave of disgust surges beneath my skin. I look at the contract on the table and shove it to the floor. I stand up, kick the sheets of paper around Ev's living room, and stomp to the guest room.

"Good night, Ev!" I yell and slam the door as hard as I can.

I haven't slept in the guest room in a while now, and I'm not looking forward to it. I know sleep is going to elude me. I strip naked and climb into the bed, anyway. Beneath the sheets, I toss and turn for what feels like hours. I look at the clock on the bedside table. It *has* been hours. I can't seem to find any comfort without Ev beside me.

My unexpected, extended stay with Ev has got my mind all mucked up. I've never spent this much time with one woman. I may not know Ev's secrets, but I know her routines, her habits, what drives her. And I like it. I can't help thinking that meeting Ev and winding up with the injury that kept me here is the kind of fate Devon is always talking about. It's like the universe wants me to realize what I've been missing without a steady lady in my life.

Did I have to get hurt to get to know Ev?

I huff, flip to my stomach, and cover my head with a pillow. If Cork Screw hadn't dragged me around that arena, I would have been outta New York City lickety-split. Ev would have been a one and done notch on my belt, just another number on my long list of women.

Being Ev's project is making me realize what it's like to be used, and I don't like it one bit. I hate admitting to myself that I've been doing the same thing to women for a very long time. I throw the pillow across the room, flip on my back, and stare at the ceiling.

What is happening to me?

The next day, I notice Ev has collected the contract I'd scattered around her living room. It's neatly stacked on the kitchen counter with a pen on top. I give it the finger.

I hate being her project.

50

Ev expertly avoids me for the next two days. She's gone before I drag myself out of the guest room and doesn't return until evening. When I hear the key in the lock, I retreat to the spare room and leave her full access to her home. My gut tells me she isn't interested in tripping over the likes of me after a long day at the office. I feel even more like an intruder now that we aren't even talking to each other. My mind's too scrambled to face her.

I use my get-out-of-jail free card from my doctor and my physical therapist to keep myself busy. I've taken to strolling the city streets during the day.

Ev slipped through my fingers. So what!

New York is full of beautiful women. As I wander the sidewalks, I notice one after another. It would be so much easier to go back to my playboy ways. I've considered throwing good sense to the wind, talking a lady up, and bringing that lucky someone back to Ev's apartment to test out the guest room mattress. That would show Everly Mitchell that she hasn't gotten under my skin, and prove I've still got my swagger, but I change my mind each time I'm about to strut up to another woman.

What happened to me?

Instead, tucked behind sunglasses and my ball cap, I busy myself with seeking out and admiring my billboards. I get a kick out of seeing my face around town. When I tire of that, I wander around Central Park, petting people's dogs and watching the carriage horses cart people around. I'm still missing the country terribly, but it's nice to be out in open air.

In the evenings, I mull over what I'm going to say to Ev. We are going to have to talk eventually at this stupid event she's got us going to. I know nothing about having a serious conversation with a woman. I've never really had to. It isn't a particular skill I needed to learn because all I've ever had to do is smile in order to get my way with the ladies. Most my life has been spent on the road traveling for the bull riding tour. My days involved making the eight followed by nights in bars, where a man like me could meet a buckle bunny who would be happy to make the bed in my clunker trailer less lonely. I remember those times all too well, although now it feels like someone else's life. If I hadn't gotten hurt, and was still living it, I wouldn't be dealing with the Ev situation right now.

Still, regardless of how different or ill-suited the two of us together seem, the chemistry between us is real. It's like nothing I've ever experienced. I can't help thinking that by the way Ev responds to me, it might be the same for her, even though she denies it. It feels so weird to suddenly want a woman so much. I've never considered myself able to fall for someone, but there's no denying I have.

I still don't know what I am going to say to her though.

Saturday has finally rolled around, and I'm high above the city streets on a massive rooftop. I'm feeling glum over the fact that Ev sent a car to retrieve me. It wasn't my plan to arrive at this spectacle separately. I'd wanted to get a word in with her before I had to parade around, meetin' and greetin'. I anxiously search the crowd for my redhead, but I have yet to see her here. I shift my hat down low over my brow.

What is a cowboy like me doing at a glitzy New York City pool deck party?

I watch Ev's niece, Missy, flit about the crowd, networking with the fashion industry executives. I'm sure she and Ev rode here together. For the last half hour, I've played my part wandering among the guests, tipping my hat, and shaking hands with the various folks Ev has introduced me to since I came to this forsaken city. I reckon it would please Missy to know that I'm using some of the manners she taught me in Ev's kitchen. Across the illuminated pool, Martin Bloomberg catches my eye through the crowd of partygoers. I haven't seen him since the night at his restaurant and bend my brim to acknowledge him, but I'm not all that thrilled to be his next target.

I've got my mind on conversing with someone else.

It must be my lucky night because Missy zeros in on Martin. I can't help but smile as she heads him off before he can cross the deck to speak with me.

That Missy is a real go-getter.

Stealing a moment for myself, I lean against the bar, finish my third glass of whiskey, signal for another, and mouth 'top shelf' to the bartender.

I am getting used to the good stuff.

When Ev and I first started off together, I never imagined any of this. Ev certainly lives in a highbrow world. I am a part of that world now. I look at the larger-than-life-sized poster of my naked torso pasted to the side of a Manhattan high-rise across the street and don't feel fazed. Seeing myself posted all over town and beneath ground in the subways took some getting used to at first, but the streak of joy at seeing one always feels the same as it did the first time. I hope that electric feeling never fades. Ev has certainly made me a nice nest egg, and I'm glad to be adding to it with my face for the time being, rather than busting up my body on bulls.

I thought I would miss the action of the bull riding circuit, but truth be told, the flashing of those light bulbs during a photo session is all the excitement I need right now. I think about that unsigned movie contract and shudder. Turning my thoughts to the task at hand, I scan the crowd for Ev's head of crimson hair again. Instantly, it's as if the crowd parts, and standing at another bar across the party is Ev. I drink her in: tall, thin, and shapely with emerald green eyes and razor-sharp cheekbones. She notices me over the shoulder of a guest she is speaking to.

The woman is utterly remarkable.

Trying to contain myself, I stroll to where Ev is standing, a fresh drink refill in hand, and brush her elbow. At my touch, Ev politely excuses herself from the conversation she's having.

"Can we talk?" I ask.

"We are to be on our best behavior tonight. Remember?" she murmurs with suspicious eyes.

I nod and guide her around the pool to a more private space on the mid-deck. I lean against the cool railing and look up at the elevator climbing the side of the building to the rest of the upper floors.

"What's on your mind, JD?" she asks.

"I'm looking forward to taking you up that elevator to my room. Don't know why, but they gave me a key when they checked my name off the guest list."

"All the platinum guests get a comp room. The hotel wants celebrities to post about the party to their social media profiles."

"A wasted effort on the likes of me. I don't do social media, but I do enjoy messing up a motel room. What do you say? Wanna get outta here?"

I'm a little tipsy and awfully nervous. It's not what I planned to say, but I figure if I can get Ev alone, the words will come out easier.

"We aren't doing dirty anymore, JD. This is supposed to be a business event. You and me. We are just business."

"It's never been just business, but if that's what you're callin' it, I'm here to tell you I can't do just business with you anymore, Ev."

"And why is that? Am I not making you enough money?"

"Nope, that's not it. I've got plenty of money. Thanks to you. We can go upstairs and roll around in it if you'd like." I grin and take a sip of my drink.

"Are you ever going to stop with this silliness, JD?" She rolls her eyes and drags her fingertips through her loose hair.

"I'm trying to tell you something here, Ev."

"And what is that?" Ev puts her fists on her hips. I clear my throat and look deeply into her eyes.

51

"I've fallen for you."

Ev's eyes widen for the tick of a clock. I reach out to touch her cheek, but she shakes her head. I drop my hand. She starts to walk away, but I hook her elbow gently. I don't want to draw anyone's attention. Ev stiffens, but stays put.

"I'm not doing this," Ev sighs.

"Listen to me, please. I've never put much stock in the idea of long-term relationships, not after all the loss I've seen, but I've been noodling on it the last couple of days. I've hated not talking to you. I don't like the silent treatment. I realized I don't want to know what it would be like without you in my life, Ev."

"This isn't happening," Ev says, pinching the bridge of her nose.

"McKennon meeting Devon has changed him for the good. I can't deny that meeting you has changed my life, too. I didn't mean to fall for you, Ev. I especially wasn't planning on admitting it to you, but it's true."

"I chose you because I knew it wouldn't get emotionally complicated. Please don't make me wrong about that."

"I'm in love with you, Ev." I say it with conviction.

I'm in love with her.

"Have you lost your mind, JD? Thinking you're in love is a dangerous way of thinking for a confirmed bachelor."

"Just because of how I lived my life in the past doesn't mean I'm not capable of falling in love. I didn't expect to fall in love *ever*, but here I am, confessing my love for you. You aren't a conquest to me. Well, not anymore. You are amazing, Ev, and I'm in love with you."

"That was awfully sweet to hear you say, but I'm more of a fleeting romantic entanglement type." Ev laughs and retrieves a champagne flute from the server, passing us with a tray.

"Ev, I just told you I'm in love with you."

I can't believe I'm groveling. Must be the whiskey.

"How many times do I have to tell you I don't do relationships, JD? I do projects, and you've been a good one," she says it icily and takes a sip from her glass.

"Things change, Ev. I wasn't the relationship kind either. Until you."

"I don't do love, JD. I thought you didn't either."

"You're lying," I reply through clenched teeth.

"I know hearing that is inconvenient, but it's the truth. I'm going to ask you to cowboy up and take this information square on the chin. I'm not interested in breaking anyone's heart. That was supposed to be the beauty of our arrangement. I don't want to mess with your head and have you believe anything other than what is true. I am not capable of love, JD."

"Wow, you really know how to deflate a guy's tires." I remove my hat and run my fingers through my hair.

"I'm glad this is happening now that you are on the mend. I've been lying awake at night wondering how I am going to end this thing with you. I let it go too far. I'm sorry about that."

"I don't believe you."

"Believe me," she replies.

Of course, I would fall for someone as incapable of love as I am.

I rub my temple, replace my hat, and chew my cheek. I don't have any words. I am badly bruised, but I will not show it. Rejection has never come easily to me. Hell, I've ever experienced rejection from the opposite sex before. I don't lose, but right now, I feel like a loser. I'm going to remedy this.

Immediately.

"Go find your next project then, Ev," I growl. "I'll find mine."

I shift on the heels of my boots, turn my back to Ev, and scan the party deck. I am a man obsessed with winning right now — any prize will do. I lick my lips and spot my target. Focusing in on the miles of lean leg just waiting for me, I let out a long, low whistle. I tip my head from one side to the other as I examine the length of them ending in her strappy black high, high heels like a pot of gold at the end of a rainbow. I conjure up what's left of my swagger and strut up to the fit blonde in a white tube top and silver sequined mini-skirt. She puffs on a cigarette. I recognize her as one of the many models I've encountered since coming to New York City. I'm not really interested in her though.

I am interested in pissing off Ev.

I always win.

"Howdy, good lookin'. Can I bum a smoke?" I ask the model when I reach her poolside table. I grin when she suggestively uncrosses her legs.

"Help yourself," she purrs, pushing the pack across the tabletop. "Have a seat."

"What's a beautiful lady like you doing sitting at a party all by her lonesome?" I pull a chair out. My back is still to Ev, but I can sense she's standing where I left her. I can feel her stare penetrating me from behind.

Good. I don't care.

"Nothing has tickled my fancy ... yet," she sighs, shrugging her shoulders with a plump-lipped pout.

Direct hit.

"Well then, I'll plan on being your plans for the evening, miss" I conclude, striking her book of matches boasting the hotel's branding. I hold the flame to the end of my cigarette. "Reason being, I know a thing or two about tickling."

This comment makes her smile. Her interest is evident.

"What's your name?" I drawl.

"I'm Amanda, and I was plenty bored with this party until you sat down here." She leans forward and flicks the brim of my hat. "Are you a real cowboy or is that hat for show?"

My eyes linger on her cleavage for a moment, trying to figure her cup size.

"Hello?" She lifts my chin with a fingertip. "Are you a real cowboy?"

"Oh, yes, ma'am. I'm the real deal all right." I grip my brim and give her a proper bend of it. Her eyes wander down my torso, and I adjust the sizeable silver buckle at my waist for her benefit. I force a sultry smile, but I feel anything other than sultry. Ev's words have cut deep. I've never had my heart trampled on by a woman. I've always been the one doing the ditching.

I can't let Ev get away with it.

"I've never been with a cowboy before," the blonde muses, blowing out a stream of smoke.

"Go figure. Well, that's a darn shame, Amanda," I reply as she extinguishes her cigarette.

"I might just be drunk enough to go to your room." She moistens her lips and hooks a pink painted fingertip in the waist of my jeans.

"Is that so?"

"Yes. I've decided it is so. You are way too handsome, mister. I feel all gooey inside, especially when you smile. I can't imagine how I'll feel when you take your shirt off."

Jackpot.

I've been with beautiful women before, but Amanda is *really* beautiful. She's the kind of beautiful that men satisfy themselves to in dirty magazines, but not the kind they actually ever get to spend a night with. This woman is like an exotic, endangered species. It kills me that I don't even remotely want her.

I want Ev.

While Amanda nibbles my earlobe, I look over her shoulder for my redhead. I spot her hovering at the bar. My eyes travel the open back of the sexy, black dress she chose for this special occasion. She's speaking with Missy and Martin, but to my glee, she's positioned so she can see me in action. Vengeance rears up in me.

Showtime.

I extinguish my cigarette and lift Amanda out of her seat gently by her arms. I scan her lovely peach face. It's dusted with a shimmery powder. A rosy glow has grown deeper on the apples of her cheeks. Her supple lips are parted just the right way. I shoot Ev one last lingering, angry look, and put my mouth on the model's. It takes a lot of effort to forget that the woman I love is standing just feet away, but I am able to lose myself momentarily in the kiss. Breathlessly, Amanda breaks from my mouth, bites her lower lip, and then takes my hand.

"Ready to get wild, cowboy?" she asks.

I am flattered, and at the same time, I'm offended. Amanda is willing to come to my hotel room but hasn't even asked me my name. I brush off that fact, quickly realizing she probably has seen my posters all over town and doesn't need to hear my name from me. This isn't about getting to know Amanda, anyway. This is about getting back at Ev for not loving me. This is what I do. It will never change because no one will ever love the real me. All I'm ever good for is a roll in the hay, so I put the wheels in motion.

"Do I get to taste more than that mouth?" I ask, running my fingers through her hair and down her back. I rest my hand on her ass. Over Amanda's shoulder, I see Missy's mouth drop open. Martin raises his glass in my direction. Ev is examining her fingernails.

"I need to cool off," Amanda says near my ear.

My attention returns to the woman at hand, and her glossy lips curl into a wicked smile. Before I know what is happening, she tugs me by the belt loops over the deck's edge, and we plunge into the empty, aqua pool. Once we are underwater, Amanda wraps her arms around my neck and guides my hand under her skirt.

She isn't wearing panties.

Mission accomplished.

When we come up for air, I hear the gasps of the partygoers. Given that the swimming pool is the centerpiece of the rooftop party, this is an even bigger spectacle than I intended. I am momentarily blinded as the flashes of cameras light up the night. I smirk, realizing that this might be quite the scoop for the tabloids, so I turn up the heat. I wrap my hands in Amanda's wet, long blonde hair, tug her head back, and kiss her hard. She gasps into my mouth as I move my hand up her leg. The water skims over her ample breasts, and I finally feel myself stir.

That'a cowboy.

"Your room now," Amanda says. She hastily shoves my hand out from beneath her skirt and wades into the shallow end of the pool.

I don't say anything. I just follow. We are both fully dressed and soaked to the bone. It feels delightfully sinful.

I certainly picked the right girl. I win.

Once we are on the deck again, Amanda removes her heels, takes my hand, and tromps barefoot with me in tow through the whispers of the crowd. Giggling, she presses the up button to the hotel's glass elevator.

When the doors separate with a ding, I sweep her into the lift and press her back against the glass window. I pause to let my eyes wander over her. Dripping wet with her shoes dangling from her fingertips, I can see the outline of her breasts through her top. She's the ultimate male fantasy.

And she wants me.

Instinctively, my lips move to her mouth. I let my hands wander over Amanda's backside, up her spine, and over her shoulders. She tips her head back, and I nibble her exposed neck. I hear each floor chime as we pass it. Still, I keep one eye open on the deck below, and I'm flooded with a mix of emotion. Ev is watching us leave the party. Her mouth is agape.

I have my revenge.

Cameras are pointed at the elevator. Flashbulbs continue to go off. This is going to be front-page news in the fashion world.

Pure. Cowboy. Debauchery. That will show her.

I plan to use this model up and get the hell out of this city at daybreak.

This glitzy place has lost its gloss.

Hours later, I lie there in the bed next to the model with my guts wrenching. Mulling things over in my mind, I'm not so sure if I dodged a bullet or just lost the love of my life. I've surely ruined Amanda's career. She'll never work in this city again after Everly Mitchell is finished with her. I likely won't be working anymore either.

What have I done?

I jump when there is a knock at the door. Amanda moans in disgust, waves a limp palm toward me, and tugs a pillow over her head. I slip out from between the sheets and grab a towel from the bathroom on my way to the door. I wrap it around my waist and peer through the peephole.

Holy shit. It's Ev.

Foolishly hoping she'll want me back, I open the door. All I can do is drop my jaw when she tosses my rigging bag at my feet and holds out her hand.

"My key," she says. "If you're going to act like a stripper, I'm going to act like a bouncer."

I open my mouth to say something, anything.

"Don't say a word, JD."

I shake my head, roam back into the hotel room, and pull the key from the pocket of my crumpled jeans at the foot of the bed. Defeated, I walk back to the door and place the key to Ev's apartment in her waiting hand.

"Goodbye, JD," she says before turning on her heels and heading down the hall.

I click the door closed and squeeze my eyes shut. I can't help wondering who she will replace me with, now that I'm through.

Goodbye, Ev.

52

U nder dark clouds and towering grey skyscrapers, I slither down the sidewalk. I'm making my way toward Ev's parking garage to retrieve my monstrous green truck and drive myself back to Green Briar.

I'm heading back to where I'm wanted.

My intention is to pull away from the city undetected, but I stop in my tracks when I spot Missy walking toward me. I duck my chin and plunge my hands into my pockets, even though my cowboy attire is a dead giveaway. I don't think I've even seen another cowboy hat on a head in this city, except on that chap in Times Square who plays a guitar in his underwear.

"JD," Missy calls out as she hustles up to me.

I instantly tense in anticipation of a confrontation. She's Ev's niece, after all. I reckon I'm gonna get an earful this morning.

"That was quite a spectacle last night, cowboy," Missy says somberly, pointing in my direction the closed umbrella she's carrying.

"Yeah," I say with a shrug. "I expect you're gonna give me a talkin' to right about now."

"Nope. It's none of my business. By the looks of you, I expect you are beating yourself up plenty. You look terrible, JD."

I feel terrible.

"Is she all right?" I ask, not meeting Missy's eyes. I scoot a boot tip along the crack in the sidewalk.

"I'm not sure, to be honest. I stayed with her last night, but she didn't say much. She just now sent me out for *The Post*. She wants to see Page Six this morning. She figures the gossip column welcomed the photos of your sultry swim last night. If her name is mentioned, she will have a mess to clean up. What on earth did you do that for?"

"I told Ev that I love her," I sigh.

"Making out with a model in a pool at a celebrity party in front of the woman you say you love is a pretty funny way of expressing that, JD," Missy remarks with a shameful shake of her head.

"She doesn't feel the same way," I mutter.

"My aunt is a tough cookie. She has reasons for the things she does."

"It doesn't matter anymore. I'm leaving the city. I'm going back to where I'm wanted. You take care of yourself, Missy. Look after Ev," I say. I start to walk away, but Missy catches my arm.

"If it helps any, she *was* different with you, JD. I know this really isn't my business, but I thought you should know that none of her projects have ever stayed in her apartment. She always put them up somewhere else. I have a feeling she might reach out. If she does, I'd hear her out if I were you."

"There's nothing more to talk about. She made herself perfectly clear. See ya, Missy. I need to get on the road before it rains," I reply, tipping my brim to her and heading into the parking garage.

As I climb into my new truck, my heart sinks. I buckle myself in and take a deep breath. I'm going back to my old life. I console myself that it will be a great, long road trip – an opportunity to contemplate where my life has taken me, to put a woman I can never call my own behind me.

Why couldn't I turn off my emotions this time?

I turn the key in the ignition and feel a gnawing in my gut that I'm doing my best to fight through. As I drive out of Manhattan, the grey sky opens up, and it pours. As the wipers zip furiously across the windshield, I can't stop replaying my time with Ev like a movie through my mind. I realize over the past months, I've never experienced this kind of yearning in my chest, nor ever felt this sort of connection to a woman, not since I was young. I shake my head and suddenly turn cool with foolishness reflecting on my exploits with Amanda the night before.

What was I thinking?

I've never had to actually think before. All I've ever had to do was climb up on the back of a bull, hope the animal couldn't get me off, and if he did, make sure he didn't step on me. I remove my hat, set it on the seat beside me, and touch the new scar on my forehead.

I sure screwed that part up.

The reality is that I'm struggling with a palpable fear that I've lost my nerve for riding bulls, and I'm afraid all the future holds for me is becoming just a dumb model. When Ev didn't reciprocate my feelings at the party, I blew any chance I had of winning her heart by returning to my playboy ways.

Really loving Ev? Never riding a bull again? Retiring? How stupid can I be?

I can't stop the questions reeling around in my head. Going back to Green Briar will bring me back to earth.

I hope.

As the rain pelts my truck, I force myself up straight in my seat and clutch the steering wheel. I adjust the radio to a heavy metal song. Once I'm on the highway, the storm lightens up, and I roll down the window to allow a burst of air to rush my face.

The anticipation of working at Green Briar again is the only thing that gives me any peace of mind. I can ride on the cash from my short-lived career as a model. I've got plenty of time to figure things out.

Maybe I'll open a bull riding school at Green Briar with the money I earned. If Sophia will have the idea, that is.

I distract myself by thinking up a plan to get McKennon on my side.

Yes, that will make the pitch to Sophia a lot easier.

Pushing my face to the open window, I steal another deep breath and light raindrops sprinkle my skin. The air smells cleaner already. There are just some things that money can't replace. All the money in the world won't be able to take the country out of me.

I'm heading back to where I belong.

53

My eyes flick from the pavement to the digital clock on my dashboard, and I realize I've been driving for almost 24 hours. I only stopped once to relieve myself and grab an energy drink from a vending machine. I caught a quick nap in the rest area parking lot. I only have two more hours to go. When I see it – the sign for my exit — my heart turns over in my chest, and I feel a deep sense of relief. Green Briar is just a few miles away. I've been driving in a haze with no actual sense of time or place.

I have been inside my head, or perhaps my aching heart, that all that time has passed without my being aware. It's time to put all that bellyaching behind me. I have to swallow the fact that Ev doesn't love me. I know I never belonged in that city. I can't wait to ask for my old job back. Not because I need the money, but because I need to work the ranch.

I need to do something real with myself.

The sun is bright as I pull into the tree-lined drive and hear the familiar crunch of the gravel. I feel the weight lift from my shoulders.

I am home.

I throw my truck in park outside of the barn and step out. I just linger there for a while, inhaling the fresh country air.

This is exactly what I need.

It is warm — warm and beautiful at Green Briar. I take a gander around. There isn't a grey high-rise in sight. My eyes travel along the white fence line. The leaves of the trees stir in the breeze, and the birds in the branches sing the sweetest song. The sun shines upon the backs of horses out to pasture, and flowers bloom across the wide green fields at their feet.

After a while, I rummage around in the backseat of my big truck and sift through the swag the sponsors have given me. I grab a couple Lariat pearl-buttoned shirts and a few new pairs of jeans. Arms full of goodies, I make my way to the barn. Inside, I look left to right but don't see anyone. Moving farther in, I peer over stall doors and finally find the man I'm seeking.

McKennon is sitting silently in the deep bedding of Willa's stall.

"Hey, brother," I whisper, trying not to surprise him. In my haste to get out of New York, I hadn't bothered to call to let anyone know I was coming. Wasn't particularly interested in having the conversation as to why either.

"Well, look what the cat dragged in," McKennon drawls, rising to his feet and dusting the shavings from his pant legs.

"That foal sure is a looker," I say, admiring the Palomino colt bashfully blinking at me from behind his momma.

"The breeding program is off to a strong start," McKennon agrees. He smiles, gives Willa an appreciative scratch, steps out of the stall, slides the door closed, and extends his hand. I shift the clothes to one arm, take his palm, and give it a proper pump.

"What 'cha got there?" McKennon asks, scratching his jaw.

"Thought you could use some new duds with a little style," I say, shoving the garments into McKennon's chest.

"Mighty kind of you, JD. I reckon I'm due for some new threads. I gather these are courtesy of your endorsements?"

"Yep, I got an even bigger surprise from them out there in the parking lot," I beam.

"You wanna tell me what you're doing here?" McKennon asks, admiring a plaid shirt from the pile and holding it up to his torso.

"I'm back for good this time. Hoping for my old job back," I reply.

"Is that so?" McKennon gives me a hard look and squints his eyes. I know he's about to inquire why, but I pull a fast one before he can start asking.

"Why don't you come see my new truck before we get into the negotiations," I say, heading out of the barn and leaving McKennon standing there with his new clothes. I glance over my shoulder to make sure he's coming. McKennon sets the stack on a hay bale, lifts his hat, runs his fingers through his hair, sighs, and follows me out into the drive.

Dodged that bullet.

"That's a hell of a shade of green," McKennon drawls with wide eyes at first sight of my free truck.

"So everyone will know it's mine," I reply, hopping up behind the steering wheel.

"Listen, JD. I'm glad to see you and all, but ..."

I interrupt him before he can start asking questions.

"Listen to this," I hoot.

I turn the radio up on McKennon, hop out of the truck, beaming my rock star smile, and do a little jig in the driveway to the tune blaring through the speakers. The horses in the pastures jerk their heads up at the radio, roaring. McKennon shakes his head and crosses his arms.

"JD, turn that down. You're spookin' the dang horses."

A moment later, Devon appears from the direction of the pastures, and Sophia scurries down the hill from the main house.

"What is all the commotion?" Sophia asks, covering her ears with her aged hands. I instantly turn the stereo down and rush to embrace her.

It is so good to be back with my Green Briar family.

"We have a celebrity in our presence, Sophia. Our boy JD here got himself famous by taking off his shirt, slipping out of his jeans, and riding an energy drink can," McKennon says with a smirk. He wraps an arm across Devon's shoulders.

"Yes, I saw the magazine you were in when McKennon and Devon came back from visiting you. How are you feeling, dear? What are you doing here?" Sophia inquires.

"I'm back at Green Briar, Sophia. I'm here to work the ranch. Do you like the tune, Devon?"

"I'm not sure I've heard this song before," Devon replies, recovering from the sight of my green monster truck.

"It's the new album by an alternative band called Wise Guys. I got a prerelease copy in this giant swag bag from a celebrity party Ev took me to, and I can't stop jamming to it."

"Money looks good on you, JD," Sophia comments.

"Heck, I'm still a jeans and T-shirt guy. It's just that now they have a designer label sewn inside and the softness that comes with it."

I know I'm showing off, but I can't help it. I don't want anyone to see what's really eating me.

As if on cue, McKennon steps forward and flips my hat off of my head. Devon and Sophia giggle.

"I suppose I deserved that, being so full of myself and all. Sorry, guys," I say, sweeping my hat off the gravel drive and replacing it on my head.

"That sounds about right," McKennon replies. "Now if you'll excuse me, I've got to go see a fella about a tractor. JD, we will talk later." He squeezes Sophia's shoulder, kisses Devon on the cheek, shoots me a look, and jingles his spurs back in the direction of the barn.

"McKennon, supper will be ready in about 20 minutes," Sophia calls after him.

"I'll be there with bells on," he calls back over his shoulder.

"What 'cha got cooking, Sophia?" I ask. My stomach turns thinking of her good old down-home cooking.

"Why, I'm hosting one of my barbecues, JD. What a perfect time for you to visit," Sophia chirps.

This isn't a visit.

"In fact, I should really hustle back," Sophia continues. "I've got a peach pie in the oven, but we'll have ourselves a good catch up over dinner. I can't wait to hear all about your big city adventures. You've gone all Hollywood on us."

"It's a deal, Sophia," I say through a forced smile.

"See you all in 20 minutes," Sophia reminds us. Devon and I watch as she happily floats back toward the main house.

"It's a surprise to see you, JD. How are you doing?" Devon asks.

"I've made a pretty fine recovery, if that's what you mean. I've got the all clear from my doctors, not for riding bulls, but for doing work. It's a start."

"That's splendid news, but what about your work with Ev in the city?" she presses.

"I belong here. At least until I head back to the bull riding circuit."

If I head back to the bull riding circuit.

I tuck my hands in my pockets, rock back on my heels, and make sure I don't meet Devon's eyes. She will see right through me.

"Did something happen?" Devon presses.

"I don't know. Not really. It's just seeing my face plastered on billboards all over the city really got me rattled. I kept asking myself what the heck I was doing in New York City," I reply. I know it's not the truth, but I'm thinking fast on my feet.

"Well, basically a big city female mogul kidnapped you and turned you into a male model," Devon teases.

"Yeah, something like that," I chuckle. "The truth is, I never intended to be in New York longer than the three days of my bull riding event at Madison Square Garden, maybe a few days after that, but then the injury happened. I've been out there for months now. Things got under my skin. I've been feeling homesick. I needed me some wide-open spaces."

"I can understand what it feels like to miss Green Briar. Are you really OK though?"

"Yeah, I'll be fine. Give me a few days." I'm telling another lie.

"Where is the philandering JD I used to know?" Devon asks. "I'm worried. You haven't stuck your package in my face once since you've been home."

"You're a married woman now."

"Yeah, right, JD. That never would have stopped you before. What's really going on with you? Is it Ev?"

Stifling my urge to offend her like I so often do, I opt to tell her the truth instead. I take a deep breath. It's time to turn a new leaf.

"It's funny. All I've ever been interested in was eight seconds or a good roll in the hay. Ev's changed all of that. I want to matter, Devon. I thought I would matter if I won the million or saw my face in those magazines, but I've realized it's more than that. I want to matter to *someone*."

Devon's eyes go wide, but she doesn't respond right away. She bites her lip. I can tell she is mulling over what to say next.

"What are you saying, JD?" Devon finally asks, twisting her wedding band.

Something about that ring on her finger makes my heart start racing, and I lose my nerve to be truthful.

All of this is still too fresh.

"Don't think too much about it, Devon. You hear?"

Devon opens her mouth, but then closes it. I hope that means she will drop it because I'm not ready to admit to anyone else I'm in love with Ev or that I screwed it all up before it even got going. I look toward Sophia's house, stuff my hands in my pockets, and chew my cheek for a second.

"C'mon, there's some good barbecue waiting for us up at Sophia's," I say.

"You are right there, Mr. Hollywood. Sophia's cookouts are the best. She's tickled pink that you are some big-time model dude now. You do realize that you're going to have to spill the beans, eventually. I want to know what happened between you and Ev. I want to know why you aren't still in the city. I'm not letting you off the hook that easily, JD."

"I know, I know. I can never get anything past you or your husband, but right now, all I can think about is all that meat waiting for us up there. I just know it's slathered in Ken's signature sauce."

I shift on the heels of my boots, hightail it toward the barbecue, and away from this particular line of questioning.

I gallop up the gentle slope of the grassy knoll that leads to the main house. Sophia and McKennon are already seated in chairs that circle around the bonfire. They slow their happy chatting and look up as I settle into an empty chair across from them. Devon arrives from several paces behind me and leaps into McKennon's arms. A smile settles across Sophia's luminescent face as she watches Devon plant a happy kiss on her cowboy's lips. It reminds me of the type of smile you'd see a proud parent wear during their child's wedding day vows, and I feel something like envy swirl inside of me.

"Welcome home, JD. I'm so glad you're here." Sophia nods to me, and the fire sets an orange twinkle in her eye. "It just so happens that I've made your favorite."

"You made your famous baked beans?" I ask.

"Indeed, I did. It must be fate. We've missed you. I can't wait to hear your tales from the big city. Let us make our plates." Sophia clasps her hands together in anticipation like she so often does.

I sense my cares melting away, if only temporarily, as we fill our plates with heaps of brisket, sausage, ribs, and pulled pork. As I hoped, it is all slathered in McKennon's homemade barbecue sauce. It's just like I remember, laced with the perfect amount of heat and sweet.

Sophia's beans bubble and spurt from an ancient olive green crock-pot, and I can't wait to shovel them into my mouth. When I do, they melt on my tongue. I savor the taste of brown sugar and maple syrup. McKennon offers me a brew from an icy tub.

The southern evening air is heavier than it was in the city. There is a hovering humidity that I never noticed before, but the fire accompanied by a light breeze keeps the mosquitoes away. In fact, the temperature is perfect.

This moment is perfect.

We eat, drink, laugh, and talk at the base of Sophia's big white house where not so long ago Devon and McKennon had their wedding reception and my whirlwind adventures with Ev began. I tell my favorite stories from the city, leaving out the details of my accident and the rooftop pool party. I'm not ready to face those topics. I particularly enthralled Sophia with my tale of the bull riding photo shoot on the New Jersey beach.

As the last bit of flame grows low and loses its luster, Sophia rises from her perch across the fire and makes her way around the pit toward me.

"When will you be leaving us, JD?" Sophia asks, laying her sapphire eyes on me with a serene smile.

"I'm not planning on leaving," I say, looking up at her. "There's nothing for me back in the city. I'd like to stay on at Green Briar and resume my position as a ranch hand. That is, if you will have me. Will you have me on again?"

Sophia's eyes glisten, and she looks to McKennon for a moment. He nods, and she returns her attention to me.

"Of course, we'll have you here at Green Briar, JD," Sophia replies softly.

"Would the part about the city have anything to do with Ev?" Devon inquires.

I shoot her a 'don't you dare say anything' look, and she giggles. She doesn't realize how serious my situation is. Sophia and McKennon look at each other with interest, but they hold their tongues and don't ask about Ev.

Thank heaven.

"Shame it's gettin' so late," McKennon says, shooting me a wink. "We've still got so much catching up with you to do. I'm too stuffed to listen right now though."

I know he's just gotten me out of a rapid succession of questioning. I toss him a grin and let out a sigh of relief.

"What do you say, wife? Shall we hit the hay?" McKennon asks Devon.

"Yes, husband. I think it's time for some shuteye. I'm not through with you though, JD."

"No, I don't expect you are," I grumble.

"JD, will you be staying at the house?" Sophia asks.

"That would be mighty nice, Sophia."

"I thought you'd like that. I made up a room for you after I took the pie out. It's the same one you and Ev shared at the wedding," Sophia says, mischievously.

"That would be terrific, Sophia. Thank you." I swallow hard. I feel heat rise under my collar at the thought of the night I spent in that room with Ev.

Go figure.

54

I wake feeling rested and ready to take on the day. The morning light is bright, and so is my spirit. Rising from the bed, I gather jeans and a T-shirt from my rigging bag. I hastily dress, eager to return to my ranch hand chores. I intend to lose myself in work and put Ev behind me. Settling my cowboy hat on my head, I jog down the stairs and spy Sophia gazing out the window, sipping a cup of tea.

"Good morning," I say, wandering into the kitchen.

"Well, good morning, dear," Sophia replies. "There's coffee on for you. I hope you slept well."

"I slept like a brick, Sophia. It was a relief to not hear any sirens in the night. I can't even explain to you how dang noisy New York City is." I help myself to a cup of Joe and lean against the counter.

"It is a noisy place, indeed," Sophia agrees. "I felt small and vulnerable there, but then I met my husband at a horse show. I count my blessings every day that my sweet Andrew brought me here. Rest his soul."

I set my mug down and sweep Sophia into a hug.

"I know you miss him," I murmur.

Missing someone — it's something I can comprehend now.

"Fate has a way of bringing people into our lives when we need them," Sophia says, stepping back from our embrace and gazing upon me steadily. "Andrew, and then McKennon. Both of them arrived in my life when I needed them to. It's important to open your eyes and see what fate is showing you."

"Yes," I reply. My mouth has suddenly gone dry. I reach for my mug and take a swig. My head feels heavy again with thoughts of how I ended my time in the city.

Did fate bring Ev into my life?

"You've been through quite a lot in a brief span of time. A bull riding accident, a modeling career that resulted in substantial endorsement deals, and living with a woman in New York City is a lot of change and quickly. The enormity of it all, I imagine that's been a great deal for you to handle, dear?"

"Yeah. It definitely has been a whirlwind." I bite my cheek and mull over the last few months.

"I sense there might be a bigger reason you've returned to Green Briar. Could it have to do with Everly?" she asks gently. There is a glimmer in her eye.

I don't want to talk about this. I want to work.

"Ev ..." I hesitate.

"How is Ev?" Sophia presses.

Great question.

"I was a project for her," I croak.

I clear my throat, finish my coffee, and set the mug in the sink.

"Project?" Sophia asks with a raise of her brows.

"It was just business with Ev, and we've finished our business together, so I'm back. I'm thinking on what's next. Planning my future and all that."

"I see," Sophia says. "Well, that's too bad. You two seemed rather drawn to each other." Sophia gives me a hard look, and it makes me uncomfortable. I feel ashamed and sneak a gander at the front door.

I need to get out of here.

"Well, I'm going to head out to the barn and catch up with McKennon. I reckon it's time to find out what needs doing around here."

"You go do that, JD."

"Yes, ma'am." I turn toward the door, but Sophia puts a hand on my shoulder.

"While you figure out your future, there are accommodations here for you at Green Briar. McKennon's just finished installing an apartment above the new barn. It's scheduled to be furnished this week, and it's yours for as long as you want to stay here. I won't have you staying in that trailer of yours when I have something nicer to offer you."

"That'd be mighty swell, Sophia." My heart expands at her offer.

"And, if you want to talk about what's really going on, I'm here for you. We all are."

"I know, Sophia. Thank you. I'll see you later."

I sweep in, swiftly kiss her cheek, and bolt for the door. I desperately need to clear my head. Sophia has a way of implying things without actually saying the words. Everything I'm trying to suppress came rushing back during that talk. I miss Ev something fierce. I miss the feel of her skin, the silk of her red hair, the sway of her hips through that apartment of hers, the way she smells. I love her sharp mind, and everything else sharp about her. She is a lot to miss, but I have work to do.

There's no time for missing when there is work to do.

Shaking my head, I make my way out onto the porch. I take a deep breath of Green Briar air, head down the front steps, and strut across the lawn toward the stables. I tip my hat to McKennon as I enter the barn.

"Mornin'," he drawls, tossing a flake of hay into a stall.

"Feels so good to see nothing has changed too much around here. There's been way too much change in my life lately," I reply, grabbing flakes of my own to assist with the morning feeding.

"What really brings you back to Green Briar, Mr. Superstar?" McKennon asks.

"New York is a bizarre place," I begin, and then clear my throat. "It's easy to lose touch with reality there. Did you know I got offered a movie part?"

"No, I hadn't heard that. JD McCall, the bull riding movie star. Kinda has a ring to it," McKennon razzes. He tosses the last flake of hay into a stall, crosses his arms in front of his chest, and leans against the wall.

"Stop teasing, McKennon. It really freaked me out," I say, sitting on a hay bale in the aisle across from him. "Posing for pictures is one thing, but the pressure of being in a motion picture. It got to me. Thank heaven I never signed that contract."

"Thank heaven? Didn't figure you to be one to turn down that kinda attention," McKennon replies with a raise of his brow.

"I admit I enjoy seeing myself up on them billboards, but a movie? That's just too much. I had to get home. I don't want to read from a script and speak someone else's words. I'm just a country boy. I missed the country. Feels like springtime year-round here because everything is growing and blossoming, even in the dead of winter ... you, Devon, the horses, the business, and the family we created with Sophia. I miss belonging to Green Briar. The city — it's just cold. Grey. All. The. Time. My favorite thing ever since I was a kid was the smell of the horses, the bulls. It's livestock that I love. I love the smell of livestock. You don't get that in the city."

"No, no. You certainly don't get that in the city. New York sent two people hightailing it for Green Briar with their tails between their legs. Sent Devon here and now you, too. I figured you'd come back one day, but not quite so soon. You seemed happy as a pig in mud when we left you there."

"Things changed," I murmur.

"Life has a way of doin' that. You're healed up enough to catch a couple mid-tier rodeo gigs. Got your sights set on any of those?" McKennon asks.

"Nah. Think I'll stay put for a while. Sophia offered me the loft above the new barn while I figure things out. I'm taking her up on the offer."

"In the past, you would've been antsy to get back out on the road where you can drink hard, ride hard, and find an endless supply of anonymous women to fill your time. What's changed?" McKennon inquires with a scratch of his jaw.

"I've traveled all over the country following the National Bull Riders tour, but I've never found another place that felt like home. Green Briar is home. On the road, what I did or didn't do meant nothing. No one who mattered was ever there to see it. Green Briar and this town with all our history tied to it, good, bad, and ugly, is home. I have no doubt about that now. I missed it something fierce while I was cooped up in New York City. I never really had time to ponder that sort of thing. I was always just racing off to what was next. The accident changed me. Reckon I'm ready to settle down, brother. Stay in one place."

"You? Settle down? How hard did you hit your head in that wreck?" McKennon chuckles.

"I'm serious, McKennon."

"Want to know what I think?"

"What's that?" I ask.

"You're running away. You don't run from something unless it scares you. I think all this has got something to do with a certain redhead."

"Maybe I'm ready for a little of what you and Devon have."

"That so?"

"I started thinking I might have something special with Ev, but the truth is, I was the one being used this time. Got a good dose of my own medicine. It hurts like hell, I'll tell ya. Ev was just playing a game of cat and mouse with me. She doesn't feel the same way I do. It is always easy to walk away from the young ones. I guess with older ladies, it's a lot harder."

"I don't think age has anything to do with this, JD. What you're talkin' about is a woman who you want to respect, a woman that you actually want to keep around for more than one night. You haven't learned how to play your cards right with a woman. You always go straight for the easy catch. You aren't willing to bait the hook and wait on a good one. Thing is, that fact that you think Ev might be the one for you, well, that has me scratching my head."

"I never wanted something that might last, McKennon."

"Exactly. Keep your chin up though, brother, because the right one for you will not go by you. Devon was right for me and no matter how I tried to avoid her, we ended up together. So, I reckon if Ev is the right one for you, it will work itself out somehow. That is, if you are serious about wanting something that will last," McKennon says.

"I do. I want something that matters. I want something that lasts. I don't want to live without that anymore. The accident helped me see that riding bulls doesn't give me time to think, and I like not thinking. The wreck on Cork Screw gave me time to think."

"It's about time you started using your noggin. Better late than never," McKennon replies with a smirk.

"For the first time in my life, I'm not living on luck and hoping for the win, event to event, day to day. My life isn't a blur of highways, truck stops, and fairgrounds anymore. I can afford luxuries now that I never knew existed. I don't have to finish any more rides and cross my fingers to make the placing with the paycheck. That's because of Ev. She saw something more in me and helped me have more."

"But that high from making the eight is what you love more than anything, isn't it?" McKennon asks, rubbing the back of his neck.

I know I am confusing him. I don't sound like myself at all. Heck, I don't even recognize myself anymore.

"I fell hat over boots for that redhead," I admit.

"I know the feeling. I fell spurs over Stetson twice in my life." McKennon rubs his chin thoughtfully.

"That wreck really did something to me," I continue, trying to explain it all. "I'm tired. I'm tired of the road and bustin' up my body on the back of bulls. I'm tired of beddin' women I hardly know and runnin' out the door with my jeans barely zipped up. I'm tired of searchin' for the next adrenaline rush. I'm ready to start a new chapter."

"Sounds like you are looking beyond eight seconds for the first time in your life."

"I am, and I'd like to start fresh by working at Green Briar full time. That is, if you'll have me?"

"Sophia's already given you the green light, so I reckon we can work something out ... if you are serious." McKennon gives me a stern look. I've let him down in the past.

Not this time.

"You have my word, McKennon. It's funny, I always thought I'd make my fortune winning that cool million off of the National Bull Riders tour. I never figured I would make any money with my face. Things have really changed. I've changed."

"Well, I reckon that's the thing about change, brother. People try to hold change back by building routines and believing they are a certain way, but change always comes," McKennon philosophizes. "I went through it when I lost Madison. I avoided it when Devon came around. I tried to fight change, but I've learned that it's best to embrace it. Seems like you have. If what you're saying to me is true, you've changed, and I think it's for the better."

"I know I've been a total train wreck most of my life. Growing up was a spectacular disaster. My uncle died right in front of my face. My father is a tough bastard and made my mom run off. I lost my childhood sweetheart, and then Madison ... it's an awful lot of loss for one guy to handle. Now this thing with Ev has me rethinking my entire existence. It's really thrown me for a loop ..." I swallow hard. "I think she broke my heart."

"You are kind of a train wreck," McKennon drawls to make light of the situation, but turns serious at my serious face.

"Over the last few years, I've been screwing up all over the place. You or Devon are always the first to call me out."

"Well, you're right there. Devon and I do call you out, but that's because we love you. You're family. I'll admit I've been a little hard on you about gallivanting about with your pants around your knees, but I believe when people go off the rails, it's usually for a reason. That Ev. She seems like a hard dog to keep under the porch," McKennon says, adjusting his hat.

"Yeah." It's all I can say.

"Sounds like she's the one that revs your engine, though. Are you planning on running frantically after her?"

"No."

"Well, then, maybe you aren't in love. Maybe this is just the opportunity you needed to open up to the idea of loving someone more than yourself, more than your bull riding career?"

"I told her I love her, McKennon. She told me she didn't feel the same way. That I was only a project for her."

"Is that so?"

"Even if she had feelings for me, I done messed up. I was angry when she said it was just business. I felt used, and I wanted to hurt her, so I did." Everything I've been holding back since coming home is gushing out of me. "I went off with another woman and got the hell out of town the next morning. I'm not proud of what I did. I thought it might make it all hurt less. But it hurts more."

"Hm. I certainly don't agree with how you handled the situation. You got yourself into a hell of a spot. I can tell you actually have feelings here, so how can I help?" McKennon asks.

"How do I get her back?" I blurt.

"I reckon if you want someone to love you back, the first step is you don't chase them away, you give them something to come around to. We always make our way back to the things that really matter. The universe is funny that way. We always end up exactly where we belong. It's why you are back at Green Briar. It's why I'm married to Devon."

I can't help but smile. McKennon once was a man of few words. His marriage to Devon sure seems to have loosened his tongue.

"This is all of that fate stuff everyone seems to always be believing in, isn't it?"

"Yep," McKennon says, resting a hand on my shoulder. "It's time to be the man that you claim you want to be. Start being that man, and love follows. I had to learn that particular lesson the hard way. It seems you do, too."

My thoughts travel back to Ev. During our time together, she has become everything for me: a friend, a caretaker, a business partner, a lover. All I have given her is an ill-planned 'I love you', and then a slap in the face.

I'm an idiot.

"I really do want more, McKennon. I want people to see me as more. I've spent a lot of years perfectly content with being as irresponsible as possible, but the problem with being irresponsible is that it's useful until it isn't. You're right. If I really want to be treated differently, then I have to act differently. I'm ready."

"Wow, brother, you may just be growing up after all. I'm mighty glad to hear you say that, and I'm happy you came home. Green Briar is the best place to start. We've got your back, and if you really mean what you're saying, we'll hold you to your word."

"I don't doubt that for a second," I chuckle.

"Not to mention, my son's gonna need a responsible uncle." McKennon's eyes glimmer. He unleashes the biggest grin I've ever seen on the man. As the news settles in, my mouth draws open, and my throat feels tight.

McKennon is starting a family.

"I'm gonna be an uncle? Did you say son?"

"Yep, on both counts. We don't have a name yet, so don't ask," McKennon huffs. "That's the first question dang near everyone asks. I do know, however, that Devon is 22 weeks along, so we got plenty of time to ponder names."

"Well, I reckon M&D Quarter Horses is gonna need a solid investor the way it's growing with horses and humans. Now I can help you with more than being a groom at shows or building barns. I'd like to be your moneyman. I've got it coming out of my ears after that New York whirlwind. Got more than I know what do to with now."

"I like you groomin' and buildin' barns, JD, but investin' in the business? That'd be awfully kind of you. We need all the help we can get. I like the idea of not havin' to go to Sophia or the bank for growth loans for once. The business sure is expanding," McKennon says.

I can make a real difference now for my Green Briar family.

"Now I can do more good than damage around here," I say, puffing out my chest. "Proud to do it. In fact, I'd like to talk to you about startin' up a bull riding school here. Do you think Sophia would support somethin' like that?"

"I think that sounds like a fine idea. You really are thinkin' about the future, brother. I bet Devon would help you write up a business plan. Get somethin' to me, and I'll speak with Sophia."

"I'd sure appreciate that, McKennon. I'm feelin' awfully inspired right about now. I'm throwin' my cowboy hat into the ring here."

"Happy to hear it, brother, and I'm dang proud of you." McKennon extends a hand. I take it. We seal the deal with a grin.

55

EVERLY

3 Months Later

As they fly past me, traveling in excess of 180 mph, my heart races. I can literally feel the rumble of the race cars vibrating through my body. I adjust my earplugs, twisting them in tighter. It already sounds loud on television, but it's nothing compared to the roar of the real thing. In the stands, I bear witness to the incessant bumping that goes along with stock car racing. I know it can victimize even the most expert of drivers in the blink of an eye, and that knowledge keeps my attention glued to a single car. This sport is dangerous.

I seem to have a thing for men with dangerous professions.

As the green flag run continues, my stomach is in a twist. I say a silent prayer for the man inside car seven. I know, as a race car driver, he'll likely lose some paint off the side of his car, perhaps a tire, and surely exchange positions in the pack more than a time or two. Unless he runs flawlessly, but I don't kid myself. Flawless hardly ever happens in car racing or in life. As long as he finishes in one piece, no matter the position, I'll be satisfied.

I've been warned that even the best stock car drivers are expected to hit the wall at least once in their careers. I don't even want to think about that happening. He's the most fearless person I've ever known. He doesn't seem to fear anything. He certainly wasn't afraid to put a ring on my finger after a swift courtship. I twist the ring around, admire my left hand, and smile.

I'm pulled from my revelry when the crowd around me roars and the thunder of the cars becomes louder. As they come out of the far turn, my eyes return to the track and seek out car seven. I watch it surge from a seventh-place starting position to third after 12 laps of the track. My eyes widen as the car and driver continue to make their move.

He's running in second place now, and only a few yards behind on lap 13. I can't contain myself. I bounce to my feet, pump my fists in the air, and shout 'go, go, go!' The leaders of the pack start into the next turn, and I clench my teeth. Car seven is bumped. Hard. I cover my mouth and send up more silent prayers that he'll keep the car under control.

Car seven jerks right and left, but the tires find grip again. Relief floods me momentarily, but my nerves fray further as the car nudges forward. It's a strong move to take on the lead car. The battle ensues inch by inch until the lead car delivers another vicious bump. As the front tires of the two speeding cars collide, I feel lightning pulse in my veins. The crowd gasps, and I gasp along with them.

Horror overcomes me when car seven skids sideways. Smoke billows from the track beneath it. I shriek. It's clear that he has lost control this time. I watch helplessly as car number seven somersaults over the hood of the car behind it. My worst nightmare is happening in front of me. I see that seven on the hood, see the undercarriage of the car, and then I see the seven reappear just before the car slams into the thick concrete wall.

I feel like I've gone under water. A deafening silence fills the air. Stunned, I race from the stands, force my way to the infield, and with great relief, I see him get out of the car. Its wheels are still spinning, and the hood is on fire.

I fight tears as my husband approaches me in his racing suit, flames bursting behind him. His handsome face is serene. When he reaches me, he touches my cheek, a soft smile lights up his face, and he catches a tear that made an escape down my cheek.

"Everly," he whispers.

"You're here. You're OK," I gasp, frozen in space and time. Over his strong shoulder, I can see safety personnel extinguishing the inferno and hustling to cut the roof off the car.

"Please look at me, Everly," my husband whispers.

Stricken by his voice, I tear my eyes away from the fiery scene behind him.

"I want you to be happy, Everly. Are you happy?" he asks.

"No, I'm not happy," I cry, shaking my head.

An ambulance speeds into the scene, pulls onto the track, and blocks my view of the smoking, twisted piece of metal that no longer looks like a race car. I see the medics extricate his body from the burning wreck.

"You can still love, Everly," he murmurs. "I want you to love. I want you to be loved."

"It hurts too much," I sob.

I gasp for air and reach for my husband, but he fades from the raceway. My surroundings go hazy. I know I am about to split in half and experience two different outcomes. Now, I am hovering near the ceiling in a dark room. I'm looking down on myself. I no longer recognize the man whose hand I'm holding. It can't be my husband. This man is charred and bandaged from head to toe. I don't know this person. There are tubes in his mouth and arms, and he's hooked up to a machine that's doing the breathing for him. I scratch at the ceiling, trying to get back to the man on the track.

I can't be here. I can't do this again.

Suddenly, I drop from the ceiling and am sitting in a chair. The darkness has lifted, and the light in the room is too bright. I squint my eyes. I am holding a clipboard. I am signing papers. I am watching the medical team turn the machines off. I see that straight line. I hear that horrendous flat tone. I hear my own wailing fill the room. No one is there to offer comfort. I am alone.

I am so utterly alone.

I bolt upright in bed. I fear I may have stopped breathing. I clutch my chest, struggling to suck in a breath. I bury my face in my hands. I sit just filling my lungs with air. I will myself to keep breathing.

My sheets are damp again. My apartment is still dark. I am alone, so utterly alone, just like in the dream that keeps coming for me night after night. I've been having the same dream over and over since that night at the pool party. My husband is trying to tell me something from the other side of the grave.

My husband was a successful stock car driver until he wasn't. He died doing what he loved. I understand now. He loved racing cars, and he loved me. He wants me to love. I'm certain he won't stop coming to me in my dreams until he gets his message through. Although it is part blessing to see him whole in my dreams, I can't stand the idea of reliving his death again and again. I can't have this dream again. I have to do something to make it stop.

I will make it stop.

I clamor for my phone on the nightstand. I hit the number on speed dial. I'm relieved when the other side picks up after a single ring.

This is why I only hire the hungry. They are the best in the business.

"Book me a flight to Texas," I say to my assistant. I know where JD is. Missy ran into him in the street before he left the city. And I get updates with Devon's page submissions. I bark out the rest of the information and then launch myself from the bedding. I stomp into my walk-in and fling open my carry-on outside of the closet door.

I thought I dealt with the loss of the man I loved. I replaced him with empty lovers and protected myself from ever feeling that kind of pain again. His dangerous profession caused us to miss out on all of our plans: traveling, having children, growing old together. I got left behind. I lost a wonderful, irreplaceable man. There was nothing he wouldn't do for me then, and now he returns to me in a dream over and over asking me to love again. It took a long time to put myself back together after he died.

Can I love another man with a dangerous profession?

The reality of it is, I already do. I didn't think it was possible. Didn't want it to be possible. I can't afford to lose another man I love. JD's absence has made that all too clear. I miss him. I miss him waiting for me when I come home. I thought these unexpected feelings would fade, but they have only grown stronger, with the reoccurrence of this dream and with my husband's encouragement from beyond the grave. It's too quiet now. I'm not enjoying being on my own anymore. Since JD's been gone, I've been lying to myself, telling myself I like it like this. Telling myself I'll only hurt him if I pick up the phone and call. Telling myself that this is the way it is supposed to be. How I designed it to be. But I don't want another project. I want JD.

My work filled the void my husband left when he died. I carefully created a life that suited me, one that protected me. I didn't think it was in me to love a person again, so I've had my career, my business, and my power. It's all been good for me. I have been in control of everything.

Until now.

I never questioned the way I live my life. I just stayed on my path. I thought I would go on forever the way things have been. It never occurred to me it could change, but it has. I'd rather give love another chance than head back to a padded room. I know if I don't do something soon, that is where I'll be heading.

I pull myself together in the bathroom and then drag my suitcase out into the kitchen. I pick up *The Post* from the counter and thumb to Page Six for the hundredth time. I flood with a mix of emotions as I read the headline again, *"Top PR Executive Dumped by Younger Cowboy Model at Rooftop Pool Party."* My eyes scan the accompanying photo of JD's lips locked on the model in the center of the pool. The whole scene has been a bear to clean up. I've been calling clients for days now, but they are sticking with me. I'm that good, but I know I caused this. I'm to blame for the ding to my reputation. I'll recover. I always do, but I caused all of this by pushing JD away.

He loves me.

Perhaps it was an error in judgment when I brought him into my home. JD was supposed to be a project. By design, I take on projects, so I can have all the physical pleasure with none of the emotional pain. I firmly believe a woman should always be allowed her pleasure. I should have been able to let him go, like the rest of them, but then he told me he loved me. I didn't give him any reason to think I loved him back. Maybe I didn't really know that I did. Then the thing with the other woman happened. It was the opening I needed to extract him from my life, and I did. I toss the newspaper in the trash and head for the door.

Now I find myself going to Texas.

56

JD

In a hurry, I gallop down the stairs from the loft, pulling my T-shirt over my head. McKennon and I have been seeing who can beat the other out of bed every morning. When I enter the barn, I see he's got me licked once again.

"Good morning, sunshine," McKennon calls with a one-sided smirk plastered on his face. "We've got horses to feed, a load of hay to stack, and a whole herd of mares to check in on."

"I'm gonna beat you one of these days, brother," I reply, slipping on my leather work gloves.

"Wanna wager on that?" McKennon asks.

"I'll put my truck up as collateral," I say with a smirk of my own.

"That lime green atrocity? Bet's off the table," McKennon replies with a shake of his head. "Wouldn't catch me dead driving that thing, even if I won it fair and square."

"Figured that'd shut you up," I tease.

"All right, Mr. Smarty Pants. Let's get to work feedin' the horses, check in on the mares, and then we'll work on the bales."

I give him a nod, and we start in on the chores for the day. McKennon and I work well side by side. We breeze through the feeding and then ride out to check the pastures. With an all clear in the fields, we untack our mounts back at the barn and turn our focus to the sky-high pile of hay on a tractor-trailer in the driveway. I guide as McKennon backs it up to the outbuilding, and we work at it for a good long while. I've been happily lost in my work all morning. Realizing I haven't thought of Ev for the first time in months, I lift my cowboy hat and wipe my brow.

I'm making progress.

Like a machine, I return to the task at hand and heave bale after bale of hay off the back of the trailer. My attention is diverted when I hear the gravel crunch on Green Briar's driveway. I look over my shoulder and out the open doors of the pole barn. I see the tail end of a sleek town car slither by followed by a wave of dust.

"We aren't expecting any clients or deliveries," McKennon says, checking his watch.

"Be right back," I tell him.

Could it be?

My gut is in a twist. McKennon acknowledges me with a lift of his chin as I strut past the tractor-trailer in the car's direction in the driveway. I can sense McKennon is wandering after me. He knows it isn't a delivery or a client. He saw the town car, too. I imagine he's probably still trying to figure out what happened to the kid he used to know. The one who has always been dangerous with the bulls and the women he chooses. I haven't been my old self at all. I'm working on being something new, hiding out at Green Briar, asking for more and more work to do. I glance back at him, and he clears his throat.

"If I've learned anything in my life, it's that you can't time love. You just have to live it. I'd say this might be your chance to do just that, brother."

Before I can reply, McKennon drops his gaze, grabs another bale of hay, and disappears into the outbuilding.

Moving McKennon's words around in my mind, I walk on. The car's driver opens the back door, and high heels emerge from the backseat. I clench my teeth when I reach her. Standing tall in front of me, her flame-colored hair lifts in the breeze. She's cut her thick hair into a bob and dyed it a darker shade of red. I have to blink at her beauty.

It's so good to see her.

"Ev," I say with a tip of my hat. "You changed your hair. I like it."

"I thought it might help me be a different person, maybe help me forget you."

"Did it work?" I ask. She shakes her head.

"Can we talk?"

I shrug, rub the back of my neck, amble over to the bench seat at the front of the barn, and settle in the shade. As Ev joins me, I watch her driver sit behind the steering wheel and close the door.

"What are you doing here?" I ask.

"I heard you're thinking about not returning to the bull riding tour."

"Devon told you, did she?" Ev nods.

"Are you sure that's the right choice?"

"It'll take some gettin' used to, but I reckon I've lost my nerve. I'm figurin' out my future. Looking at my options while I work here at Green Briar."

"What if I offer you a better career path? You still haven't signed the movie contract. The offer is still on the table," Ev answers.

"Is that why you're here? *Business*?" I sneer through gritted teeth.

Ev's arrival has blown my mind to confetti.

Am I angry? Am I happy?

"Yes. Filming begins early next year, so you can fulfill your current obligations here. It is perfect timing for a deal like this. We'll get you some acting classes if that makes you more comfortable."

"Acting classes? Ev, you came all the way from New York City after how things ended to push the movie contract on me and sign me up for acting classes?" I'm flabbergasted.

"I think so," Ev pauses, then folds her hands in her lap, looks down, and sighs. "Actually, I don't know. Here it goes, OK?"

I nod. I don't want to say anything that might spook her. I'm mighty spooked myself right about now.

Gosh, it's good to see her.

Ev presses her lips together as if trying to find her words.

"You and I are not the kind of people who say I love you. Or at least, I didn't think so. You don't just meet your perfect match, and then everything is beautiful, and life works. I know better. If anyone understands that, it's you and me."

"Uh, OK. What exactly are you saying? I'm having trouble understanding what you are getting at right now."

She reaches for my hand, green eyes intense.

"This thing ... you and me ... it turns out it's more than I expected," she murmurs.

I hesitate. I am afraid to interrupt the moment.

Has something shifted for Ev?

"Yeah," I finally say. "You already know that it is for me, too."

"I create obstacles out of my past," she continues. "I've come to realize that we might work, but it's going to be work. If you and I are going to move forward together, I want you to know it's going to be hard work."

"Ev, are you saying you want this to work?" I ask.

"I'm saying that I thought it would be easier to walk away from you than to work at loving you. The feelings I'm having are messy and scary. You scare the life out of me."

"You are confusing the hell out of me, Ev." I shake my head.

"Stay right there," she urges.

I watch her pick her way across the drive in those high heels. She ducks back inside the town car to retrieve something. When she reappears, she cradles a puppy.

"This is for you," she says, plunking the pup in my arms. I awkwardly accept the dog and shake my head again.

What the hell?

"Why did you come back here, Ev?" I ask, trying to avoid the pint-sized heeler attempting to lick my face.

This little dog will not make me smile.

"It's a girl," she says, nodding toward the pup. "Now you have a committed female companion. Am I off the hook?"

"What are you talking about? This is absurd. You bought me a dog? I don't remember telling you I wanted a dog. Come on, Ev. What are you doing here? What is this about?"

"You can tell a lot about what people keep hidden by the way they treat animals. When you were in the city, you always had to stop and pet a dog. When they put a dog in your lap after your accident, something shifted in you. I think you have a lot of affection stored up in you, cowboy. No matter how deeply buried it is."

"So ... you bought me a dog?"

Suddenly, I can't help it. I stroke the puppy's head and put it down on all fours in Green Briar's drive. The little furball waddles over to Ev with its tail wagging and plops down on top of her foot.

I am not going to smile.

I turn a cold eye toward Ev and raise an eyebrow.

I want an answer.

"What's your problem, anyway? What's with the tough woman act all the time? It's off putting. What happened to you, Ev? Why are you like this? Why are you here darn it?" I *am* angry with her.

"I want to explain," she murmurs, looking down at the tiny canine perched on her toes.

"Explain what? What is there to explain? Today was the first day in a long time that I didn't freakin' think about you, and now here you are. I didn't always make the eight when I was on a bull; I can accept failure. Everyone has to fail once in a while. I went out on a limb falling for you, and I failed splendidly. You broke my heart."

"Please don't say that, JD," Ev murmurs.

"Why not? It's true. What I can't accept, though, is you not trying. I actually tried with you. Why didn't you try, too? What we had was more than lust. I know you know that." The muscles in my jaw ache as I spit the words through my gritted teeth.

"I lost my husband, JD," she whispers, dropping her head into her hands.

I think I heard what she just said. She is trembling, and I can feel her body heat. It takes everything in me not to pull her to me, but I can't touch her and lose her again.

"What?"

"My husband. He died. It ruined me."

"What?" I repeat. "How?" I swallow hard.

"He drove race cars." Ev's eyes go unfocused, and I can see her suppressing the urge to cry. "I liked fast back then. Hell, I still like fast. Even after I lost him, I never planned to slow down or settle down, but I promised myself I'd never fall for a fast man ever again. I didn't want to risk that kind of loss."

"And now?" I encourage.

"I'm finding myself at a crossroad. My heart tells me you are too unpredictable. My head tells me your line of work is too dangerous. Your accident and the time in the hospital brought up a past I thought I had put behind me. I had to sign the papers to take my husband off life support. I was afraid I'd have to do that for you, too."

"Ev, I didn't know. I'm so sorry."

I reach out to wipe an escaped tear from her cheek. My heart hurts knowing this information. It's a new sensation.

"I thought I could control it all, but I'm realizing I can't control anything. I've made a habit of being attracted to fleeting romantic entanglements where I call the shots, so I don't have to worry about being in situations like that."

"You mean your projects?" I reply dryly.

"Yes, my projects. I don't get hurt that way. When my husband lost control of his car and lost his life, it changed me, JD. I saw him go up in flames. I signed the papers to end his life. I didn't even recognize the man in the bed when I did. I couldn't see the man I loved anymore."

My jaw tenses up, and anger swells inside of me.

"How could Devon not tell me this? She's supposed to be my friend." I ball my hands into fists.

"Devon doesn't know," Ev murmurs. "She came into my world after I lock and keyed that chapter of my life."

"Missy knows, though?" I ask. Her words from the day I left New York come flooding back to me, 'I have a feeling she might reach out, JD. If she does, I'd hear her out.'

I will hear her out.

"Few people know about that part of my life, but, yes, Missy knows. She's family. I've lost touch with the friends we had when he was alive. It's been my mission to keep that part of my past in the past. I built my business. No one in my new life knows. Not Devon. Not my clients. Not any of my projects. I certainly didn't want to tell you. It was a very difficult time for me. The only way through the pain was to grin and bear it. Be tough. I learned how to be tough, emotionless."

"You are one hell of a tough woman. I want to know what happened. If you'll tell me that is." I scoot closer to Ev. The puppy wanders off into the flowerbed and flops down among the flowers.

"I was just a young thing in my twenties when I married. My husband was 10 years my senior. I loved him desperately, but I hated that he was a race car driver. When he crashed and burned away, he left me everything, but it wasn't enough. I couldn't go on living without him. I suffered a deep depression. I had to go away for a while. I needed professional help. It was a very dark time in my life. Eventually, I got myself together. I started my business with the life insurance money and the earnings from his racing career."

Ev looks out in the distance for a while. I take her hand.

"I vowed to never care about a man again. But here I am. I've found I care. I care about you, JD." Ev's green eyes are hopeful as they meet mine.

She cares about me.

I remove my hat from my head and hold it to my chest. An unusual ache washes through me. This news is not what I had expected, especially since I've been trying so dang hard to put this woman out of my mind.

"I ... I don't know what to say, Ev," I murmur.

"There isn't anything you can say. I can't risk that kind of depression again. That's why I wanted to keep things light with you. I promised not to care about another man after Jason died. That's why I don't fall in love, and that's why I grab what I want by the balls — men, career, and life. I'm tough now. I don't want any regrets, and I don't want to be vulnerable to loss again. That's why I pick the wild types to fill the void when I get lonely. That's why I picked you. The fast guys rarely stick around long enough to get attached. You, though, you surprised me. That is, until I rejected you at that party, and you left with that model. I couldn't get that image out of my mind for a long time. I know it wasn't your fault. I made you do it. I deserved it."

"You didn't deserve that. You should know that I didn't sleep with her. I couldn't do it. All I could think about was how much I wanted you. It's all I think about still," I admit.

"You didn't sleep with her?"

"I didn't. Will you forgive me?"

"Well, I forgave you for not remembering me the first night we spent together. I suppose I can forgive you for going off with another woman and not sleeping with her. You are kind of perfect for me. You're the male version of me."

"Why are you here, Ev?" I ask again.

"I don't know."

"Come on, Ev. You don't leave the city for no reason. I know that much. Tell me."

"Maybe I want a little bit of what Devon's found. I realized I'm not ready to give up on loving someone again. I've let some time pass. I've survived these last months without you, somehow, but I miss you."

"You miss me?"

"Yes," she answers with soft eyes. "You know what the worst part is?"

"What?"

"I can't even remember the last time we kissed. You never think the last time is going to be the last time. You think there will be more. You think you have forever with people, but you don't. It's the same way I felt when I lost Jason. It woke me up about us."

"Is that so?" My throat is tight.

"Yes. I've been having dreams ever since you left. My husband comes to me in them and tells me it is OK to love again. I fought it for a while, but I think it's time to listen to him. I'm not broken. I am able to love, and I want a second chance at loving somebody. Being driven has its perks. I'm proud of what I've done for you, for Devon. I've been using success to replace love. I build careers for people. Working every second of the day, going to fancy parties at night, and then coming home to an empty penthouse isn't necessarily good for me. It's not what I want anymore. I enjoyed having you to come home to. You were always more than a project, JD."

This is unexpected. This amazing woman who has been so guarded just told me everything. Explained everything. I reach out and hold her face. My eyes search hers. My insides are in tangles.

"If you don't want me to kiss you right now, please say something," I whisper.

When she doesn't speak and fixes her gaze on my lips. I lean forward and graze her mouth with mine. When she shudders, I deepen our kiss until Ev breaks away.

"Come back to the city with me?" she breathes, touching my forehead with hers.

"Stay in the country with me?" I murmur.

"I can't, JD. I've built an empire there. I can't leave all that behind. The city is where I belong. Come back with me. Please."

"I can't. New York is addictive. The lifestyle you live is addictive. Heck, you're addictive. I was hooked, and I couldn't think straight. I broke the habit when I came back to Green Briar. The country is where I belong, Ev."

"Where does that leave us?" she asks.

"Is it me you want or are you here for the money I can make for your empire?"

"Of course, it's you."

"Answer me this. Did you really come here to get me to sign that movie contract?"

I'm shooting straight from the hip. My heart pounds while Ev contemplates her answer.

"I'm here for you, but I can't leave everything I've built for you. I can't."

"I'm not asking you to. How's about we enjoy the time we have here and now? I'm not opposed to trying the long-distance thing. I've got plenty of money now and plenty of flexibility. We can go back and forth, and you can keep running that business of yours. It seems like a simple enough solution to me."

"And if it doesn't work?" she asks.

"What if it does?"

"Aren't you ever the optimist?"

"Listen, Ev. We'll cross that bridge when one of us decides we want something more, say a permanent address together."

"Are you suggesting a relationship, JD McCall?"

"I reckon we should at least give it a go. A wise cowboy once told me if you want someone to love you back, the first step is you don't chase them away, you give them something to come around to. We always make our way back to the things that really matter. The universe is funny that way. It seems we've made our way back to each other. Never met someone quite like you, Everly Mitchell."

"I'm scared. This is scary for me," Ev replies. She bites her lower lip.

"I'm pretty darn scared myself. If you and I decide to be together, really be together, which I really want, I know I will probably do something to screw it up."

"Oh well," Ev says, shrugging her shoulders. "Let's screw things up together then. I don't want to lose you because I'm afraid to love you."

I lean forward, grab her lovely face, and kiss her deeply.

"So, you really think this will work?" Ev asks, breaking from our kiss.

"I don't know. I've never done this before. I reckon we owe it to ourselves to give it a try," I say with a shrug.

"Hmm," she taps her lip with her fingernail. "I like the idea of being a part-time country girl. It'll give me a chance to wear all those boots I bought the last time I was here."

"And a chance to relax," I add. "You need to unwind that brain of yours every now and again. Not to mention, wind those long legs of yours around me."

"I like the way you're thinking, cowboy," Ev whispers.

"I'm breaking rank because for the first time in my life, I'm interested in things that last more than eight seconds. How old are you, Ev?" I ask.

"I'll never tell," she whispers, burying her face in my shoulder. "Aren't you going to miss all of your buckle bunnies?"

"I think I've sown my oats enough to know that you're the one I'd like to go through time with from here on out." I wrap my arms around her and kiss the top of her red head.

"JD McCall. Playboy reformed. Who would have thought?"

"Took an awfully special woman to rope the likes of me," I say with a chuckle.

The puppy barks and runs a circle around the driveway.

"What did you name her?" I ask.

"Hope. As in, I hope I can learn to love again."

"I hope you can, too. It'll be nice having little Hope here to remind us of that. Thank you for the gift. Didn't know I needed a dog. Didn't know I'd get a girlfriend out of the deal either. How long do Hope and I have with you before you head back to New York?"

"I have to be back in the city in a week. The holiday campaigns are about to kick off."

"I reckon we can work with that," I say with a smile. I'm already imagining stripping her naked in my loft apartment and taking my time kissing every part of her body.

"So, what do we do now?" Ev asks.

"Easy. We get you out of that dress, start kissing a little more, and talking a lot less."

"That sounds lovely," Ev breathes. "To tell you the truth, I like myself better when I'm with you."

"Me too, Ev. Me too."

As the town car pulls away with a wave of Ev's hand, I take her hand, carry her suitcase in my other hand, and lead her toward the barn with the little pup tagging along at our heels.

"You'll still consider the movie though, won't you?" Ev asks as we take the stairs up to my loft.

"I knew it wouldn't be long before you mentioned that again," I chuckle.

"Just because I'm in love with you doesn't mean I'm going to let you blow a lucrative business deal, JD. It's who I am. It's what I do."

"I know, and I wouldn't change you for the world, Ev."

"Will you consider it?" she asks.

"You're my agent, aren't you?" I reply.

"I am," Ev answers.

"Well then, I reckon you can talk me into anything."

She already has.

I open the door, and Hope scoots inside. I set the luggage in the hallway and lift Ev into my arms. I plant a kiss on her lips, carry her over the threshold, and kick the door closed behind us.

I've never thought beyond eight seconds before. Now I am.

JD and Ev's story continues. In the follow-up to *Beyond Eight Seconds*, you'll start exactly where this book left off and continue your journey with all the members of the Green Briar gang.

Want more romance? Get instant access to exclusive, previously unreleased deleted scenes from *In the Reins* when you join my Readers' Group.

You'll also be occasionally notified of giveaways, new releases, and receive personal updates from behind the scenes of my books. Get started here: **https://www.carlykadecreative.com/bonus**

ACKNOWLEDGMENTS

Thank you to my readers — I couldn't have written book four in the *In the Reins* series without your kind words, emails of support, and positive reviews. Writing a book can be hard. You keep me going!

To my horse, Sissy. You are the inspiration behind the *In the Reins* series. You've taught me that good horse(wo)manship is a journey, not a destination. Thank you for keeping me on my toes and perpetually teaching me something new.

To my editors, Ann and Laurie. You improve my books and are irreplaceable friends. Thank you for being such positive contributions to my creativity.

To the equine authors, bloggers, and journalists who have supported my author dream and have been guests on the Equestrian Author Spotlight podcast. I learn so much from other writers and appreciate how unique our writing journeys are. It is important to support each other and share knowledge among us. We are stronger working together to expose this "niche" genre of ours. Let's hear it for equestrian books and blogs!

ABOUT THE AUTHOR

Photo by Shelley Paulson Photography

Carly Kade is an award-winning author, horse owner, and the host of the Equestrian Author Spotlight podcast. Creative writing makes her spurs jingle! Her books are for people just like her — crazy about reading, horses, and handsome cowboys.

facebook.com/carlykadecreative

twitter.com/CarlyKadeAuthor

instagram.com/carlykadecreative

Made in the USA
Monee, IL
23 September 2022

14547192R00194